No replacement

James Hayward-Searle

A

A KIT MARTIN SPYTHRILLER

Copyright © James Hayward-Searle 2019

All rights reserved. No part of this publication may be reproduced, stored in a retrieval system, or transmitted in any form or by any means, mechanical, photocopying, recording or otherwise, without prior permission in writing of the author.

ISBN: 9781073477999 (paperback)

Other novels by the author:

Deep secret

Carlos II

And so to return

The meeting

Acknowledgments and many thanks in respect of research to:

J. Lupton (The Gun Room)

A. Holmes (The Shooting Lodge)

Lynn Broadbent

Chris Briscoe

One

Late summer – London

It was early evening, now growing cool, damp, with the dusk gradually closing in upon one of the last days of September; to be exact the twenty-seventh day; for England, it had been a much-needed late Indian summer. In Hyde, the Royal Park in central London mists hung and swirled mysteriously over the waters of the Serpentine lake, the surrounds of which now displaying the golden autumnal shroud of oak, beech and ash, a slowly dying season, in this bustling capital.

Yet for all this, the pleasant evening was lost on the face and character of the man that looked out through a dark half-curtained window, hidden in the growing darkness of an unlit small three-storey mews apartment. He was on the first floor, standing back from the window his shadowed face looking out patiently to the scene displayed below and across the cobbles, a scene that was to be set deep within the rooms opposite. His vision would be slightly distorted by its half-drawn lace curtains, but it was better than nothing.

Kit Martin was waiting, silently watching. His features rugged and tanned not by Mediterranean holiday sun, but by constant training in all weathers, pounding the moor land and hills of Yorkshire, endlessly honing his senses and skills. He would show no emotion – that weakness had long gone. He could wait, wait forever if necessary, maybe tonight, maybe never, but he could and would wait.

'Alone' was to him no hardship, indeed it was heaven. He confided in few, trusted less than a handful. That way he knew he could always survive.

He was a tall, six ft. plus, well built with dark hair not yet intruded by grey. His startling sharp sapphire blue eyes and broad infectious smile flashed of Irish ancestry. He was a smart dresser, if perhaps a little conservative, with the echoes of Establishment hard to shake off – a code of dress which stretched from Turnbull & Asser, his Jermyn St shirt maker, via Burlington Arcade to his Savile Row tailor, both often military in style and approach.

For all this, the city style did not disguise him, it did not even blend him away. He made a striking figure, a figure of presence. One that would not escape notice in this, a select part of Knightsbridge.

Aware of his magnetism as a new arrival, he had arrived early, before the professionals; the bankers, stockbrokers and barristers of the City returned to their week day home, drained by their toil.

As luck, would have it, Kit, in accordance with his brief of some days before, had managed to rent the small mews apartment in this picturesque and trendy area – Pavilion Road. Its colourful window boxes, uneven cobbles and overhanging eves all added to the charm and flavour of a London mews, so close to the city centre, yet country 'cottage' in appearance.

In the past, these had been stables and coach houses, backing onto the well-to-do properties of the time. They were now in great demand. But more to the point, this particular property was within twenty yards or so – according to a tip-off from the obsequious and, due to his not so discreet nature now 'moneyed' estate agent – of this furnished supposed love nest, so recently rented by a cabinet minister? Such is confidentiality. But for Kit it was just another 'target' for surveillance and one not of his wishing.

Cabinet Minister? He thought to himself, standing there looking out through the half-drawn curtains of the upstairs window, there was doubt in his mind, indeed a great deal of doubt. Rank stupidity was something that Kit could not get on with.

On a table to his side lay an old but reliable Nikon 901 S camera, its telephoto lens pointing ominously outward from a tripod, out across the cobbles, directly toward the apartment that was nearly opposite. The ever watchful; the all-seeing black eye of Cyclops, waiting unremittingly for its shutter to click, creating a record of scene and time. The curtains of the first-floor apartment opposite were equally half drawn, a clear photographic shot, the evidence he required would be difficult, but not impossible

'Supposed' was a word that had been used so many times. Kit wondered idly, how stupid a minister must be to become 'involved' nowadays, to have an affair. That was of course, if the Minister was? With so many political sex scandals rocking the government, Profumo still fresh in the memory, it didn't add up, however, 'his was not to reason why'.

Among other equipment that lay close by on the pine bedside table was a pair of Helios-201, night binoculars and tonight with luck if need be he would see.

Some twenty-four hours earlier he had discreetly entered the 'target' apartment. Deftly and easily for him with his height he had removed the curtains, delivered them to a waiting seamstress, an Indian lady in Soho and there had them altered to half the width, returned and hung them within the afternoon. Now they could not fully draw, thus for the moment giving him a reasonable and less restricted view of the main front bedroom, and also of the downstairs area. He smiled to himself, he had done it before and for a few days it worked.

He doubted that it was going to be satisfactory for long, a couple of days at most, but the estate agent had assured him that as yet the couple had not used the apartment. Indeed, the lease to the property had only just been signed. They had only just collected the keys so this was probably to be their first evening, if not he would wait for the next, but human nature he knew well and the eagerness of whoever he was sure would outweigh poor curtains and modesty.

Kit was just beginning to ponder how boring and drawn out this surveillance may be, when suddenly and unusually taking Kit by surprise, from out of the misty September shadows a figure of a man came into view. Kit stiffened, his senses becoming alert.

The man was purposeful, looked powerful, yet slim, his triangular frame moving briskly, yet softly, cat like and keeping close in the shadows of the buildings. He moved impressively like dark silk in an Arabian breeze, his body language indicating his experience. There was a certain air of dominant supple confidence about him, yet maybe too much Kit thought. 'Cocksure' sprang to mind as the man came down the mews toward Kit's watchful eyes. But for all his arrogant surety, it was obvious to the trained eye that he knew what he was doing – at some time for sure this man had been trained.

He slowed, tried the door and with a flash of hand, key or instrument Kit was not sure, but in seconds the man had skilfully and quietly let himself into 'the' apartment. He melted back into the dark doorway, enveloped in the darkness of within and disappeared as the door closed. Strangely, no lights came on; all remained quiet.

Kit was surprised; this was not the man that he had been suspicious of expecting. Intrigued he settled back to wait.

Within half an hour and with the evening mists now noticeably clearing, visibility improved. Down the cobbles toward the apartment came a smart and new looking, dark metallic-blue Ford Escort Cabriolet; it drew up gently. A dark leggy female climbed out gracefully and looked around somewhat nervously. She then deftly flicked her key fob and, with a smile remotely locked the car. There was no one around, she visibly relaxed as the Ford's lights flashed momentarily, the twin door locks clicked in, her self-consciousness now gone she was happy, pleased with herself. She fumbled deeply in her Prada bag, presumably for keys – once found she examined them, turning them in her long delicate hands reading the tags. It was quite obvious that they were new to her. The correct one found she opened the white Georgian-style door swiftly, and left it ajar, flicked down the light switches and the room burst into light, shafts of which flooded out either side of her and into the mews. Insects awoke and began to dance in the sudden luminescence.

Too bright, she must have thought, as she moved forward and dimmed the lights down to a seductive low glow, the shafts of light and shadows disappearing from the mews as she closed the door behind her. A police car or ambulance wailed away in the distance.

Some moments later a black London cab came rattling down the mews cobbles and pulled up noisily behind the Cabriolet, its brakes squealing; it sat there chattering noisily in a cloud of diesel fumes.

A distinguished-looking gentleman climbed out, stood tall, stretching himself, his greying hair glinting in the half-light, his complexion was possibly a little florid. He was wearing what appeared to be a dark suit, no doubt the ubiquitous pinstripe of Savile Row? He also seemed to be carrying a large briefcase and, by his laboured movements it looked to be heavy. He politely paid the driver, and glanced at the Cabriolet as he waited for his change he then handed back one presumes an appropriate tip.

The taxi growled its way once more down the cobbles, the familiar yellow 'For Hire' sign now illuminated.

The gentleman was now standing alone in the street. He looked nervously left to right, up and down the mews, he too, in equally unfamiliar territory, but when satisfied that there was nothing untoward, he checked the door number and looked again at the Cabriolet, cautiously he backed into the doorway, his hand fumbling behind him for the brass handle. He watched the street all the while, the door opened and light cascaded onto the stone cobbles once more.

Carefully Kit held the remote-control button of the camera between finger and thumb and waited, exhaled his breath and held; the door continued slowly to open as if he was unsure, now a little more light from within shone upon the face of the visitor, a face Kit instantly recognised.

'The Minister,' he muttered, shaking his head in disbelief, a face that deep down he did not really want to see.

In that fleeting moment of time, Kit squeezed, the camera motor drive activated with a whine and clattering shutter, rattling off six rapid shots. Kit released the button, silence resumed. Inside the noise seemed loud, deafening as the camera shutter had clattered at three or more frames a second, the 'motor' drive giving off the high-pitched whine; but that sound he knew would not carry outside.

In these sordid circumstances, he felt distinctly uneasy about being a snoop, a 'peeping Tom'.

'This is a man's private life, for Christ's sake,' he muttered to himself. Then again, a Minister is a public servant. Kit glowered out of the room, attentively looking opposite.

The Minister moved nervously into the house and the door closed behind him. Once in the subtle lighting of the dining room Kit could see him quite clearly, albeit framed by the multiple panes of Georgian glass in the bow window. The minister then cocked his head as if calling upstairs.

Kit was right; after a moment, the leggy lady came slowly, seductively down the open stairs that were just visible to the back of the small but elegant dining room, its miniature cut-glass chandelier twinkling, enhancing the enchantment of the meeting.

She was wearing little, yet sufficient, it looked expensive and was certainly tantalising – even at this distance. Kit imagined her perfume and admired the long dark hair that was clipped on each side and flowing over each shoulder, glistening around her throat. He knelt down and looked through the lens zooming in; she had among other things a beautiful, bright, sparkling smile!

A small silver tray and two frosted flute glasses of what surely must be champagne were held in her bejewelled hands. It was a scene that was quite exquisite; class personified, or nearly so.

Nearly so? This scene played out before him told Kit something. A 'lady', a true lady would never have opened the champagne; a 'lady' would have waited for the gentleman to do it for her. This girl was used to working for others.

Had Kit been more alert he would have realised that there were just two glasses. But this was only a casual surveillance. He did not need to be on his metal. Yet three people had gone into the apartment! However, Kit was distracted, his mind curious, fascinated by the spectacle that was being played out before him.

The couple embraced in a dignified manner, then suddenly with a flinch she appeared to giggle, twist and move away having spilt some champagne. With a cunning devilish smile, the Minister deftly, with a flamboyant flourish removed a white handkerchief from his breast pocket. Gently he dabbed her ample yet firm breast. He then placed the hanky within his cuff, the white Egyptian cotton showing.

Half turning, he nodded toward the window: was he afraid of being seen perhaps? She appeared to counter his action, his worry, by offering the stairs. A choice, he willingly seemed to accept, all caution vanishing. Kit now watched intently.

Some moments later they appeared at the entrance to the front bedroom, the door now opening fully as she led him in. She again adjusted the lights Kit adjusted the lens of the Nikon.

Bemused, he watched the Minister give a tug at the curtains, which produced a scowl, and another tug followed by a shrug as he realised that in any event they were not wide enough. He would no doubt give instructions to have them altered. Again, Kit smiled to himself.

The light was not good, and the angle not the best. So, leaning forward Kit reached for the night glasses, focused them, but quickly put them down. The eerie green tinge that these created to his view was not to his liking. For the moment, at least, and with what natural light there was, ordinary glasses were preferable to him.

After a time, his fascination began to wane, Kit felt quite sad as he watched them frolic and eventually settle on the edge of the bed, a mock, glitzy, semi four-poster, of polished wood and brass, all decked out with drapes in white lace.

Kit now wondered why the hell he had agreed to this. Others would have been far better 'peeping Toms' than he; some he mused might even have enjoyed it. He most certainly did not. Raising the glasses once more he looked back into the room.

He saw her take the Minister's glass away, placing it on the glass-topped side table. Then slowly and exquisitely he watched her undo her lover's shirt, having wasted no time getting him there. Maybe time was short. Kit watched, fascination returning, as she took what appeared at this distance to be two or more pairs of chrome handcuffs from her bag. Gently she laid him back onto the pillows and kissed his forehead. She then smartly cuffed him by the wrists to the uprights of the bed, one to the left, one to the right. Then without further ado she bent forward and started slowly to undo his belt, remove his trousers, his underpants, then his socks one by one, each pulled off and stretched from the toe before they sprang off, for maximum effect. This achieved she cuffed his ankles to the corners of the bed, one to the left, and one to the right.

Kit imagined he heard the locks click, he shuddered, not his style at all.

Then slowly, delicately, quite delightfully she pulled her small, jewelled, crop top over her head, finally releasing a pair of large yet firm upright breasts. For a moment, Kit wondered where they had been hidden. She unclipped one side of her hair and with a seductive shake of her head let it fall forward, cascading over him and her breast, the remaining bare breast swung free with the shake showing all who cared to look, an upright nipple seated in a large tightening chocolate brown aura, the other side of her hair was unclipped and cascaded down; As she moved on her man Kit's vision was now difficult. She slowly leant forward over the Minister's genitalia, covering him as a Falcon mantles over its quarry. Her narrow waist and backbone were clearly visible in the half-light, the pale orbs of breasts protruding either side by her elbows through her fallen hair, either side of her backbone, muscles were flexing glistening in anticipation of the events to come.

Trapped! Trapped! The Minister must have felt so, visibly squirming with delight as she caressed, fondled, smiled and then deeply manipulated her man. The brass bed head steadily began to move, to rock and sway

Kit imagined with callous amusement that it would rap tap on the wall, a sexual Morse, in an urgent code for those who wished to hear.

Events had moved so quickly that he had completely forgotten that there was a third party, the other man, the one he had seen enter the apartment.

'Jesus,' he said under his breath as his brain caught up, 'now where the hell is he?' Then as if by a second sense, a premonition or foreboding, he knew not, he began to rise tensely, slowly from his chair, his eyes never flinching, intently watching the scene all the while.

He didn't like it. He knew something was wrong and, with a sense of apprehension, all too late he saw the door, from what was maybe the other bedroom, or even a bathroom, he knew not which, slowly start to open! He watched now, half out of his chair and coiled motionless, like a cobra ready to strike.

Kit instantly recognised the blunt black barrel of a silenced weapon, its dull black shape came ominously into the apartment around the door. Immediately he pressed the Nikon into auto action; again, the shutter clattered and the motor whined, simultaneously he athletically uncoiled fully to his feet. In a single springing leap, he left the room, ran to the landing and plunged headlong down the stairs grabbing the rail as he went, falling urgently onward downward toward the door two or three steps at a time, cool air rushing up to meet him. Suddenly he heard a dull thud from across the street. The bloody latch! Unlock the door, damn it, unlock; it took time, too much time, but the bloody latch finally gave.

Kit powered himself out of the door and into the street, that sound again he knew only too well. That lead-heavy sound, the sickening thud of a slow-moving bullet from a silenced weapon, travelling less than 700ft per second; the awful open-nosed plop of a 'hollow point' lead bullet on soft flesh. The sound had come from the dull-lit room above and across the mews; the love nest. A chill greeted him as he slowed, slid, stopped, then dodged an oncoming car, then dashing forward again across the cobbles, twisting around her Ford Cabriolet and on towards the apartment door he went.

As he arrived the door flew open a man crashed viciously through taking him with a crushing gasp to the floor. Christ the man had been fast; it was all too fast, too sudden even for Kit to see clearly. Two men equally startled meeting head-on. The assailant had the advantage and hit Kit a hard yet glancing blow across the side of the head, his knees buckled as he went down, then through surging nausea Kit heard the hollow click of a hammer falling on a dead round; luckily for Kit, a misfire. He heard the slide being pulled back the dud round hit the floor, his hands grappled upward to the weapon it did not reload. With huge effort, the assailant wrenched the weapon free and hit him again across the head; he could actually smell the pungent gun oil as with impact it sprayed in the air. Then all he saw was a blinding flash in his brain, of red and white pain, as momentarily he went down further with a bone-rendering crack to his knees.

His hands feebly rose again skyward in front of his face, grappling in thin air, searching desperately for that shadowy unfocused black muzzle. It's one black eyed look into oblivion. There was a brief second as the man struggled and fiddled with the weapon, cursing he joggled the top slide yet again, then another mechanical click as the hammer fell thankfully to no avail.

Whatever it was, whatever he'd been hit with, it was now smashed into Kit's hand, tearing a finger to one side, and then with a grunt and curse, the assailant was gone.

Kit struggled uncertainly to his feet and crashed into the doorframe cursing as he fell dizzily inside the open door and across the dining room. He sidestepped the table, knocking over a chair as he went; grabbing the rail he pounded up four or five steps before he stopped momentarily; he pulled himself up, collected himself, his senses returning. Steadily he climbed the remaining stairs, listened intently, motionless and caught his breath, heart pounding in his breast, ears ringing as if the only noise, he cautiously continued and slowly entered the only room that was lit.

He was greeted by the sickening stench of explosive and the sweet and sickly scent of warm blood and perfume. A fly was already buzzing greedily in the room, awoken violently for a sickly feast. There was a fading wisp of pale white gun smoke; cordite. It still hung in the air, as a mist of death, a rising spirit, a torn soul, in shocked ascendance.

He gathered his breath and looked around, hearing the tragic sound of blood and smashed body fluid dripping relentlessly to the floor. He hesitated again for a second, not because of the horror before him for he'd seen plenty before, but to take it all in, to memorise it forever and to miss nothing.

The sight was not pleasant. She lay, no longer beautiful, across the Minister's white, dough belly, which heaved with gasping short breaths. Blood spread slowly across the white sheet.

The top of her head had gone; most of it was on the wall.

The Minister groaned, trembled below her, open mouthed his eyes wide and rolling too frightened and in shock to scream.

'Don't move,' Kit murmured as he assessed the damage. Then with more than a little apprehension asked urgently, 'Are you hit?' He looked down upon the sad sight that was laid there before him, the Minister did not seem to have been hit.

'Are you hit?' quietly yet directly he asked again.

The Minister began to shake his head slowly, his bottom lip shaking and flopping about like a tired horse. He looked pathetically up at Kit. His public bluster now gone, he was pale and terrified.

'It wasn't me,' Kit said to him quietly. 'I did not shoot.' Then, trying to offer hope, 'I was just passing when I heard a shot,' he lied. 'I'm in security, er, an official,' he lied again; the Minister seemed to relax a little and looked up, dazed but thoughtful, wondering.

'Help Me,' he croaked.

Then as Kit unlocked the Minister's left wrist, as if thinking aloud, he said,

'I must make a call.' He was looking at the phone.

The Minister suddenly became alert. 'No police!' he said urgently, then again, 'No – no, police please,' quietly, with a broken voice.

'Don't be bloody daft, man! I'll have to,' Kit exclaimed, aghast at the suggestion.

'No,' the Minister repeated again, urgently. 'No police! I didn't do this thing, how the hell could I? Let me free, let me go, do you know who I am? I demand it.' The Minister's voice then began to rise as he panicked at his entrapment.

Then suddenly as an afterthought Kit took the key sharply out of the last remaining cuff, the one that held the Minister's right wrist firmly to the brass bed head, and snapped it loudly, visibly and aggressively shut again. Demand, did he?

Kit now stood up. The Minister looked up at him in utter horror, one wrist again firmly and securely cuffed to the bed!

'So, tell me about it then,' Kit asked, relaxing as if he had all the time in the world. He pocketed the keys with a flourish whilst stubbornly giving the remaining cuff a yank to prove to both it was firmly locked.

Kit wanted his attention and would make sure the Minister got the message; there would be no relaxing for him, now was the time for some answers.

'So, who did it and why?'

'I can't tell you!' The Minister whined, now nearly in tears, 'I don't know! I don't bloody well know! I tell you.' The sight was pathetic as he tugged hopelessly at his cuffed wrist, so that it chaffed red and started to bleed, dripping onto the sheet. Kit took no notice.

'Then if I can't, you can. You can tell the police,' He growled through gritted teeth, his face so close that spittle flecked upon the Minister's forehead.

He then leaned back and passed the telephone receiver to the Minister's free hand, simultaneously punching in the three 999 emergency numbers.

'Speak,' Kit boomed.

'No, no, please listen. Listen, please get me

out of here, *please*' the man begged desperately. 'You do and I'll tell you all, I will!' He was near purple. Kit noted, more likely to die of a coronary than a bullet.

'So why, why should I?' Kit said awkwardly, slowly replacing the receiver as a voice asked which service he required.

'You tell me *now* whilst I've got you.'

'Got me! Who the hell are you?'

All this time, the body was grotesquely sprawled out at the foot of the bed, crimson human flesh visible, the last cells of life now fading, changing, shading, flickering, its surface marbling as life ebbed away. Cerebral fluid hung suspended in a viscous drip. Then with a sudden terrifying gurgle and groan, as if in a final effort, the remains of the body started to move again, to twitch and shudder. With a sickening thud a leg dropped from the support of the bed to the floor.

In utter horror at the spectacle the Minister's eyes rolled wide, his mouth opened and he emitted an ear-splitting, blood-curdling scream which came again and again, shattering the night silence, echoing round the mews. He was going into shock, but not for long, for with a flat open hand Kit hit him hard, time and time again, until the Minister fell silent.

The Minister now spat saliva, clearing a fleck of blood from his broken lip, gingerly licking the salt.

Everything became silent, the Minister's breathing now coming under control whereupon Kit answered the Minister's question.

'Now we have got that over with, who the hell am I? You may well ask. So, I'll tell you,' he growled, 'I'm a friend; and believe me now, *Minister,* you bloody well need one, now more than ever before. As for the police, well we will have to see -----'

Kit smiled, just, for the first time.

Two

Yorkshire

Two weeks earlier whilst in Yorkshire at The Manor, Beamsley, the telephone had burst into life, unwanted and rudely invading Kit's guarded privacy, its dull tone echoing, accentuated by the high oak-beamed ceiling of the great hall.

The call though was not unexpected; he knew it would come; it was just a question of when. It had taken some time, but when it did come he had no quick answer, no prepared statement and no excuse. But his mind had instantly flashed back.

It was now some time since the tragic death of Stuart, his oldest and closest friend, head of department, confident, and in some ways a restraining influence. After all, years before it was he, Stuart who had recruited Kit. They had been at school together where they had shared the traumas and excitement of growing up.

The memorial service was one of the worst; as for the funeral, itself, Kit was still involved at the time with the *Carlos II* affair and had unfortunately been abroad, but he had reflected from afar that it should surely have been him lying there with arms crossed in that dark oak box with the brass handles that would only be held twice. Stuart after all had come to warn him, to tell him of the wrongful suspicions about him that were circulating within MI6. He would willingly have changed places, in that box.

A little later at the memorial service many damp and questioning eyes had looked deeply and searchingly into his looking for reason. He had wondered if they too had felt the same. That it should have been him in that polished oak box, all those weeks ago.

He remembered that the Old Man had never spoken to him that day; he had kept his distance. He had seen him look toward him thoughtfully for long periods of time, his dark, warm yet piercing eyes shrouded by greying eyebrows, prone to frown. Yet now, weeks later, here he was, the man himself on the telephone from London.

He forced himself back to the present, yet he could still imagine the Old Man, sat as always at his desk, a tower of strength, and a figurehead for all on the top floor. Long polished corridors containing many secrets. Large and powerful, he would be turning in his favourite high-backed Chesterfield, the burgundy leather matching the inlay of his desk, he would be craving for a smoke, wishing that he had his pipe. He would no doubt as usual be cursing the doctors.

From the telephone receiver Kit, could hear the deep steady breathing, if now a little harsh. The Old Man was waiting for him to speak, waiting for the first move in this deadly game.

'Still smoking a pipe, I can hear,' Kit had remarked idly, listening to his 'rasp' whilst trying to break the ice, score a point. There was a stifled cough at the other end.

'Certainly not,' was the quick and curt reply, then after a moment, 'Kit, will you come up to London, meet me?' the Old Man – Sir Edward – had then asked, in softer tones.

Without consideration, Kit had refused point blank.

'The last time that I went to meet anyone from the service it ended in tragedy,' he said firmly. 'I've told you, I've retired,' he added, more politely

'Then I must come and see you,' was the firm, authoritative reply; and with a hollow plastic clatter the phone went dead. However, it did not sound, as a landline telephone should, there was no density to the sound.

Moments later the buzzer of the main gates echoed in the hall. Without hesitation or surprise Kit rose and spoke into the communication phone to the gates, inwardly knowing!

'Good evening, sir,' he said as he simultaneously pressed the grey button that lay next to a surveillance monitor on which he watched the gates open. But there was no answer to his greeting. He replaced the receiver and watched the progress of a large dark car making its way up the poplar-lined drive to the front of the house.

The fact that the Old Man was not in London was of no surprise to him.

Sir Edward did not ring the bell and consequently Kit took his time to open the thick, iron-studded oak door. When he did, he opened it slowly, deliberately, the flat iron draw bars grating noisily in their clasps.

Sir Edward stood there; looking a little older, yet still a strong and impressive figure. Kit thrust out his powerful hand.

'Welcome to Yorkshire, sir,' he said, smiling with a small bow whilst moving to one side; Sir Edward walked in.

'On your own?' he said quietly, looking around.

'Indeed,' Kit answered, closing the door after him; as he did so he could already see the chauffeur in the car making himself comfortable, clearly thinking that it may be a long wait.

'I'm sorry to hear about Camilla,' Sir Edward said softly.

'Don't be,' Kit snapped. 'We should never have been married in the first place. She's happier now. The not knowing of what I was up to, the secrecy in the end got to her. Women want affection, children and a nest called home! Anyway, it interfered with her, er, social life, not to mention the odd tennis pro. That is, my being here, back at the estate and not in London or wherever, it did not suit her lifestyle, I got in the way. Divorce is never easy, they say, but for us I think it was a merciful relief.'

'You're a hard bastard, cynical too.'

'I am, sir, and quite intentionally so, but at least I'm realistic, whereas many are not. The service has a lot to answer for.'

The Old Man had then looked at him, raising one eyebrow in a moment of thought, as he had done many times before; Kit wondered if it was an affected habit one which gave him the extra millisecond of time to think. 'Probably' he growled.

'Kit, I've come to ask you a favour.' His tone and manner changed. We were no longer playing polite games, Kit thought. It was now business as usual; the trivia was dismissed, done away with and not open for discussion. Marriage, divorce, unnecessary social niceties were now firmly in the bin.

'Quite frankly, I need you back in the service. You might say desperately, er, for a while at least. What with the death of Stuart, your retirement and the Liam fiasco, I am three men down.' Kit began to object but the Old Man held up his hand. 'No, please don't forget, you and Stuart were key players both in practical and administrative areas. It was 'one for all' and we worked together as a team. It's left a big hole, one difficult to plug,' Sir Edward spoke sombrely.

'Would you care for a drink?' Kit asked somewhat dismissively of his plea, whilst playing for time and showing no emotion, or little interest.

'Brandy,' Sir Edward had answered irritably, noting this non-committal attitude.

It was a rare occasion to have the head of MI6 in your house, a little wrong footed and somewhat beholden. Kit was not necessarily enjoying it but he was damn well not going to capitulate straight away, if at all. He was out and wanted it to stay that way.

He poured a brandy, a Hine Antique, and one for himself, which was not his usual tipple before dinner, after yes. They both swirled the caramel-coloured spirit thoughtfully. Whirls of spirit wormed their way down the warm balloon glasses. Silence prevailed. The atmosphere could have been cut with a knife.

'Sadly,' Sir Edward said, 'Stuart's files are very much as he left them. Liam's, and your old files too, for that matter. Although of course with the move to Vauxhall we went through everything.

Liam was a very clever man; he left no clues to his duplicity and he was good at his job too. To me it was a complete shock, but you knew all along, didn't you? Uncanny! Your father was just the same.'

Sir Edward sat staring ahead, lost in thought. Then he muttered irritably whilst looking around the old hall, curiously examining it.

Old oil paintings hung off the walls lit by dim picture lights. Game trophies, old guns of another era, adorned the ancient stone walls.

'Damn it, man, you can't sit alone in this bloody great house. It's like a museum.'

'I can, I do and I like it,' Kit countered stubbornly, returning his stare; there was a stony silence. 'You're not driving back to London tonight, sir.' It was more of a statement than a question; playing for time again.

'No, I'm staying at that, er, country house hotel close by, The Devonshire, isn't it?' he said, knowing full well what it was called – several senior government figures had stayed there in the past, old Willie Whitelaw when up for the grouse for one, and protection had to be arranged, placed in order. He knew precisely where he was staying.

'You'll enjoy it,' Kit said nonchalantly, standing and walking toward the tall mullioned, transomed window. He looked out thoughtfully at the lengthening shadows of evening that were cast from old horse chestnut trees scattered thoughtfully for this very purpose in the parkland. Cattle stood in their darkening shade. They were nut brown and white – Ayrshire. It was a typically English scene, relaxing to the eye, with the fast approaching night, gentle autumn colours soon to be bleak.

'I was going to have a holiday in the Balearic Isles, maybe look for an old farmhouse in Mallorca. Possibly buy an old finca, grow olives, grapes and make wine,' he said, turning and looking directly at the older man.

'Then do, be my guest,' Sir Edward had interjecting, smiling 'We all need a break.'

'But I want to retire, a complete change of direction, I really would like to, I'm serious,' Kit had expounded, looking directly at him.

'You never will, fully, that is. These situations are in your blood and you of all people love it, you always will.'

Kit had already been feeling the mounting excitement, the curiosity that was a drug to him. He now knew that what Sir Edward said was right.

'Listen,' Sir Edward said, finishing his brandy with a flourish. Rising, he made it plain that he was tired of this banter. 'Join me for breakfast in the morning and we'll talk then, it'll give you a chance to sleep on it. I'm worn out,' he sighed now, somewhat dejectedly, 'I need a good dinner and sleep.'

He looked it and suddenly Kit felt a little guilty for not being more accommodating, but without further ado, he shook the large, powerful hand, and the Old Man had left just as suddenly as he had come. All was now quiet.

Morning broke in true Yorkshire Dales fashion. A cock pheasant called loudly, voicing his opinion of the morning mists that were hanging ghost-like over the River Wharfe, no doubt of interest to an unseen hen pheasant or two which would be close by.

In the distance a farmer was calling his sheep from the craggy hills, their plaintive bleat audible along with his voice, echoing down the long narrow Wharfe valley that nestles on the softer side of the Pennines. The river gently meanders its way toward Ilkley, then to the famous brewery town of Tadcaster, and on to York the Humber and the waiting eager sea.

It was late August, nearly time to separate the yews from their lambs, with market beckoning. He wondered idly if today was the day.

After making a strong freshly ground coffee, he took a deep breath and rang; the phone was quickly and politely answered, 'The Devonshire Hotel.'

'A message for Sir Edward,' he said. 'I would

like to take him up on his offer of breakfast and will be there at eight.'

On the dot, he had walked into the small, bright, airy dining room, a former orangery, the 'metals' on his shoes clicking on the polished Yorkshire stone flags.

Sir Edward was wearing a conservative brown tweed suit, looking very much the country gentleman. He predictably sat in a corner reading the Telegraph, as expected it was held sufficiently low to take in all that was happening.

'Good morning,' he beamed, looking refreshed, rising as he spoke. 'I'm delighted you've seen sense.'

'That remains to be seen,' Kit complained, 'but be that as it may, I've decided to help. You knew bloody well I would anyway.'

The Old Man smiled, folding his paper.

'I'd have been shocked if you had not,' he said and with that the waiter, who had been hovering in the background, came across to them. They ordered two traditional English breakfasts.

It was a convivial atmosphere in which to gently put one's head back into the noose, to climb gracefully out of country life, back into service. Not to mention the new business ventures he had recently looked at; these would now surely have to wait. Promises broken; retirement was now once more on ice.

'When can you come up to town?' Sir Edward asked, looking up hopefully and wasting little time.

'Within twenty-four hours or so, I suppose' he replied. Sir Edward visibly showed relief.

Then as an afterthought, he pointed out, 'But I still need a break, I have arranged things.'

Sir Edward had looked at him wistfully; his furry eyebrows twitching.

'But of course,' he had crooned quietly, in the manner that a praying mantis would to its dinner.

Three

Several days later Kit had walked along a top-floor corridor, high above the bustle of London, just as he had done so many times before, to knock on the Old Man's private door, but this time with an escort and in the new department building, nicknamed 'The Block'; it felt odd.

The Old Man's secretary had met him at the door as after all he was no longer official, he'd resigned. Would he have to be reinstated?

The knock was greeted curtly, but as he pushed open the heavy door over the thick pile carpet, Sir Edward's manner visibly mellowed.

'Welcome,' Sir Edward had boomed with a rare smile, settling deeper into the burgundy Chesterfield, its polished leather gently creaking.

Then getting straight to the point and somewhat brusquely, Kit asked, 'Did you ask me back purely to sort things out, or did you have something else in mind?'

'You mentioned a holiday, Kit,' he smiled 'I see no reason why we cannot combine this with a little trip, if it materialises as I think it will.'

'Where to?' he asked, curious.

'Not just too sure yet, but the PM is worried. A senior MP – a good man too, it may be nothing of course – but he could be having a little, er, shall we say affair, a small indiscretion. The PM wants a damage limitation exercise putting in place immediately; you know, stop it in time before it gets embarrassing. If need be, have a private word with the silly man.'

'Do I know him?' Kit enquired.

'You do.'

'Hell, sir, it's hardly my field, poking through keyholes watching some old minister in a sex romp,' he complained. 'It's more for some 'understrapper' or some 'deniable' guy. Even for a young lad in MI5 home affairs back at Curzon St; give it to him to cut his teeth on! It's hardly MI6.'

'Not exactly,' Sir Edward corrected thoughtfully, 'There could be an awful lot more to it, and we need someone to be, er, a little diplomatic, shall we say, someone we can all trust, someone who will not blab to the staff. No, it must be kept in-house at a senior level; he deserves that, because you see he is at the very highest level, and more importantly --- 'He smiled, looking hard at Kit, his eyes piercing. '***He's a friend of mine!***' Sir Edward boomed, his voice filling the room. Kit took the point but bravely replied, 'Then why don't you ask him yourself, sir?'

'Well, if he isn't having, er, some kind of affair, he'd be very offended, that is, to think that I have had him under surveillance, me, prying into his private life. It's also extremely out of character. Then again, he may of course be being set up, its happened before! And that's where you come in, for the moment at least, it is just you, and I.' Then after a pause the Old Man said, 'I believe she's Russian.'

'Means nothing,' Kit had said with a shrug, 'London's full of call girls from the East. Now that the wall's down, the knickers seem to come down faster.'

'Quite, quite,' the Old Man uttered, sounding a little ruffled and not amused at such flippancy. Then he said, 'But then of course she may be a little special, the Minister would want that.'

'What, dancing off the top of the wardrobe, that sort of thing? Or running around on all fours mooing?' Kit had continued facetiously, not ingratiating himself. Now out of order, but really not wishing to be at all enthusiastic over the proposed assignment, his excitement was wilting.

Sir Edward had tapped his forbidden pipe furiously in the bin, as if to bring the meeting to order.

'No, damn you, Kit, you know precisely what I mean,' he said raising his voice crossly.

'No, I don't' he had countered, yet again being somewhat obtuse. Not a good start, he thought.

'She reputedly comes from good stock, that is the point; may even be related to royalty I'm told,' said Sir Edward.

'Most are dead, the communists saw to that in 1917,' Kit answered sharply.

'And, sir, with all due respect I have never met one who has not been related to royalty! It's all part of the bloody package,' he went on cynically, and this time Sir Edward listened with interest.

'Is that so.'

'Yes, it is, sir. They arrive, seem to wish to shake off all the shackles of communism in a breath, and who can blame them, but they strut and pose around London, complete with the necessary kit, Cartier handbag and scarf, not to mention the gold Cartier watch dangling from their wrist. Oh, and of course the obligatory designer clothes, with the odd title thrown in, London is a prime target.' Kit said knowledgeably.

'Target for what?' Sir Edward said curious and mystified, as if it were all totally lost on him.

Kit sighed. 'A new passport, a false one of course, a new identity, a new life, social benefit, money and ultimately an influential partner, who can blame them, but it's all crooked, all forged, multinational fraud.'

'Ah, crooked, multinational, forged you say. Then that's precisely where we come in. Multinational! Well now, that brings us full circle

Kit!' Sir Edward announced proudly, pleased at having manoeuvred Kit into this position; he smiled as he would at winning chess.

Kit knew instantly that he had said too much, his brain was not as sharp as it should have been; he really was out of practice.

'Fell into that didn't you, admitting they are crooked, forgers and *foreign*: that IS our department, MI6, not the Police. You do indeed need a holiday!' he grinned happily, leaning forward and passing over a blue folder.

Kit undid the pink tape and opened it cautiously, only two pages of typed un-headed paper lay inside; he took a deep breath and started to read. It was not long before he looked up.

'There's still no name, or names,' he said, not that he had expected any in print. Sir Edward leant forward again, pushing a small piece of paper over. Kit read it and raising his eyebrows passed it back, countering the older man's stare. Sir Edward immediately lit the small piece of notepaper and dropped it in the wastebasket. Kit knew there would be no other paper in the bin to catch fire; Sir Edward left no paper trail, just ashes.

'I see,' Kit said thoughtfully while taking a deep breath, adding sarcastically, 'and where have the loving couple supposedly been seen.'

'Trader Vicks at The Hilton Park Lane, just for a start,' was the reply. Kit winced.

'A pleasant place I like it, good rum punch too, a 'Planters', but not the subtlest place for a romantic rendezvous for a man like that,' he pointed out shaking his head in disbelief at such folly. 'Any pictures of the said lady?'

'No and it may of course only be a rumour.'

'But big enough for some well-meaning, friendly chap to whisper in the PM's ear though? And a big enough rumour for you to bring me in' Kit said, not for a moment believing Sir Edward's third hand information and apparent naivety on the subject.

'Quite.' His tone said it all.

'How will I recognise her?'

'Find him and I surmise you will find her. I have also scribbled an address for you at the bottom. You know Knightsbridge well, so you will have no bother, and of course you will unfortunately recognise him. He has apparently been to look at this, er, mews apartment. There may be nothing in it but you never know. I'd check it out with the estate agents, it's er, Langley's of Knightsbridge.'

'Indeed! You seem to know a great deal sir' Kit said trying to dig out more information.'

'I know enough not to give it to anyone else, but of course as yet I don't know enough and my suspicions may cloud your judgment if you see what I mean. So, will you take it on? Of course, you will?' Sir Edward asked, as if now needing to be reassured by a reticent Kit, who was curious, if not staggered that a minister of this standing could be so lax in his affairs. There had to be some reason, some ulterior motive.

That morning, now several days ago, he had accepted the Old Man's offer cautiously, and yet he was intrigued, curious. With that he had gone to London where Sir Edward had briefed him more thoroughly. It all seemed quite straightforward so as a 'one off' he had agreed to go on 'watch' as it were. He would be reporting directly and only to Sir Edward, working as normal somewhat out on a limb. He would find out what was going on even though he had not as yet been officially reinstated.

Four

'Slide your legs slowly from under her and off the bed, but be careful, I don't want her to be moved,' Kit told the Minister. Although thinking to himself he really didn't know what difference it would make.

He looked down at him, with his small, sad and now shrunken piece of manhood, like an old acorn.

'Not quite so much fun now, is it, Minister? Get in the shower,' he ordered as he un-cuffed the man at last, with a certain unceremonious disdain. The Minister's trousers lay over the back of a chair, so Kit rolled them up and folded them under his arm. The Minister watched curious.

'Just for now, I'll keep these so you don't scamper off into the night,' he said smiling, answering the Minister's unspoken question. He crossed to the bathroom and found it exactly as it should have been, tidy and no sign of any recent occupation. Kit left him alone to run his shower and went into the adjoining second bedroom. Turning on the light, his eyes took in a smaller double room with one bed creased in a small area at its foot; someone had been sitting on it, and had left a slight aroma of a Pine aftershave, BO and the smell of pumped up nervous sweat. This was where the assassin had sat, waiting, anticipating his kill.

The white door with its gilt handle was still ajar, leading back into the master bedroom. Not wishing to disturb anything, he moved carefully. By the far wall and on the floor, lay the glinting brass case of what appeared to be a 7.62 mm round from an automatic pistol. He stooped to pick it up and held it between his fingers, turning it slowly. Its primer was copper in colour and noticeably not quite flush with the brass of the case head, indicating to him a non-factory round thus a reload. It would have been loaded specially, the barrel pressures brought down to sub-sonic levels, to give a bullet speed of less than 700 feet per second and specifically for use with a silencer. And there would be another close by, possibly two, for he had certainly heard two shots.

But what was even more surprising to him was that what had appeared to be a 'hit' by a trained and proficient assassin was not! What on earth was he doing leaving behind the empty cases? He had not even fitted a 'collector' to the weapon, a device to collect the spent cases as they were ejected. They could be cumbersome and sometimes caused a stoppage, but to have one would have made sense under the circumstances, strange he thought! Maybe this was his first hit in real life.

The weapon; Christ! He suddenly remembered it had been thrust in his hand during the scuffle. As if to recall the incident he felt his damaged finger. He had discarded the weapon in haste with a clatter onto the dining-room floor as he had dashed through.

There was suddenly a hiss of water as the Minister turned on the shower. Kit straightened and went carefully down the open stairs into the small but ornate dining room. Locking the door leading onto the street, he wished now that *he* could draw the curtains!

The pistol lay under the table where he had cast it only minutes before. He bent down and picked it up carefully, film star style with a pen through the trigger guard. He then held it delicately in his handkerchief and pulled the slide back. A heavy round dropped onto the floor. He stooped to pick it up, examining it, turning it in his fingers thoughtfully. It was a 'special', as he had guessed. It was a reload, for use with a silencer, a slow lead bullet no doubt.

The shell was imperfect. The copper primer was barely dented. It was marginally recessed so that the firing pin of the weapon had not hit it with sufficient force to cause detonation. The open chamber and magazine of the gun now stared up at him glaringly empty. He had been lucky. But why empty? Another amateur mistake as the weapon should have held fourteen rounds. Empty? Hence, the reason it had been thrust into his hand. Did the hit man wish to swing the blame? Was it intended for him to be blamed for the murder? He looked at it again; it was a Russian Tokarev 7.62 auto complete with a short fat silencer, a Carter, cumbersome but deadly.

He went into the kitchen, found a flip-top bin liner and enveloped the weapon in it, wrapping it carefully.

Whilst the Minister was still in the shower he dialled Sir Edward from the kitchen phone, and told him of the tragic events; after a long pause, the answer was totally devoid of surprise or emotion.

'Thank you,' he said quietly and thoughtfully. Then 'Please escort him to his home, I will be there when you arrive.'

'What about the body?' Kit asked, surprised.

'Just lock the door and, er, bring all her identification with you.'

'What about her car she had a nearly new Escort Cabriolet? It's sat outside.'

'Did they both arrive in it? Surely not?'

'No, he arrived by taxi, still not very discreet!'

'No not really, anyway use it, come here in it, get it away from the scene and then I may relieve you of it.'

'Where's here?' Kit asked.

'David will direct you, just insist that you take him home, don't let him change your mind.'

'Some chance. Sir, may I ask something?'

'Go ahead.'

'Is this not now a civil case? for the police'

'What case? Oh, I see, m'm, probably, but not for the moment, I shall make a decision I'll be waiting.' The phone was put down crisply and the line went dead.

Kit replaced the phone slowly and stepped out of the kitchen. The shower was still running above. Holding the pistol in the black bin liner he unlocked the door, slipped out and moved quietly across the street to the apartment opposite, where he placed the liner and pistol safely for the moment under the cushion of the settee, then turning and locking the door he walked quietly back.

As he entered he heard the shower above being switched off. With a sigh, he pulled himself up the stairs and met the Minister coming out of the bathroom; he threw him his trousers.

'I'm taking you home,' Kit told him, 'get dressed.'

The Minister began to do as he was told, but for a moment hesitating, he asked again, 'Who are you?'

'I've told you, a friend, but it would appear you also have friends in very high places' Kit answered with a wry smile.

'I have?'

'You have.'

'Who?'

'Try Sir Edward for a start.'

There was a silence, an awkward silence save for an airliner clawing its way overhead; the Minister did not move.

'I see,' he said quietly to himself, visibly shocked, then a little louder to Kit, 'Sir Edward knows about this?' he said incredulous.

'Does now,' Kit answered casually. And leaning forward he gently drew a sheet over the top of the body. Looking around he collected her bag and checked what few clothes she had been wearing – little, but however small Gucci and La Perla come expensive.

The keys for a car and possibly an apartment jingled at the bottom of the bag; the blue Ford logo emblazoned on the black plastic fob. Interestingly, there was also what looked like a new passport; a British passport. He removed it, raised it to his nose, it smelt as new, freshly embossed, his eyebrows rose. Deftly and unnoticed he also removed what appeared to be the non-Ford key and slid it into his pocket.

Then as if the whole sequence of events was

just beginning to dawn upon the Minister, he looked across at Kit who was holding up the new British passport and looking at him. He purposefully sniffed it again.

'New,' Kit exclaimed. 'Funny, I thought she was Russian. A little present for, er, services rendered, perhaps eh Minister?' And he slipped it into his inside pocket, watching the Minister all the while. Maybe that had been the key to her passions, thought Kit.

'Oh, my God,' the Minster now muttered, holding his head in his hands; he was shaking.

'Come on, get a grip, man! Let's get out of here,' Kit said with slight annoyance, with obvious distaste showing in his voice.

There was little else in the bag; a notebook, a clip of business cards and some cosmetics, so he left the bag and cosmetics but kept the notebook and cards. The Minister rose, completed dressing, straightened his tie and began to look more composed, his inner strength returning.

'Come on, I'll drive you home,' Kit said again, impatiently. 'Where do you live?'

'Chelsea Harbour,' the Minister answered.

'Wet?' Kit inquired facetiously; the Minister did not smile but then added quickly, 'Hell, where's my briefcase?'

'Never saw one,' Kit answered with a genuine look of concern, 'Is it important?'

'Very, yes, very. There's a laptop computer in it, it's full of information.'

'They generally are,' Kit said quickly, looking round the room.

'It was right here in the dining room,' the Minister sighed, now beside himself, looking around with anxiety and in obvious fear of his folly.

'We can't stay here all night! I have got to get you away from here. We have to go, now! I'll come back later,' Kit offered pushing the Minister out of the door and into the street; he did not lock the door. Predictably the Ford keys fitted the Cabriolet, and Kit swung open the passenger door unceremoniously bundling the Minister in. Within seconds they were accelerating away in silence towards Chelsea and the Harbour development. The car smelt of perfume, her perfume; it was unmistakably Issey Miyake. The perfume she would never smell again. Sadly, it was her last scent.

Five

Chelsea Harbour was a hive of activity even at this hour. The local restaurants and bars no doubt helped, it is an area for celebrities to be spotted, this mystique all-adding to the Marina's popularity.

Kit, who seemed quite undisturbed by the events of last hour or so, looked across at the Minister.

'How the hell can you live in all this noise, this blaze of bloody humanity?'

'I've never really considered it. I often sit late so I miss most of it. 'Miranda', er, my wife, likes it here,' he added as an afterthought.

'Your wife!'

'Yes, my wife. I trust I can count on your discretion,' he added, his pomposity also returning rapidly.

'We'll see, for the time being anyway,' Kit said guardedly. 'Whereabouts are you in all this lot?' he asked somewhat disdainfully as he drove past the Conrad Hotel. A Liveried doorman stood outside, waiting.

The Minister gave him directions to the left and into a small, open residents car park, which was surprisingly, poorly lit.

'I live over there,' he said pointing towards an attractive modern block of white apartments, terraced backwards artistically at angles, overlooking the Thames and the Harbour.

'Anywhere here will do,' he said as Kit simultaneously found a slot. 'Are you coming up?' the Minister asked hesitantly.

'I'm going to deliver you to your door, if that's what you mean,' Kit said, abruptly looking at his watch. The trip had taken nearly an hour and the traffic had been heavy.

'It isn't usual for my driver to come to the door, my wife might be suspicious,' the Minister complained.

'First time for everything,' Kit said, being totally non-committal to the man.

'And anyway, I'm not your bloody driver.' He climbed out and followed the Minister towards the bright foyer with its electric doors and lifts, noting that he pushed the button at the top of the panel; no name just 'The Penthouse Suite' was registered there.

They arrived quickly at the floor with a rush of air, the Minister moving first as the doors hissed open, his confidence gathering all the while. He punched in his code into the door panel opposite, there was a click and the Minister opened the door to the happy, excitable sound of a female voice.

'Darling, we have a guest, and you'll never believe it,' she exploded. 'Just passing' he said, 'Although I doubt it.' And she burst into laughter of genuine delight.

Kit stood by the door as the Minister went inside briskly to meet his wife and their surprise guest, Sir Edward. She held Sir Edward by the arm, leading him towards the centre of the spacious and luxuriously appointed room, which looked out over the lit Harbour. They both held drinks. The Minister held his cool and, showed no great surprise that Sir Edward should have been there.

Kit followed the Minister inside, his trained eyes wandering, assessing quickly. It was not an apartment that exuded family charm and warmth; there were no family photographs he noted, just maybe the one on the corner table. From this distance, it looked like somebody in uniform at a passing-out parade, maybe the Minister as a younger man, he mused. Other than that it was all books, polish and 'Minister.'

There were no tell-tale signs of a young family; just blatant luxury. The place was immaculate but far too modern and clinical for Kit's taste; there was nothing out of place. There was no dog, no log fire, no worn-out sofa, no dust, no old shotgun hanging on the wall; it was not for him.

'I've also brought a friend,' the Minister smiled, gesturing toward Kit who had been politely waiting. He snapped out of his thoughts. At the same time the Minister's other hand, with the practised ease of a thousand insincere handshakes, shot out to shake Sir Edward's. Then suddenly realising he did not know Kit's name, as after all they had hardly introduced each other, the Minister faltered momentarily. Kit, equally experienced in guile, quickly took up the cue and introduced himself politely to the lady. He held her hand softly.

'Kit Martin,' he smiled.

'Mm, Kit, and I'm Miranda.'

'How very nice to meet you.'

She smiled, stepping towards him, offering him her cheek, and still holding his hand. He looked upon an elegant lady, probably in her late forties, her dark hair quite long; tinged with grey only adding to her timeless pedigree, bone structure and beauty. Pearls glistening upon the fading tan of her summer, Cannes would suit her Kit thought.

'And this of course is Sir Edward' she exclaimed with a mock bow, and a waft of the forearm across her middle, 'an old friend of David's.'

'David,' Kit repeated, acting as if he did not know the name and turning slightly to the Minister, who nodded in acknowledgement. Miranda, busy chattering to all, did not notice.

'We *are* acquainted,' Kit answered, raising an eyebrow whilst now facing Sir Edward and proffering his hand again. It was a light, non-committal shake.

'We're the odd ones out, er, Kit,' David stated, taking over the conversation and out of character, fussing a little.

'So, a gin then?'

Kit flashed an indiscernible glance at Sir Edward; in reply, there was an equally indiscernible nod of an approving 'Why not, what the hell'.

'Thank you, plenty of ice,' Kit replied, turning to the Minister, now 'David' his host. He was amazed as to how the Minister could continue as if nothing had happened; it was quite amazing. All his insincerity and turned-on charm, professional political guile, coming to the fore to help him in his hour of need. None of these particular charms endeared him to Kit, or for that matter, to Sir Edward.

After the usual fifteen minutes or so of social banter of 'Oh! What a coincidence' and 'How is Lady Jane?' 'The family, oh! University, good, good', with Miranda chattering loudly, yet absorbing nothing, she suddenly turned toward Kit she asked, 'So how long have you known David and Sir Edward, Kit?'

Alarm bells rang in Kit's mind, for sure this was now his cue to drink up politely and go!

'Oh, for some years now,' he said glibly, waving his arm expansively.

'Well where from then?' she continued persistently, her 'woman's inquisitiveness' mounting.

Sir Edward seeing the problem helpfully intervened. 'With David's political life, Miranda, he knows everyone,' he said, throwing open his arms and laughing.

With this Kit announced that his good deed for the day was done – 'bringing David home' – and now he must depart into the night.

'May I use the bathroom before I go?' he asked.

'Certainly,' Miranda said, 'er, here, this is the nearest,' she continued and led him halfway down a beige-carpeted corridor with modern pictures of irrelevance on the walls; she pointed toward a door on the right, at the end.

The bathroom, it appeared, was en suite as another half-open door led off to a bedroom, the master bedroom, Kit surmised by its obvious size and opulence.

You can always learn about people from their bathroom; a most interesting room, probably more than anywhere else in a house. Kit knew all this, and was always using it to his advantage. You can learn whether your mark has problems from piles to pyreah, whether he or she is a health freak, a thousand other clues are there waiting for the observant. But this bathroom was totally immaculate in white marble; with no bottles or potions on display, even the sneak look in the drawers gave nothing away.

Washing his hands and having learnt little, he could not help but glance into the adjacent bedroom. It was then he noted the second and only other photograph that he had noticed to far in this apartment. It was displayed on Miranda's bedside table, next to Jilly Coopers 'Riders'.

He presumed it was her side, as he doubted that the Minister would be reading 'Riders' by Jilly Cooper. The tight white jodhpurs displayed on the cover had attracted his immediate attention.

To the left of this was an ornately moulded silver frame containing a photograph, interestingly this also appeared to be of the same young man that was being displayed solitarily in what he presumed was the main living room of the Penthouse. This time the young man was not in uniform. His curiosity was now raised. Just about to leave and turning for a last look around, hell he had nearly missed it, there on Mirandas dressing table stood another photograph in a much smaller gilded frame, it revealed two young girls in school uniform standing by two trunks. Now I had it, boarding school, hence the shortage of family atmosphere at the Penthouse. Poor girls they looked lonely, they looked like twins.

He returned to the main room, dying to ask questions but that would have belied his tarry into the bedroom. He stood tall and thanked his host and hostess, carefully placed an empty glass on the glass table, whilst simultaneously taking the keys for the Cabriolet out of his pocket, and glanced across at Sir Edward, keys dangling from his hand. There was no reaction. Kit was not surprised, so without further ado he manoeuvred his way toward the door, but on his way, he said casually to Miranda, 'Have you any family?'

In a flash, he saw Sir Edward's expression change, metaphorically feeling, as much as seeing the sudden flash of eye contact. In the event Miranda seemed not to hear his question. Maybe she did not, but the Minister did and he never said anything either...odd.

Goodbyes said, the door closed behind him and he made for the lifts, voices gradually fading away. It was suddenly quiet. He punched the aluminium lift buttons for the car park and ground floor.

Her words, Miranda's, still rang in his ears: 'How long have you known Sir Edward?' she had asked, and now he wondered just how long it was. I suppose I've known Sir Edward – well, he was just Edward then – for a long time, since the days of shooting in the British Team, or even before when training abroad with them. Hmm, what a recruit; they'd been marvellous times, he thought to himself.

Suddenly he was jolted out of his thoughts as the lift came to an abrupt standstill; polished steel doors hissed open. He stepped out into the carpeted foyer, and made his way toward the dark tinted glass doors and car park. As he approached the automatic doors opened and he moved silently out into the night.

Almost immediately a figure from the shadows approached, a slim young man, sure of himself, who gave him a smile and slack mock salute. A salute without a hat?

'Evening, sir,' he said to Kit as he proffered a small leather flip-open wallet with what appeared in the darkness to be a security pass and photo as identity of the bearer. Kit a little taken aback and was just going to question him when he spoke confidently.

'You will have some keys for me sir, I believe? For the Ford, over there.' The confident man pointed knowledgeably and nodded in the general direction of the Cabriolet.

Well done, thought Kit. At least the man sent had located the car. But he also noted that the man never took his eyes off him, never faltered. It was unusual but he could only 'presume' Sir Edward had sent him after the phone call from the apartment. Presumption, he knew, is nearly always a mistake, but these were exceptional circumstances and he was not about to go back and ask!

'So, what am I supposed to do? Walk?' Kit questioned.

'Oh, no sir' the man laughed, completely taking the nervousness out of the situation 'I've brought you a BM,' the man said, casually tossing the keys toward him Kit caught them in the air as the man pointed in the general direction of a dark blue BMW five-series, and adding, 'it's clean, and I filled it up sir.' Standard practice, and a standard comment thought Kit. The presumption and earlier worry evaporated all now seemed fine; he had a replacement car, the Ford would no doubt go for inspection, all appeared in order.

'Thanks,' Kit said raising the arm that held the keys, and sauntering off towards the BMW. Then as something clicked in his mind, he stopped for a moment, turning to observe his new acquaintance, to watch him go toward the Ford. That gait, that walk, did he recognise it? Slim wiry, no, perhaps not. After all, it was dark, just far too dark. Yet the eye contact had worried him, unusual for a subordinate to hold such contact.

He turned back to look at the BMW and as he did, he noticed that it had no communication aerial; there were usually one or two bristling skyward. So, it was just a 'transport', he thought.

His brain was ticking steadily and he wondering how the hell they had known it was that particular Ford? He had never told them but then he had told Sir Edward and that was the only cabriolet visible in the park. Anyway, the guy had known, and the 'office' had provided a pool car so that was that.

The BMW started instantly; it was still warm as he reversed it out of the lot; the guy's body scent lingered. He noted that the Ford had already gone, and if the guy had filled the car it was not done properly, as the gauge registered only three-quarters full.

Kit was now annoyed at not getting the man's name, or of checking his identity fully. But that checked out anyway, so how otherwise could the man have known? He was so cocksure of himself; his eyes had relayed no nervousness. So, Kit forced himself to relax and drove on, back toward the centre of London, the traffic not as heavy as before. It would still take a good half-hour or more. He just wished the Old Man had been more committal, but then again, in the Ministers apartment, how could he? He knew he would be in contact within the next hour or two. Nevertheless, it was exasperating.

Then checking his watch, and yet again in deep thought, he estimated that in all he must have been away from the scene of the shooting for at least two hours already. His mind was now in relative turmoil trying to piece things together. It was all very odd – too many facts just did not fit. But his was an irregular world.

He drove on frowning as curiosity got the better of him; he would not sleep anyway and the surveillance room was not cleared. With his mind suddenly made up, he swung a hard right at the next turn, with tortured tyres he headed toward Knightsbridge and the mews, the place of tragedy.

His estimation had been correct and in just under an hour he was drawing to a standstill outside the little house, the apartment that was to have been the love nest, now a morgue.

The mews was unchanged, the few cars that were parked had not moved, all was quiet.

First, he went into the apartment opposite, the one that he had rented for surveillance purposes. Unlocking the door, he moved upstairs and collected the camera and equipment. From the back of the Nikon he swiftly removed the film, placing it in his inside pocket which he zipped shut. He then placed all the equipment in an old suitcase, one that he had used many times before, and tidied the only room that he had used. Everything was now as he had first seen it. Downstairs he stooped and collected the bin liner and the weapon from under the lounge cushion. Satisfied, he closed up the property and stowed the suitcase and weapon in the boot of the BMW.

Next, he approached the apartment opposite; warily, and hopefully unobtrusively. He looked up and down the street, with hardly any discernible head movement, stretching the retina muscles of his eyes to the very limit. There was no obvious sign of him being watched from any of the other apartments or cars, no unwanted interest showed; all remained quiet; no curtains twitched.

To his surprise the white Georgian-style door was now locked or jammed. He tried the door handle again. It was locked. He was sure he had not dropped the latch, but now it would not move.

Not wishing to show alarm he quickly inserted a small piece of plastic, about the length of two credit cards, between the jam and door at the lock. Then with an experienced twist of a small steel skeleton key the lock eased and the door gently swung open. An onlooker would have not noticed any difference, maybe just a temperamental lock.

He stepped inside and closed the door silently behind him. He stood there quietly for a moment, listening and adjusting to his body responses, purposely giving his pupils time to adjust and his eyes to settle to the darkness.

As he stood there listening he could not help but notice the very slight aroma, one that he had not noticed previously. Somewhere from above a tap dripped.

Sufficient light entered the room from the mews outside for him to avoid obstacles, so he decided not to use the lights and create any more unnecessary disturbance. He moved carefully through the dining room and to the foot of the stairs. For a moment, he waited there again, listening intently. There was no sound save for the dripping of the tap from above. For all his training, all his steel, his heart still beat heavily in his breast. Quietly and stealthily he climbed the stairs toward the darkened landing; a stair creaked and he faltered for a moment, waiting, his senses stretched to their limit before moving on.

The aroma now became marginally stronger. On the landing, several doors were evident in the shadows; one was ajar, the door, he was sure, that led into the main and front bedroom, the terrible scene of earlier carnage. Kit held his breath and with slight trepidation gently eased the door open; he knew he had not closed it as it noisily brushed over the thick pile carpet. Pale moonlight shone through the Georgian sash window, the glass panes and astragals casting a patchwork of distorted shadows, across the room.

He took a breath; the room appeared to be immaculate. The bed was made and tidy, covers now straight – ***the body gone***.

Kit raised one eyebrow in calm, controlled surprise. The aroma was now apparent and little imagination was needed; it was from some form of cleaning fluid.

Six

Kit was surprised but not totally. If Sir Edward had acted the moment he had put the phone down then he would have had plenty of time to put the 'cleaners' in. The job, although unpleasant, would have been professional, efficient and with the room left without any trace or sign – which was exactly how it appeared. Yet he was surprised that Sir Edward had not given him some clue of what he had authorised; his mind was full of questions. He seemed to be protecting the Minister. Why?

There was no point in hanging around, so without further ado, he cleaned any of his prints off the door, went downstairs and repeated the procedure on the door and furniture below. He then closed the door after himself, checked it was locked, and drove off into the night, somewhat bemused, toward the Park Lane Hotel, which he had so often used in the past.

Sir Edward would know where to contact him so he would wait for the call. Strange.

The traffic by now was light and Kit was making good progress, perhaps driving a little on the quick side – spirited you might say – so much so that he had been frequently checking his rearview mirror. He was therefore more than surprised to notice in the distance the flashing blue roof lights combined with the orange hazards of what just had to be a police car.

As it came closer it was confirmed. In any event, he was by now within the limit and probably had been all along, even if the Police had been in a side road as he passed. Then again, he had not seen them. Odd! Particularly as he was an extremely alert and accomplished driver, yet had seen nothing.

For now, the police car kept its distance, yet the lights continued to flash. He had one eye on the road and one on the Police.

On his right, he passed the barracks of the Household Cavalry at Hyde Park with Rotten Row on the left. Drawn and spun razor wire adorning the high walls, it glinted ominously in the white security lights.

Suddenly the squad car accelerated up to the rear of the BMW, hesitating for a moment, tucked in behind; then finally it passed him close by and annoyingly slowed just ahead of him, its 'Police Stop' sign glowing in its rear window, forcing him to stop.

He cursed under his breath. Technically he – just like police personnel whilst off duty – did not have immunity from a speeding offence; therefore, he could always be prosecuted, just like anyone else. Then again, he thought, he had not been going that fast. If he did get a ticket, he was sure it could be sorted later. Anyway, he mused, technically he was never off duty.

'What a bloody bore,' he muttered, as he turned off the engine and briskly climbed out to greet the incoming officer.

'Evening, sir,' said the officer walking toward him whilst speaking in an authoritative manner.

'Evening,' Kit answered with a courteous smile.

'Your car, sir?' the officer enquired and nodded at the BMW.

'No,' said Kit, 'a pool car.'

'Pool car, eh?' He paused then added superciliously, 'Ah, Dorset then, as in Poole, Dorset, eh?'

Kit gave him a withering look. 'Er, no, Officer, you know perfectly well what I mean,' countered with a stony smile.

'I don't think I do,' the officer now said sternly 'Have you any identification?'

'Certainly,' said Kit, his left hand moving toward his inside jacket pocket, whereupon the officer immediately stopped him.

'Now, lad,' came the northern accent. 'I'll do

that if you don't mind,' he said, urgently, holding Kit's offending arm firmly, twisting it at the wrist and thumb. Kit let him, it was painful but he knew full well that if necessary he could turn the officer into a mystified ball of humanity and stuff him straight back in his damned squad car, from whence he hailed. Which to his annoyance was still embarrassingly flashing all its lights, while the other officer used the radio. But Kit was relaxed as there was no point in a confrontation.

The officer started to remove Kit's wallet but to his surprise it only came part way out. It was buttoned closed and attached by a black leather strap to his person.

'What's this?' The officer exclaimed suspiciously.

'Precisely what it looks like,' Kit replied. 'A security wallet attached to an empty frame of a shoulder holster, which in turn is attached to me. If you open it you will find that I am Kit Martin of Yorkshire, but for the moment I am based in London. On the opposite side, you will see an identity card – plastic. It will be meaningless to you as it's out of date anyway but as such it is, or was, MI6.' He waited for a reaction, a reaction he did not expect.

'Oh yeah, an' I'm Miss Moneypenny!' The Officer laughed in mock humour. 'Heh, Steve,' he called gruffly to the other younger officer who was just climbing out of the car, 'We got Kit bloody

Bond!' Steve sniggered childishly, not looking Kit in the face. Kit kept his cool.

Then PC Sniggering Steve dropped the bombshell.

'Yep, this is it all right, stolen about two hours ago.'

'Right, mate, let's give it another try. We now know the car's stolen, 'e just confirmed it,' the first officer said, looking and nodding at the young boy PC for support. Boy Wonder nodded back.

The officer gave the wallet another forceful wrench, but the leather held and, so did Kit's temper.

'It won't come off so easily,' he said confidently, thereby annoying the officer more, who gave it yet another determined tug, one that was obviously intended to hurt or provoke. It did neither Kit didn't move, but stood like a rock, unflinching, without batting an eyelid. The officer puffed, surprised.

'What's with the holster, mate?'

'The holster's empty, and there's no law against that,' Kit answered confidently. 'And what's more my wallet's secure in there, as you no doubt have just found out, officer,' he added disdainfully. 'May I?'

'You go careful now,' the officer stood back a little, hoping he would be ready for whatever might happen, letting Kit slowly unclip and pass him the wallet.

The officer examined the incomprehensible identity pass and documents, which proved and meant nothing to him. Kit showed no surprise, not the least bit worried, just annoyed at the inefficiency of the Metropolitan; they were always at odds. It had to be just a simple mistake somewhere in the system, at the office perhaps, a wrong computer key pressed, or a word misheard; after all there were plenty of blue BMWs in London and the Home Counties, some with very similar numbers.

The officer was not at all convinced.

'Then, Officer, I will give you an 'alert' sequence,' Kit said authoritatively, 'a 'code', a number which you will relay to your superintendent on the radio, then after he has given me a code word of five letters. I will in turn give you a nine-number sequence. Unfortunately, after that the numerical sequence will be redundant, that is, if it's not already been used today. If it has, I'll give you another, then another and so on until we get to one that's not been used. Do you understand?' he said, glaring at the officers, who gave a half-hearted nod in reply. Continuing slowly so there would be absolutely no mistake he said, 'He, your Super, will then ask you for a code word in return for the number, which I will give you. This procedure I am sure you know and understand?' They looked blank. 'It isn't so difficult, is it, Officer?'

he said quizzically, with a sigh. Then continuing, 'The code is valid for a twenty-four hour period only, or until that specific code has been used, just the once that is.'

Surprisingly, the officer had listened attentively; the clipped tone of Kit voice was never one to discount.

But still the senior officer was not sure of his ground. With a problem like this, Kit could feel the tension mounting.

'Go ahead,' Kit said, mentally pushing the issue whilst pointing at the still flashing squad car, the beacon strobe eerily flashing through the trees of Hyde Park.

He had nearly done it, nearly persuaded the man, but at the last moment the officer's nerve snapped and, sensing something very wrong, said, 'No way, mate, get in,' he simultaneously and efficiently snapped a pair of cold steel handcuffs onto Kit's powerful wrists. 'Get in the back,' the Officer said again, as Pimple Boy opened the rear door for him.

The officer placed a firm hand on Kit's head and pushed him low, down and into the rear. The door slammed shut. He blinked at the sudden darkening, noticing there were no door handles, or window winders. For the moment, at least he was trapped. Bloody annoying.

The senior officer visibly relaxed, his

charge now safe as he climbed in the front as if to drive off.

'If I were you, I would do just as I suggest and make the call. It can't harm you; also, you will end up with less egg on your face, Officer! Just think, it might even save your pension. Besides, you can't just drive away and leave the BMW here. Neither can you travel with me on your own so that Brains here can drive it back. Officer, you need a back-up, you need to use the radio!'

The officer half turned as if to speak but Kit kept the pressure on.

'This is a very important situation that you have just blundered your way into. Officer, make the damned call!'

Slowly and with a frown on his face, the officer's hand went for the radio reluctantly he made the call; after all, he had nothing to lose. Predictably the Super was out of the station; the call would have to be patched through to him, redirected. But within moments they were

'live'. The officer briefly explained the situation to his No 1; then he looked sceptically at Kit, whose large frame was slumped uncomfortably crossways in the rear of the car. There was a delay; perhaps the Super too was not sure what to do. Then, 'The number?' the Officer asked suspiciously. Kit smoothly quoted a six-figure number to him. There was a longer pause before the officer again looked at Kit. 'This may take a little time,' he muttered, probably repeating what his superior had told him. Eventually he got the word from the Super. 'Nomad,' he said.

Kit gave the officer a nine-number sequence, there was a pause, and the man's face became ashen as he replaced the mike. 'I'm sorry, sir,' he stammered apologetically, immediately starting to climb out of the car whilst whispering to his mate 'shit he really 'is' one of the bloody spooks' He helped Kit from out of the rear of the vehicle.

He climbed out and stood to his full height, whilst holding out his cuffed wrists. The officer apologised again as he unlocked the cuffs.

'An easy mistake,' Kit affirmed, rubbing his wrists. 'You were quite correct; you were only doing your job; it could have been a stolen car.'

The officer held up his hand. 'I actually still believe it is, sir. We'll double-check, but this time against the chassis number.' He nodded to the younger officer who had been listening, and gave the order to proceed.

Within moments the bonnet of the BMW was opened, hinging forward and up; quickly the chassis and car's commission numbers were written down then conveyed by radio to the central computer. The answer was the same. The car had been reported stolen some three hours earlier in

Knightsbridge, from outside a mews apartment somewhere near Harrods.

Kit was stunned, what the hell was going on! Pulling open the BM door he started to examine the interior. His mind now working overtime, he looked in the glove box for the service history. The records were there and certainly indicated a private car; the garage in the Department always held the service history of any vehicle, plus the ashtray was full and Service cars were never smoked in.

Then on the driver's floor mat Kit noticed a small strip of turquoise and white polythene, the sort that would tear off and be discarded if you were opening a hermetically sealed, sterile polythene envelope. The small strip, now stretched and elongated seemed greasy or powdery and gave off a slight aroma.

Kit brought the piece close to his nose and smelt it carefully. His heart fell, the torn-off strip smelt of Latex rubber. Then with a sigh he stood up, tall and broad in the poor light, he looked across at the two police officers watching him; pensively he shook his head, knowing that unfortunately he'd been 'had'.

He was now quite sure that the car had indeed been stolen, and by a professional. He also knew now that the perpetrator would also have left no prints, no tell-tale signs; he or she had almost certainly been wearing a pair of disposable opaque latex surgical gloves, the sickly aroma was unmistakable.

'Right, gentlemen,' Kit said authoritatively, 'I need to get going. Any objection to that?' He looked across at the two officers again, as if now challenging them.

The senior of the two replied, 'Er, no, not at all, we were instructed to be of any help that we can.'

'That's fine,' Kit answered, continuing to take control of the improved situation.

'Would you call up a recovery vehicle and trailer for the BM,' he said 'Sheet it up and get it straight to Forensic.' Then, as an afterthought, he added with a shrug, 'Even though you won't find anything.' He then nonchalantly produced from nowhere what appeared to be a pen; it was a pager. He clicked in Sir Edward's number and 'sent' it.

Sir Edward rarely carried a mobile phone, always preferring to use a pager and arrange a meeting, or at the worst use a landline. He had a distinct distrust of too much gadgetry. But Kit knew that the real reason was to give him time. Time for thought 'to adjust or to arrange'.

He then went to the rear of the BM where he took out his suitcase from the boot and placed it on the roof. He also took out a bin liner from the boot and placed it within the suitcase. The officers watched, with guarded interest. Bidding them farewell, he hailed a taxi, swung the suitcase in and asked for the Park Lane Hotel, only a mile or so further down the park.

By the time that Kit was walking to the elaborate reception hall of the Park Lane, 'Bones', a bellhop well known to Kit, came to meet him.

'Morning, sir,' he said. 'You're just in time, there's a phone call for you, they, er, have rang twice already.' He gestured in the direction of a grey soundproof cubicle just off the main foyer, 'I'll put it through to that one, sir. Number five.'

Kit thanked him and closed the door after himself; with the suitcase between his legs, he picked up the phone.

'Martin,' he said responding to the ring. As expected it was Sir Edward.

'You called.'

'I did indeed, sir. What the heck is going on? That bloody car you sent for me had wrong numbers, I was stopped; the police believe it stolen so I've left it.' There was a silence.

'I sent no car for you,' Sir Edward said slowly and calmly; there was another long silent pause.

'OK so who was the man who met me at the Minister's apartment block?' Kit asked cautiously.

'I know of no man, I sent no man,' Sir Kit said, now sounding quiet and equally guarded.

The whole saga was now beginning to turn sour as far as Kit was concerned – complicated, and very disjointed.

'Sir, we'd better meet,' he suggested, wearily looking at his watch 'And, I think straight away, sir. Can you manage that, sir, er' here? At the Park Lane?'

After a moment, Sir Edward answered thoughtfully in the affirmative.

'Yes, I can manage that,' he said, abruptly putting the phone down; as ever there was a resounding click.

Seven

Kit selected one of many vacant coffee tables in the hotel lounge, one by an open fire that flamed brightly. It all looked very comfortable and as it was still very early in the morning with few people there, it was still possible to have a quiet meeting of this nature. He drew up two old, comfy-looking, high-backed Windsor chairs and settled deeply into one to wait, his eye on the door, the suitcase by his side, tired and more than a little annoyed.

He had been staring deeply into the warm flickering flames for some time when from behind him a firm hand rested upon his shoulder; Sir Edward had entered the hotel by the rear doors from Shepherd's Market. Kit was unfazed. They shook hands again, for the second time in recent hours. With a sigh, Sir Edward sat down.

'Coffee sir?' Kit asked.

'Why not?' Sir Edward said quietly.

Kit signalled to the concierge with a raised arm and a pouring motion, mouthing the word 'coffee' at the same time. The concierge nodded back in response.

'So, what's all this about?' Sir Edward asked, looking decidedly disgruntled.

With the benefit of a photographic mind and memory to match, Kit proceeded to give an exact account of the last few hours, from the moment he entered the surveillance apartment.

Sir Edward listened intently without interruption save only for the arrival of coffee.

Kit finished his report and lay back, relaxing as he sank into the leather Windsor, looking at Sir Edward, watching him absorb and assimilate the facts he had been given. He waited for some kind of reaction, which was some considerable time in coming.

'The body's gone?'

'The body's gone,' Kit answered.

There was a pause. 'The place is clean, immaculate?'

'Just so,' Kit replied nonchalantly and with just a hint of a wry smile. There was another pause, the silence broken as a telephone rang somewhere deep in the bowels of the hotel.

Then with a groan Sir Edward with hands clasped lent forward and sighed,

'Kit, I've made a balls of it!'

'I think I'm the one who's done that, sir,' countered Kit. 'I was the one who gave the bloody car away and what's more, I've just lost a body!' Kit was incredulous at the circumstances he now found himself in. Shaking his head in total disbelief at events, his eyes flashed back to Sir Edward.

'Well yes, you gave a car away, so to speak, but only in circumstances that I believe anyone would have. Someone is being very clever, someone was taking a hell of a risk in pulling it off, some nerve.'

'Maybe, but 'I' should not have ---' murmured Kit, his voice trailing away. 'So, what now?'

'Well, we must first try and locate the car; her car, that has to be the easiest and hopefully there will not be too many bodies lying around for us to identify either. But we'll start with the car first. Therefore I,' Sir Edward said forcefully, 'will put out a search for it immediately. No doubt you will have the number?'

'I have, but it may have been changed, indeed bound to have been by now.'

'I'm sure it will, but you never know.' Then after a pause he said, 'Kit, we have to start somewhere.'

With that Sir Edward raised himself out of the Windsor, walked across the room and used a hotel phone in a soundproof cubicle. Within moments he returned, smiling.

'That's now in operation,' he said with a grim face whilst placing a hand on Kit's shoulder; then in an uncharacteristic show of self-admonishment Sir Edward said, 'It was my fault, Kit, no doubt about it. I was only trying to minimise the fuss and embarrassment for all concerned. Let's face it he was dammed lucky we had him under surveillance at the time and we know for sure that the Minister didn't commit the crime and, we had to get him out of there before plod and press. It just seemed the right thing to do at the time. Now we have to find out what the hell we have got into, and yet still keep a lid on it. The PM will be furious.'

Then in a different and happier tone, which did not suit him, Sir Edward continued.

'Kit, you look tired. Relax, come on, I'll give you a call later,' and he moved to go, standing up stiffly. But then just as Kit was about to bid him farewell, remembering something, he dug deep into his inside pocket.

'Oh, and you may want this,' Kit passed him the canister of 35 mm film that he had used in the mews earlier.

'Thank you,' Sir Edward said, putting it in his pocket, totally non-committal. He turned to go, but Kit took a step forward, saying.

'Oh, and sir,' remembering a question that troubled him, 'why did you scowl so hard when I asked the Minister's wife, Miranda, if they had any family? I felt the vibes come at me like a ton of bricks through the air,' he laughed.

'Ah, ye-es,' Sir Edward said thoughtfully as if getting ready to impart some deep wisdom. 'Er, no problem really but the boy is adopted and, er, Miranda totally dotes on him, as all mothers do. But I am not so sure that David our potent Minister does, I think he feels a little pushed out. You see, I believe that, er, he was the party that '*could not*' impotent if you see what I mean. Also, I think he could quite easily have not bothered with children. A bit of an encumbrance to him, maybe.'

'My sentiments too, but I'm sorry I asked,' said Kit ruefully.

'No, no problem, far better to clear the air and then no mistakes later, eh?' Sir Edward said with a genuine smile as he left.

Kit turned and picked up the suitcase that had been partially hidden by the high solid arms of the chair, and walked down to the dark polished wood of Reception, the lift and his room, No 319 on the third floor.

He had always tried to book this room as there had been times when he needed to come and go unnoticed. This particular room had an adjoining fire escape, which could at a push be reached via the bathroom window for covert exits and entrances. Kit liked that; he hated feeling trapped.

'*Never, ever get involved with anything or anybody that you cannot get out of…in thirty seconds!*'

was one of his favourite sayings; and so, true.

As his head hit the pillow full of the thoughts of the last few hours, he knew that Sir Edward would not sleep; it was 3.30 a.m., and he would probably be in his office till dawn. There was no point in two people worrying and not sleeping. Kit had a gift, which he used gratefully.

He turned his mind off, and for the last few hours of darkness, he slept.

He was awoken fiercely by the sharp ringing of the telephone only inches away from him. Swiftly he collected his thoughts, knowing precisely who it would be.

'Good morning, sir.'

'Good morning, Kit,' was Sir Edward's reply. 'I trust you have slept well?'

'I have,' he answered, glancing at his watch and thinking of the three and a half hours' sleep. But I presume you have not, or have even attempted to sleep.' He knew that sometimes the Old Man could be hard work.

'Correct. I have not,' Sir Edward announced proudly. 'But more to the point, Kit, it has not been an entirely fruitless exercise, my sacrifice has not been wasted.' He sounded pleased with himself. 'I have probably found your missing car, or should I say the Police may have.'

Sir Edward suddenly had all of Kit's attention.

He shot bolt upright in bed; every last vestige of sleep promptly vanished. 'And wait for it! A body, Kit, a body.' Sir Edward continued in full flow. 'Yes, but just a moment, a female body, they think, and, er, youngish too, but unfortunately badly burned.'

'Burned?'

'Yes, burned. The car had apparently left the road at speed, on a bend at the foot of a hill and crashed down into woodland in a remote part of Dorset. Hit a tree and burst into flames. They say that she apparently died of extensive head wounds from the crash in which she was trapped in the blazing wreckage. Quite tragic.'

'M'm, quite; if indeed it's ours. I can remember the head wounds all right,' he replied sombrely. 'That is of course if it's her. How did they trace it if it was burnt out? Are they sure it is ours?'

'No and, that's just it, you will have to go down to Yeovil.'

'Is this situation not more for the Police now?' Kit asked.

'Not really, we lost the car in the first place,' said Sir Edward. 'And we're dealing with a 'Minister' and a related murder, I still want to keep a lid on it for the moment' Kit noted he had said 'we'!

Then he continued. 'Listen, Kit, I need some fresh coffee and breakfast, it's been a long night for me. So, I'll tell you all over breakfast at, er, I'll see you at the Richoux opposite Harrods in say fifteen minutes?'

'Twenty.'

Kit put the phone down and sprang out of bed, his mind an electrical frenzy of action. The car found! But was it the one? Burnt out? How? If it was, he could understand. But was it her? So many questions, so few answers...

He showered, shaved and changed. Quickly yet discreetly he made his way through the hotel; the doorman was busy so he hailed his own cab. Within twenty minutes of the call he was walking through the door at the Richoux, which was not bad – but as ever Sir Edward was there before him. He looked tired, years of irregular hours and meals were beginning to tell. He pulled back a chair for Kit, beckoning him to be seated. There was a flicker of a smile. That was about as good as it got.

Kit sat down, from years of habit carefully but unobtrusively scrutinising the other breakfast customers. Continental ladies in beautiful designer clothes, splendiferous in delicate furs, were starting to gather. They sipped spa water and freshly squeezed juices, in a mist of expensive perfume, waiting for Harrods to open.

Kit looked across the table at Sir Edward, feeling infinitely the more refreshed of the two; he was smartly and conservatively dressed in a dark blue suit and crisp white shirt; but more to the point, he was ready.

'The Civil Service seems to meet eternally in restaurants and foyers,' Kit opined.

'A hazard of our particular profession,' Sir Edward added glibly. 'No proper hours,' he mumbled with a sigh. Then looking at Kit with an inquisitive eye, 'Still get your shirts made in Jermyn Street?' he enquired as he stared across the table with jealous approval at Kit's 'fresh' morning attire, whilst reflecting on his own.

'Er, yes,' Kit replied, a little taken aback 'Turnbull & Asser.'

'M'm, did you know that your father used to say that you could always tell a man by his shoes? Did you know that?' Sir Edward said as he looked down at Kit's highly polished 'glass' toes.

'Oh, the shoes,' said Kit. 'M'm, John Lobb & Co, of St Kit are still the best, and before you criticise, the ones I'm wearing are ten years old and still perfect! The leather is superb, the fit unbelievable and in the long run such indulgence is probably cheaper.'

'I'm impressed,' admitted Sir Edward. This little interlude was as near to a personal conversation as you could get. Sir Edward appeared to be nearly caring.

Kit did not continue with this banter, it had all been said before.

'Do you think it is 'the' car, sir?'

'Can't be too many Ford Cabriolets that have gone missing overnight. But predictably the plastic number plates have apparently been burned or melted, and the actual chassis and commission numbers were also melted. They're punched alloy tags, aren't they?' He did not wait for a response. 'You're going to have to drive down there. I don't think as yet that this warrants a chopper for you to play with. The car, the Cabriolet, it isn't going to go away.'

'I could fly into RNAS, Yeovil ton,' Kit offered hopefully.

'You could, but you're not. No, for the moment let's keep it simple, er, low key, Kit,' Sir Edward said, dismissing the idea.

The waitress arrived and they both ordered the special 'light' breakfast and coffee. Halfway through the meal Sir Edward raised his head.

'Your car,' he said, dismissively nodding at the window, 'it arrives.' Proving to Kit that his transport arrangements were decided long ago and that, as far as he was concerned, breakfast was now over. Kit looked across the road – on the yellows opposite waited a silver Jaguar, four short stubby aerials protruding from the rear. The man standing by the side of the Jaguar he knew to be 'George', the head of MI6 transport. So, he had followed the move to 'The Block 'too.

The Jaguar looked similar to the one that his friend and head of department, Stuart, had used. The number was different, but that meant nothing. He was about to ask, but thought better of it; he really didn't want to know.

'I'll take the bill,' Sir Edward said wearily thus indicating to Kit that he should leave immediately. 'There's a full communications system in that particular car, so keep in touch, I mean it I want to know everything' he added. 'Anything you don't understand, George will show you,' and he handed him an envelope. 'The full map references are here,' he said. 'Go straight there and then make contact when you have seen and verified the car. The Police will not do anything till you arrive. Hopefully it is sheeted up,' he added.

Kit took a last gulp of his coffee, put the envelope under his arm and said goodbye. He strode purposefully across the busy road to the waiting car, dodging the morning traffic as he went – it was rush hour.

'Good morning, George,' Kit greeted his old friend from Transport, shaking his hand.

'Are you back with us then, sir?' George enquired.

'Not sure,' was the non-committal reply 'I thought you would have retired' Kit commented.

'It has a full communication package,' George

nodded at the silver Jaguar. 'Everything you will need. Understand it all?'

'Will do by the time I get there,' Kit laughed as he climbed in, throwing the envelope onto the red leather of the passenger seat.

Wasting no time, Kit raised a hand and pulled out into the morning traffic.

Yeovil. He thought of the route; probably the M3 as he headed west out of London.

He felt better now. Suddenly there was purpose in life again. He gunned the silver Jaguar down the slip road and onto the motorway, the engine beginning to sound crisp as the revs mounted, the sound emanating from out of the cosseted silky silence of the car.

As he drove south-west he still was not sure that this should not just be a civil case involving the police, but then again, a high-ranking minister was involved, it should really be MI5 territory. But the brief was 'an embarrassment limitation exercise' and Kit would live with that he had done worse things.

He was surprised the trip was uneventful; but even driving hard and with the weather good for England, it took nearly three hours, such was the traffic. He stopped just before Yeovil to recheck his map reference.

The crash site appeared to be at the foot of a hill on a long bend on the A37 leading out towards Dorchester, somewhere near the Clay Pigeon Café.

As he approached the site, he immediately spotted the accident; a Police Range Rover and a recovery vehicle were by the side of the road, the Range Rover's blue lights still laboriously turning. He could see the yellow Police 'no go' tape blowing in the wind and two uniformed officers were standing by, patiently waiting.

Kit pulled up behind the gaudy yellow and orange 'Day-Glo' Range Rover and briskly climbed out; he approached the two officers. Not moving their position, they watched him approach, curiously.

In the recovery truck, a driver pointedly yawned and then lazily stuck a cigarette back in his mouth; he did not draw on it but just let it dangle there, enforcing his disinterest.

'Morning,' Kit said, checking his watch with a flourish; it was still morning, he noted, just.

'Kit Martin, London,' he said forcefully, extending his hand in the direction of the two officers, the older responded.

'We've been here for four hours,' the officer complained, looking at his mate.

'Sorry, came as fast as I could,' Kit replied, dismissing the remark.

'Thought you 'Special' guys could drive.'

'Can, but it looks as though they couldn't,'

Kit commented, looking down the muddy bank, nodding at the wreck of the burnt-out car, which was semi-covered with a heavy green sheet. The tyres were burnt off and it sat on its blackened sports alloy rims; the charred remains sprouting wire, of what were once tyres clung to the rims; some timber close by still smouldered.

'Yes, a bad do. The body is still in there under the sheet, just as your lot instructed,' the officer said a little sarcastically. 'Come, I'll show you,' and with that they slithered down the bank and approached the car carefully.

A forlorn, blackened wreck was crumpled up into the base of a large oak tree. Kit noted the rivulets of burnt earth that appeared to flow and snake away from the crash site, downhill, past the oak and away further down the slope.

Carefully moving further down, he bent forward and took a pinch of soil from the scorched earth of the rivulet that had been fire. Between finger and thumb he held it delicately to his nostrils. It didn't smell of petrol, but possibly oil or diesel? He wondered knowing that petrol from the tank, he knew, would have exploded.

He'd wager that this car had been set alight. The 'fuel' for the fire, whatever it was, had had time to run downhill before it was torched; having a low flashpoint, and being slow burning, it had run and burnt like a lava flow.

'No real skid marks either,' Kit commented, snapping out of his thoughts as he looked back up at the compressed undergrowth, devoid of ripped earth.

'Yeah, we've noted that too. Nothing on the road up there either; must have fallen asleep,' said the officer with a shrug. Moving forward he now slowly lifted clear and pulled back the dark green sheet, which revealed the appalling sight of a mutilated and charred body. It was hunched forward, head to one side; its teeth stood proud, lips burnt away.

'Horrific head injuries,' the officer continued. 'Not wearing a seat belt either – she must have hit the corner of the windscreen surround hard, here.' He pointed and tapped the corner. 'Here, where the hood is joined up and clipped to the windscreen – dangerous these convertibles. Oh, by the way, it is, sir, it's a 'she', the body that is,' the officer added nodding at the corpse.

Kit looked sadly at the blue-black steering wheel, its plastic with the heat nearly gone save for a charred drip still hanging from it like tallow from a candle; the wheel, its metal skeleton grotesquely twisted by the intense heat, in front of the charred remains.

It was in itself a sculpture from hell, depicting the agony, somehow accentuating and reflecting the lonely anguish of the blackened, twisted corpse.

'Yes, I've seen something like it before,' Kit said quietly. He raised his nose, a sickly miasma of seared flesh hung in the air.

He had once been told that the Japanese could smell the British soldier in the Burmese jungle; because of our Western diet we smelt of chicken; there was something in that.

The young officer, his face now ashen, started to gag. Kit took absolutely no notice.

The burnt-out, blackened, crumpled shell of what once was a car, and certainly what remained of the body, were basically unrecognisable.

'Course there's no numbers,' the officer continued. 'Everything melted, even the alloy tabs on the engine and chassis have gone in the heat. It must have been hellish hot. As yet we have nothing to trace, but the lads at Forensic will find something. Dental records for a start,' he added knowledgeably.

Kit thought to himself: if it turned out to be who he thought it was, i.e. the girl from London – the Minister's 'Lady' – and if she did turn out to be Russian, there would be no dental records. How long had she been in the country? For sure not long.

Moving round to the driver's side of the car he peered down, eyes desperately searching for any clue, damn, just one clue, he thought, that's all that was needed. Then after a moment he stood up.

'Officer, have you a pair of pliers?' The officer passed the buck and gave the order to his partner, who promptly disappeared back over the ridge to return moments later with a pair of pliers. He gave them to Kit, who in turn went back to the wreck and bent down to examine what would have been the ignition and steering lock.

There was no sign of a key, plastic fob or auto door opener, obviously long gone. Wires burnt and stripped of their insulation coating dangled loosely. But he had noticed, and indeed could just feel in the melted alloy surround, a small amount of 'proud' hard metal sticking out from the ignition/steering lock. The lock face was just not flush. The pinch-nosed pliers could barely get a grip. A little of the melted alloy dross fell away. But after several attempts, they gripped and to his delight and the officers' amazement, he extracted the steel key. It came out basically intact, having of course been shielded from the heat by being inside the alloy body of the lock. He held the key delicately in his hand as if it were treasure, which indeed it was. The key's code number was clearly visible. Looking the officer in the eye, Kit said with a smile, 'Now we'll make some progress.'

'Yes sir.' The officer was visibly impressed.

'Er, Officer, will the bonnet lift up?' Kit asked. The bonnet release handle had melted, so once again the officer this time used the pliers, successfully pulling the cable; the tortured bonnet gave in and with a grunt the officer heaved it forward and looked in on the scorched engine.

'Any oil in it?' Kit asked casually and the officer removed the dipstick. There was. He showed it to Kit. So, the oil had not caused those traces, the scorch marks that ran downhill.

As ever it was now starting to rain.

'Sheet her up,' Kit said, 'I've seen enough for now.' He then proceeded to climb and slither back up the leafy bank to the road, leaving the officers to cover the body and the car.

He climbed back into the Jaguar and turned on the radio/telephone system. There was a hum of electrical gadgetry as green and red lights flickered on the console, a fax printer set itself up awaiting a call. 'Got it right first time,' he murmured to himself and within moments he was talking to Sir Edward's secretary.

The Man himself had not yet returned; forty winks at last, Kit wondered. After polite banter, he gave her the details of what he wished her to do, but also to leave a copy of his requests for Sir Edward. Basically, it was speak to Ford Motor Co. and get a trace on this key number, the car type, colour etc. that it related to, and if possible the dealer that sold it. But more to the point, to who was it sold? He needed all the relevant addresses.

Kit would be standing by in the car, driving back north up to London.

Before bidding farewell to the two officers Kit pointed out that in his opinion Forensic should come to the site and do some preliminary tests before the car was moved from its present position. Tests most certainly should be made on the surrounding area and the rivulets of burnt earth that ran away downhill from the car. He added for good effect: 'Immediately.'

He was sure that he was telling them how 'to suck eggs' but he had to say it, just to make sure. He suspected that it would be diesel fuel that had been used as it generally burnt hotter than petrol and had a lower flash point, thus allowing it to run away from the scene more at leisure than a fierce and noisy explosion of petrol. Diesel fuel was cheap, was easily available and would be considerably less dangerous to the perpetrator too, he thought.

Eight

On the return trip Kit made better time, the big silver Jaguar eating up the miles, relentlessly heading north. It had been a fast run, 'caution to the wind', and the Jaguar was 'panting' metaphorically speaking. He pulled up on the Albert Embankment, Vauxhall, outside the new, modern, multi-storey building recently acquired in London. He drove down to the side access the Thames and the amphibian ramp, pressed an electric device and the gates on the left slid open. Leaving the Jaguar outside the underground garage, he walked to 'Reception' as such on the ground floor, where he was recognised and welcomed immediately. The uniformed concierge – Mason, a retired military man – shook his hand vigorously. 'So, the wanderer returns,' he said, beaming at Kit.

'Not exactly,' Kit countered, as the concierge called from a distance into a microphone that would lead down to the garage for someone to come and take the Jaguar to its slot in the underground park. Once there it would be fuelled, washed, cleaned checked and ready to go again. The engine of a car in commission would be run every hour, warm and waiting for duty.

'Pleased to see you anyway, sir,' Mason said as he pinned a security pass to Kit's top pocket whilst opening the door of the lift.

'Remember, I always prefer to walk,' Kit said 'But where the hell in this place?'

'Forget it, sir. In here you'll never find your way, not so soon anyway. But I do know there's someone waiting to show you,' he smiled knowingly. 'You have a new escort for today.' Kit heard Mason press a buzzer and announce to someone above that he Kit Martin had arrived, curious as it was unusual for Mason to show any expression of a frivolous nature.

Moments later he was in the reception area proper, all glass and security, the actual entrance itself a curious airlock to 'see and be seen' before final acceptance into the inner sanctum; rather like something from a beam-me-up science fiction film.

Then suddenly as if from nowhere a lithe, fit-looking young girl of average height arrived. She was unusually attractive, with a smile in a million.

She was a blond, near white short-cropped hair and this outstanding smile, a remarkably attractive girl and what was more it was evident she had been waiting for him.

'Sheeka,' she smiled up at him, offering a hand and cocking her head cheekily to one side.

'Where were you on my first visit to Lego land?' he asked.

"The block' you mean. I was helping to get your office ready.'

'My office? They want me in an office so soon?' he said in mock dismay.

Sheeka did not answer the question, but continued. 'Sir Edward, I believe, is waiting for you now, sir. He's expecting you.' Her handshake was cool and firm, very firm; she followed his gaze to the stairs.

'Er, no, sir, the lift is better as it's a long way, complicated and for security the lift is more direct.'

'The stairs.'

'They are but ----' Kit strode out and started to climb them, two at a time with Sheeka in pursuit.

'If you're getting an office ready for me I need to learn the building and, I need the exercise.'

'I don't know whether you are supposed to -----'

They arrived at the correct floor not a minute too soon. He was not out of breath but he felt the exertion, and a little sweat; he would have to become fit again, and soon. By contrast, he noticed that Sheeka was not out of breath and enjoyed showing it, her colour unchanged, her breasts hardly moving in their silk.

'You're fit!' Kit remarked, looking into her blue eyes.

'Combat training, and, er, diving, sir. I love it, but it will all be wasted if you get me sacked. We should have come by the lift, rules sir' She smiled wistfully at him, her breath and speech under complete control; he was very impressed.

'Trust me' he winked.

Corridors are corridors, but somehow this, the eighth and top floor in this section, as ever was different; it was as if the walls held some aura of deep quiet and all-enveloping power. Sir Edward was an awesome figure and this was his domain; power knowledge exuded from his very presence. The vibes could nearly be cut, but the knife would have to be sharp.

They walked quietly over the thick red pile, passing Sir Edward's private door on the left and on to the second and the first office of his rooms, the secretaries' door. Sheeka knocked sharply and Kit heard the click of the electric lock. They would now be displayed on a CCTV screen so that both Sir Edward and his secretaries would know he was there. In fairness, they would have done the moment he entered the building. Even followed his very progress up the stairs.

The door was eagerly opened by his old friend and confident Susanna Forts-Brown (Susie in her younger days, now Sue – another

Sue), a distinguished looking 'lady', a secretary who had been with Sir Edward some twenty-five years or more and would no doubt only retire when he did.

Sir Edward had two ladies in his life: Susanna his secretary, and Lady Jane his wife; they were both friends, both confided in each other and both mothered him.

'You see, Kit, we do need you after all!' Susanna winked.

'It was nice to meet you,' said Sheeka as she turned to leave, her blue eyes looking directly into his. He dismissed her with a slight bow; the door closed after her. Her look had not gone unnoticed by him.

'Some secretary?' he queried, looking back at Susanna.

'Hardly, Kit, equality of the sexes means that the female does all things possible.'

'Always did, I hoped,' he quipped with a knowing smile.

'You're quite disgusting. You don't change, in fact you're probably worse with age,' Sue said, laughing, 'She's actually training for field work.'

'Which field?' he gasped.

'I will ignore that. Yes, she is very promising; anyway, you'd better go straight in.'

They crossed the tidy office, computers as ever hard at work. The office led off to the right and to a further office of a modern open-plan design with even more equipment, its large tinted windows overlooking the Thames and Vauxhall Bridge. Susanna saw him staring out.

'Yes, it's been altered, Kit. The staff officers found the offices up here too stuffy and claustrophobic. The building is an odd design, which wasn't custom built for us. A pity we're not in America! But Sir Edward's rooms are still gracious, he's not changed his ideas and we wouldn't try to, wouldn't even suggest it! His section, er, it was sort of transplanted here.'

'Who would dare change it?' Kit countered with a raising of eyebrows.

Sue knocked loudly on the internal door; in dark oak and forbidding to the uninitiated, it stood out incongruous against the white modern office walls.

From within there was a loud 'Yes', which repeated itself on the intercom. Sue jumped a little even after so many years, then with a slightly nervous smile and a hint of apprehension she opened the door.

'Kit, er, sorry, Kit Martin' she said pushing the heavy door wide. 'You've been expecting him.'

'Indeed, I have, I have! Ah yes, Kit, come in and about time, where have you been?'

As Kit approached the large desk, Sue discreetly picked up some papers and quietly left the two men to their meeting.

'Er, yes, sorry, busy day. Right, here we go,' Sir Edward went on proudly, wafting a sheet of A4 paper. 'The ignition key and the number. Brilliant! Well done. The Ford Motor Company has been most helpful and the car has been successfully traced to the number. They say it would have been a blue XR3, an Escort Cabriolet made in Germany. It has also been traced to the Ford dealer who sold the car when it was new here in London. To a...' Sir Edward hesitated a moment, looked at his leather-bound desk diary, then clearing his throat continued, '...to a Mr Thomas Harrington of Business Office Supplies, Wembley. On his instructions, it was given a private registration number of SWR 14, nothing unusual as all his cars have some form of private plate.'

'M'm, Harrington?' Kit questioned,

'Yes, a Mr Harrington, and that's the problem. We rang his firm, Business Office Supplies, to speak to Mr Harrington saying that we were Ford dealer communications, and that there was a recall necessary for some minor warranty work. He was fine, indeed most helpful, but unfortunately, he's since sold the car on, within a month of purchase; too small or something. And he has no record of who the present owner is, or was. He sold it for cash through an advert in the London Evening Standard, and the registration number went with it. The purchaser gave no receipt and

Mr Harrington has no name or number for the person it was sold to, typically says he's lost it. The deal struck was a cash transaction and the man said he would post on a receipt, but to date nothing has arrived. When it does he'll contact us immediately, I wonder!

'Harrington's description of the purchaser was that of a man of tanned complexion. He was small and slim, with greased down black hair, possibly not English, a foreigner maybe from the Mediterranean area, a nice enough chap.

'From the price given and the manner of the transaction, they must have bartered for an hour; Harrington thought he was certainly a dealer. He apparently knew his stuff about cars and had the 'gift of the gab' just as a car dealer would, so to speak. But there the trail stops.'

'It could certainly have been a dealer if he was bartering hard,' Kit interrupted. 'We'd have a guide, a rough idea, sir, if he was as from the price he paid; he'd want his margin. He'd want to buy it at trade price or below, which should not be too hard to find out. We need to ring Harrington. But hang on, sir.' Kit suddenly exclaimed. 'Why don't you just ask the Minister who the hell she was, get an address, search the house and try tie it all in that way, then bring in the Police and leave me in peace? I am sure we will find it was her car and body. As we already decided, there can't be too many Ford Cabriolets with what was probably a female driver, dead or alive, out and about at that time of night, and with half a head blown off.'

Sir Edward looked taken aback, more than a little disgruntled, not amused by Kit's outburst. After a pause, he said in a meaningful manner,

'Kit I would sooner that we tie our end up first, get to the bottom of it all, I don't want excuses or an explanation that does not fit perfectly. Ministers are used to explaining things away and that won't do, I just cannot accept a woman being shot off the top of a Minister or anyone for that matter, it's bizarre. But a Minister Kit! Then that really is my territory and I need to know everything and exactly what his involvement was if any. Kit, we need to know, and think of this. It is also a blessing for us that she cleverly spirited away by whoever and was found in her car miles away from what we alone know as a murder scene, that is if it is her. This way the police are involved with the girl and to them an unknown, car but for the moment well away from our precious Minister. So, there you have it! We have a car, a body, a minister who is a friend of mine, and a murderer loose around London. Why?'

Kit swallowed.

'Put like that sir I am sure you are right'.

'If the murderer is still here, that is Kit thought to himself. I have the murder weapon a Russian-made pistol, as yet to go to Forensic, her passport, which appeared new, her address to check out from the number, although he doubted that it would be correct, and he possibly had a door key.' He also needed it all to fit, to hope for the right address and a house to search. Kit too was playing cat and mouse trying to gain his own space in time.

'I'm sure we can make something out of all this lot,' he said thoughtfully.

'I do hope so, Kit. Oh, and those photographs, they will be ready in a minute or two.' Then after a long pause Sir Edward asked casually, 'Well, are you happy to be back?'

'It's not my normal role, sir, but yes, since you ask, I'm happy for the moment.'

'Excellent. Then don't be so guarded, Kit, you're the only man for this particular assignment and I feel it, er, is going to get rather delicate. So, I am absolutely sure your particular talents will be needed, which is precisely why I called you.'

After a pause, he quietly repeated his last sentence, more to himself, as if it was playing on his mind; then, 'Yes, you're the only man.'

He wondered what the particular talents were that Sir Edward had in mind. Possibly the way he operated happily on his own, rarely did he need a full team and the case was always kept close to his chest, like a good game of cards, which Kit enjoyed.

But with that Sir Edward opened his desk drawer and removed a sheet of 'buff' writing paper, with an address and a crest on top, which Kit recognised, it was after all his. It was written in his own hand, it was his letter of resignation given some months before.

Sir Edward stood, then slowly walked over to the Adam-style fireplace that was between two Georgian sash windows, all recently fitted. They were no doubt of some exotic carbon bulletproof glass.

Then steadily holding the paper away from himself, with a flourish he lit one end with a classical silver Ronson table lighter. He watched it slowly burn with a blue flame, grey smoke twisting upwards. Sir Edward dropped the last corner that he was holding between finger and thumb; it spiralled, smouldered and fell from his hand. The flame now extinguished, the ashes fell into the polished grate. Sir Edward turned to look at him, then after waiting a moment to get full effect, said,

'I hope you have enjoyed your sabbatical, Kit.'

'I did, sir, but as I have said before, I am **No Replacement.**'

'For whom'

'For Stuart

'Tragic, but that remains to be seen. Oh, your office obviously has been moved here to

Vauxhall, but your files, your desk etcetera have not been touched. You will find it pretty much as before. Oh, and your 'Toys and Equipment' are all at the armoury, just as you left them too.' He looked quizzically at his agent and old friend. 'I have checked,' he smiled.

Kit stood up and shook Sir Edward's hand. Turning to go, he said, 'I'll be in touch.'

'Where will you start?' Sir Edward asked.

Kit hesitated for a moment.

'At the beginning, sir, and I'm sure you know precisely where that is, much more than I?' he added a touch cynically.

'I have no facts, Kit, only rumours. As I said, we need facts.'

'You'll get them. I'll get the facts, sir, but I have a feeling that you already know those too.'

There was no answer. As ever he was on his own. He got the feeling that if the Minister was at all guilty of some felony, Sir Edward would wish to distance himself. But until that time, that moment, if he knew anything he was not going to say, it had to be fact, hard and proven, won by himself. So, speaking to the Minister was out, the girl had to be the lead in and she was very dead, for the moment then the only leads he had were in his pocket a passport and a key.

Nine

Kit stood for a moment on the grey, polished, marble-like steps of the entrance to the MI6 building. He liked the river close by but was not sure he liked the new building; it seemed as if the service was becoming more open, almost advertising itself. The service itself was coming in from the cold, and he needed time to think about that.

He looked up at the last pale rays of a low hazy sun, now fading fast on a horizon of tall buildings. A sleek white helicopter clattered swiftly overhead. He noticed it had a retracted undercarriage, and looked like an exec Sikorsky, expensive, he thought. Perhaps he was a little envious of some corporate tycoon being shuttled home.

Some of the civvie employees from the office now came past him from behind, glancing at him nervously as they left. Some seemed to recognise him, and offered a hesitant smile, knowing that to have him back something must be important. He was such a loner, it was said, so would they ever know?

They would make way for the night shift where

there would be 'a thousand eyes' staring blankly back at computer screens throughout the night, monitoring the secret world around the globe. Its information was constant, never ending; the vision often blind.

Yes, he had missed it. But he would have preferred to have been nearer to the centre of London, and his old haunts of Park Lane, Curzon Street, Berkley Square, and Bond Street, Trumper's the famous gents' and 'Court Hairdressers', and good restaurants never far away. He had never really liked the new arrogant 'Lego block' across the river even before it was MI6. Yet he had to admit that he'd missed London itself, for he enjoyed the traditional shops, the Establishment, the old duffers in pinstripes recumbent in their gentleman's clubs; his club after all, that was London. That was England.

Suddenly a soft but assertive female voice from behind wrenched him from his rambling memories.

'A penny for them?' Sheeka said as he turned to look at her. She stood there sleek, and lithe, a well-formed body of a beautiful young woman that had been perfected by hours of training. Now outside and in the daylight, she looked even better; quite incredible.

'You wouldn't pay a penny for *my* thoughts,' he said with a laugh as his eyes flashed over her – from the ground up.

'With a look like that,' she laughed, 'I don't need to!'

'I'm sorry,' he said in a soft and flattering tone towards her.

'So, what *are* you up to here, loitering with intent?' Sheeka said with a cheeky grin.

'Absolutely, and I'm about to ask you out for dinner,' he quickly replied.

'I don't get involved in one-night stands,' she countered coyly.

'If you don't have a one-night, how can there ever be two?' he quipped

'Do you have an answer for everything?'

'Certainly do – tonight, eight o'clock at Wilton's, the restaurant in Jermyn Street, then?' he suggested confidently; only to be deflated.

'You're too old for me,' Sheeka murmured, lips pouting, her brilliant blue eyes challenging his. For effect, she shook her head, so that her soft, tousled, pale-blond hair glinted.

'What has age got to do with dinner?' he questioned.

'I'd be embarrassed.'

'I don't dribble,' he said.

'You might though! Don't look at me like that!' she gasped.

'You could learn from a senior officer,' he pointed out.

'Learn what?'

'About life.'

'Mm, is that what you'd call it? I see...eight-thirty then, at Scallini's in Walton Street, Knightsbridge. Oh, by the way, tonight!' Sheeka proposed, enjoying what she knew would be her small victory with a change of venue and time.

'You've weakened then,' Kit smiled.

'No, I'm just hungry and interested on your view of life.' With that she walked off into the bustle of humanity, an unmistakable, bright blond, a girl who would stand out in any crowd, perhaps too much, he thought, especially for her chosen career.

He pulled himself together, called a cab and went for a drink at the Hilton; Trader Vicks, just to get the feel of things, as it was one of the Minister's supposed haunts. After which he walked back through Shepherd's Market to collect an evening paper, and on to the Park Lane, just as he had done so many times before. Right at the top by Wheelers, down past Christ's church, and left again to the back entrance, of the hotel.

He felt happy, happier than he had for some time, a considerable time, since maybe his parting from Camilla. He looked forward to the evening, although he was tired, having had little sleep. But for the moment the trauma of the last twenty-four hours waned, who needed sleep? Dinner with Sheeka had vaporised such thoughts.

Two hours later, after a swift shower and change, a scotch and soda from the mini bar, and a short cab ride from the Hotel, Kit now stood at the entrance to Scallini's, it was eight-thirty and he was just on time.

Two cars – one a stretched limousine in black with matching glass – were unloading their passengers; often dark-suited Italians that he knew frequented this place. He liked Scallini's; there was a touch of the Don Corleone – the Godfather – about it. Sicilian; he liked that too, it was all eyes and padded jackets.

He was amused to see Sheeka drift out of the shadows of a nearby doorway and approach him. She looked very different, taller and somehow slinky, yet conservative, elegant in her high heels, her extra-long, dark, Italian-style coat blowing open, which tantalisingly revealed a tight black skirt slit to the mid-thigh and a white silk blouse with all the right bumps and shadows. The effect was bordering on the old-fashioned. Her dress sense had style, overtones of films from the 1960s, an impressive retro-look; there was a hint of Marilyn Monroe, if only Marilyn had had short tousled hair.

Sheeka's manner as she came close showed that she knew exactly what effect she would have on him or any other man. Kit would try and get the upper hand.

'Part of your training, er, to wait in doorways?' he smiled, continuing, 'And may I say that if I was loitering with intent on the steps earlier, as you said, we will get on well.'

'I shall forget you said that,' Sheeka laughed, feigning an attempt to kick him.

'I have to say that you look beautiful,' he admired.

'I am,' Sheeka replied looking directly at him. He could not argue.

'Shall we start again?' Kit said. 'You know, let's try string a few intellectual sentences together, make a conversation. Truce?'

'Truce,' she smiled, looking into his eyes.

As they approached the dark glass doors of Scallini's Restaurant, a flamboyant maître d' opened one briskly for them. They walked into a typically heaving and noisy Italian restaurant, bursting at the seams; luckily Kit had booked – the concierge at the Park Lane had been right when he said it would be busy.

They were led to a pleasant corner table, one that had a full view of the activity in the restaurant, played out on the Sicilian stage before them both. He had insisted, although not without some difficulty, that he required a corner table, which was a bonus. He'd remember it for the future.

The maître d' took Sheeka's long coat and placed two large menus on the table, one in front of each of them. Kit opened his and passed it to Sheeka, taking hers from her. Within moments the wine waiter appeared to give Kit a large and comprehensive-looking wine list with grapes heavily embossed on the antique leather binding.

'Wine?' he enquired looking at Sheeka.

'Is the Pope a catholic? Of course, wine! Red.'

Ignoring her quick retort, he enquired politely, 'You don't prefer white?'

'Red, or should I say Rosso?' came back the definitive retort. 'I would recommend Colli del Grasimeno which is produced by Feruchio Lamborghini as a hobby; it gets him away from his cars and tractors. It's, er, quite delicious, and is from Panicale, Perugia. Anyway, white is for poofs and girls,' Sheeka smiled devilishly.

'You're not a girl then?' Kit queried, but got no reply. 'The wine,' he said again, 'is Italian?' trying to break the ice with a smile, but being more than impressed by her knowledge than he ever dare admit. He had heard of it, but only just!

'Are we not in an *Italian* restaurant, by any chance?' Sheeka retorted facetiously.

He looked at the wine list again, and of course it was there so he quickly ordered it! Sheeka could be hard work, he decided, wondering then if he had done the right thing by inviting her to dinner. Was she just a clever bimbo, in MI6 just for an interesting ride? Many were; it had happened before.

He continued to browse through the wine list in silence, deliberating

'I went out with an Italian once,' she announced loudly after a moment, breaking the silence between them. 'He was dark and handsome, a real trendy from Milan. He owned a restaurant right here in London. He taught me a lot,' she smiled, watching and waiting for his reaction. Uncharacteristically for Kit it must have showed, just the very slightest change of expression. A glimmer of disappointment or mild jealousy must have flickered on his hardened face.

His thoughts raced, along the lines: Oh hell! Is this a mistake? Is she just another good-time girl on the London circuit? Security has made yet another 'cock-up'. Yet was she not the bright, intelligent, one-man girl from MI6, the career girl that he had imagined. Then again, what damned right had he to think like this? He was no bloody saint. There must have been a good few, a score or more that he had never seen again, after the morning shower that is.

'You're jealous! And you don't even know me,' she burst out into laughter. Their own private silence was now broken again, as slowly her hand went out toward him. He was a little taken aback by the swift turn of events. He took it and held it; it would have been rude not to! Then, 'I never screwed him if that's what you think, if that's what you're worried about.' He suddenly smiled at her openness. 'I told you I rarely have a one-night stand and I don't get involved. I have a career to think about, one I am going to be good at,' she continued. "We,' in our chosen way, don't have too many friends, do 'we'. We are taught that it might one day not pay? We are loners,' she said tightening a little on Kit's hand.

'I can't believe somebody as attractive as you, and dressed as you are tonight being a recluse,' he laughed.

'I did this for you, really I did,' she expounded, gesturing expansively at her blouse and dress. Kit now suddenly truly believed her, she was not dishonest. He was truly flattered.

'Even for an old man?'

She smiled back, a radiant beauty.

From that moment on they were the best of friends, as if they had known each other for years. Both talked furiously, often frenziedly, both at the same time. Their rush to explore each other's minds, their wit and charms, to explore, knew no bounds. Both were totally enamoured with each other, the age difference vanished, melted in pleasure.

This was a real man, with a rogue of a smile, but nevertheless a real man, she thought.

Dinner ordered, dinner came, dinner went, and it could have been anything; Cold Cod or Hot

Frog! They would not have bothered, minded or noticed. So much at ease in each other's company were they. Kit had never actually felt like this before, not even with Camilla.

It was not until the coffee and a couple of complimentary flaming Grappa had arrived, that they even started to relax. Sheeka sat back in her chair looking at him, her long legs just touching his. She brought the conversation back to herself and back to her career interests.

'They say that you may be coming back to MI6, on a full-time basis? Er, head of department, maybe?' Sheeka asked cautiously.

'Have you not read the little notices on the phones about idle gossip?' he jovially reprimanded, then added softly, 'We'll have to see. I'm not sure and I have never been asked, but I do have something to finish, a loose end to tie up, so I'll be around for a while – perhaps.'

'Mr Non-Committal Maybe,' she grinned. 'In this country?'

'For the moment, at least,' he looked thoughtful.

Sheeka looked at him, he's a great thinker, she thought now watching him closely, and calculating too, his expression giving nothing away. He makes his words to fit your mind, clever.

'No tell?' she said.

'No tell.' He smiled and the subject was dropped.

She now knew her place, the game was over and she did not want to offend him; she had lost. She wondered idly if he even cared.

When the bill arrived Sheeka wanted to go 'Dutch' and split the bill; she still saw no reason to be beholden to a man even though this man was different. But he refused to let her contribute and she gracefully thanked him. They both stood as the waiter held her chair back for her.

'For the moment, I'm staying at the Park Lane Hotel' he said.

'I'm delighted for you,' Sheeka answered with a knowing smile. 'I have a small flat here in Knightsbridge, which one day you might like to see. Anyway, thank you again. I have loved the evening.'

'Me too,' he replied cautiously.

She leant forward on tiptoes, balancing on her front leg, and she kissed him gently on the cheek. 'Till tomorrow. Will you be at the *office*?'

'The Block? Could be,' he replied nonchalantly, dying to say yes; and with that he started to hail a cab for her.

She turned and walked off into the shadows and the night.

When he looked round she had gone.

Ten

Kit returned to his room at the Park Lane having walked back through Knightsbridge and Hyde Park; it was quite a long way but he enjoyed walking at night, it cleared his mind. When he arrived at his room there was a hand-delivered letter waiting for him, which had been pushed under the door. Sitting on the end of the bed he opened it. The sheet of paper was a tear-off from a tele printer, which read: -

---

Kit. 17.50 hrs
The first owner of the Ford rang in at 17.04. He remembers that it was sold to a firm called Sea & Sea Motors? Or similar. The only firm of that name that we have on record makes underwater cameras! Any clue?

E.F

Kit thought for a while and then laughed out loud. Sea & Sea? Hell no, that would be

C C Motors, situated out of London – north, on the way to Hatfield, on the old A1. Their full name was Connaught Cars hence the abbreviation and the letters 'C C,' he thought, and yes, if memory served him correctly they dealt in very low mileage, nearly new cars and sporty ones at that. The Cabriolet would have nicely fitted the bill.

He was tired now but that would be the morning's first task; a trip out to Hatfield. He turned in; tomorrow was another day.

For London, the morning was unusually bright and blue. He walked briskly into Shepherd's Market for a paper and hailed a cab in Curzon Street, requesting Vauxhall Bridge. On arrival, there he walked across the bridge and into 'The Block'. Today he would need a car. But instead of going straight down below to the garage section, he made his way across to Reception, ever hopeful but alas there was no sign of Sheeka. She no doubt would be up in the 'Gods' with some new guru training her to a point of mental exertion, such a pity.

There was no point in going up to see the Old Man either, as he would have no news as yet. Disappointed but not particularly surprised, he turned, telling himself to get a grip, women could wait. Pushing her to the back of his mind, he made his way down to the garage.

An hour later found him travelling north. He had not been out on this old historic road for some considerable time. It used to be the normal route north, until the advent of the M1 and a host of other motorways.

After about three quarters of an hour C C Motors, a mid-1960's-style garage with obviously defunct petrol pumps and a tatty canopy came into view on the left. He pulled on to its multi-coloured bunting-adorned forecourt, the little flags blowing aimlessly in the light wind. Judging by the cars and registrations on display, he was right, the present owners, even if it had changed hands, had kept the tradition of nearly new sports cars.

He climbed out of the immaculate silver Jaguar, which although it glistened expensively, might have appeared slightly sinister with its tinted windows and four aerials, but probably not to a car salesman such as the man who now briskly approached.

A smart, dark man with pencil-moustache and of ebullient character greeted Kit. He was small, slim and sharp, reminding Kit of the spiv in the TV series 'Dad's Army'. He looked like he should have been selling ladies' stockings in a London pub during the last war; he probably was.

'An' how can I 'elp you on this lovely morning, squire?' was his opening gambit. He approached with a swagger, a blue Barclay chequebook protruding from one side of his bright waistcoat, a used car guide from the other.

'Just information,' Kit said with a shrug.

'Cor, you're not the bleedin' 'Bill', are yer?'

'No, relax, I just need some help and then you will never see me again, I promise.'

'Go on.'

'Ford Escort Cabriolet, blue, registration number SWR 14, I think,' Kit said hopefully.

'Lost yer bird then, eh mate?' the spiv laughed causing the thin pencil-line moustache to twitch, his bright rat-like eyes giving away the fact that he remembered the car all right, and mention of the word 'bird' telling Kit that it probably involved a girl or woman. Bulls eye for C C Motors, he thought.

'So now you can have a laugh at my expense,' muttered Kit, continuing,

'Yes, you're quite right, she's gone to live with another guy. He bought her the car, I shouldn't wonder, and put her in a bloody flat somewhere! You haven't got the address, have you, mate, by any chance? I, er, need to see her.' So, saying he blatantly took his wallet out of his pocket. As expected, the spiv's eyes clocked the wallet, like a Magpie's first egg of spring.

'Address, mm, only what'll be written on the order sheet, but you're very welcome to that.'

He nearly licked his lips as he saw a twenty note being extracted, but Kit deftly palmed it and followed him into the showroom.

'She was a tall girl with long dark hair, wasn't she?' he said smoothly and once again the spiv fell beautifully right into it.

'Yeah, most of these foreigners in London are, not the Afros, I mean, but the Russkies. Why, you fancy a Russky then? She was Russky, Ukraine or something, wasn't she?' the spiv asked.

'Oh yes, Russian, but from good stock, you know, not really Russian, though she came from the Royal family of Georgia; South Ukraine, isn't it?'

'Possibly, but they all do,' the spiv replied with a knowing smile, in the same manner Kit had to the Old Man.

'They're all bloody Royals,' Kit smiled back. Where had he heard those words before?

'You seem to know a lot about them?'

'Naw, not really, mate, but there are some who operate out of the Chelsea Girl escort agency in Knightsbridge. I know it, been there, er, with a customer of course.'

'Of course,' Kit echoed, helping him.

'And anyway,' he continued, 'if she wasn't one o' them, her mates would be.'

With that the spiv handed over a completed green MAA (Motor Agents' Association) order form, which he'd taken from a battered old grey cabinet that supported a vase of faded plastic flowers on its top.

On the pale green MAA form that would once have been in triplicate was a description of the Ford Cabriolet. Also, clipped to it was a copy of the firm's guarantee, which on glancing at, Kit saw was more of disclaimer. But in any event the car was still under factory guarantee by the maker, Fords, typical, but at least it was signed, albeit the signature illegible. However, the order form itself was typed and stated her name as a Miss Vicky Sutcliffe of 14 Harbour Way, Chelsea. Close, Kit thought, so close that it might even be correct. It must surely be near to the Minister's penthouse in the Harbour proper, they may even have met there, at the Harbour, though he doubted it.

'May I have a copy,' Kit requested.

'Sure,' the spiv said, looking pointedly at where he knew the palmed twenty to be.

'Er, did she come here by taxi?'

'Naw, mate, with a geezer in a black Daimler; bit pompous he sounded too. I could hear the way he talked to her. How did you lose her to a guy like him; money?'

Kit said nothing.

'Anyway,' he continued, 'I didn't actually see him so I can't help yer, see. He didn't get out of the car. With all that tinted glass, impossible. Bit of a sugar daddy, eh, I'll bet? An' he didn't want to get out anyway; wouldn't.'

'No, I don't suppose he would,' said Kit thoughtfully.

With that he passed the order form to Kit, who studied it, cursing himself for not bringing the passport and key with him. Was it her car? Was it her signature on the order form? And if so was it the same as the passport. Was it her real address on the car order form? From what he could remember of the passport signature, he thought it was. What about the key? Only time would tell.

Once back in the car Kit placed the papers into a grey slot on the communications console, which was installed neatly in the walnut on the passenger side of the dashboard, he adjusted it to A4, pressed No1 and then the red 'send' button. A faxed copy of the order form would now go straight to Sir Edward, it would chatter out by the side of his desk.

With that done he drove quickly back to his temporary residence, The Park Lane, hoping that Sir Edward would be picking up the tab! Once there he collected the brass Chubb door key that he had removed from the ignition key fob of the Ford Cabriolet, along with the passport from her handbag. Only a few days had passed but it now all seemed a long time ago.

A quick glance confirmed that the car order form from the dealer had the same signature as her passport. So, she had obviously felt secure with her identity and this address. If the Minister, a man of such standing, was involved, could this be the reason? Was the new passport genuine? Or had she just got a replacement, or her residency? He thought not from the very look on the Minister's face that night when he had taken it out of her bag. When he had held it up and smelt the newness, the freshness of the print. That said it all; now to try the key.

The doorman of the Park Lane, dressed in customary grey livery, held open the Jaguar door for him, and within moments Kit was accelerating hard, skilfully and unobtrusively through the West End traffic, out towards Chelsea and its harbour village. He had no idea exactly where 'Harbour Way' would be and although he could easily have used a street map he wished to assess the area. With that in mind he parked the Jaguar some distance away from the main harbour development and walked back down King's Road to make some enquiries.

On a corner, there was a small, colourful and trendy pub, its offerings of food and real ale chalked in multi colours on propped-blackboards that leaned against the outside of the building – an ideal place to start. He was greeted by a merry, over-powdered, somewhat puffy landlady, whose make-up and paint would have done justice to Scotland's famous warrior, William Wallace. That said she put him in the right direction, her huge, brilliant, ruby red lips pouting hopefully, willing him to stay.

He soon found the street, Harbour Way, which was for one-way traffic, either side of which were the old dockland warehouses. They appeared to have been converted recently into apartments and studios, enhancing the one-time gloom of a dying industry.

He walked casually down the street, his eyes and ears alert. Number 14, with a mahogany door and brass period fittings, was halfway down on the right as you approached the harbour.

He tried the door at the same time as he fitted the key into the lock; it would have been suspicious to an onlooker for him to knock first. As it happened it was locked, so he turned the key and entered without delay into a darkened room with its curtains drawn, closing and locking the door behind him.

He stood there waiting, listening; there was not a sound from inside. Carefully he felt for the light switch, and with a click the room burst into subdued light. He did not move, waiting for his eyes to adjust, and to take in the scene; the only sound, although controlled, was his breathing.

The apartment appeared to be just a single large room divided off into a bedroom, a bathroom, and dinette with breakfast bar and a soft-furnished lounge area, all in the more modern Laura Ashley style. The walls were mostly of exposed red brick, black metal braces and beams, some glazed, some matt; it was a tasteful conversion if a little sparse.

A tourist poster hung on one wall depicting what looked like St Petersburg with the river Neva flowing under a bridge in the foreground. On another wall was St Peters square and a faded green Summer Palace of the Tsars.

A telephone with its red answer phone light flickering was on the antique pine breakfast bar, to his right. Nearby a little red address book lay open, with a pen to one side. The apartment appeared to be just as she would have left it. It seemed no one had been there, nothing looked to have been disturbed.

He moved further into the room, wary that it might still be occupied, moving slowly and stealthily until he could be sure. Then when he was satisfied he was alone and only then did he start to relax, to breathe easy. So, was this her apartment? A trace of an unmistakable perfume lingered; once again, Issey Miyake? Sadly, he thought so.

Reducing the volume, he played the answer phone back, there were many calls, twenty in all, mostly men saying they'd call back. But two messages, including the last one recorded, were from another girl. Her voice came quietly from the machine.

'Hi Verkuska, its Hella, where are you darling? This is the second time I've rung; give me a call. Oh! And Olga wants you to give her a ring as well. Where are, you hiding? Hope he's nice, you naughty thing,' and with that the phone clicked off.

Now he knew her 'real' name, or part of it, 'Verkuska'. Surely it was Russian. Just as it had been said on the last recorded message. With that knowledge, he took a gamble and dialled in 1471. It came back as a central London number, which he noted down to try later; it could well be the number of her girlfriend who had rang and called her 'Verkuska'.

Rising from the tall pine stool at the breakfast bar, he closed the small telephone address book that lay nearby and put it in his inside pocket; she wouldn't need it any more.

The mirrored bathroom gave little away; it was typically female and showed no signs of her having an occasional male guest. Kit checked the waste bin but there was nothing untoward.

Her bedroom, with its silk drapes and mirrors, was as exotic as it could be given the present surroundings. The small dressing table stood alone, somehow now sad and forlorn, as if it knew of her fate. It displayed an array of powerful and expensive perfumes, lined up like toy soldiers waiting for her, waiting for her to use them, but she never would.

As he thought of her now, her beauty gone, her lonely disfigured remains lying in some cold morgue, he was absolutely certain that the charred body he had seen was hers. Whatever you are, or whoever you are, no one deserves that end. He felt a certain sadness creep over him; he had after all seen briefly what a beautiful girl she had been.

Feeling slightly depressed he took a few dark hairs from her hairbrush, putting them in an envelope for Forensic to check out. He also took two small items of underclothing from the wicker laundry basket in the bathroom and placed them inside a newspaper; he would take those too.

He glanced at the large bed, which was made and tidy. He turned, but as he did so he noticed from the corner of his eye a small framed photograph on the bedside cabinet, nearly hidden by an ornate bedside lamp and its large flowered shade. He went over to look. Somehow it was vaguely, cut to shape from a larger photograph; it had not been done perfectly and it did not fit the beige card mount properly it was now at an angle within the silver frame.

The photo was of a smartly dressed young man; broad shouldered and dark, he was leaning on a sports car, an old one judging by its style. Kit was just replacing it when suddenly he looked at it again. This is just not possible, it can't be, he thought to himself. He was surely being mistaken. How could this poor photograph be familiar? Dismissing it from his mind he placed the frame back on the polished wood of the bedside table.

Next, he pulled open the bedside drawer below, which revealed little. But then right at the back amongst a packet of Kleenex tissues, some loose, was another photograph, this one unframed. It had also been cut from another larger one, the scissor line was not straight, but he was sure it would match the one in the frame. He picked up the frame and eased out the photo of the man. They were indeed from the same larger photograph! He held the two together and there they were, two people leaning against the same sports car. It was a remotely taken shot and therefore a poor photograph, but Kit could see that she was certainly beautiful; just as he and others would want to remember her. That particular day she was casually dressed, her hair styled in a different way. But she still looked wonderful, just as he had first seen her on that fateful night, when briefly, and mistakenly, he had watched her at her best. That night she was holding a glass of champagne; she had been alive, young and laughing in the mews dining room. Yes, it was certainly of Vicky or Verkuska, taken some time before with this smart young man. The photograph had been taken out in the country, or in some park. Judging by the leaves and colours in the background it was summer.

He looked again at the photograph. Was this her 'real' boyfriend framed by the bedside? Then what of the Minister? Somehow it troubled him. But no, surely, he was mistaken; he didn't know this young man, had not seen him before; it was not a good photograph anyway, but could he be sure?

Suddenly the silence was shattered by a knock on the door.

In the quiet it sounded very loud. Kit froze as he stared at the door. The brass door handle moved up and down, agitated as the door was tried and tried again; the knocking continued.

His heart began to race, pounding as his breathing quickened, but within seconds he was back under control, ready for whatever might happen.

A small piece of paper appeared under the door and a moment later he heard footsteps moving away; the distinctive rap-tap, rap-tap of high heels. He dashed to the window and slowly eased back the curtain just one tiny and indiscernible fraction to see a tall blond girl with long flowing hair climbing into a taxi. She looked about twenty-six, of the same striking calibre as Verkuska, the same style, and the same dress code. Kit relaxed as the noise of the taxi faded away into the distance. All fell quiet once again.

Bending forward he picked up the piece of paper, which read simply: 'Verkuska, Olga wants you to ring' and it was signed 'Hella'. A piece of the jigsaw had fallen into place.

The apartment disappointingly had not revealed much, but as he walked back to the Jaguar Kit was not in the least surprised. Perhaps he should have given it a more thorough search but somehow going through all her personal clothes and belongings did not appeal to him. He believed she was the victim of some appalling circumstances and not the real perpetrator of some terrible crime. However, he now had an address book, which he would laboriously analyse, and there was always the last number on the answer phone, probably Olga's.

When he got back to the Jaguar he found that there was a message waiting for him; the red 'message' light was flashing urgently on the communication console, but not wishing to be seen longer than was necessary in the street, he wasted no time in moving swiftly off into the traffic. As he drove he pushed the receive button; it was the voice of Sir Edward, wanting an update.

Kit rang in to the office but not for the Old Man. For the moment, he was wary of making any direct contact, as the case was only just hotting up and he preferred to present Sir Edward with some concrete evidence first. When the phone connected and the operator spoke he asked to speak directly to Sheeka. Her extension was promptly answered.

'I thought you might have made contact,' he complained.

"I'm not allowed to,' she replied, 'and anyway it's not my style. You, sir, are of course my superior.'

'How superior am I?' he enquired with a laugh.

'Once again, Kit, I'll forget you ever said that. Er, sorry 'sir'.'

After a pause, he continued, 'Dinner tonight then?'

'Busy,' she replied quickly.

He felt deflated but he rather expected it.

However, after a pause during which he could hear her breathing, she continued, 'But seriously, I would have really loved to.' His mood lifted immediately as she sounded genuine. Then as an afterthought she said, 'I know we don't have lunch as such in the Service, but tomorrow I have to go out at one p.m. to collect some files that should be ready. I could see you then for a snack.'

'Right, Harrods oyster bar at one-fifteen,' Kit commanded.

There was a gulp at the other end of the phone. 'Oysters?'

'Yes, oysters. Nothing less, they're good for you,' he said trying to sound less officious.

'Er, good for what? Is there anything else remotely edible?' Sheeka asked.

'For you, Sheeka, I can arrange anything.'

'I can't wait, I'll look forward to it,' the phone was put down with a clatter. She doesn't waste words, he thought admiringly.

The traffic had been heavy and by now it was late afternoon. He was tired as he approached the Park Lane, so without further ado he parked the Jaguar in the hotel garage at the rear, locked it and went into the hotel through the foyer, through Palm Court lounge and into the Brassiere Bar where he ordered a Scotch and soda. He selected a comfortable chair in a corner and settled down;

opening the address book he had taken from Verkuska's apartment.

After about fifteen minutes of perusal it had revealed little, other than a maze of numbers but very few names. Some of the telephone numbers had little ink drawings next to them. Only she would have known whose name they really represented. But some he could guess. There was a hangman's noose; was he a client, a judge perhaps? Or just bad news.

Kit wasn't overly suspicious. If she were some form of call girl or high-class hostess, which he was now beginning to believe, then this practice was commonplace, to preserve clients' anonymity. Also, the trade of prostitution would be more difficult to prove if she was ever in trouble with the law.

He snapped the red address book shut with a resounding 'smack', knocked the residue of his whisky back and left the bar for his room. Some of these numbers needed ringing.

Once settled he rang several to no avail other than passing sordid interest; one was a solicitor in Harrow, another a doctor. Then he rang one that stood out as a fairly recent entry: the page was clean and against it there was a top hat penned in what looked like fresh ink; it was a mobile number. He punched in the numbers using a direct dial from the hotel room, the 141-code included as a prefix before, so as to withhold the dialler's number. After a moment, it was answered by an aristocratic, arrogant and slightly pompous voice.

'Hello, Stevens here, Stevens, hello,' the voice shouted. He recognised the voice immediately it was David, the Minister. 'Bull's-eye,' Kit muttered, not bad and for the second time today things were getting better, a chance in a hundred or more. He smiled to himself as he put the phone down. David Stevens indeed!

So now he knew! Another piece, he thought as he dialled in a further number, the last re-dial from her phone. There was no answer. Then he thought for a moment, what was that name, what was the name of that escort agency? The one the car salesman had mentioned when he was at C C Motors. Then it came to him, yes, the Chelsea Girl. He promptly did a 192 and dialled Directory Enquiries who gave him the number. He dialled it in, and the phone was answered instantly.

'Good evening, this is the Chelsea Girl,' Came the reply.

'You're an escort agency, aren't you?' he said, deliberately sounding a little hesitant, nervous.

'We certainly are, sir! How can we help you, would you like us to send you a girl, or would you prefer to come down and view?' Came the quick and eager reply.

'Er, no, no, I'll come down and view. Whereabouts, are you?'

'Beauchamp Place, Knightsbridge.'

'Er, I like Russian girls. Do you have any?'

'Certainly, sir, the best in the City,' was her standard reply. 'If you come at about eight this evening you can see for yourself. Most of the girls should be here by then, OK?'

'I'll be there,' and with that Kit replaced the phone, poured another Scotch from the mini bar in the room, then spun the antique brass taps on a large Victorian bath. Hot steaming water gushed in. He lay out a blue blazer and flannels on the bed, which was just about as casual as he ever got.

An hour later and approaching 8 o'clock he was walking expectantly down Beauchamp Place in Knightsbridge. Finding the premises above a continental restaurant, he climbed the twisting stairs to a half-open door, inside which a charming lady 'of a certain age' greeted him. A retired escort, he thought. Girls of all shapes, colours and creeds scuttled off into an adjoining room closing the door behind them, shutting the giggles out, their perfume mingling with cooking smells and garlic, all emanating up through the boards from the restaurant below, a battle royal.

He was asked to sit down on a large and comfortable chaise longue. When he seemed comfortable, it was then tantalisingly explained to him that the girls would come from out of the room opposite one by one and parade before him.

If there was one that he wished to have as an 'escort' for the evening, then he should say so. They would then be introduced, and of course terms would be discussed. The madam was just about to call a girl in when Kit asked, 'Have you a girl called Vicky or is it Verkuska working here? Er, she was you see er, recommended. I understand she's Russian? I just love some of the Russians,' he uttered, rubbing his hands nervously. He presumed one did that.

The woman was clearly un-phased, and gave him a comforting smile.

'What a girl! We do, yes, but our girl Verkuska, she is not very regular now. A real beauty, but because of that she's a law unto herself. She's Russian all right. A lot of girls here are. But it's also a common name. Anyway, we haven't seen her here for a few days, although of course it may not be the same girl, we do have others.'

Kit just knew he had to keep her talking.

'Yes, of course I understand. It's just as I said, I was recommended by a friend and he mentioned her name. He met her at Trader Vick's. Did she ever go there, do you know?'

'Possibly, a lot of the girls get taken there, it's a meeting point too. But probably not our girl, though, she's been busy! I think, well no, I'm sure, that she's got an attentive and unsuspecting boyfriend, totally kosher. I think it keeps them stable. It's surprising how many girls in this profession do, you know. They go out and about as normal, saying they're secretaries, au pairs or something, and the boys never catch on. They don't think logically enough when they have a lump in their pants. You know 'where is she getting all the money'?

'Ang' on a minute you're not a tax man or the 'Old Bill' are you?

'No, no' Kit laughed, 'It's just that this pal of mine said she was fantastic'

'Well she is and she also had, of late you might say, a bit of a sugar daddy hanging on too, best of both worlds. It was from here he met her. So latterly she did not have too much time for this job, 'a bit beneath her', if you see what I mean.' She laughed heartily at her own joke. 'You know, darting between the two of them, you know 'the stud and the paymaster, 'she laughed again.

'Anyway, she's probably lying in luxury somewhere, sipping iced Pina Colada, under some palms on a white Caribbean beach, resplendent in the sun. Probably doesn't need us anymore. They all get established here, then move on to better things,' she added nonchalantly. 'Could even be your mate.'

'Perhaps,' said Kit. He hoped his expression would not give him away, as he couldn't believe his luck – surely this was the same girl. The little car salesman's information was spot on.

'Anyway, listen enough is enough, would you like to see the girls now?' the madam asked impatiently.

'I would,' he smiled settling down into the chaise. With that the woman pressed a button on her modern desk, which in turn created an inconsistent buzz in the next room – both of bell and chatter. On cue the first girl came slinking into view.

'I'm Kirsty,' she smiled, 'from Scotland.' She lent forward, proffering her hand for him to shake. She swayed before his very eyes in her high heels and very little else, balancing with some difficulty. Kit made a move to stand up for the girl but the lady at the desk waved him back.

'If you do that each time you'll be up and down all night.'

'Isn't that the idea?' he answered with a knowing smile.

As Kirsty bent forward, he peeked a glance through her wide, ample and extraordinary cleavage; he could see down to her toes. He doubted her dress to be any more than three feet in total length, from shoulder to thigh.

They shook hands and smiled remotely, automatically. And so, it continued, from Kirsty to Linda to Susie and so on. Twenty gorgeous girls all clad in various stages of undress, it seemed, large, small, pendulous and pert; round, leggy, blonde to black, east to west, and not forgetting the deep, deep south. All in turn and ever hopeful, they teetered toward him. But disappointingly no Russian girl was there at the moment, or so it seemed.

'Have you a girl called Olga?' he said to the woman at the desk as the last girl wobbled back into the next room, her bum working as if by remote control.

'I'm Olga,' she replied. There was a pause as Kit's brain exploded with annoyance, why the hell hadn't he thought of that? Of course, it was obvious this would-be Olga ringing in for her girl. Verkuska was needed for duty, to work at the agency.

'Which girl would you like to see again?' she questioned. 'Oh, and I, er, don't work anymore, that is not unless you particularly want an old Olga!' she replied quizzically maybe hopefully.

'Er, the first one, Kirsty, she has a certain unbalanced look,' he said. Olga smiled back at him. The buzzer went again and one of the girls popped her head round the door.

'Kirsty please,' Olga said to the girl who promptly frowned.

Disappointed, she called Kirsty. In a flash, Kirsty came through the doorway and tripped across the floor to unfold herself resplendent on the arm of the chaise longue. As they discussed terms Olga discreetly walked into the back room to join the remaining girls and left them to it.

Kit was not bound to take a girl, but he thought it rude not to. He could certainly have refused. But maybe she could be of use. She might even have known Vicky.

'It's £400 for two hours,' she announced. He blanched, his mind changing. Then Kirsty whispered her trade and sweet nothings excitedly in his ear, her tongue licking his lobe as she simultaneously fondled him knee to thigh.

'Did you know a girl called Vicky?' he asked, unmoved by this sudden display of financial lust.

'Phew, Vicky the Rusky? That's what we called her. But no not really – we've normally a few Russian girls floating about here but they keep themselves to themselves, stick together, they do. You see, I doubt they're all supposed to be in this country. They get visas and false passports or whatever and then vanish in the city! Never see em again.'

'Is that all you know?'

'Yes, I don't get involved, none of us do, it's just the way they are. The Czechs are the same.'

'What about passports, where do they get those from?'

'Here, you're not a copper, are you?' she grimaced.

'No, certainly not,' he laughed, giving her a squeeze. 'Just interested' With that she homed in on him again, brushing his crotch.

'But what about us, what about us tonight?'

'£400, it's a lot of money!'

'It is, but I'm a lot of girl.' She pulled her shoulders back – the overall result was just amazing.

'I can see that,' he blinked and smiled as they jostled for position under his very nose. 'But, tonight I have a problem. I'm supposed to see somebody at nine-thirty,' he lied, 'and I don't see how I can fit it all in, er, if you see what I mean.' He smiled back.

'You could try,' she winked.

He shook his head with a look of mock remorse.

Her face fell. 'You mean I've been wasting my time?'

'Not exactly maybe tomorrow,' he uttered hoarsely.

But he really didn't think that she had that much more information left in her anyway. With that he took a pre-counted and folded wad of twenty-pound notes – £200 in all – and pressed it into her hand.

'Now we've met, some other time maybe, I'll call I've got your name' he said as he got up, left before Olga reappeared with another offering and Kirsty could complain. Although now she seemed happy enough, counting her cash.

Eleven

The following morning over his wake-up coffee Kit considered the events from the start to the present time. He had some facts, but as yet nothing like enough; and he had no motive or clue as to who the assailant was. Or for that matter to what extent the Minister was involved, if at all. There must be a connection but what was it? Or was she just his lover?

Was it the theft of the Minister's computer that started it all? He doubted it. To achieve that, a murder was not necessary. Was she herself the problem? A Russian with a new British passport certainly posed some interesting questions.

It was ten past nine and he rang Sheeka, purposely still avoiding the Old Man, arranging to see her at Reception an hour later.

Showered, and with a breakfast of kedgeree, toast and Cooper's vintage marmalade to support him he walked with his briefcase to meet her.

As he approached from Vauxhall Bridge, he could see her on the steps where she turned, even that movement was athletic; she smiled radiantly. He would have loved to give her a welcoming kiss, as a gentleman would, but instead he held the door open for her and they moved discretely just inside the doors, where she looked up into his eyes and in lowered tones said,

'We're still all right for lunch, aren't we?'

'Wouldn't miss it for the world – your first oyster?'

'Er, we'll see about that,' she winced.

He opened his briefcase, then said in a commanding tone to which she responded, 'I want you to take this package to Forensic,' and he handed her a 'Jiffy' type envelope containing the items and hair that he had removed from Vicky's flat, adding, 'They're expecting it.' Then he gave Sheeka the passport saying, 'Check this out for me, can you, Sheeka, and see if it's genuine?'

'Yes, sir,' she said with a laugh, snapping her heals to attention with a mock salute.

'See you at lunchtime and, er, don't mention you've seen me, unless asked, that is, which you won't be,' and with that he was gone. At this stage, he still did not wish to get involved with anyone else at the moment, as he needed many more facts. In this business if your knowledge is imparted too early an unwelcome smoke screen could be put up. Never give them chance, the dangers may come from inside from your own camp.

Harrods was as busy as ever. It was a store and an institution that Kit enjoyed, especially the food halls. His view on life was: 'You have to eat to live, so make every meal an interesting gastronomic trip,' and why not? It did not need to be expensive. So much education and history was contained in the food and wine from around the world, and he felt it was a sin to miss it.

He approached the Oyster Bar and selected two empty stools at the end, where his back would be to the wall and he would have a full view. Force of habit meant that he did not like people behind him. To the side was a view he admired; a huge selection of magnificent fish and crustaceans, artistically displayed.

Two Japanese tourists were being dissuaded by Harrods security from taking photographs as it's against the rules of Harrods.

Kit sat down to wait for Sheeka and ordered a glass of green label Harrods 'house' champagne from the bar manager, who greeted him as an old friend. Indeed, he had known him for many years, from when the man had started as an apprentice at Bentley's of Swallow Street. There he was trained to perfection and had become well practised in the art of opening oysters, becoming au fait with all the different varieties of oysters and other seafood, and their preparation. Harrods had done well to get him.

Kit had just started to relax and observe the lunchtime trade from his prime position when a voice from nearby called.

'Kit, it is, Kit, isn't it?' He turned on his seat in surprise, only to see the Minister's wife Miranda standing there laden with green and gold Harrods carrier bags. On recognising her he immediately stood up, giving a slight bow. There was no possible way that she could shake hands.

'May I help you?' He quickly relieved her of some of the baggage.

'Thank you so much,' she gushed breathlessly, whilst proffering a tanned cheek for him to kiss. 'What a pleasant surprise. Do you eat here often?'

He was now rapidly trying to recall what he had used as a cover story when they first met, whilst delivering her husband, the Minister, home. He didn't want any mistakes.

'Yes, I do, its handy and uncomplicated. May I get you something?' Her eyes flashed as if by magnet at his glass flute.

'A glass of champagne would be fabulous,' she smiled back, placing the rest of her baggage on the floor between the stools with a sigh and sitting on the one next to him. 'Well, what a surprise!' she exclaimed still breathless, more so now with excitement than fatigue. 'I seem to get more to carry every time I come here,' she groaned.

'The problem of a store having everything under one roof, I suppose.'

'I wouldn't like your account,' Kit replied.

'Neither does David,' she giggled, 'So, what do you 'do' for a living?' she questioned. This time he did not have the Old Man to get him off the hook.

'Oh, I'm just a civil servant.'

'On champagne?' she retorted.

'I'm thrifty, I save up for these little luxuries.' He winked wickedly.

'Mm,' she was not in the least bit impressed with the excuse. But she squirmed a little at the wink and the glib manner. 'But then I suppose that's how you know David.'

'Exactly,' he smiled, as he looked over her shoulder, now intent on changing the subject. 'The fish, the lobster and crabs, that display, isn't it fantastic?' he continued showing an open palm at multi-coloured display of seafood, all intermingled with a fountain that played at the centre of the spectacle. A display that was all encased within a huge shell of a South Sea clam, at least five feet tall. 'Isn't it just fantastic?' he said again as they looked upon the glistening array. 'Look,' he pointed. 'The fountain, it's making its own rainbow amongst the coloured spotlights.'

'Yes, many tourists come just to see this, and of course they try to photograph it,' Miranda added.

Just then, as she turned back to look at him, he noticed over her shoulder, from the direction of the Tea, Coffee & Patisserie Hall, the elegant figure of Sheeka approaching. Hell, what now?

She made her way through the mass of people, heads turned, men stopped to admire. Kit felt a little jealous.

When she got near to them he caught her eye. She was just about to smile and greet him when she noticed the virtually imperceptible shake of his head, his eyes just widening for a second. She understood and walked past looking at his guest, her tongue just protruding a millimetre from her delicate lips. They moved just a fraction to an equally faint but cheeky smile. Sheeka moved on and past and melted away, lost once more in the crowd.

Kit's attention quickly returned to Miranda who had not noticed the exchange and was watching oysters now being opened in front of her.

'Would you like some?' he asked. 'I haven't eaten as yet.'

'I have to get back really. We have a dinner party tonight, hence this lot.' She nodded at the green bags heaped on the floor.

'Don't worry, Miranda, do have *something*,' he suggested as persuasively as he could. 'And if you will, then I can save you time by giving you a lift back. I'm going through Chelsea later, is that any good to you?' Miranda readily accepted the lift and agreed 'it would save a lot of time', visibly relaxing now at the good news, settling in for a mini session.

Miranda ordered a prawn and smoked salmon salad. He ordered a dozen oysters, small French 'Papillion's' served with brown granary bread, no butter, and a further glass of champagne for Miranda.

'I haven't seen oysters eaten since Mallorca,' she said nodding at his plate, 'Do you think they will all work? People do say that Casanova used to eat three dozen every night,' she added with a coarse laugh.

'It's the zinc you know. Mallorca! m'm a lovely island, do you go often?' Kit asked.

'Not as often as I would like. But we have a small holiday home there, up in the hills. Like many ministerial families, we need to get right away. It is somewhere to go when Parliament is in recess, when you need to get away from your constituency. Many ministers go to Provence or Tuscany, but we still prefer Mallorca. Away from the maddening crowds, up in the mountains and hills of the Tramontana, it is truly beautiful.'

Kit and Miranda got on fine; she was chirpy and he imagined a lot of fun, quite naughty really. As lunch came to a close he managed to order her yet another glass, which promptly caused her to move up another gear, starting to chatter away as if they were old friends. He was delighted – having broken the ice, more information would soon flow.

Rising slowly from his stool he said, 'I do apologise but please excuse me, before I forget I must just go and get a little 'Fresh and French' – Foie Gras – from the other food hall for this evening, er, my supper. I won't be a moment. Then if you wish we can go.'

Miranda took a drink from her new glass without answering. This was fun.

Kit called for the bill; as he did so he caught the manager's eye and surreptitiously nodded at her glass, knowing that on his return it would be full. With that he made his way briskly to the other food hall and pulled out his mobile phone. Damn, no signal. He quickly moved in search of a better signal, the west entrance, and was nearly there at the doors before two bars lit up on his phone. He quickly punched in the 'block' number, urgently asking to be put through to Harold down in the garage. Once through he asked Harold to send a car immediately to the west entrance of Harrods, the driver to stand by the car until he saw him approach and make eye contact. He would be with a middle-aged woman and carrying her shopping bags. Harold laughed out loud.

'I never thought I would see the day. I`ll be there myself to witness it, standing by a blue

Jaguar; similar to the one you're running. Oh, and where's yours, crashed?' Kit didn't answer. This was no time for pleasantries, and he knew that Harold in conversation could take forever.

He folded the phone, put it in his pocket and strode back to the food halls, not forgetting to buy his excuse on the way, four ounces of fresh French Foie Gras and some brioche. Supper would be a delight!

On his return, Miranda's champagne glass was full, and she was in full flight chatting ten to the dozen with the manager, who smiled knowingly at Kit, visibly relieved that he had returned.

'Ah, there you are,' she exclaimed, now looking a little pink round the gills. Not dissimilar to some on the display close by! 'I thought you'd left me!'

'No, certainly not, just a little queue that's all,' he replied.

He did not have another drink, but politely waited for Miranda to finish hers. The car he knew would take just a little time, there was no rush and he wished her to drink up fully. Maybe even loosen her tongue a little more. He was ashamed of his actions, but the result nevertheless was effective.

Then with a flourish she threw back the glass and Kit lent forward collecting her bags, he now checked his watch; with a slow stroll through

Harrods to the west door they should have wasted just enough time for Harold to arrive.

'Right this way,' he smiled guiding her gently to the west entrance, glancing at the odd counter as they went.

Once out on the pavement in the afternoon sun Kit spotted Harold. With perfect timing, he stood as promised by a blue Jaguar parked on the yellows; the moment their eyes met Harold moved away into the crowded street. The key would be on the floor.

Kit walked to the car, put the bags down on the kerb and made out as if he was unlocking the door.

'Lucky you didn't get a ticket,' Miranda remarked looking surprised, but her expression soon passed as she could not really have cared less. She'd had lunch, a good one, with champagne; she'd got a lift home and this was some good-looking man! Her Harrods bags lay on the back seat of a Jaguar; she was settled and on her way toward Chelsea Harbour and its village.

Then Kit spoke he had remembered Sir Edward's words about their child being adopted, but he was curious as to why Sir Edward indicated that it was such a taboo subject. After all the Minister certainly had sex drive!

'Any family any children, Miranda?' he asked remembering that last time he had mentioned this she had not answered and even now for that split second there was a falter, indiscernible to most, but to Kit a definite falter. He was determined to pursue, to make her subconsciously answer before she had time to think. 'Sons or daughters?' he asked making it easy, continuing the roll.

'I have a son, 'Charles' of whom I am very proud.' She looked across at Kit, smiling distantly with her doe-like eyes, a mother thinking of her family, her son. 'Yes, I have a son,' she purred.

He noted interestingly that she seemed to put the accent on 'I' rather than 'we'.

'At school and doing well, I trust?' Kit continued.

'Oh, good Lord no!' she exploded with laughter. 'You are a flatterer. He's away, up and running now, fled the nest. Charles went into the Army after University. Now he's on loan, or training with, or to be with, the Special Air Service, at Hereford I think. But it's all hush, hush, he doesn't really say.'

'That *is* an achievement, I am very impressed,' Kit replied genuinely, and he was impressed, for anybody who achieved and passed the rigours of the selection procedures, training and trials for the SAS was worthy of note.

He himself had done some training with them. He was as good in many respects, especially with weapon usage and instruction. But to his continual annoyance a leg injury achieved some years before, in a car accident, had prevented him from keeping up the pace and the time required, during long-distance training, which included running with a full pack or Bergen through the Brecon Beacons and Welsh Mountains, tabbing out day after day, night after night, with no respite, often in streaming rain; the overall weight was just too much, training at 50 lbs and rising, with an MI 6, plus ammunition and extra kit, could in extremes go to the weight of another man on your back! And for good reason, for one day you might have to carry the same.

'Yes, it's a tremendous achievement, you must be very proud. You married early then?' he said again.

'Foolishly I started young, but yes I am proud. Yet I think David has pushed Charles very hard, maybe too hard. They don't really get on very well. David was, no is, jealous of him, jealous of his fitness. But when he's finished all this, he wants him to be in the Civil Service as an ambassador and he can help him achieve that. But for all the family arguments, he's proud of him in a way, I'm sure he is; he just doesn't show it.'

She did not take him up on the 'early marriage' question; indeed, she seemed to dismiss it. She was not convincing with her testimony of David's affection towards his son either. The tone of her voice was just not quite right. He hoped he had not put his foot in it. He had wanted her to talk and she was a little reticent.

Unfortunately, he knew that some fathers did not always take to these circumstances as readily as their spouse; a man is not as paternal mores the pity.

That must have been the reason why Sir Edward thought it necessary to mention; he must have known of some acrimony lurking somewhere between the two. Interesting, he thought to himself.

The conversation had been absorbing and it did not seem long before Kit was swinging the Jaguar into the car park and looking for a space close to the entrance and the lifts.

'You must come up for a coffee and let me return the compliment of our wonderful 'surprise' lunch,' Miranda said eagerly, hopefully, whilst walking toward the lifts. I just can't leave you here.' Kit dutifully followed carrying the green Harrods bags.

Once inside the penthouse apartment he heard Miranda run the water. From a distance, he watched her quickly fill a small Gacia Italian espresso machine; the gorgeous aroma of fresh ground coffee flooded into the room.

Eager to see the view now in daylight he turned, the large panoramic window beckoned.

He looked out onto the harbour, admiring the sight, a lot to take in, it was much bigger than he had thought, attractive too, full of powerboats, yachts of all sizes and colours, a maze of masts and aerials. In his imagination, he could hear their halyard lines tapping away on the masts, flags cracking as they blew in the breeze. He had always wanted a yacht in his retirement and he wondered now when that would be.

Some minutes later he heard the coffee machine start to rumble as steam began to hiss. He heard Miranda in the kitchen with the cups, saucers and spoons, the sound of china against china.

'Milk and sugar?' she called from the kitchen.

'Just black please,' he answered.

Not before time he belatedly moved to the kitchen area, to help with the coffee.

It was then; just then, as he turned that he saw it! He froze, stunned, the photograph, the framed photograph! He remembered that it had been in her bedroom that night, the night he had brought the Minister home. That was the first time he had seen it and now it was displayed on the glass-topped table to the left of the picture window.

The photograph; it was of the same man, the same man whose picture was mounted and framed by the bedside at Verkuska's apartment! The same man he was sure. He slowly picked up the photograph and looked at it closely, the hairs prickling on his neck, his chest a little tight. There was absolutely no doubt.

The photograph was of a young, good-looking man, powerful and broad with piercing dark eyes, which stared back at him, hard and quite disarmingly from out of the silver frame. The young man exuded more power from this frame than the Minister ever would.

'Yes, that's Charles,' said Miranda loudly, proudly, as she entered the room holding a tray, which displayed delicate translucent china cups of fresh ground coffee, the scent of which was quite intoxicating.

He looked again at the photograph in his hands. As he put it down he could not help noticing there was a surprising resemblance to Miranda, an extraordinary likeness for an adopted child. Yet again a cold chill ran up his spine. The effect as he held the picture was chilling, the room seemed to go cold somehow it was quite eerie.

Yet acute likenesses happened, he knew that with love, children often grew just like their foster parents.

'That was taken just after Charles had left Oxford, when he took a commission in the Army. He looks fit, powerful, doesn't he?'

'Mm,' he said thoughtfully, 'he certainly does; dynamite. Did you go to university too?'

'Yes, the same Oxford, and you?'

'Er yes, but unfortunately Leeds. I read psychology,' he spoke somewhat reluctantly, 'and I'd rather not say any more,' he smiled. 'As they say in Yorkshire, 'nuff said'.' Miranda nodded understanding.

'I studied economics, then after my degree I took a year off, a sabbatical. After that I went into local government; that's how I met David. He was very ambitious then, a rising star, still is, I suppose, but he'll not make Prime Minister now.'

'No?' Kit was curious.

'No, he's changed, he's not as caring, well not toward me, and he shows no humility which is needed every now and again, for the electorate at least.'

In the last half-hour, he had learned a great deal. He wanted to close this conversation, get to the car and to its communications systems. He knew he needed to set the wheels of research in motion, fast whilst his mind was fresh.

But he certainly did not wish to appear rude to Miranda. Indeed, he wanted to leave the door open with her, possibly see her again just in case he needed to coax more delicate information unwittingly from her. It seemed a bit abrupt, but rising from his chair, looking purposely at his watch as he did so, he covered his action by saying, 'Terribly sorry, but I really must go; such great company, I just didn't know it was so late! But I'd love to take you for lunch again soon. Maybe a little more organised next time.'

'That would be nice,' Miranda replied, sadly rising with him.

They walked across the thick pile carpet to the door in silence; Kit's mind a whirl with new thoughts.

Once outside Kit made his way swiftly across the car park to the Harbour security office. After much persuasion, and several phone calls by the very reluctant security officer; Kit was now walking back towards the Jaguar holding a 24-hr VCR tape of the night that he had so embarrassingly *'lost'* the Ford Cabriolet.

He knew that for insurance reasons alone, these tapes had to be kept a certain length of time for an eventuality such as this. So, despite the arguments the security officer had to have the record.

Inside the car, Kit instantly dialled the Block and asked to be put straight through to Sheeka.

'You don't have to apologise just because you have been able to 'pull' an older woman, shopping bags and all! I told you that you were too old for me. Where were the kids?' Sheeka demanded down the phone.

'You will be surprised just how helpful older

women can sometimes be,' he retorted, his voice set in a tone the Sheeka had not heard before.

'Right,' she said, guardedly, and waited.

'Sheeka, pen and paper,' he said before continuing, 'I want you to find out the maiden name of David Stevens wife, Miranda.'

'The Minister?' she coughed.

'Correct, oh and this enquiry is absolute top security, don't even leak it by mistake at your end, their present matrimonial address is just the 'Penthouse' at Chelsea Harbour. I also need to know exactly where she was educated, er, latterly, I believe it was Oxford where she studied economics, but we need to be sure.

'I need to know everything about her, everything. You'll have to go to Oxford. I'll cover your tracks at the block; for the moment, you're working with me.'

Sheeka felt herself stand taller, somehow more important than before, as she listened to Kit on the phone, and received her first operational orders. Official or not she knew she was working with the best, if not the most conventional.

'It's a long time ago, twenty-five years or more maybe, but I need to know of any boyfriends she had, who they were and what her social life amounted to? I need to know who she slept with, when and why? I need to know her down to the colour of her knickers; I need to know everything. There may even be some old professor or lecturer still there who remembers her. If not, and he or she has retired, find them, go and see them. Look on the old team lists, hockey, or tennis; she may have been in one. Check committees, library records, anything like that. Try finding anyone who knew her, trace her friends and her enemies to their present addresses. Enemies are often by unwitting mistake, more help.

'To help you, I think she took a sabbatical after Oxford, but we need to be sure; find out if she was alone, where she went, anything. Follow it up and miss nothing.'

'Well I'll try, but isn't it all a long time ago?'

'You'll find something, I'm sure. Start with an enemy, believe me, they'll love to knife a minister's wife. It'll all revolve around the university, I just have a hunch Sheeka, just a hunch.'

'Er, what do I tell my shaven-headed boss, my guru at this end?'

'Nothing at all, I'll get the old man to, better if it comes from the top. I'll speak to him, and tell him I've pinched you!' Then perhaps Kit would not tell him, he did not like refusals.

'Pinched me? Ouch! He might get the wrong idea. Shall we say requisitioned?'

Kit did not respond to that, thinking more of the pinch, but continued, 'Also, those items I gave to you for Forensic, please check if there is a match. They'll know what I mean.'

'Yes sir', she said raising her voice. He could imagine her standing there by the phone and giving a mock salute.

'So, give me a call in the morning and let me know how you are going on.'

'Going on! In the morning? Sheeka exclaimed'

'Yes, my dear, start now! Kit said a little condescendingly 'Get a car from the pool and go to Oxford now. Start straight, away stay overnight, get me some information, dig something up dig – let's see how good you are. I want results, Sheeka,' he spoke very much in the tone of an order, which she acknowledged.

'By the way,' she said nearly forgetting 'There's a memo on your desk. The passport was correct but was only issued in the last month. The memo says that you will notice the oddity of it all.'

'Thank you.'

Kit leant forward and slid the VCR tape that came from the security office into the tape deck in the console. A small 5-inch screen, where the glove box would have been, flickered into life. He would watch it now, and make a copy later.

The car park in which he now sat appeared ghost-like on the screen. Security lights shone like stars, brightly distorting the clarity of the picture. It luckily showed the area where, from memory, he had parked the Cabriolet. It also covered the entrance doors to the lifts and apartments, but frustratingly it missed a large chunk of the car park that was offset at an angle. Had somebody cleverly worked this out? Possible.

The area was badly lit and this was where he was sure that he had been offered and had collected the BMW 5 series. All from the unknown man, who was posing as an officer on that fateful night; once again, he was not amused at his own mistake. Yet in this closed, secretive, cloak-and-dagger world of real unrehearsed life, operatives even at his level made mistakes and this was no exception, although it was highly unusual for him because he preferred to work on his own, but now Sheeka? Well we would see.

Feeling uncomfortable in the car park and rather than remain conspicuous sitting there in the Jaguar, he moved off into the late afternoon, keeping one eye on the screen. He would pull over and stop as soon as any cars appeared on the video screen.

The fact that Miranda's son Charles was with, or was training with the SAS intrigued him. A lucky man, no he thought, 'a man makes his own luck'; nevertheless, he would not mind meeting him, or at least seeing him.

With that thought in his mind he quickly pulled over, the tyres objecting with a squeal. He had the sudden urge to turn around and head immediately northwest for Hereford and the SAS base and training camp.

Miranda had mentioned Hereford and as chance would have it, that was where a friend of his was stationed; Colonel Simon Stewart was the CO at Hereford. Although the friendship and privilege had been stretched to the very limit when he had trained with them, they still kept in contact.

Luck was still with him, as now at a standstill at the kerb watching the screen, the Ford Cabriolet simultaneously appeared on the flickering video. He watched intently. He saw himself get out of the car and move quickly round to the passenger door to escort the Minister home. He watched himself turn around when he reached the self-opening doors in the foyer, and check to see if he was being followed, before going forward to select a lift; all looked quiet for the moment, there was no other movement. Then a minute or two later, as if it had been in hiding, waiting for Kit to disappear into the building, a BMW with its characteristic grill cautiously entered the car park. It could well have followed him.

He immediately recognised the car although he could not make out the number. Surprisingly there appeared to be possibly two people in the car but the faceless shadows were indistinct. The car missed one space and drove forward into another parking space, still in the shadows and now nearly off screen.

This was consistent with Kit's memory of where the car had been positioned. The doors opened and the interior light came on, definitely two people, but only dimly illuminated from the shoulders down. As they got out it was impossible to see them clearly as their heads soon moved above the roof line of the car and thus into relative darkness.

He watched the video screen, fascinated as the two men walked purposefully towards the Cabriolet; they knew exactly what they were looking for. Their features were still not discernible, but the larger of the two men walked ahead of his accomplice, his broad shoulders moving with a noticeable self-assured gait, or even swagger. He peered into the Cabriolet and quickly raised a hand seemingly to warn his friend not to touch in case of alarms. They then melted swiftly back into the even poorer light. Frustrated, Kit fiddled with the contrast, the picture now poor. The larger of the two men, the one who appeared to be in control, pointed at the BMW, and his friend went over to wait close by, appearing to lean on the boot while the other man disappeared into the darkness. Leaving no doubt in Kit's mind that if their little plan of a car swap had not worked, he would certainly have had a fight on his hands.

He watched the video continue until he saw himself come out of the lift and foyer, to be greeted almost immediately by the man who had been leaning on the BMW. Having watched Kit come out of the lifts and into the marble foyer the man had approached him in an amazingly self-assured manner as if he knew precisely who he was and pointing casually at the BMW nearby. There was a brief conversation and with a friendly shrug he threw the keys to Kit, who caught them deftly in the air. Annoyed, he watched himself toss the other man the keys for the Cabriolet. The swap was now complete!

It had all looked quite professional, as if they were on familiar ground. Nevertheless, it was some gamble, a dangerous game that they had played with him. He was impressed – but not by his own performance. He would have to redeem himself; that he knew.

He watched and saw himself climb into the BMW and reverse out of the slot; meanwhile the Cabriolet in an obvious hurry easily beat him away, the tail lights flickering as it went with a bounce down the ramp and onto to the street. During this time, he would have been presumably adjusting the seat and mirror, hence the delay, as there had been no need to hurry. He presumed the Cabriolet must have picked up the other man on the way out. Who the hell were they?

He reflected for a moment that they surely must have known the Minister. But more to the point, they must have known him! Seen him. Why would the elaborate car swap have been made in the manner that it was? His mind was now ablaze with possibilities.

During all this time the Jaguar engine had still been running. He looked up into the rear-view mirror. A traffic warden was approaching, pen poised, the obligatory notebook in hand. Without further ado, he spun the leather-bound wheel of the big Jaguar on a finger to full lock and powered the car around with a squeal of tyres in the road, the bonnet rising as he flattened the accelerator.

He was now annoyed with himself and in a slight temper after watching the tape. For him it had not been an epic movie.

The traffic warden stood there, all yellow and black, like an angry wasp, frustrated and with a look of disapproval at the manner of his hasty departure. Bollocks.

Kit headed northwest out towards Wales and Hereford.

From memory, he dialled in the technically non-existent, ex-directory number of Colonel Simon Stewart.

Twelve

The Brown Cow at Hereford he remembered always served an outstanding Welsh breakfast. Today though Kit was a little miffed as his favourite was not available – Laverbread or Bara Lawr, is seaweed boiled for hours before being rolled in oatmeal and made into a sort of patty, then fried in bacon fat, a delicious Welsh delicacy and supposed to be very good for you. He was not too sure about the fat. However, after making enquires they said he needed to be much nearer to the coast, possibly Cardiff or Penclawdd, further west, they said. He was not impressed, the winds of change.

However, his mood lifted dramatically as Colonel Stewart wandered casually into the breakfast room. He was dressed in jeans, a round-neck sweater, a tan cord jacket and soft leather 'Timber' boots. He looked more from Texas than Wales.

'Do they insist on this sort of disguise, or do you actually dress like that normally?' The over-conservative Kit asked as he rose to shake hands whilst looking his friend up and down.

'I like it! You're a stuffed shirt, too much of London and fancy restaurants, no action other than in a bloody bed, that's your problem, Kit,' the powerful man joked, crushing Kit's hand with his handshake, clasping his wrist with the other. There was something in what he said.

Simon Stewart was not as tall as Kit, not as suave, but square jawed, handsome and ruggedly unforgettable.

'So, what's the problem? You don't normally pay me visits when you're so unfit,' he observed, looking at Kit and holding his own paunch in. Kit got straight to the point.

'Do you have a guy named Stevens in the squad, well 'a' squad?' He said looking hard at the Colonel.

'You know better than that. We don't discuss names, or people, we don't exist,' he said arrogantly.

'Yes, yes, I know, but cut the crap, this is official,' Kit, grumbled.

'Official, on whose say so, I have seen nothing?'

'Shall we start again?' Kit said pleasantly. 'A coffee?'

There was a pause whilst the Colonel idly poured himself a cup.

'You know whose son he is, don't you?' the Colonel queried.

'I do, and may I presume from that you have him based here?'

'Yes, he's not a bad lad either, tries hard and is very fit. He was one of the best in training, one of only seven out of nearly a hundred and thirty. Some never even got to the physical side of training.' Kit raised his eyebrows and looked at the Colonel who continued, 'He's psychologically deep though. Do you want to borrow him?'

'No, it's really more a case of seeing him, er, without him seeing me!'

'Problems?'

'I don't honestly know,' Kit, answered thoughtfully, 'How can I get to see him? I don't want to go into the camp, or for that matter to be seen with you.'

There was a long silence before the Colonel spoke. 'There's no real problem, he'll be training, running I shouldn't wonder at about eleven o'clock this morning. There will be a few of them out. My car won't be suspicious and anyway you can use glasses to keep your distance, is that any good to you?'

Two hours later they were sitting in a drab and battered green Range Rover, the Colonel's own. From within the tatty tan interior, Kit raised a pair of Carl Zeiss Zena 7x50 binoculars to his eyes. He watched a group of young men approaching, steam rising above them like morning mist, some 400 yds away to his right.

They were in full kit, their backpacks looked full, straps taught and straining as they ran and swayed, toiling along a steep rough track, strewn with boulders; it looked like a dry stream bed leading off snake like into the dark bleak hills, unforgiving. It came back to Kit, the dire memories of his own nightmare here.

He now recognised the leading runner from the photograph that sat on the glass table in Chelsea and also at Vicky's bedside at 14 Harbour Way. It was unmistakably Charles Stevens.

But what surprised him most and now troubled him greatly was the slim man running next to him, for he also looked vaguely similar to the character who, just few nights before, had tossed him the keys for the BMW, the man who had ultimately driven away in the Cabriolet. And yet looking again there was no way that he could be certain, in fact the more he looked the more he was sure he was not.

'Is that Stevens?' Kit asked, passing the Colonel the glasses, not wishing to give anything away even to his friend.

'The leader, the one at the front?' The Colonel refocused the glasses. 'Yes! That's him, a keen lad, he likes to be up front he's a leader.'

'Fine,' Kit said in a non-committal tone, 'M'm, oh, and who's that guy running next to him?'

'Oh, that's his pal, 'Wiley Riley',' the Colonel laughed, 'He's got more front than Blackpool, believe me he is going to be very useful to us. He should have been a bloody actor!'

'Probably is,' Kit muttered with certain suspicious feeling.

'Pardon?' said the Colonel. Kit, let it ride; there was no need to answer.

But the Colonel continued, 'Yes, mm, that's Sergeant William Riley and an equally good lad. They go everywhere together, a hell of a team.'

'No marks against them then?'

'Kit, you know the bloody answer to that. If they had, they wouldn't be here!'

He'd no wish at the moment to open up his mind to his friend the Colonel, but just casually remarked after a moment's thought, 'Mm well, so that's him. Hell, they all look fit.'

'They are, and they have to be, you may have forgotten?'

'How could I.?' Kit said, remembering his personal hell and the pain that went with it.

'So why did you need to recognise him, Kit? Is the minister requesting his protection or something? If so there's no need, he can do that for his bloody self, believe me!'

'I'll tell you in a day or two. By the way, Simon, do they still have fairly easy access to weapons?'

'Well yes, but the access to weapons is controlled, movements are logged in and out by the armourer', the Colonel said, concerned.

'Lost anything recently?' Kit asked.

'Should I be looking?' asked the Colonel, curious.

'Maybe'.

'Time like an ever-flowing stream'; it was now nearly 12 o'clock midday and they were driving back, surprisingly rapidly in the Range Rover, the typical uneven beat of the enlarged and modified alloy V8 engine making it enjoyable; originally not the most powerful of engines, a bit old fashioned, basically an old Buick design, but now displaying an unusual amount of power, a 'Wolf in sheep's clothing'.

Once back at the Brown Cow Kit was dropped off by the somewhat curious Colonel, who waited for Kit to speak.

'Don't forget to call me,' he said trying to goad Kit into speech. 'I want to know what you're up to,' he said as they parted. Kit called across the car park

'Will do' in an unconvincing manner, raised a clenched fist in acknowledgement and climbed back into the Jaguar. He watched the Range Rover and the disgruntled Colonel drive away, the vehicle's twin exhausts giving a snarl from the Buick-derived V8, as if in rebellion.

He was suddenly brought back to reality as the phone beeped loudly in the car, accompanied by a red-light flashing; it was Sheeka, an excited Sheeka!

'Well, have I got news for you, sir, and in such short time too. Aren't you pleased?'

'I might be if I know what it is, you haven't told me yet, but it's nice to hear your voice,' he said cynically.

'Well, from the beginning then,' she exploded, excited.

'Absolutely the best place,' he answered patiently, now focussed.

'Your Minister's wife Miranda, OK? She was a Miranda Gibbons, a girl full of life and a lot of fun, a good student and a member of various committees, no problem there – she was easy to find. However, her lifestyle got the better of her and sadly towards the end of her time she fell pregnant; she had the child but it was all hushed up.

'One theory is, that the boyfriend at the time was supposed to be a wealthy Lord or something, an aristocrat and he did not really want to know; he disputed he was the father, complained that she had many lovers. But several casual observers did not think that was so.

'Anyway, the bastard left Oxford and left her in the lurch – just typical. Two other friends I have spoken to say they didn't know the father, but that she was faithful to somebody at the time, indeed quite in love, but that itself was a mystery.

Anyway, I haven't got to the bottom of that yet, but believe me, I will! However, they didn't marry. It's all very sad. Apparently, she had the child about her for a short while. Then she went off to do a sabbatical, just disappeared. When she came back, bingo, no child!'

'How did you find all this out?'

'Long story but really I just dropped lucky. I've now got to prove it all for real, but it looks correct. Are you going back to London?'

'I think Oxford for dinner tonight, don't you? Are you anywhere near?' he joked.

'Sounds marvellous, and I should have some more news by then. But I've nothing to wear.'

'Then don't!'

An hour and a half later and thirty miles out of Oxford Kit's phone burst into life once more, it was Sheeka.

'Don't get excited about dinner!' Her voice echoed round the Jaguar. 'I'm off to Yorkshire.'

'Yorkshire,' Kit repeated, lifting his foot off the accelerator, the Jaguar's bonnet visibly sinking and his heart with it.

'Yep, Yorkshire,' she laughed. 'I've found out who the Lord was the bloody aristocrat!'

'What who?'

'It's Lord Strutt, whoever the hell he is, or was.'

'How on earth do you know?'

'The old lady in the newsagents remembers

him; she's been there for forty years or more! Would you believe it?'

'A good find.'

'A terrific find, unbelievable! Anyway, yes and "e's tall long neck with a large Adam's apple, very aristocratic 'e was,' she remembers. He always received the 'Shooting Times' magazine each week every Thursday, without fail. 'An' there were ructions if it did not arrive,' she said. Really, that's why she remembers him, the 'Shooting Times' magazine and all the fuss that went with it, she told me.'

'So, he's a shooting man then?'

'Hang on, wait for it. So, he is, yes, and now is the shooting season, glorious twelfth and all that. Grouse, right?'

'Right.'

'So, I thought about that for a moment; guns and the names Purdey, and Holland & Holland sprang to mind, you know the gun-makers in London. I rang Holland and Holland but no joy, but then I rang Purdeys at South Audley Street, spoke to a Mr Beaumont, Nigel, told him a bit of a story and he was very helpful.

'So, yes, Lord Strutt indeed had his guns serviced there, a pair of Purdeys and they were delivered back to Gowthwaite Hall only a month ago, which is where he usually stays for the grouse season, then comes back to London. He returns later for the pheasant in November. So, how's that? That's how I found his address; it must be him.'

Kit was highly impressed, although he was not absolutely sure where all this would lead, delving so deeply into the Minister's wife's private life. But he had this hunch and, it just would not go away.

'I think you've done remarkably well, but I will miss dinner.'

'Well, I'll be stuck in some country pub in the middle of nowhere tonight. Am I not worth waiting for? Er, dinner I mean.'

'Keep in touch, whatever. I'll go back to London, call me as soon as you have anything.'

'Will do, bye.'

He heard the phone go down. The progress she was making interested him and put him into a good mood as he headed back towards London.

As Sheeka drove out of Oxford and glanced down at her tights, she could make out a ladder slowly making its tickling and twisting way to her groin. Damn! There might of course be a spare pair in her overnight bag, but she couldn't remember, it had all been such a rush. What she did know was that she would most certainly need a change of clothes; there was no way that she could drive north and try to get an audience tomorrow at the Hall with His Grace looking like this. No, she would need something new, and more feminine. If she was quick she would just have time to purchase a new skirt, blouse and a pair of shoes. Her long coat for the moment would have to do.

The following morning, and with some trepidation, Sheeka approached the huge wrought-iron gates that formed the imposing entrance to Gouthwaite Hall. She had located the Hall late the previous night, before she had booked a bed as discreetly as she could at a small country house hotel a little further away in the next village.

It was a bright morning and the gates were open; two large lichen-blotched stone eagles glowered down at her, their carved talons gripping the tops of the massive stone pillars either side of the entrance. Sadly, they were crumbling a little with age; cracks were showing with the odd weed protruding.

There was a single-storey lodge either side of the entrance, both covered in ivy that was now turning a deep autumnal red, one had a little wisp of grey smoke curling up out of its chimney; the scent of wood smoke lingered in the air as a tan and a white Jack Russell terrier peeped and started to bark from behind old frayed lace curtains at the window.

The gravel and tarmac drive had seen better

days. With grey water-filled potholes, it disappeared winding its way into the distance, passing through wheat stubble as it went. Pheasants pecked for old grain. Further on chestnut trees with a distinct autumnal tint lined either side, but from this angle there was no sign of the Hall, if indeed it still stood, so far it did not look promising.

Sheeka did not falter but drove steadily down the drive dodging the potholes as she went. An old retainer waved vigorously from the lodge door as if to stop her, but she smiled and waved back, ignoring his gesticulations.

After about half a mile she rounded a bend in the drive and in front of her was an old balustrade bridge spanning a narrow part of a clogged lake which reached away far to the right of her. Brown bull rushes clawed at the bridge, intermingling with the ivy and moss. In the distance, further still to the right stood proud was what could only be Gouthwaite Hall. Sheeka had not seen many, but this sight was one, which took her breath away. It was a stately home in the Palladian style, with five tall pillars at the front and multi-paned windows stretching away like white lace either side. The masses of elongated chimneys fingering the grey clouds above were uncountable. In the distant hills behind, high above the once formal park, oak and beech woods were scattered on green and copper hillsides for pheasant. Higher still

Sheeka could see the fading purple heather still lingering on the bleak Yorkshire grouse moors.

Sheeka stopped for a moment to take in the scene, which was rare and quite beautiful, from a forgotten age.

Getting an audience with His Grace was not going to be easy. After a moment's thought, she slid her hand into the middle of her shoulder blades and with a slight smile undid her bra, hunched forward and with a shake freed her bosom, placing the discarded underwear beneath the seat. Her breasts were free, her ammunition loose and she felt good.

Delicately she straightened her white blouse, pulled the silken material down from within her skirt, back and front, so that it was now tight and wrinkle free. She could feel the pressure of silk on her nipples, which began to harden. As if she were a young racehorse, a filly being introduced to her first stallion, her vagina gently twitched, just once. Her pulse quickened; and so, to battle.

Sheeka drew up outside in the shadows underneath the vast stone portico which was supported by the five fluted pillars. She felt very out of place, dwarfed in the little Rover saloon bristling with aerials. Nobody was about.

The lawns were cut, not perfect, but recently. The ornamental garden was now small; a fraction of what it would have been a century earlier.

She could see where earthworks had been sculptured to enhance the view. Old walls, a ha-ha and a gazebo had all been part of the vast gardens of the past; a lonely statue stood on its own, its former glory gone, surrounded now just by grass and sheep, a plinth remained where another had been. An obelisk stood high on a hill, a round and pillared temple on the one opposite. Capability Brown, the famous eighteenth-century landscaper came to her mind. Was he responsible for this beauty? Scores of staff would have laboured here in the past.

She climbed out and drew her long dark coat tight with the belt around her. For the moment, she was discreet, her secrets concealed.

She strolled up the steps and towards the massive double doors, one of which was slightly ajar. There appeared to be no bell so without further ado and taking a deep breath, Sheeka walked into the hall. To her it seemed like she had just entered the dome of St Paul's in London; it was vast and cold, with no carpets, just worn Yorkshire stone flags, polished only by time itself. There was a staircase spiralling its way around and down, upon it centrally the remnants of a threadbare carpet, its bright polished brass carpet rails creating a contrast to the dilapidation. The walls were lined with old oil paintings depicting probably ancestors, most in military dress. There were stuffed fish in glass cabinets, with the odd big game head mounted in between. From out of a dusty case the glass eyes of a moth-eaten falcon stared back malevolently.

Standing halfway down the stairs and much to her embarrassment and surprise stood a tall man, resplendent in tweed britches. He was wearing odd slippers and his ample body hair was protruding upward out of his collar-less shirt; it had a tear in the sleeve and looked more like an old pyjama top. He was some hundred feet or more away, no distance in that hall.

He faltered at her sudden presence. In some degree of shock and surprise he turned in

mid-stride and glared at her. Taken aback at this unusual and unwanted intrusion he thought for a moment, his Adam's apple bobbing up and down like a clucking hen. After a moment to collect himself and adjust, he spoke.

'Who are you, and what the hell do you want?' he boomed sternly, his voice echoing round the great domed entrance hall. She expected bats to flutter out from above.

'Er, I'm looking for Lord Strutt,' she declared, mustering up her powerful voice. It did not sound very convincing, much too weak and inadequate on this huge stage.

'Did you say looking for, or looking at?' the man barked back, in true military fashion.

'Er, looking f-for,' she began to stammer.

'Well, actually it's at,' he boomed back, his red and rugged face glowering.

Suddenly at this juncture, an ageing, pale and dusty butler, dressed in ancient livery, shuffled into view, apologising profusely to His Grace for the unwanted guest, this untimely intruder. 'It will not happen again sir.' His obsequiousness made it an obvious and frequent occurrence.

He tried half-heartedly to usher Sheeka to the door, whereupon His Grace raised a hand in tired dismissal. Shaking his head like an aged Labrador the butler shuffled off into the gloom from whence he came.

'No matter,' Lord Strutt now said calmly. 'What can I do for you, young lady?' His eyes searched for her form beneath the coat.

He would not be disappointed, she thought, but not just yet. That salvo, the battle of eyes and flesh could wait.

'Could you spare me the time for a few questions?' she asked with a sultry look.

Lord Strutt, now instantly and visibly on his considerable guard, answered in a pained tone, 'Oh, you're not a damned 'anti' are you?' he said shaking his head. 'You know, blood sports and all that.'

'Er, no sir, I'm not,' Sheeka said raising a smile. But now knowing she had to metaphorically fire the next shot, up the ante she said. 'But does

Miranda ring a bell with you sir, er, a Miranda Gibbons, now a Miranda Stevens, the wife of David Stevens the Minister?'

His Grace's face twitched, his left eyelid flickered. He gave a nervous little cough.

'I see, mm' there was a pause 'will you come into the study young lady,' he said coming down the stairs into the main hall and leading the way to an open-door opposite. His slippers sounded like a dying fish as they flapped along the stone flags. He held the door open for her. The room smelt of dogs.

'Sit down,' he said as he closed the door. It was an order, not an invitation. The room oozed character from another era. An unfortunate lion's head looked down at Sheeka from above His Grace's ancient and battered leather-topped desk. He sat on one corner of it; he had to, as a dog sat in his chair. Another peered silently and blindly upward from under the desk. His Grace looked at her for some time, a tick now flickering in his cheek.

'I hope you're not wanting money?'

'Not a bit of it, sir. What I have to ask is in the utmost confidence. I've been sent here by Sir Edward Ferrensby of the MI6.' She had told a story, a fib, but the base line was indirectly true.

'Then why did he not call me himself?' he spoke sharply. 'I know Sir Edward well, he's shot here, and I in return have shot at Ferrensby Hall; we're friends.'

Sheeka had not bargained for this. She had made a mistake underestimating the 'Old Boy' network; it stretched a long way.

'He's had to go away, on urgent business,' she answered quickly and quite convincingly.

His Grace was not warming to her and she could see that he did not really believe her; he was suspicious. He had after all interviewed thousands, probably commanded them too. He was a man who could not be fooled easily. Yet for all this, he was captivated by Sheeka's beauty. She had noticed his eyes had tried to undress her more than once. As if in thought he reached across the desk for the black Bakelite telephone.

Time to play her trump card and quickly! Sheeka stood up and removed her coat with a flourish whilst walking across to the window, where she lay it across the back of a chair. When she turned slowly to look at him, to hold his stare, his mouth dropped a fraction before he gained control; all thoughts of Sir Edward Ferrensby had vanished. The phone, un-dialled was quietly replaced on the cradle. Unashamedly he feasted his eyes on her body, which was exquisitely displayed in the gentle mysteries of silk. Having now got his attention and not letting him catch his breath Sheeka spoke.

'Miranda had a child whilst at Oxford, did you know?'

There was a long pause before he quietly said.

'Yes, I'm afraid I do, it was a boy.' He bowed his head and with a sigh stood up and walked to the window, the window that Sheeka had just left. He looked out across the ancient parkland. 'I was accused, but I did not believe it, and I suppose now for some devilish reason you've come to chastise me, after all these years. The guilt, if it was true, is already my living penance.'

'Were you not the father?'

'It was never definitely proved,' he said a little pompously.

Sheeka was not impressed and after another long, silent pause asked softly

'What happened to the child?' She could feel his emotion, the atmosphere in the room now enshrouding them both.

'That's a long story and one that has never been told.' His Grace half turned. 'Is this really necessary?'

'It could be,' said Sheeka, although she didn't know why; perhaps she was being too inquisitive. She stooped and took from out of her folded coat her identification and placed it on the desk. He did not turn again, but just glanced casually from over his shoulder.

'It's all such a long time ago. I couldn't marry,

I was far too young; my position, and my parents, they would never have understood. It would never have worked, never have lasted, so I did the best I could.'

There was a long silence only interrupted by the movement of a dog as if it too were preparing to concentrate and to listen to its master.

'Really, do please tell me and it may help you, secrets like this are not always meant to be locked away inside you, it can do more harm than good' Sheeka reasoned, her voice now nearly a whisper, head a little bowed. She did not have eye contact.

Slowly he continued.

'As you say, Miranda had the child and stayed at Oxford for a time, but the situation was far from ideal. There were social pressures of the worst kind, you know. She was going to have the child adopted; it was the best thing.

'Then suddenly, quite out of the blue, my gamekeeper's wife had a baby boy, which was premature. Tragically and within the month the boy was dead. They were devastated, all the estate was shocked.

'Quite by chance one weekend I brought Miranda to see them, and she stayed overnight. For her there were no pressures in the country, no fingers pointing. They were friends almost immediately and she stayed for some considerable time, living with them in the keeper's cottage and working on her degree, it was a sort of sabbatical. When term started, she left the child with them, first for a few days during the week, then longer, even a week. It was not intentional but they became sort of unofficial foster parents; in the meantime, thankfully the keeper's wife became pregnant again.

'In an obscure way, I was happy with the situation because I was still in touch with Miranda and what may well have been my son. But Miranda and I then slowly drifted apart, although she still came every weekend to stay with the child. Then she started to date another chap, a chap I knew from Eton, name of Stevens, a complete cad'

Lord Strutt suddenly spun round. He'd been crying, tears were rolling down his rugged face. He held on to a nearby chair back, allowing it to take some of his weight.

'That's why you're here, that's why you're here, isn't it? David Stevens is now the Minister of Defence. There's going to be a scandal,' he said hoarsely.

'At the moment, there isn't going to be any scandal at all. In fact, just the opposite; that I can assure you. So how does it all fit together?'

Sheeka was not convinced.

'Do go on.'

'Well, Miranda continued seeing David and eventually she married him, yet she kept on coming here every weekend on her own, not to see me you understand, but to see the child. What on earth she told David I shall never know.

'But after about two years it was found that he could not sire any children. He was devastated, of course highly embarrassed. Then I believe after an in-house battle for many months, Miranda persuaded him that it was not the end and they should go to an adoption agency.

'David was always busy, and also a little shy or ashamed about their predicament. As an MP, he did not want others to know. So, the agency, or so he thought, came to see him; it was I believe the gamekeeper's wife suitably dressed and turned out, armed with a host of 'acquired' or duplicate adoption forms, I know not which.

'The 'forms' were duly 'processed' and weeks later, by mutual agreement, along came a son; her actual son Charles, and maybe mine. So, there you have it.'

There was another long pause and a sigh. Sheeka was amazed; whatever her preconceived thoughts had been, they were nothing like this.

'For one reason or another, I never married,' he continued sadly, then with another sigh, 'Guilt maybe, who knows? But then I may well have a son.'

There was a long silence as Sheeka took in the relevance of it all and tried to make sense of what she had just heard.

'Would he inherit if it were made public, if he found out you were his father?'

'If it was genetically proven, er, yes he could inherit.'

'Would it really have to be genetically proven?' Sheeka said, playing the Devil's advocate.

He hung his head a little, then after some considerable time said, 'No, maybe not.'

'Would he inherit the estate and the title?'

'On my death, yes, I suppose he would.'

'Don't you want that?'

He did not answer. Sheeka felt sorry for this lonely man on his vast estate; she leant forward and kissed him on his cheek just as another tear rolled slowly down his rugged face. She tasted the salt.

'Thank you,' he murmured, and squeezed her hand. She returned the pressure, stood, turned and slowly laid her coat over her arm.

'I'll be in touch, but for the moment I don't think any of this will come out, it's only an enquiry.' She smiled up at him and turned for the door. He remained silent and did not attempt to follow her.

As Sheeka let herself out, somewhere in the bowels of that enormous stately home another dog howled; her neck prickled.

What a revelation! But only Kit would be able to piece together her news, which might or might not be relevant to this case. She was desperately excited and needed to make contact.

Thirteen

Kit had driven back up to London and on the way, had called Forensic, just as he had thought, the hair and items taken from Vicky's flat had proved to be a genetic 'match' with that of the charred body found in the burnt-out Cabriolet. But predictably as far as the weapon was concerned, there were no prints.

At least now he knew who she appeared to be and where she had last lived, but why the murder? It seemed excessive to say the least, what was the motive? Who was she really? Was Verkuska her real name, how valid was her new passport?

It was time to speak to Sir Edward and bring him up to date. That was the least that he could do. After all he had purloined Sheeka and she was now somewhere in North Yorkshire chasing a bloody Lord. It was probably only tittle-tattle a dead-end, but all very necessary – it could be another piece to this puzzle.

On ringing the Block at Vauxhall, he found that Sir Edward was out at a meeting and leaving instructions not to be disturbed there. Thursday, of course Kit had forgotten, he would be with PM, where no doubt over lunch there would be more lamb and claret and a discreet question from the PM, about the Minister.

There were no messages for him and he said that he would report in at eleven the following morning, if that were convenient, to see Sir Edward.

It was Friday morning and London seemed busier than usual as Kit returned the second Jaguar; he drove across the bridge, turned left and on down into the garage. Just as he did so the phone rang; it was Sheeka.

'Good morning,' was her excited cry.

'Where are you?' he asked with equal pleasure and curiosity.

'Right now, I'm halfway down the long drive of Gouthwaite Hall, must be a mile or more in length. This place is a stately home! You've never seen anything like it. Oh, and I'm sat in the Rover talking to you!'

'Have you scrambled this transmission?'

'Er, I would if I knew how to, sir.'

'Press the purple button.'

'Right, OK,' she sighed. 'I'll start again. I've just had a remarkable conversation with His Grace, a sad and eccentric man, but with a good heart.' With that Sheeka recounted to Kit word for word Lord Strutt's description of what had happened all those years ago, Kit listened intently, fascinated and wondering, just as Sheeka did on how it would all now fit together.

He asked Sheeka to type out a report on the communication console whilst it was still fresh in her memory. Then fax it to him in the car, giving her the number of the other car that was languishing in the garage at the Park Lane Hotel, and for the moment the one he was in. The fax would not be printed out, but would be held in code so he could read it later. Now he would have a hard copy.

'I have an appointment with the Old Man shortly so I'll call later. When are, you coming back to London?' he asked.

'Straight away, I'll call you when I'm there.'

He sat for a moment absorbing all that he had just heard from Sheeka. It was complex and may yet have some bearing on the overall picture. Looking at his watch he saw it was 11.05, which meant he was late for his meeting.

He checked in and used the stairs at speed as usual. It was a personal thing; he had done it many times in various offices over the years. The Old Man was always on the top floor and Kit liked to see if he could arrive at his door without being out of breath, and he did. He winked at his secretary and she nodded at the door. He knocked and walked in, late.

A glare at the clock in the corner confirmed that it had not gone unnoticed, so he apologised. He was shown the usual chair with a casual wave. Many people had remarked over the years that it always seemed to be positioned lower than Sir Edward's chair, but it did not work with Kit as he would sometimes hook a leg over the arm which he knew infuriated Sir Edward, but at least he knew that the 'playing field' was levelled somewhat.

With an imperious wave of his arm, Sir Edward indicated that Kit should proceed with his report. As ever Sir Edward listened intently, his bushy eyebrows twitching as he concentrated, glowering at a leather-bound pad as he made notes. He was totally unimpressed by the antics of his friend the Minister.

'Your friend, Mr 'B' Minister is a loose cannon,' Kit said, summing up as he finished the verbal report. There was a short pause. He then sat back relaxing in his chair, the leather squeaking as he waited for a reaction, one that was not long in coming.

'Well, Kit, it's a sad business, it is strange and odd' said Sir Edward grappling for words and sitting back in the big Windsor, shaking his head. 'Now with your thoughts on the matter it makes even less sense and leading you towards his son Charles you say, or should I say stepson? Not to mention this pal Riley. It really does not make sense Kit' There was a long moment of silence. 'It's a hell of a tale Kit, you're sure it was this chap Riley on the video?'

'No sir not at all – be careful. I just said it was like him, there were similarities. No, I'm not sure at all. The video is not clear, far from it, it was just a likeness.'

'Well, Kit, we have nothing absolute, nothing concrete, it's all supposition – you never actually saw any person or shadow that actually looked remotely like his son Charles in the video'

'That I suppose is correct.'

'You say you could not get a positive identification of the assailant at the scene, the mews apartment even – correct?'

'That is also unfortunately correct.' Kit shook his head and looked directly at Sir Edward 'I'm sorry but I say again, sir, is this now not a job for the Police, the Chief Inspector?'

'Definitely not' he snapped back 'In fact the more I think about it for the moment definitely it is not! Kit, if I am to believe you, we may now have two of our own men from Hereford involved in this. Which I doubt, but nevertheless it is serious stuff and that in itself is right off limits for the Police.'

'I see,' said Kit thoughtfully, not at all convinced.

'Mm,' Sir Edward paused, 'there is something else I have not told you. David came to see me yesterday.' There was another pause.

'And?' Kit said expectantly.

'He apparently was carrying a laptop computer with him, to allow him to work when he got home that evening.'

'If he had the energy,' Kit observed with a rueful smile.

Sir Edward scowled but went on, 'He thinks he left the computer on a table downstairs, and that it was apparently stolen in this fracas.'

'He did mention something about it to me, but he didn't seem overly concerned at the time, er, to me that is.'

'Anyway, now the problem is this, it contains information, very important information, he tells me and er' we are the only ones he has told, by the way.'

'May I enquire what was in it?'

'You may. I believe it was the, er, details of the satellite and telephonic surveillance that goes on in conjunction with the Americans at Menwith Hill in Yorkshire, near Harrogate. Right on your doorstep, I believe.'

'I know it well, any details?'

'No, not yet. Section Eight is looking into it, but only just to see how important it might be. I personally don't think it's much to worry about. It's all to do with our contribution to the site, or rather what we get out of it – information, communications monitoring etcetera. Interestingly it is actually an RAF base but we have only a token commander there and a handful of staff, the rest are the Yanks, its theirs really, but it could still be rather embarrassing. I doubt there is anything lost! The Americans keep us ill-informed and by the time it gets to our Minister even less! It seems he downloaded some details from the main computer which is available to him and, of course he shouldn't have done that.'

'That's a breach of security in itself,' Kit pointed out.

'It is, but as I said previously, he had wanted to work at home as he felt he had some questions coming up in the House and needed to be prepared. Correct and swift answers at question time are important whilst in Government,' he said dismissively, as if in support of his friend.

'Is that it?' Kit said, incredulous at the lapse of security. 'A mistake like that is no excuse, or so you once told me!'

'Mm, probably not, but we will have to see. I actually think it is all a bit of a red herring on his part.' Sir Edward was unusually noncommittal.

'Trying to blame the murder on the theft?'
'It's a thought'

Kit, mindful of this last comment, did not press the point. They went over all the facts again, and with a big sigh Kit asked, 'Well then, what am I supposed to be after now, a computer, an assassin, a rogue or a long-lost son?'

'Find one and you may well find them all – unfortunately. Oh, and try be discreet, Kit,' Sir Edward requested, with certain feeling.

'I'll try, sir.'

'I'm afraid I've something else to tell you.'

'Yes, sir?' Kit said in a weary tone.

'He, Charles, the Minister's son that is, he is my god son.' There was a moment of silence that you could have cut with a knife. Kit, astonished, spoke first.

'It's a real family cock-up, sir.'

'I will pretend, Kit, that you never said that,' Sir Edward growled as he stood up, his chair scuttling backward. He added, 'Keep in touch.' Kit took the hint and left, wishing now that he had not made that glib comment. It had wounded Sir Edward. He went out of the building hurriedly, not wishing to have a conversation with anyone now.

Back at the Park Lane Hotel and in the Jaguar, Kit punched his code into the console communicator. The waiting fax from Sheeka came chattering out, virtually word for word what she had related to him previously.

As he thought of her his mind painted a picture. It was a masterpiece, a Michael Angelo of a pale blond girl with tousled hair, near white, a laughing cheeky face with brilliant blue eyes. All of which distracted his thoughts. He hoped he would see her that evening.

Then, as fate often does, it took hold of him, as he suddenly realised that he had not got a photograph, a positive ID, of Charles the Minister's son. It would be useful, if not essential, not only for him, but Sheeka would need to see who she might eventually be dealing with. She would be curious, in any case, to see the supposed son of a Lord, the adopted son of the Minister.

He could probably get a photograph from Hereford but only by using official channels. Thinking about it, he preferred not to. Anyway, it was far from normal for the Special Forces to release photographic records. Then it clicked – he would go back to the apartment at Chelsea and lift the framed photograph that was by the bedside.

He felt for the apartment key, it was still in his pocket. Motivated, he quickly fired the Jaguar up and left the car park. The engine being cold, the timing chain on the old XK 4.2 straight six engine chattered, the steering rack hissing a little on full lock, its drive belt squeaking. It irritated him and he would as ever report it to service tomorrow.

It was late lunchtime by the time he arrived. He had driven down the King's Road and turned off just after the Worlds End, the pub of previous delights.

The area of Chelsea Harbour was busy with diners. This time he took the car closer to 14 Harbour Way, estimating it was about eight doors down from him. He parked inconspicuously between two equally modern cars, of similar bland computer-generated colour and size. Apart from the Jaguar's aerials the car melted in. He was lucky, as in this area he noticed most cars appeared to be of a more personal nature, displaying the owner's personality. There was a trendy Suzuki Vitara 4+4, colourful and flowered. A Citroen 2CV, a 'Deux Cheveaux', displaying a faded sticker of 'ban the bomb', he noticed an old and patched grey Guernsey sweater covering its tattered seat. This was an art and craft area with auction rooms for antiques with display 'Shoppe', it was all 'yoghurt & sandals'. Across the road by an antique dealer's, he noticed a very tidy yellow Alfa Romeo Spider, a 1750 model and no doubt somebody's pride and joy, now a classic. They handled well in their day, he mused.

He remotely locked the car and made his way to No 14. As before key in hand he nonchalantly placed it in the lock, turned it and pushed the door. To his surprise, it stuck, so he pushed again hard, it moved a little. Then, on examining the door casing, there appeared to be some form of adhesive between the door and the frame, which was odd – it looked like cream-coloured builders' foam, liquid polystyrene, the type you can buy in a spray can from any hardware store. He bent to touch – it was still a little tacky and as yet it had not fully 'gone off', or dried.

He pushed harder and the door slowly began to give. His suspicions were now aroused, he was wary he didn't like the situation as, coming from the inside and now wafting out onto the street was a smell, a pungent stench. He pushed a little harder, but now with considerable care. Suddenly the door shuddered forward, just opening as the foam gave and cracked, its adhesion failing. He applied more pressure and slowly the door broke free from the case in accompaniment to a sound akin to that of Selotape being peeled from plastic.

The stench of domestic gas swirled round him. Was this a suicide, if so whose? The room was in total darkness. By human instinct his hand began to reach to the wall, preparing to grope momentarily for the light switch. But he then froze, his movement never completed, as training took over. His hand stopped midway, he made no further movements; for a split second, he stood motionless.

Then checking the door and its casing for

any wires or further obstruction, he very slowly opened it fully – the stench of gas was unbearable as unseen waves wafted into the street.

From the doorway daylight now flooded into the rooms. Once again, he checked for pedestrians, checking left to right, but there were none to be seen. In this short street, he appeared to be alone.

Before carefully entering, he took off his shoes so as not to cause any spark, friction, or static and moved slowly through strips of bright sunlight and dark shadows towards the closed curtains opposite.

Expertly he checked for wires or devices, but there were none that he could see. Slowly, very slowly he drew the curtains back a little so that shadows danced as more daylight flooded in.

Now desperate for breath he staggered back the way he had come, carefully moving through the room and back into the street, eyes streaming. He needed air, God he needed air.

Still mercifully there were no pedestrians, but he had to act quickly. One over curious member of the public complete with cigarette, or spark from a shoe and he would be history – so would the apartment and any evidence therein including the photo.

Sufficient daylight now shone into the apartment as the density of gas depleted, allowing him to make his way towards the darkened kitchen where, predictably, a row of gas taps on the polished, trendy, brass and iron cooker lay crosswise and appeared to be fully open, from which gas with a low dull and ominous sound rushed into the small kitchen. Urgently but carefully his eyes were looking, searching, watching all the while for any form of booby trap. Slowly, carefully he closed the taps down. Then in the gloom, out of the corner of his eyes, he saw it; carefully he ducked away in a calculated movement from an electric flex which hung down menacingly from a ceiling light unit.

This was not a suicide attempt by anyone. A wire, an extension wire at that was hanging from the light socket? Leading to where? And the builders' foam! That door had been closed from the outside after the intruder had left; the residue of foam was cut and cleaned. No suicide had been planned by anyone.

He quickly moved over to the two kitchen windows, carefully drawing back more curtains. As he did he checked them for wires or triggers and then carefully checked the window frames for the same.

Kit knew what he was looking for and now he was not disappointed. A row of red-tipped matches held under tension were taped to the base of each opening window frame, with sandpaper stuck to the main base frame – all of which had been casually hidden under a newspaper and behind a row of earthenware condiment jars. With practised skill, he carefully unstuck and removed the matches from each window frame.

Had the windows been opened, the matches would undoubtedly have struck and ignited. They were in effect a 'second trigger', a back-up for whoever. He now carefully inspected the latch and opened the two windows. Fresh air thankfully gushed in, flowed through and across the room in a cleansing breeze.

Gasping for breath he held his head out and breathed deeply. He looked out onto a small but tidy back yard, with a barbecue area and an old wooden beer barrel, now a water butt. He could see the towering white blocks of the harbour development in the background.

He checked the back door and its casing, the lock and the key. It had been taped airtight but surprisingly there were no other untoward signs of tampering. He opened it slowly, carefully; whoever set this little party up never expected the person who entered the building to get this far.

With the flow of air now going through the apartment, the gas was beginning to disperse completely, and the apartment was light so that he could at last see easily. He was able to relax now that the apartment was no longer in an explosive state and he no longer stood in a bomb.

He turned to take in the scene. From what he could see of the rooms, they still appeared untouched and tidy, just as they had been before, all except for a table lamp which he now saw was connected to the ceiling light holder by the flex, a black extension wire – the wire that he had ducked past earlier and, he now realised would in effect have been the first trigger of the now averted bomb.

The table lamp was on the floor close to the oven. He knew precisely what it was, and why it was there. Squashed into the oven was a blue plastic bucket, the type you would put in a sink unit to wash crockery, but this one was full to the brim with a dark yellow glutinous substance, like a dark lemon jelly. He knew through experience that it would be very sticky and would also smell of gasoline – which it did. It was a highly inflammable mixture, not unlike napalm, a flaming jelly used by the United States in Vietnam, a most heinous creation. This would have been easily made with household substances available from any hardware store and gas station

He took the lamp into his now gloved hands and examined it. The glass of the light bulb had been delicately broken away and the zinc filament laid bare. He immediately broke the filament.

The 'first trigger', the sequence would have been this: he, or another unfortunate, would have entered the house which would have been in total darkness. The intruder would naturally have reached for the light switch to turn on the lights. The table lamp, which lay near the cooker, would have been activated and the filament of the broken bulb would have glowed red hot for a moment, then burst into a short-lived, brilliant, magnesium flare. The cooker and the surrounding rooms being full of gas would have exploded violently. The napalm-like substance in the plastic bucket would have cannoned forward out of the oven where the greater density of gas was and, the oven's inside restricting its immediate expansion, it would have left the oven as if from the barrel of a mortar. It would have exploded devastatingly into the room, showering the area and any intruder with a fiercely burning jelly, sticking to any human flesh, burning and flaming, eating its way deeply into the body. Very nasty.

All traces of occupation in the apartment would have been destroyed, as would the unfortunate and unwanted intruder.

Collecting his thoughts and now clear in his mind, Kit looked keenly around once again. Everything else so far still looked fine, just as it had – nothing more appeared to have been moved.

With that digested he moved carefully into the bedroom, which was just as he remembered it – neat and tidy with a large central bed with silken drapes. He moved on into the room watching, listening, seeking all the while for any tell-tale signs of a hidden trap. He went carefully around the bed and to the bedside table – and stopped short, staring. The photograph, the ornate silver-framed photograph which he supposed was of Charles Stevens had gone!

Had he got the right side of the bed? His eyes flashed across to the other bedside table, nothing. No this was the right side, the side he remembered well.

He looked closer at the bedside table. There in the very fine film of dust on the top he could see where the frame and its support leg had been. The photograph had been carefully lifted upwards and away leaving no smear in the dust, it had not been dragged off. He looked down at the drawer below. Its gilt handle stared back at him tantalisingly, coaxing him into a mistake, but looking too obvious a trap – a 'third trigger' perhaps?

Slowly and carefully he examined the edges of the drawer, the tiny gaps where it slid into the frame. There was no visible sign of any trap, no wires, no tape, no tell-tale marks, nothing hung down underneath or protruded from the back.

Heart pumping his hand moved to the gilt handle – ammonium tri-iodide? He faltered. Near invisible and if painted on the handle it would blow his hand clean off at a touch. No, whoever was the perpetrator wanted any intruder dead not maimed.

Once again, he reached out and gently, between finger and thumb, gripped the little gilt handle. Taking a deep breath, he slid the drawer centimetre by centimetre carefully towards him, so he could see inside from an angle. He then nervously slid it open all the way. There was no bang, no heart-rending flash, no seared flesh.

He gently exhaled and looked inside, all was as before but with one exception. Although the Kleenex tissues were still there, the other half of the photograph, the torn jagged half, the other half to the young man. That had also gone!

If it had been me, he thought, I would defiantly have booby-trapped that drawer, it was a natural, so why not do it?

He was puzzled. To him it was a mistake.

At least he was now building up a picture, a character picture in his mind of the sort of person he might be dealing with. It wasn't easy. Whoever it was had wanted to kill the intruder to the apartment, but why? He or she had also removed the pictures – why? Had they incriminated the perpetrator? Surely that could be the only reason. Yet in some ways this was a half-hearted effort. They hadn't gone all the way. It was as if he or she really deep down did not want to do the 'job'.

Kit continued to search the apartment but to no avail, there was nothing unusual. As a precaution for others who might follow, and knowing the jelly-like substance in the oven was soluble, he carefully lifted the bowl out of the oven, carried it outside and dumped it into the water butt in the back yard. There it would lie harmless, dissolve and evaporate.

He checked once more that he had missed nothing, moved out into the street and tried to close the door after him. Predictably with the builders' foam still making a seal it did not close easily. He bent down to clear some away and it was then he noticed in the corner by the doormat, stuck in some of the yellow foam, was a piece of turquoise and white polythene, a tear-off strip from one end of a polythene packet. Picking it up he immediately knew what it was. It smelt of latex and had at one time been the seal to a pack and pair of translucent surgical gloves. The same tell-tale piece from a pack, the same type of seal that he had found on the floor of the BMW those few fateful days ago, the person was also careless.

Not only was he involved with someone who was perhaps not fully committed to what they had started, but one who was also lax in covering their trail – could it have been on purpose? Once he had the door closed, Kit turned and walked briskly up the street, taking in the scene. He had not heard an engine start or a car move.

But the little yellow Alfa Romeo had gone.

Fourteen

Kit was on his way back into London when the car phone burst into life, it was Sheeka, also on her way back to town, it was a welcome call.

'Sir, can I call you Kit?' she asked.

'Everyone else does.'

'So, dinner you asked?' she continued.

'Yes indeed,' he answered 'we have a lot to discuss and I always prefer to do it over dinner, I think better, it is less restricting'

'Pardon?' she laughed. 'Over dinner, anyway, fine by me. But Kit, I would just like a straightforward steak, not your damned oysters and whatever goes with them!' She laughed again.

Kit was a little taken aback; rarely were his tastes challenged. But as a gentleman he conceded willingly.

'Where then? You choose.'

'The Topo Giggio in Soho. It's an Italian, I like Italians.'

'Most girls do!'

'Don't be jealous, I'll see you there at eight.'

The light banter of unofficial conversation

with Sheeka lifted Kit's mood, it was an interesting contrast to the thoughts going through his mind. Spontaneous happenings like that were often frowned upon, but for Kit these helped his thought process.

Kit arrived just before eight o'clock having made his way to Soho from the Park Lane via Piccadilly. It was a good walk, which he had enjoyed, but for some reason he was uneasy. Was it the gas-filled apartment playing on his mind? He knew not, but several times he had thought he was being followed. He did some counter-surveillance moves but spotted no one. It was just an odd feeling he had, one he did not like. His instincts were usually right.

Soho was heaving with tourists of every type and creed, some peering nervously into the strip joints, hoping against hope that they would not be noticed. Others looked nervously over their shoulders, as unwittingly they entered conversation with a streetwise prostitute. Neon lights flashed; there was a stench of cheap and over-used cooking oil, of roasting mutton that posed as lamb kebabs, blue flames licking the sides as it turned on a spit in an open window at a nearby restaurant. The street was strewn with litter from the daytime market. Pimps lurked.

The Topo Giggio, the best of the rest even with its gaudy sign, came up on the left. Through the dark damp window, Kit could see trademark of Ruffino Chianti wine bottles hanging in their raffia baskets from the ceiling; the place looked traditionally Italian. Sheeka would no doubt be happy.

Then suddenly from nowhere she appeared, startling him.

'Why so nervous?' she laughed. 'Did you think I was a 'Lady of the Night'?' she smiled, the flashing neon reflecting in her equally flashing blue eyes.

'No, but for the last ten minutes or so I was sure that I was being followed, just a curious feeling, that's all.'

'And?'

The street was noisy, but from amongst the cacophony of sound were some that Kit knew yet could not instantly discern. What had they been? A thud, a whoosh? A closing door? He knew not, but the hairs on his neck had been more perceptive than his ears.

'And?' Sheeka said, again trying to get his attention.

'Well, no sign,' he said looking around, his eyes searching for the slightest hint of abnormality. Then they focused on her. Now she had his full attention as all other thoughts started to melt; women his down fall. It was often said they would be the death of him.

'Boring! No blood before dinner, bloody boring!' Sheeka said with a fabulous toss of her head.

All worries vanished and for Kit with an uncustomary shrug he held the door of the restaurant open for her. He looked again up the street one last time, knowing that he too had now been lax, somebody was out there, who?

The restaurant was not too full, so with a polite gesture he ushered her into the dim pillared room and chose a discreet table hidden in a small alcove, all before the headwaiter could intervene with an easier but for Kit a less convenient position. The waiter was about to protest until he saw the glare in Kit's eyes. He swiftly backed off.

Her words 'a Lady of the Night' stirred in Kit's mind like a delicate worm, eating, seeking, finding its way through his grey matter, searching for a solution to his thoughts. Once achieved, it became more like a maggot. He smiled to himself; it was shocking;

'Sheeka, have you ever felt like being a 'Lady of the Night', you know a hooker, a prostitute?' She was predictably and visibly taken aback.

Aware that her face had registered shock, she blanched, then as if to brazen it through and throw the gauntlet down to him she said, 'Why, you paying?'

'Er' no, not exactly, Sheeka.' He smiled. 'No such luck, but just listen for a moment,' Whilst thinking to himself, I wonder how much she'd charge? Instantly ashamed of his thoughts, he kicked himself metaphorically for the lapse.

She knew by the tone of his voice that this was a serious question, not frivolous and in some perverse way within the call of duty. He now had her full attention; she was interested, if a little apprehensive.

'I'll tell you,' he continued, and moved closer to her across the table, nudging a glass of wine to the side.

'We have a problem,' and with that he proceeded to outline all the facts to date.

'So, we have a lot of pieces in this puzzle and I'm not sure as yet how they are all going to piece together, or even if some are related. But what I am sure of is we need to know more about the girl, the Minister's girlfriend and the only way I can achieve that is through her friends at this agency. Right now, it's our only source. I just can't barge in asking questions – well not yet anyway. So Sheeka, I need you or someone to get involved just as if you were one of them! I need you to find out as much as you can. I need you to find out if the Minister had any other girlfriends? Was this his first? How did he get introduced? Is there anyone else involved? All this we need to know. What do you say?'

Her answer surprised him.

'Should be fun!' Sheeka said, followed by a chuckle and a large gulp of her wine. Kit sat back and admired her beauty, wondering if he was doing the right thing; he hoped he would not regret it. After a moment, he said, to reassure her and probably his own conscience.

'I'll watch you all the way.'

'I'm not sure I'm into that yet,' Sheeka said with a screech of laughter.

'No, you know what I mean, I'll be on hand all the time, in the same restaurant, in the same hotel or whatever. I'll be at the next table, or the car behind. I don't want you to go all the way, you may have to feign an illness, be sick or something. Don't worry, I'll show you the ropes.'

'So, when do I start? Where is, this place, this den of iniquity?' she said.

'I'll take you there straight after this meal, you could make enquiries then.'

'You don't mess about, do you?'

'Neither did her murderer'

Sheeka nodded solemnly.

Two hours later Sheeka was walking down Beauchamp Place towards the escort agency. She climbed the steps and as she opened the door there was a scuttle as the waiting girls moved off at a dash into another room. Then suddenly realising that it was not a client, but another girl and a stunning one at that, they came drifting back one by one into the room to have a look at her. It was obvious even to the untrained eye that by this time of night the best had long gone.

Undaunted Sheeka looked round the room, her eyes resting on the cluttered desk and the woman who sat behind it and a pile of tab ends. There was a mixed aroma of exotic perfumes, cooking from below and female odour; she was not terribly impressed.

'Are you the boss?' Sheeka enquired, not looking the woman in the eye and purposely acting a little nervous.

'You could say so, deary, you could say so. Main boss Olga ain't 'ere, she's sick, so it's me. How can I help you?'

'I'd like a job!' Sheeka exclaimed shocked by her own voice.

'Would you now, mm, a job.' The 'madam' nodded cheerfully. 'A job, mm, sit down, luv, sit down,' she gesticulated, patting a chair. 'An' you lot buzz off, go next door,' she shouted at the onlookers, 'girls in waiting'. 'Don't frighten this, er, little lovely off.' With that she proceeded to tell Sheeka the terms of business, finishing with 'Oh and, er, we have certain, gentlemen you might say who like nice 'new' young 'uns, unmolested like, you know, like yerself'

The deal the madam offered the girls appeared to be this. The girls paid her £100 a night each for the privilege of being here on display, so to speak, and the madam also got an introduction fee from each client. After that it was up to the girl, who kept what she earned and made her own arrangements with the client.

'That's it then,' Sheeka said.

'Just as easy as that, love,' the madam cackled. 'When will you start?' she was rubbing her hands.

'Um, tomorrow I think.'

'Fine, get here at about seven-thirty, luv, an you'll get the wealthy businessmen up in London for the night, an' if you're lucky wanting to take you for a meal as well, an

that way luv, you'll get fed and fucked on the early shift.' She laughed coarsely. Sheeka nodded apprehensively and stood to leave.

'May I just have a word with the girls, you know, see how they go on?'

Deal done, her interest waning, the woman waved her away to the waiting room to speak with the remaining girls.

Ten minutes later Sheeka was back outside in Beauchamp Place walking towards Kit who was waiting by Bill Bentley's, a wine bar at the end. In acknowledgment, he flashed the Jaguar's lights and Sheeka made her way down and climbed into the front seat. There was a moment's silence before she spoke.

'Well I hope for your sake this works.'

'And if it doesn't?'

'I'll personally rip your balls off!'

He coughed,

'Ouch! Now we wouldn't want that, would we?'

'We?' she said turning, smiling, and looking at him.

'When do you start?'

'Tomorrow, 7.30 got to parade before the customers when they arrive, sort of

'View before you screw"

Kit laughed out loud, he liked her humour.

'Mm, then I need to get you sorted – a distress beacon, a two-way radio / and microcassette at the very least,' he said. Sheeka scowled.

'Don't panic! They'll come disguised as a powder puff, a pen or whatever.' Then thinking aloud, he said, 'But it might be advisable to double up on this lot just to be sure. We'll use a small trendy handbag as well, to hold another miniature two-way radio/cassette and a miniature video camera if we can, then at least I can see what's going on.'

'Pervert.'

'Also, a ladies' watch, again as an alarm. Er, you've passed out at self-defence, haven't you?'

'You know I have!'

Then after a pause he went on, 'I also want you to purchase a pot of Pond's cold cream, too, you know it's in the white opaque glass jar.'

'I never use it! Didn't know they still made it. Would Clarins do?'

'Listen to me Sheeka! These are things they don't tell you at school.'

'Sorry.' Suddenly she went quiet.

'Yes, I suppose Clarins would do but the glass is important it must be opaque, and the seal is also important. Be careful to leave the seal on and unbroken, intact, so that as you unscrew the cap if you hold the seal and the cap firmly they will unscrew together, then lift off as a whole. Don't separate them, keep them intact. That's why I recommended Ponds; I know it works that way.

Remove all the cream and clean the jar and lid. Then fill it with tiny chopped vegetables, colourful ones. You can actually buy shredded veg, carrot and the like in a jar at most supermarkets. Chop it up even more, then add coriander or curry powder, vinegar and olive oil. Olive is also important it has colour and it sticks better; the rest is just for the smell.'

'Smell?' she said, screwing up her nose.

'Yes, smell. Listen to me seriously Sheeka, this could get you out of a jam. To feign a sickness, you might have to be sick – someone has to believe you, so take your saviour, take it with you in your handbag, in the Ponds jar.

'The lid now replaced and with the seal unbroken no one will know from the outside; the glass is opaque so no one can tell. It will look unopened, new. You may of course be searched, indeed you're certain to be if you get involved with a wealthy Arab or similar, most have bodyguards. So, when you have the need to get 'sick', excuse yourself and spill a little on your front for maximum effect. Make sure you wear a white blouse so it stains and can easily be seen. Leave some in the toilet, on the bowl or seat, believe me they'll check it out. Also, have it on your breath, swill some in your mouth, leave a little on your chin, it'll work and it should get you out of an unwanted situation.'

'You are a mine of information.'

'I've had to be – and I'm still here.' He wished he hadn't said that. His mind flashed back and he thought once again of Stuart's death during the Carlos II episode. He looked down at his watch, a white-faced Audemar Chronograph all dials, date and moon, gold hands and Roman figures specially ordered. It reminding him of when he and Stuart had both bought them on the same day. 'More discount for two,' he had said. Stuart, he remembered, later bought his wife one, a smaller version of his own. An extravagance and tragically now it all seemed a long time ago.

The following evening, and not without a certain amount of trepidation, Kit went through his final instructions with Sheeka – how he would cover her safety and what procedures would be triggered if something went wrong. He told her he would be able to trace her movements on the monitor and, providing she left her communicator on, he would never be far away. Worryingly, he was also fully aware that he had not got all this sanctioned by the Old Man – but then he never would, so he never tried. He needed a result.

Kit dropped Sheeka off at Beauchamp Place and drove to the end of the street watching her in the driving mirror as she walked away, swinging her bag nonchalantly, blond hair blowing in the evening breeze, confident and complete with all her electronic gadgetry – and the jar. Without looking back, she turned left into the agency, her pulse rate quickening, yet controlled.

At the end of the street Kit turned the Jaguar round, checked the monitor for her movements and waited. The screen filled the car with an eerie green glow so he turned down the brightness and fitted the cowl.

Sheeka was greeted by the woman in a notably less friendly fashion than on her previous visit, and was casually told to go and join the girls in their waiting room, the door ajar. They would be called as and when they were needed, she said. Sheeka then dropped a hint, sowed a seed for the benefit of anyone listening, by saying, 'Tonight of all nights I don't feel too good, what bloody luck.'

'Hope it's not the curse, deary,' was all the reply she got. No one was interested – they all had their own problems.

However, it was not long before a gentleman apprehensively pushed open the door of the agency. Soon the buzzer sounded, the call for the girls to parade through the open door, one by one, to greet their prospective partner for the evening or night.

No way did Sheeka want to get involved so soon she had learnt little! She wanted to speak to the girls, find out what she could – and for that she needed time. Quietly she sat down, clutching her stomach; predictably no one had any sympathy, the thinking being: one down, especially an attractive one, the more for the rest. It was written on their faces as the eager girls filed past into the lounge. Clearly it was not going to be easy to befriend them, as very obviously, most were in competition with each other. However, in only a short time they had chattered inanely, a babbling troop. It seemed endless, so all one had to do was sit, listen and smile, throwing in the odd comment and trying to glean something.

Luckily the ploy of 'unwell' worked and

Sheeka did not go through with the others, nor was she asked to by Madam. Her condition was accepted and she just watched the proceedings.

The suited gentleman selected a young Australian girl who was going around the world. 'These, er, stop-offs,' she said with a wink, 'supplement my minimal expenses allowed by my father.'

Her father it later turned out was a man of the cloth in Queensland.

Sheeka soon realised that it was the more casual workers who were going to be friendly and useful, so she targeted a young girl who looked nervous, wrongly as it turned out.

'Do you like it here?' Sheeka enquired.

'I've only being 'working' a few weeks,' she answered. 'The money's good' and as she pointed out, 'I'd be doing it anyway, so I might as well get 'paid and laid'.'

'Do you have a boyfriend?' Sheeka asked.

'Oh sure,' was the comment 'He's useless, couldn't earn a penny – but I like him, he's good in bed, knows all about foreplay which makes a change in this game, and he has a big 'todger', as if I need any extra,' she laughed, 'and what's more, he doesn't know of my activities, he thinks I'm an actress.'

She probably was – no, had to be! thought Sheeka with a smile.

She managed a desultory conversation with the girl and eventually when the coast appeared clear mentioned the Russian girls working in London. 'Are there many working here?'

'Oh sure,' came the reply. 'But none are here tonight as yet. They'll be after much bigger fish – they want husbands, money and most of all a British passport so they can stay! I mean, who the hell wants to go back to Russia? Some of these girls have had a rough time, you should hear the stories – but once they see the big stores in the West End there's no stopping them. They look good in all their designer gear and they are attractive no doubt. They get their share of the more 'well-to-do types'. They're so damned persistent, they just hang on in there for the odd Lord or whatever; they try hard all right, don't give up. You know, some old guy working on a debate in a late-night session at the Houses of Parliament, he's tired and wants company his guard is down, not to mention his pants.' She laughed. 'An' he's easy meat.' With a smile, her long tongue flicked across her glistening lips.

During the next couple of hours men came and went, some selected a girl or girls, some did not, others paid up then off they went into the night. The room became less and less crowded so that Sheeka was becoming more conspicuous. She sat there rubbing her stomach, feigning sickness and talking to her new-found pal Streak – so named after a dare at Lords Cricket ground whilst full of champagne and in the company of another gentleman. Streak was a wild, athletic-looking girl with auburn hair and a laughing smile; she was lithe and willowy yet at the same time she seemed to be very well endowed, to say the very least.

She had not as yet been selected, indeed she had not tried too hard as she'd been chatting willingly enough to Sheeka – for her it was good to have a new friend, especially in this game. But enough was enough, the Madam now pushed her head around the door and glared at Sheeka.

'Why haven't you buggered off, eh? No bleedin' home to go to?' she said gruffly. 'You'll not get better sat there.'

'I'm not well. I'm sorry, but I'll be OK for tomorrow night,' Sheeka muttered.

'You'd better be! I don't like hangers on – we ain't got time luvi.'

Suddenly the door to the main salon was pushed open again and the Madam briskly closed the door to the girls 'waiting room'.

'Now then, sir, how can we help you? Got some lovely girl's – did you ring earlier?' could be heard through the door as the woman addressed the new client.

'Right, sorry, enough of the chatter,' said

Streak 'Your name Sheeka wasn't it,' she was suddenly alert and now very determined, 'I'm hungry, and what's more I need a few quid – this guy's going to be mine, might be the last tonight. Give me a ring tomorrow, not early though he might be rough!' Streak laughed, continuing, 'an' we'll have a coffee!' She quickly scribbled her mobile number on a cigarette packet lid, tore it off and tossed it over. With that she took her bra off and stuffed it in her bag, quickly followed by her panties – what little there was of them.

The remaining four girls had not seen this remarkable 'sleight of hand', all being too eager to clock the new prospective client.

The call eventually came and one by one they filtered through. Streak was the last to go. Rather than shake the man's hand, as they were instructed to do, she promptly sat on his knee; the delighted punter put his arm round her instantly able feel to her warm, unhindered flesh radiating through her thin garment. To him and to all the onlookers she was plainly wearing no bra, while her tight mini-skirt covered little. The others had been slow off the mark – Streak did not return to the 'waiting room'.

Kit sat patiently outside the premises in the Jaguar. Thanks to Sheeka he now had all that had taken place on tape. He had just seen yet another man leave the premises, this one with what appeared to be a very interesting girl, that is judging by the way she kissed him in the street whilst gently massaging his crotch, almost the entire length of her naked legs protruding from her extremely short skirt.

As the two wobbled off into the night, Sheeka appeared and immediately saw Kit. As arranged she walked off in the opposite direction for a discreet pickup, when both were sure they were well clear and a block or so away.

Kit saw her raise her compact to her face. His radio burst quietly into life.

'Can I go home?' Sheeka whispered, in an acted and forlorn manner.

'No, it's time for a coffee.'

He pulled up alongside Sheeka who climbed in.

'You didn't fancy it tonight then,' he remarked glibly.

'If you weren't my senior, I'd hit you.'

'If you wanted to, you would,' he replied with a smile as he pulled out into the traffic, 'Coffee?'

Fifteen

As promised the following day at lunchtime, Sheeka dialled Streak. A few moments later the musical tone of the mobile was answered and after an obvious rustle of bedclothes Streak spoke. As agreed they arranged to meet for coffee in a Shepherd's Market deli, an Italian.

Sheeka arrived early. The cafe was small and not very private, but she chose the best of the few available tables, not too near the counter and service area, where background noise would affect a tape transmission. The display looked delicious, bristling with sandwiches and rolls with every filling imaginable. There was also the inviting aroma of roasted coffee beans being noisily ground and packed for re-sale.

Twenty minutes or so later Streak arrived. Sheeka stood up and went to meet her, only to discover that Streak had brought a friend with her, a startlingly attractive Russian girl named Hella, complete with hourglass figure, long legs and straight long blond hair. They were introduced.

No pan-flat Slavic features on this girl, her

face was more southern Russian, close to Italy or maybe even Georgia, Sheeka decided. Predictably she was dressed to the nines. Hella stated with a heavy accent and forthright speech that she had been bored and needed to go out shopping and for a chat. She had been waiting in her flat for a call from her friend Verkuska. She normally always went out shopping during the day with her friend, Verkuska, she stated. But now surprisingly she hadn't seen her in days. She was cross, annoyed as they shared their secrets and now where the hell was she! Some bloody man, no doubt, and they weren't worth it. They had one good thing and it was not between their legs, it was in their pocket – a wallet.

The three good-looking girls all nodded in agreement, moved back to the table Sheeka had selected and sat down. They attracted glances from all sides, some not so subtle; Hella preened.

An overwhelmed young boy of a waiter, slim and tanned, took the order for coffees, one with a large vodka for Hella. As the vodka arrived first she promptly ordered another, whilst slipping her arm around the boy's thigh.

'So, young, so vulnerable,' she smiled with a sigh as she let him go.

Kit sat reading the early edition of the 'London Evening Standard' just two tables away, watching and listening as best he could. In any event

Sheeka was recording the conversation. He could have used an earpiece but for the moment a recording would do as after all, these were just girls out having a coffee and a chat, not selling secrets.

To start with Sheeka found the Russian too full of herself, while in a strange way she was also aloof. It was difficult to extract answers to the innocent questions that she posed during conversation, disguised as they were as light-hearted inquiries into the girl and her friends' lives here in London.

Something was lost in the translation for sure, but nevertheless Hella was a wary soul and avoided any straight answers, giving nothing away, except that generally they, 'the girls', did well in London.

However, as the vodka began to take its toll she became a little more relaxed. Indeed, she began to take over the conversation in her slow, clipped accent. Excitedly she said, 'My friend Verkuska has even been dating a real live Parliamentarian, yes a minister of England no less,' She had said previously that she had not seen her for some time and she had not answered her mobile, although there was nothing unusual in that. Certainly, if she was with her lover the Minister, she must appear to be his lady. After all there had been talk of a car, even a flat for her. She must not lose that! Hella boasted of her friend's good fortune.

Yet on a personal level she was annoyed because Verkuska's involvement with someone else meant that she was not always available to work and this affected their joint act when two girls were requested, as they often were.

When Sheeka heard this, she could hardly contain her expression of friendly interest, of trying to appear helpful in welcoming a foreign girl to London; one who by now needed to go to the Ladies room.

Streak then lent across to Sheeka and said,

'Don't worry, she's always guarded, that is till she's had a drink or two. They all are, its years of the KGB looking over their shoulder and all that crap, but then they forget and get loud and they don't stop drinking. I reckon she's an alky!' Streak said in an informed manner. Sheeka nodded in casual agreement. Streak then continued, 'Anyway I've something to tell you, er, about tonight, can't now though as she'll be back in a mo.'

Kit immediately thought he had recognised the Russian girl, his heartbeat stepped up a gear. But was she the girl? Yes, he searched his memory for her name, yes, Hella, it was Hella. She had signed the note, the blond girl who'd come by taxi to Verkuska's apartment at Chelsea Harbour; she was the one who knocked on the door and left the note for Verkuska, asking her to contact Olga, who he now knew ran the agency. Hella, yes, he'd recognise those legs anywhere. Last time he'd seen them they were getting into the back of a taxi.

As he casually looked across in her direction he noticed her dark flashing eyes, the 'blond' was probably out of a bottle.

He was having great difficulty in hearing and understanding Hella's accent now that she was eagerly and speedily chattering away, the alcohol making it worse. Although he trusted Sheeka implicitly, he desperately hoped that the tape was running.

Later that afternoon Kit watched Sheeka enter a phone booth by Selfridges as the other two girls wandered off excitedly into the store. Seconds later his mobile burst into life, Sheeka was ringing to put him out of his misery by telling him that she thought the tape would be fine. However, she had now agreed to go off shopping with the girls and might not be able to speak to him for a while. She said that the Russian girl was continuing to burble as the vodka by now had a firm hold. Sheeka would try and get her to have some more to keep her talking.

Kit replied cautiously saying.

'No problem. I can wait for the tape when you're free. Just be careful and remember, I'll never be far away.'

That evening Sheeka arrived at the agency in Beauchamp Place promptly at seven-thirty, having just had time to pop back to her apartment and find fresh clothes suitable for the job in hand, although she had few that would actually suit. Streak was already there and dressed to kill with today's new kit from Selfridges. Smiling widely, she came straight over to Sheeka.

'Great, I'm glad you're here,' she said quickly. 'Listen, 'Madam' has just had a telephone inquiry from some guys, two girls wanted now, straight away, hey don't scowl!' she exclaimed 'We know em' they've rang before they're big payers, foreign, Arabs or something, doing their entertaining maybe. It's always at a private house or apartment I think, though I've never actually been, but other girls have. The two Russian girls have for sure many times, an' it's sort of first come first served. Hella and team aren't here an' I don't want to miss it, it's good money, great money. Fancy going with me eh?'

Sheeka was somewhat taken aback. But there had to be a first time and Streak for the moment was her main contact. It was unlikely Hella would appear tonight judging by the state she was in when they left her, so no further gain there and there would be safety in numbers she told herself.

If Hella and co. had been 'involved' on such a date before, then there might be a connection somewhere. Kit had said, 'If the remains in the burnt-out car were of the Russian girl, the Minister's 'Lady' as we now believe, then we need to know her associates, her friends; we need to know everything about her.' So, with a great deal of trepidation Sheeka answered.

'Yes, sure I'll come, but you only if you look after me; I've never earned money this way before.'

'No problem really,' said Streak with a nonchalant shrug, as she dashed into the other room, closely followed by Sheeka to tell the 'Madam' the good news. The woman promptly dialled what appeared to be a well-known number to her. It was engaged. Streak excitedly nudged her.

'You might even enjoy it I sometimes do,' she giggled. 'It's nothing to be ashamed of, sometimes we all need it and tonight to hell with it, I'm looking forward to it.'

Sheeka did not answer but watched the Madam dial again, her podgy fingers prodding the phone. She could tell by the prefix number that it was a mobile, and she tried to memorise the ten-digit number in full.

Within ten minutes or less a smart but small and facially ugly man pushed open the door; the other girls scuttled away. He smiled weakly at Streak and Sheeka standing there, Streak as ever leaving little to the imagination.

'Gorgeous, just bloody gorgeous. I'm Michael, Mick,' he said unconvincingly. Then under his stale aromatic garlic breath, he muttered with a chuckle, 'He's gonna be a lucky bugger tonight.'

Who's going to be lucky? Sheeka thought, doubting the creep's real name was Mick. She could name him, she thought to herself.

The man was obviously well known to the Madam, she smiled greedily near salivating as he gave her a small wad of notes and simultaneously waving the girls out of the door.

'Limo's just outside, me beauties,' he gestured again towards the door with a sickly smile. He had large wet red lips that rolled and furled outward, as if ready to drool.

Streak quickly teetered off confidently down the stairs. Sheeka followed warily trying to remain calm. As the man followed, his hand felt her bottom. She would love to have broken it finger by finger.

Outside waiting was a stretched limo, a Fleetwood, all shiny black with mirrored glass, a mist of moist exhaust fumes hung in the air. Once the door was opened Sheeka could see there was a driver in uniform at the wheel and another man in the front seat; the girls climbed into the back with their escort. The chauffeur said nothing, but the other man who sat in the front, a big broad man not unlike a bouncer from outside a London club, turned.

'Hi, I'm Bill Delaney.'

Sheeka believed him, he looked smart and clean-shaven, ex-military with his short neat hairstyle. 'I'm just here to see these two goons don't molest you before you get there, the boss likes his goods freshly wrapped.'

'Like his newspaper, freshly ironed,' muttered the chauffeur.

'Who are we seeing?' Sheeka inquired.

'Oh, the boss I suppose. I don't know if he has any guests tonight, he ain't back yet. Delayed by a late and boozy lunch maybe, but I don't really know we only see him briefly. He's probably with some celebrity. You might even meet somebody famous tonight,' he said with a laugh. 'They get about, these celebs.'

'Is he foreign then, or English?' Sheeka enquired, while not wishing to seem too curious.

Rubber lips coughed and stared pointedly at Bill Delaney who never answered, he just turned icily to watch the traffic. Sheeka didn't think Delaney cared either way, but the conversation abruptly stopped. He had said too much.

When the road was clear they pulled away from the kerb and into the night. Sheeka and

Streak settled back into the pale cream leather, their feet buried into the deep pile of the carpeted interior.

Sheeka drew out her compact, applied lipstick and checked her make-up. Streak was adjusting what little dress she had, rather like pressing a handkerchief. In the mirror of the compact that reflected back through the tinted rear screen, Sheeka saw the Jaguar pull out to follow some distance away. She thought to herself, 'Thank you, Kit,' and closed the compact thoughtfully. A little happier now with the make-up compact activated and Kit behind, she now hoped he would hear everything and be able to monitor her movements on screen. As he had insisted, she was also wearing the mock gold 'Cartier Tank' watch as a back-up. If activated it would also quietly warn him of whatever danger she might be in. Idly she wondered what he would do.

The unlikely 'Mick' passed them both a glass of champagne from the cocktail cabinet, Dom Perignon, ice cold and very welcome. Then with relish he helped himself to a glass. Annoyingly he clinked their glasses together, glaring at them with the trademark sickly smile; this time he did dribble.

They had not been driving long when they slowed and turned right into a narrow road with high walls to one side. It was a residential area, but she felt it must be somewhere within the West End as only minutes before they had passed Marble Arch. Sheeka did not know the area.

On the left, they came upon some tall wooden gates with black iron studs. The gates were already beginning to open as they approached; the security lights came on lighting up the quartz chippings in gravel.

They slowed to turn in and she saw from corner of her eye the Jaguar drive past and away; it did not seem to have been noticed, but then a Jaguar in London was commonplace.

Once the limousine had stopped in front of an impressive entrance hall they were ushered out. Incredibly two very large (re-pros, she presumed) Ming vases stood sprouting flowers either side of the double doors. Through these Sheeka could see a huge glittering chandelier hanging from the black ironwork of a glass-domed roof, bright adornments were twinkling back through the windows. It was without doubt an expensive residence but it did not exude good taste. Yet for all this, it appeared quite private, the high wall enhancing the effect. Sheeka noticed the odd security camera dotted about but there was certainly nothing unusual in that. London and indeed most cities were riddled with them.

It was now quite evident that the men with her were all employees and none wished to be found wanting. Sheeka could sense they worked in genuine fear of someone much senior.

Streak however did not seem to have any thoughts on the matter, just a '£' sign firmly registered and multiplying in her brain, the till was ringing.

In the entrance hall Sheeka was overwhelmed by the heat and slid out of her coat as did Streak. Two lithe and attractive girls stood there in very little. Sheeka was not embarrassed she saw it as a challenge. But the heat told her something; their host had to be from warmer climes.

'That's what we like, eager girls,' Mick spluttered. Sheeka would have loved to have smashed him in the face, but had to content herself with smiling back at him knowingly. He licked his abundant lips.

The chauffeur, another big man who had mostly kept silent save for his 'ironing of the morning paper' comment, had not followed them in. Now it was the other man's turn to speak.

'He's not back yet, so I don't know if----' The sentence was never finished as an internal phone chimed into a sort of coarse musical jig on the brash gilt table next to him. No one moved. Sheeka stared up at the huge chandelier with a bored expression on her face. At the other side of the hall sat a large polished golden Buddha.

Streak thrust her breasts up and forward.

'Spoke too soon,' Delaney uttered to anyone who would listen, 'he's back, an' he's on his own.'

'You shouldn't say that you don't know who he's with,' snapped Rubber lips, spraying all before him, mouth like a frayed garden hose. Delaney shrugged with disinterest.

'Oh, they come an' go don't they, bow-wow you faithful 'Poodle dog,' Delaney snapped back at him.

This was the first sign of any dissent between them. Sheeka made a note of it; if the going got tough it might be put to could use. She did not like any of them, but if there was a choice Delaney it appeared was different, more humane and the near total silence and robot-like movements of the chauffeur had been weird.

'Anyway, you're to get the girls some drinks, normal kit, so he says, and that means not me, mate. That's your job and of course the usual as well, he says, an' oh' he's in the bath, having a bloody swim.'

'Come, come girls,' said Rubber lips, now opening two huge white and gilded double doors leading into a sparsely furnished yet homely lounge which surprisingly had a large fire burning at one end. Sheeka noticed there were no personal items so far anywhere in the house that she had seen.

Rubber lips was now feeling Streak's bottom,

so she pushed it quivering back into his expectant open palm. He could hardly contain himself.

Meanwhile Kit parked the Jaguar away from any lights and under the greater darkness offered by some large leafy branches that protruded from mature trees the other side of the high wall.

He checked the hand-held monitor and zipped it into his inside pocket, threading the wire under his shirt. With the miniature earpiece, he could now hear the voice of one of the men, and the chatter of the girls; for the moment, they seemed happy and unconcerned. He waited for a moment watching and listening, not trusting the switch he then removed the car courtesy light bulbs so as not to cause alarm if the doors opened.

Ten minutes or so later curiosity got the better of him. In darkness, he eased himself out of the Jaguar and locked it by hand with the key so as not to flash the remote hazard lights. He checked the road again for passers-by but there were none; he scanned the wall for cameras, but again there were none visible.

Then in a flash he was on and up the wall, melting into the top, lying flat along its surface surveying the scene; small pieces of broken glass set in the wall topping dug into his clothing. From where he lay it all looked quiet. Then without a sound he rolled like a falling leaf off the top, landing silently he sank to his knees.

He held his breath listening, motionless. He rose slowly keeping amongst the trees and their shadows. Moving stealthily forward he approached the house at its nearest point, using the cover offered by the rhododendron bushes in the large garden.

Then looking to his left and up he saw a dark camera on the surrounding wall. Nothing really unusual in that, for it was a substantial house and would need security. He looked at the angle he imagined it would cover, took a gamble and moved off in the opposite direction but again toward the house itself. Once there he hugged the dark walls and crept to one of the many large Georgian-style windows.

The curtains were not fully drawn and allowed light to flood out. As he approached from the shadows he could see Sheeka and her friend standing there talking to a man with an unfortunate protruding mouth and lips. He looked like a fish or a toy, something you could pick up and stick by suction to a mirror. Amused at the analogy, he smiled.

Then his senses suddenly heightened and he stiffened as his eyes focused on the man who was now slipping some substance into the drinks. Then quite unashamedly indeed deliberately, the man offered more of the same to the girls. As if to give confidence to them both, the man now took one of the tablets himself. Kit saw Sheeka deftly and unnoticed fumble with the belt of her dress. Then, just as he had told her, she palmed the hidden strip of cut cling film and surreptitiously rolled the tablet with one hand in the superfine wrapping.

She made a great show of placing the pill, or whatever it was, into her mouth, sucked it in through pouting lips for all to see, her eyes rolling in feigned delight, then she swigged down more champagne with a flourish. He knew she would now have to be reasonably quick about getting rid of it somewhere as cling film is not infallible, it can soon unravel and lose its surface tension inside the mouth, and thus expose the pill, powder, potion or whatever to her bodily systems.

Another man now joined the person with the unfortunate face. Kit recognised him as the man from outside the Chelsea Girl agency, the one who had opened the limousine door. He was a big man and his body language showed that he was uneasy, unhappy with this or some other recent situation that Kit had not seen. The big man also showed noticeable disdain in regard to this other fellow.

Kit now saw Sheeka holding her stomach, rubbing it a little and frowning, play-acting toward her companions, as if complaining to Streak and the two men.

The big man quickly spoke to Sheeka, then politely it seemed he showed her through a flush-fitting door that blended perfectly with the trendy washed-white effect of the panelling. Kit had not noticed it as it was near invisible. He presumed it would lead to a downstairs bathroom.

His pulse now quickened as a light came on some distance further down the house wall, just to one side from where he crouched. He moved off in the direction of the window, which would presumably be the one to the bathroom about to be used by Sheeka. To achieve this, he had to pass several others; he guessed that there must be another surveillance camera by now somewhere up there on the garden wall.

The illumination from the house was growing and as he watched another light flicked on, reflecting onto several gravel paths of limestone chippings, the quartz fragments of which twinkled in the artificial light, which he had to cross.

He picked his route carefully and proceeded quietly step-by-step, but to him his footsteps seemed to be a cacophony of sound. Could he get there before she left the bathroom?

Then suddenly just as he was about to duck under a window, an un-curtained one, yet another light came on. He froze, melting immediately back into the shadows. Then curious he watched a small broad-shouldered man slowly approach the window; he was wearing a white bathrobe with gold piping, wide sleeves and a tightly drawn belt. On the breast pocket was a blue and gold monogram, which was plain to see.

The monogram, a padded, embossed shield of blue silk, was of a golden dragon entwining a sword and with what could only be his initials: T H.

The man had a thick short neck and pale yellow skin, topped by an ominous shaven head, shaped not unlike a giant goose egg. He seemed to be comparatively old. Lizard-like, he moved forward towards the window as if to peer out into the gloom, as if to search for an intruder, an intruder who pressed himself hard against the wall below, as if to be ingested by the very stone and shadows.

Kit looked on. The man raising himself onto the balls of his large naked feet stretched his arms, a hand showing a large gold and ruby ring, diamond and ruby trinkets, crowned by an ornate watch, he looked out unseeing into the night. One hand clasped and pulled the gold braid sash by his side as he slowly drew the heavy curtains. The ambient light dimmed, the shadows becoming as one for the moment goose egg had gone.

He had disappeared behind the drawn curtains as if on stage and taking his last bow. His eyes momentarily seemed to meet Kit's, they were cold blue-grey eyes, unfeeling oval slate pebbles on a bleak Welsh shore.

Kit knew by experience that he could not be seen by the naked eye from where the man had been standing in the well-lit room. Yet it was if the man who looked out had a 'second-sense'. Those cruel eyes had stared out unblinking into the night, staring, unmoving yet searching. His arm had slowed as he closed the curtains, looking thoughtfully out into the blackness, as if waiting.

He should be thoughtful too, Kit considered. He had recognised the man, a man he had not seen for many years. He'd had hair then, black and tightly cropped. He was a ruthless financial billionaire, a manipulator of people, governments and states. It was Tai Hock, no less, an arms dealer, entrepreneur a Mr Fixit of the East; older now, yes, but nevertheless it was him and for whatever reason he was in London Tai Hock would be just as lethal just as deadly.

Now Kit's own second sense kicked in and made him turn just milliseconds before an axe handle swirled down past his head and shoulder, the draft of which he felt as he grabbed the arm that clung to the pale wooden shaft, a shaft that would have reduced his skull to pulp with one blow.

He clung to the arm and wrenched downward, twisting it and the shaft up and over. His assailant's grip broke and the chicory wood pick handle clattered noisily to the floor. They continued to struggle and whilst maintaining the momentum, Kit's other forearm swung forward and up, powered through his body from the ball of his opposite foot his forearm struck viciously and with a deadly force smashed into his assailant's larynx; his head flew back and Kit felt the cartilage shatter with a sickening crunch as his elbow passed through.

For a moment, there was silence, followed by a gasping groan emitted from the mouth of a small smartly dressed man as he fell to the ground; he was wearing a double-breasted suit – the dress of a chauffeur. Blood welled up on his lips in crimson bubbles, and dribbled onto his front to ruin his neat white shirt. With sad susurration, his life started to bubble away.

Kit shook his head to clear it. The man had been easy he had shown no signs of being a trained bodyguard, which was odd for Tai Hock. That was the last thought Kit had. He was just straightening himself when he felt a sickening blow, a searing nerve-shattering pain to his head and shoulder. His head seemed to explode in a myriad of stars, then fading, fading as he went. Mind blank – numb – he crashed to earth with a groan, momentarily unconscious. His brain subconsciously shut down his systems as it rapidly tried to assess and guide deep-rooted bodily functions to repair its own immediate damage.

※

The big bodyguard Delaney let his pickaxe handle fall to the ground as he hauled Kit to his feet, curiously looking at him in the light, only to let him slump back to the ground like a heavy sack. He was out cold.

Quickly Delaney stooped to check Kit's pockets for some kind of identification. Finding what he was looking for he turned again to what little light there was, cursed and stood up.

Disbelievingly he looked at Kit's ID again before replacing it in the inside holder that would normally have held a gun, too late. He cursed again.

Delaney moved over to the chauffeur and looked down at the sad sight. The man was conscious but gasping for breath, eyes bulging, clawing at his own throat to allow much-needed air to enter. But it could not.

Delaney leant down close to the man. His

larynx was crushed; he was choking, dying, lonely on the cold gravel.

Kit began to stir. Delaney spun round, put the weight of his knee onto Kit's throat whilst twisting an arm from the wrist he brought his face close to Kit's and, with a hand over his mouth he whispered.

'Keep quiet! I'm not here to harm you,' Delaney hissed as he felt Kit's muscles tense, his senses returning rapidly. Delaney knew a fight was coming, one he did not want. Although Kit was older, it could still be one that he, Delaney might not win. This guy could kill in one blow, shit he'd just seen it!

'I'm an undercover guy, Special Branch,' Delaney hissed, desperately trying to avoid confrontation. 'I'm here posing as a bloody bodyguard from an agency. I'm going to open my jacket,' he said urgently, 'and prove it to you. I'm going to show you an ID, do you understand?'

Kit was not impressed and wanted to rid himself of this character, big as he was. He wanted out. Yet there was something in his expression and the urgency of his voice that made Kit hesitate.

'Go on,' he said, curious, watching the man and getting himself ready to go for a body roll, ready to kick out at the man's knee side on and break it, fell his man and attack back, another forearm smash would send him down.

The man slowly produced a well-known – to Kit at least Metropolitan Special Branch identification, at the same time relaxing his grip on Kit.

'Special Branch,' said Kit, stating the obvious. 'Certainly, bloody special,' he added holding his neck, feeling the torn flesh.

'Tai Hock, the man here,' Delaney said with a nod of his head, 'we have him under surveillance when he's in London, er, fairly often.' Now he completely relaxed his grip.

Kit rolled away and adopted a springing squat, looking very athletic as he bobbed on his haunches, arms ready and not betraying fact that he felt terrible. He looked at the pseudo bodyguard Delaney, assessing this new situation.

'Why the hell are you carrying identification if you're supposed to be undercover?' Kit asked shaking his head disbelievingly.

'Wrong, I know,' Delaney answered. 'But maybe just as well with you around,' and he began to smile.

'And him?' Kit nodded towards the chauffeur, who was now quite still.

'Just a straight guy, believe me,' Delaney answered quickly. 'A chauffeur, a married man and you've killed him.'

'Are you sure he's straight?' Kit snapped abruptly.

'Absolutely,' Delaney replied. 'He's just from

the staff agency here in London, poor guy. He comes complete with the limo. Tai Hock takes it from the agency every time he's in town.'

Kit looked down at the chauffeur who was now blue and lifeless except for the slow movement of his feeble fingers, still clutching, digging hopelessly at his throat.

A sudden decision galvanised Kit into action, his pain vanishing as the adrenalin kicked in.

'Get a pen, a tube or something!' he demanded urgently, at the same time peeling off a small knife from a Velcro band at his ankle. With a metallic click the knife blade flicked open. Unceremoniously holding back, the chauffeur's head by his hair, he wrenched open his shirt and tie; buttons flew. Then without hesitating he quickly felt for the soft skin between the thyroid cartilage and the cricoid cartilage of the throat. The evil little knife glinted in what light there was. Gently, carefully he forced the blade between the two, making an incision. There was a sudden rush of air as the lungs reacted to their own desperate fight for life. Kit held open the wound.

'Well! Got a pen,' he demanded.

Delaney fumbled in a pocket and passed him a marker pen. 'Will this do' he said nervously.

'It's a start if it is all you have'

'Lucky I had one at all, lucky I had anything' he said, gaping open mouthed as he watched.

Kit said nothing trivial comment at this moment was unnecessary. He just got to work, broke off the end of the plastic pen and quickly flicked it so that the inside fell to the floor. In the same deft motion, he turned over the shaft of the plastic in his fingers and cut off the plastic stopper at the other end. He then inserted the now unobstructed hollow plastic body of the marker into the incision he had made in the chauffeur's throat and windpipe. It was messy but worth a try.

Kit squeezed the man's chest. Slowly and with a horrible sound he began to react evenly, to gasp weakly for breath and life. Kit then rolled him onto his side into the recovery position; blood spurted out but soon cleared. The man's breath was now a little more even, although his pulse remained high. He needed a larger inlet, but for the moment he would live.

'What now?' asked Delaney, 'I'm paid on as temporary security and we were supposed to take whoever we find back into the house. You set off an alarm, then you came up on the screen as a camera turned on to you. The boss will go mad, he will know somebody is here.'

'Who is the boss? Tai Hock?'

'No, he's the 'Number One' my boss is another guy, a bit of a pervert actually but he works all the time with Tai Hock, provides him with his women and of course women for his friends or clients. He goes everywhere with Tai and another dangerous man called Koetz, he's his personal bodyguard. He has several heavy gofers but he's his main one.

"The Koetz as we call him, his personal bodyguard, has taken the car and gone into London a special trip to collect someone, another late-night guest. Must be important to send Koetz, that's why the chauffeur was free. The person rang earlier demanding in no uncertain terms to see Hock he sounded very stressed but posh, important.

There are two girls already here, so I suppose it will be someone he's now trying to bribe or impress.'

'Is this a regular occurrence, I mean guests and girls?'

'It is the way he works, likes to control the situations.' Delaney said with a shrug.

Sixteen

Sheeka unnoticed, had managed to contain the tiny cling film package within her cheek and after a suitable delay had feigned another stomach upset. Streak had laughed at her saying 'Oh no! Not again,' remembering Sheeka's stomach rumblings from the night previous.

The big tall guy Delaney had felt sorry for Sheeka and it was also plain to see that he didn't like Rubber lips and whatever games he was playing for himself or his boss. He had after all come instantly to Sheeka's rescue and taken her politely to the bathroom. Once inside she had locked the door and she heard Delaney walk away, back to the hall. Delaney was ok, she decided. She even quite liked the big man; he was not like the other two she had met.

Suddenly all hell was let loose, an alarm was sounding off somewhere in the house and she could hear Rubber lips shouting at the top of his voice for Delaney and the driver. Internal doors banged and there was the sound of feet running urgently through the house. Then came the sounds of bolts being drawn on the heavy double doors that led to the courtyard and gardens outside, the creek of polished brass hinges as the doors were opened and closed. Footsteps vanished into the distance, and then silence reigned once more.

Sheeka looked around the bathroom seeing nothing of interest but she did not wish to appear too curious, just in case she too was on camera. Once settled she got rid of her package, being careful how she did it, a surreptitious cough into her hand was sufficient, to take it out of her mouth by hand could have been a fatal giveaway.

Next, after two or three uncomfortable coughs she feigned being sick, just in case there was a two-way mirror, or an ever-watchful camera. The next trick was a little more difficult to hide from view. Removing the jar of 'Ponds Cold Cream' she pretended to tidy her face while making sure she had unobtrusively spilled some of the contents of the jar on her white blouse and had left a trail of the concoction around the toilet, just as Kit had said. She was playing this scene out to an unseen camera; there probably wasn't one, but she was not prepared to risk it. These people were deeply involved with drugs and if she got caught out she would have no control of her actions, she could blow her cover, she wanted 'out' and now. Doped she would be of no use to this operation. Somehow

Kit must have sensed this, he had given her the instrument of release and she had used it. He was no fool, she thought. Sheeka returned to the room dabbing her mouth, looking pale and frail.

'I'm sorry, so sorry,' she said to Rubber lips while Streak looked on embarrassed. 'Don't know what came over me. I've had this problem for a few days now.' She shook her head in mock disbelief, whilst holding a handkerchief to her face.

Rubber lips looked at the expanding stains on her silk blouse. There was an unpleasant pungent smell of garlic and vinegar, not to mention old crushed vegetables emanating from her.

'That's horrible, quite horrible, you're disgusting,' he announced, 'you'd better go, you stink. I can't send you in looking like that, more than my job's worth.' Then as an afterthought he added 'Dirty bitch,' said with feeling. He now looked on in disgust and wanting to rid the house of this obvious stinking tramp. He dialled for a taxi and with his job on the line it could not come soon enough.

During the short wait Sheeka tried desperately to find out who she had been destined to meet. 'Could I meet him another time, after all I'm attractive, am I not?' There was silence, nobody answered not even Streak, her time was over.

Once again, the double Georgian doors of the house burst open and light flooded onto the courtyard.

Opposite the doors some thirty metres away were the tall security gates, the entrance Kit had seen from the road. They were painted black with gold spikes on top. There was a small CCTV camera on top of each of the stone gate pillars. Servants or tradesmen's doors were in stone arches set into the high wall at either side of the gates.

At the first sound Kit dropped to the floor as if wounded, re-enacting the scene when Delaney had 'axed 'him. Luckily the immediate light did not cast his way. Delaney stood in the shadow of a large tree watching, worrying, but well within earshot of him.

The ugly man that Kit had seen earlier now came down the steps with Sheeka. He was hunched forward and was holding Sheeka roughly by the arm, muttering as he escorted her to the main gates. Once there he quickly unlocked one of the small tradesmen's doors in the wall by the side of the gate, and thrust her unceremoniously out into the street and the night. The door banged firmly shut behind her.

He heard Sheeka shout out aloud.

'Well fuck you, Lolly lips.' He smiled liked her spirit and personality it was the right thing to do, she was tonight after all a whore! Sheeka strode off before the ordered taxi arrived.

The man muttered to himself as he returned to the house and its brightly lit doors. Once there he looked apprehensively over his shoulder at the gates and into the blue-black night towards Kit and Delaney, standing there blinking, listening for a moment on the steps. Had he heard them? Now there was the sound of traffic outside and jets above heading for Heathrow, it was difficult for him to hear an intruder. Anyway, that was Delaney's problem he thought. He turned, entered the house again and closed the doors after himself. The lights to the courtyard went out and darkness was resumed.

Delaney breathed more easily, then as he turned his mouth fell open yet again. Kit was rolling in a flowerbed and wiping soil over his shirt, face and hair. He then took out a small silver flask of brandy and gesturing towards Delaney he had a little swig, before regretfully pouring most of it over himself.

'Get me out of here,' Kit ordered, 'If we get caught, I'm a drunk. Tell them I just wanted to doss somewhere, or even break in, sort your own tale out!'

'He'll want to see you.'

'Can't see me!'

'Then what about the bloody chauffeur?'

'Get him to hospital before he dies anyway of ink poisoning!' Kit grimaced, 'tell them that there was an accident, that you hit him in the dark by mistake.'

'That'll make me look a fool.'

'Such is life' Kit said with a smile.

Even as Kit looked at him the quartz security lights that focused onto the courtyard suddenly burst into life again. With an electronic hum and metallic grating the entrance gates started to open. A black limousine was edging, nosing its way forward. It held Kit's attention for a millisecond and that was more than he ever needed; he turned to look at Delaney.

'Goodnight,' he said with an impish smile and a wink that was more in character with an irresponsible schoolboy rather than a senior member of MI6. 'I expect to see you in the morning, at Vauxhall. You know where?' Delaney nodded. 'Can you make eleven?' Kit then added ominously, 'And if you're not who you say you are, I'll hunt hell for you! And we wouldn't want that now, would we? Er, Mr Delaney.'

'Won't be easy, but OK, eleven o'clock. I'll try,' was the curt reply.

'Do.'

With that Kit rolled out of the muck, sprang to his feet and he was out of the gates and gone, acting small and stooped, dishevelled as an old drunk would once he was away from the shadows.

For all this he did have time to notice the heavy build and shoulders of the driver in the limousine, who he presumed would be 'The Koetz', the bodyguard. He looked a handful, but Kit would remember him.

In the back of the car, which was dimly lit by a reading light, was another man. By his rather upright, arrogant posture he clearly thought himself important, his square chin thrust forward, dressed as he was in a dark suit with blue polkadot tie. He was unconcernedly reading a paper. To Kit a give-away; he must have been here before.

As the car moved slowly past he could see the man's face more clearly. To his sudden shock, sat there cosseted amongst leather and East of England cloth was the Minister.

Just as the gates were about to close Kit slipped unobtrusively out of the grounds; once in the street he vanished into the shadows, turned and waited to see if he had been noticed, or if he was being followed.

He had to make a decision about the Jaguar. Should he go to it, or have it collected later? He heard the electric locks on the tall double gates click shut behind the limousine; after a few moments, the security lights went out. A further five minutes later, all seemed quiet so he shambled off; he would risk taking the Jaguar, it was too important to leave.

Once by the car he dropped to his knees and with a small shrouded pencil light glowing green between his fingers he checked under the car. It was 'clean'. There had been no tampering, no wires, no packets, and no suspicion, as yet. He worried momentarily as he turned the key, but there was no heart-rending explosion, no brilliant flash of death. The well-mannered Jaguar, settled into a quiet tick-over.

He pulled out, turned left at the main road and then back towards Marble Arch, his mind full of thought. On the console his red communication light was flickering as ever there were messages waiting.

Half a mile down the road a young scantily clad girl walked along swinging her bag looking eagerly over her shoulder. As he approached she held out her arm with a raised thumb for a lift. Kit pulled over, leant across and pushed the door open.

'What kept you? Its bloody freezing,' was Sheeka's frosty greeting.

'Sorry I, er, got sort of held up.'

'I thought 'Highwaymen' were a thing of the past.' She looked across at him as he drove on. What she saw made her jaw drop, 'Christ it looks more like you've been held up! What a bloody mess, what the hell happened? There's blood dripping onto your collar and you're all covered in dirt and mud,' she exclaimed.

'Who'd be a 'Peeping Tom'?' he smiled back whilst gingerly feeling his neck, now a swollen warm sticky mess, not to mention his shoulder, which was going stiff and hurt like hell. He clammed up, biting his lip. Sheeka knew there was no point in continuing with that conversation.

'I must congratulate you, your idea saved me from an unknown fate,' she said trying to cheer him up.' Do I still smell?' She was considering her own situation.

'Rather, I never knew that it was so effective.'

'You'll gather I left somewhat early,' Sheeka continued, 'but they fell for it beautifully. I hope you're not too mad, but drugs were coming out and I was not sure of how I could take it and keep my head. I thought caution was the best answer, if it all went wrong I could easily have blown my cover and not even known. But I'm worried about Streak, although I have to say she was set to enjoy herself, not to mention the money.'

'Don't panic. I fancy she'll know her job if you see what I mean. You did the right thing, Sheeka; Lord knows where it might have ended. It's time we all had a meeting anyway to see just where this operation is going.' There was a pause before he continued, 'I'm going to drop you off at your, er, apartment, isn't it? And we'll meet in the morning. In the meantime, I will have had a session with the Old Man,' then correcting himself, he said, 'er, Sir Edward.'

'You need to hang a left here, if you really are going to drop me off,' Sheeka said.

He pulled into a pleasant mews area not dissimilar to where all this had started, with the Minister and his late lady friend. Kit raised his eyebrows in appreciation of her good taste. If ever he got time he would look for a similar property again.

'A nice area,' he commented, as he looked at the neat little line of 'old antique red brick' terraced houses, the type you only really see in Southern England.

'I share,' Sheeka explained, as if to justify the type of property, 'with another girl, that is she thinks I'm a student.'

'Tomorrow,' Kit continued, 'come in late if you wish, unwind. I have a meeting about eleven, so I'll see you about twelve. By then I will have come to some decisions.'

Sheeka looked at him almost fondly, not as a fellow agent should. Then with a sigh and a big smile she got out of the car, all legs muscles and firm bosom. He squeezed her hand on the top of the seat back as she lent in to say goodnight.

Her beauty still astounded him but he

reluctantly bade her farewell. Could he detect a look in her eyes that said come in, come for a coffee? He believed there was but he did not pursue it, he was in a too much of a mess. Abruptly he decided he must go and sadly noticed that she had changed her mind too, it was business as usual.

'Before you come in at twelve see if you can speak to your friend Streak, find out if there are any developments we should know about.'

She nodded back as she silently left. Was she a treasure in waiting for him? But something now said not. For some reason, it seemed like it had been the last chance.

He needed above all now to clear his thoughts, see the Old Man and get back on course. He had not mentioned to Sheeka that he had seen the Minister in the back of the limousine. That little treat would be saved for Sir Edward. Face to face.

Kit puzzled over the whole affair. The Minister had been warned in the most callus manner. For sure his affair was over and the murder of his 'lady' was now a job for the Met. So why wasn't the Minister quietly returning to the normal life of a respected MP, forgetting if he could his affair?

Handled carefully nobody would be any the wiser, which was of course why he, Kit, had been brought in; now a certain amount of discretion was needed. After all he, the Minister, did not murder the girl, she'd unfortunately been blown off the top of him so to speak. It was someone else. Of this there was no doubt; and then the man had taken the Minister's laptop – maybe that was the reason for it all.

No! It couldn't be. Why shoot the girl? The laptop had been downstairs. Or had she over a length of time persuaded the Minister to rent the mews apartment so that an accomplice could carry out the theft? And therefore, was she killed because of what she knew? That was possible. Had her knowledge been a liability, been her death sentence? After all there had been no reason to kill her, as the laptop had been downstairs? A theft could easily have been accomplished without the added problem of a murder.

So, what now was this new turn of events, this meeting between Tai Hock and the Minister? Was it official business, or was it just a coincidence that he had been going to see Tai Hock at the same time that Tai had invited two hookers to his house? Tai after all was hardly dressed for a board meeting, or to see an official.

Tai Hock was an arms dealer; the Minister was involved with defence. Was that the connection?

Deep in thought he nearly drove past the Park Lane. What he desperately needed was a hot bath, then a phone call to Sir Edward and sleep. Tomorrow was another day.

Then suddenly, as he was walking through the hotel, for what reason he knew not, he decided to ring the Minister's home, lengthening his stride till he got to the room. He dialled the Minister's number and just as he imagined, Miranda answered it. The long-suffering wife, he thought.

'Good evening, it's Kit. Do you remember me?'

'How could I ever forget oysters and champagne, not to mention a lift home. Course I remember you. So, how are you?'

'I'm well,' Kit lied smoothly. 'But as much as I wish I had rang 'you' and, I know it's late but I've actually rung to speak to your husband David.' Kit wanted it to sound official, as there was no real reason to ring Miranda.

'On a Thursday?' She gasped 'You must be joking, he's always in the House it will be some damned debate or other and usually every Thursday, never gets in till Friday, ever.'

Kit wondered idly if it was a Thursday when David's girlfriend had been blown away, but couldn't quite remember the day, but he would bet it was.

'Pity he's not in, I, er, just wanted a quick word.'

'Then why not come for one.'

'It's nearly ten o'clock,' Kit said, surprised.

'A good time for a nightcap then! And you

can speak to David when he arrives, if he does, so don't dilly-dally on the way,' Miranda laughed as she sang, slamming the phone down before he could object.

He was just about to call back and say it was totally impossible, he ached like hell and was in an awful mess, yet he realised there may be some information to glean. So, he would go, after all, he had an invitation.

An hour later saw a suave man, showered and dressed, very English in blue blazer and cream slacks, a cream handkerchief flamboyantly protruding from his breast pocket. He took the lift up to the penthouse suite, curiously looking forward to meeting Miranda again; she was after all quite a character.

She opened the door and nothing could have shocked Kit more. She was dressed just as she would have been when she was seventeen, in a tiny white mini skirt, a low-slung top, high heels and nylons, just as if she had stepped out from a 1960 Beatles album, or perhaps Cliff Richard's 'Summer Holiday'.

Kit's surprise must have registered.

'Think nothing of it,' Miranda declared with a wave of her hand. 'David likes me to dress like this at home, gets him going! I used to wear this kit in the sixties and I can still get into it so I'm quite pleased, although I think it makes me look a little like something off a street corner. But I sometimes think David likes that! In private, that is, he likes me to look like a tart. What do you think?'

Kit was suddenly thinking a great deal.

'I could never think that,' he said politely, absorbing this wild apparition that was now gyrating before him. He was only just getting over the shock.

'A drink,' Miranda prompted, as if he were about to escape.

'Scotch and soda.' Kit closed the door after him and walked into the bright modern room that he remembered. It was not to his liking. No log fire, no dogs lying within its radiance, no wood smoke. Such is London.

The picture of her son in the deeply embossed antique silver frame was still there, which prompted him to ask.

'How is your son, Charles, isn't it?'

'Oh, he's fine,' then after a pause she turned back to him and in a concerned tone said, 'well since you ask me, no! He isn't really; he's a bit low just at the moment he seems to be brooding over something. Well you see his girlfriend has vanished!'

Kit blanched.

'Vanished?' He reacted, his hair tingling on the nape of his neck. The silence hung there as her statement sunk in. He was not sure how to continue, his trained mind worked over time it was curious, but his carnal instincts also kicked in. He waited for a lead and watched Miranda, who he decided had a very shapely back, he noticed she had poise even now as she was making his drink at an elaborate glass mirrored cocktail bar. He liked most bars, but to Kit this one was in the height of bad taste. Bad or not, he weakened. He had to, her pert breasts were reflected in the mirror. To enjoy the scene, he lifted out one of the four chrome-legged stools, their tops covered in snakeskin. He relaxed, yet felt the uneven snakeskin penetrating from beneath him. A myriad of colours, nature's camouflage stolen, now wasted serving only to be a prickly, spiky problem through his slacks.

He looked again into the mirrors at Miranda and thought of the unfortunate snake he now sat on. Kit liked snakes, but not dead ones.

Her outline absorbed and the conversation stopped so he continued to probe.

'Vanished? Really, how?' he asked again.

'Don't really know how, he only met her a couple of times or so. Charles brought her here once with his pal Riley. I was not too impressed; David though was very taken with her. I believe it was a shock to him.'

'A shock?'

'Oh, for sure and I was the only one who noticed. A Mother's intuition you know. When David came in through the door and saw Charles's girlfriend stood there in all her diminutive finery, David stopped in mid-stride and visibly blanched. The surprise or shock was mirrored on her face also. Charles never saw it, but I did.'

'So, what are you saying?' Kit's brain cells were now at fever pitch. 'Did they know each other? Or had they met before?'

'It's hard to say, I mean he genuinely sees so many people, he's so much in the public eye; he meets scores of new people every week. So, it's difficult for me to feel concerned.'

Kit took another sip from his drink, waiting for more.

'She's an attractive girl, foreign though odd name something like Verkuska'

Kit listened intently his pulse skipped a beat. 'It reminds me of foot fungi, Russian I think. Well from Georgia she says, not really Russia, is it? But near enough, I suppose.'

He nodded knowledgeably.

'How did Charles meet her?'

'Oh, that was easy. She was having lunch with some old crony here down in the Canteen Restaurant. According to the boys he was far too old for her. Charles and his mate Riley plus a couple of friends were all there so they all got talking together; Charles won the day and arranged to see her later. You see, the old duffer could not compete. Well, only with his cheque book, of that there is no doubt. But she is too sure of herself Kit. My Charles is still unfortunately a little naïve regarding women. Especially with something like her to contend with!'

'Once your husband had got over his surprise or whatever, did he like her?'

'Oh, yes and I think the feeling was mutual too! She was very interested in the workings of government, fascinated even. But towards the end of the evening I don't think that Charles was too impressed by all this. I actually think David was jealous of dear Charles, jealous of his son indeed!' Miranda said with a laugh, throwing back her head. 'Jealous of Charles and his girlfriend! Could you believe that?' she said again, laughing. 'What a silly old man.'

'Some young girls do prefer the older man,' Kit advised, mindful of his own age.

'And you?' she asked turning, her head cocked impishly to one side, tongue just protruding from the corner of her mouth.

Then, precocious as a young girl and dressed as one, Miranda came from behind the bar, handed him his golden drink, the soda bubbles amongst the whorls of whisky, ice clinking against the cut crystal.

'Mm, yes,' he murmured thoughtfully, looking deeply now at the amber mixture, remembering the last time he had seen what must now have been Charles's girlfriend Verkuska, sadly with half her skull blown away, the grey remnants of which writhed like a fisherman's bag full of seething grey maggots.

'Yes,' he repeated, snapping out of his thoughts and taking a needy drink as the memory and the horror of it all came flooding back.

'He'd been on a training exercise somewhere in the East, the poor darling. Brunei maybe, I forget – he did tell me. But anyway, when he came back there was no sign of her. So, he's a bit miffed.'

'He would be.'

'Anyway, he spent last weekend here working on his little Alfa with his mate Riley and he didn't mention her at all which was very unusual really. Normally he does, continually. I do know that she was often difficult to get hold of, and that annoyed him too. He's very possessive, dangerously so. Anyway, now I suppose it must be over.'

'His mate Riley, does he come here often?'

'Oh, quite a lot they joined up at the same time so they have helped each other in training. Very competitive the two of them together, but Riley's a bit jealous, you know, a little of the green eye'

'Really?'

'Yes, the first time he came here he was amazed with the 'Penthouse' never seen anything quite like it. I remember particularly he said to David that he would do anything to have a place like this. 'But how could I ever earn the money for this in the Army,' he had commented.

I don't really like him but David does. The rivalry between the two boys, I think, has helped them both. But in some ways, I think that David, my perfect husband' she raised her eyes to the ceiling. 'Well he actually acts as if he prefers Riley to Charles and it's sad because it's so noticeable, I mean when Riley is here David always talks about the Army to him, asks how he is going on, encourages him to do more. He never talks to Charles like that, but I suppose once again it's jealousy somewhere along the line. I sometimes think David is actually envious of Charles, well no I'm sure of it.'

Changing the subject Kit continued, 'You mentioned an Alfa?'

'Yes, his favourite hobby is his cars. Charles loves old classics, a little like his father,' she said dreamily, smiling.

'The Minister is a car buff didn't think he would have time?' Kit replied.

She looked at him slowly, her expression quizzical.

'No, not exactly,' then again, 'No----' and she

faltered stopping mid-sentence before continuing, 'but Kit I'll tell you soon and more than you will ever expect.'

He looked at her expectantly.

'Yes, Kit you, why you after all this time? That, I don't know; but give me time and I will. Maybe I'm tired of it all maybe I need a shoulder cry on – metaphorically speaking.' She was visibly now a little embarrassed.

Kit would have loved to have somehow kept the conversation going but he let it slide. As she said it would come out in time, but enough was enough and after such a strong hint, he would wait.

Miranda gave a little wet sniff before saying,

'Charles restores his cars when he has the time. He's got this yellow Italian thing. It's a convertible to me, although he says it's a Spider and I thought they hung in the corner of dirty rooms. Anyway, it was all tuned by Mango or somebody years ago,'

'Mangoletsi?'

'Yes, that's amazing, just amazing! How did you know?'

She was happier now and forgetting her lapse.

'That's right! How the hell did you know?' She said again spiritedly whilst looking up at him. She was visually impressed.

Kit smiled back casually.

'Well, I have an interest too, er, in old classics that is.' He looked down at Miranda stood there dressed as if she were about to go to school, St Trinian's.

'Cheeky,' she laughed, catching his devilish glance and sharp quip and squeezed his hand just too late for philandering.

The alarm bells were beginning to ring in Kit's mind, quietly at first and then bursting into an urgent crescendo.

So, that could have been the car in the picture, the one at Verkuska's apartment! Yes, it could have been an Alfa Romeo 1750 Spider all right. He remembered the flat line of the boot! He remembered thinking at the time that the man he now knew to be Charles, the Minister's son, was leaning on some classic car to have the photo taken and the car had a certain classic style or line to it. In their day, they were quite sought after, probably still are, he mused. The Alfa Romeo was a good little sports car, if a little short on power, but they handled well.

His brain heaved, Christ! Had he not also seen an Alfa Romeo Spider in the area the other day whilst in Chelsea? The day he went to investigate her apartment. Had it not been yellow? He was damned sure that it was.

This whole situation had suddenly changed; the investigation had now been stimulated, unknowingly, by Miranda. In these few minutes, it had leapt forward a quantum leap. He knew now that he needed to have a chat with the 'Mr David Stevens' as soon as possible. He did not even wish to dally here.

But as alcohol coursed through the hardening veins of Miranda, increasing her desires, decreasing her modesty she moved closer. Her leg slid between his and her lips parted as she kissed him delicately on the mouth, he resisted a little, but then she kissed firmer, her tongue immediately searching, not a fleshy mound but a sensuous and firm tip darting two and fro deep and shallow. He now weakened by this sudden delicate and beautiful onslaught, she felt him relax and Kit responded, his hand slid round her trim waist and held her close; he could feel her nipples go hard beneath her blouse. Her stomach was flat and firm. She groaned and now too relaxed in his arms, her mound of Venus pressed and gently squirmed against his thigh. Her scent was of a delicate, 'Lily of the Valley', young and vibrant. Carefully and slowly she led him uncaring towards the bedroom, unresisting as they passed the photograph of Charles.

'I won't make love in another man's bed' Kit whispered as she closed the door.

'You don't have to he sleeps next door, snores you know'

'Convenient!' Kit was not sure he believed her but as she turned to undo Kit's shirt her few clothes were already falling to the ground there was little time for conscience as she let go his belt and he stepped out, standing there naked and powerful. Foreplay was fast and furious but so much was the urgency it worked for both. Kit would never consider himself an affectionate lover but he always tried to be gentle, his sheer size as he entered her demanded this. She moaned biting into his already wounded neck, double pain double pleasure. Her nipples like bullets trying to penetrate him. Lovemaking was a cacophony of sound an explosion of movement and wet drained exhaustion. After an hour, they slowed and began to relax slowly gently moving away rolling onto their backs. As Kit lay there warmly thinking for a moment then turning he snuggled up to her once more and in the half-light over her shoulder he noticed the photograph.

'Your son looks very much like you,' he whispered into her neck. She snuggled back to him and kissed.

'He should, so now I'll tell you,'

Seventeen

At eleven prompt the following morning the phone rang in Kit's new office at the Block; No. 89 The Albert Embankment, Vauxhall Cross, London. One he had vowed some months ago, never to go to. He had just arrived; it was clean and smelt of new paint and some effort had been made to welcome him back. He wondered though, somewhat idly, if the office was really 'clean', or if someone in counter-espionage had bugged it for his predecessor. If so, was the bug or microphone still in place and conveniently forgotten? Maybe not, but later he would check it out, he would 'sweep' his own room.

A red light was flashing urgently on the beige internal phone. Another phone on the other side of the leather-inlaid desk also rang. It was all that he hated and just as he remembered, this urgent discordance of raucous, unwelcome sound.

Someone else had also tried to make him welcome. A pale lemon china vase of cream-coloured lilies with their prominent phallic yellow stigmas protruding, was displayed on the sill that overlooked the Thames, lilies were his favourites. It was an exotic explosion of scent and colour, which seemed to be frozen in time. He used to have them before, in his old office, which somebody seemed to know.

The aroma of fresh ground coffee mingled enticingly with this exotic scent, the mixture hanging in the air, all seeming to come from the adjoining door. He was just about to investigate when the phone rang again. This time he picked it up, casually looking out over Vauxhall Bridge. A blue and red barge was passing underneath, its wash lapping the muddy shore. Gulls hopped back in annoyance.

The call was from the ground floor reception desk.

'A Sergeant Delaney from the Metropolitan to see you sir, shall I bring him up?'

'Please, but give me a minute.'

Kit had been reading his messages, realising he had been a little neglectful in not contacting the office sooner; he quickly read the memos. Most had been relayed to his car, but the most recent was from Colonel Simon Stewart of Hereford. It would take a minute or two for the Sergeant to arrive.

Kit was curious; he needed to know. So, he dialled the Colonel and was put through immediately; the switchboard at Hereford would have been briefed that the incoming call from the Block was cleared.

'So, you've returned,' said Stewart. Kit heard the scrambler kick in. 'I tried your car. Was she nice?'

A little too close to the bone, Kit thought, however he replied, 'That's for me to know, and you to wonder, Simon!' his mind flashing back to the previous evening with Miranda and his newly acquired knowledge. But he quickly changed the subject.

'So, Simon, what have you got for me? You don't normally ring me to gloat on my sad love life.'

'Quite right! I really do pity you, you're a lucky bastard, but then you always were. Anyway, I can but dream.' He heard Simon take a deep breath, then after a pause he continued, 'Remember when we last met, you asked me if I thought anything had gone missing at this end?'

'Yes,' Kit said, now alert.

'Well, I have to say that there may just be. The Armourer came to see me yesterday, but you must realise that on some exercises, due to the very nature of our circumstances, things can go missing, or get destroyed. Anyway, we're down on one, an automatic pistol, a silenced Tokarev 7.62.'

'Do you know who the weapon was booked out to? Or for what operation?'

'I do, but I think it better that you come and see me; today!'

'I'll be out there as soon as I can. Answered Kit'

'By chopper?'

'No, nobody here'll think it's that urgent,' he lied. 'I'll drive.' After a little more banter, he replaced the phone.

Simultaneously there was a knock on the door and he called out. The door opened and to his astonishment it was his old secretary Sue, who had left when Kit resigned or rather when he thought he had!

'Welcome back, sir.' She stood there and smiled enjoying his surprise, her long dark hair cascading over her shoulders as ever, and her high cheekbones amplifying her elegant looks. 'A Sergeant Delaney to see you.' She led the Sergeant into the room and he stood casually, glancing around the room.

'Would you like two coffees? I, er, took the liberty of re-acquiring 'your' Espresso coffee machine and some Maragogype beans, gently roasted from Fortnum's.'

After Kit, had recovered from his surprise, he said

'That will be fine,' and smiled, giving her a friendly glare.

'Sir Edward said that you might need me, so he asked me to come back,' she explained, looking a little guilty.

Did he now, the cunning old ---. And no doubt within hours of my 'quasi' acceptance, Kit thought, as he turned to look at Delaney.

'Morning, Delaney,' he said, curtly standing up and rubbing his bruised neck.

'Only doing my job, sir. After all, you were an intruder,' he pointed out whilst staring at the vivid bruise.

Kit did not respond.

After a short chat, with carefully loaded questions, he realised that Sergeant Delaney of the Metropolitan Police drugs squad did not have much to add to what he already knew. Indeed, to probe too far would have weakened his-own position. The Sergeant had been undercover posing as a bodyguard and gofer for Tai Hock. The powers that be had insisted that on information received Tai Hock must be involved in some form of drug racket, money laundering or whatever and they were curious to know what. Sergeant Delaney was to keep the drugs squad informed, but so far there had been little evidence available to him, although Tai Hock and his cronies did use drugs themselves.

This annoyed the Sergeant in the extreme as he had seen the effects, some of them unpleasant and he was annoyed that he could not make an arrest for these offences alone. But he was told that this might rock the boat; the powers that be wanted bigger fish, all the fish, they said.

Kit knew that Tai Hock's enormous wealth came mainly from arms dealing. This was not to say he shunned drugs in his nefarious activities, but as yet there was no tangible evidence and in Britain you need cast-iron proof.

No, the acknowledged fact was that the ruthless arms dealer, manipulative he would do almost anything to earn money, fame or favour and Kit personally thought he probably had more sense and kept away from mainstream drug running.

In short though he would stop at nothing. His methods to achieve success in whatever field knew no bounds. If only he and his accomplices could be caught.

It was also apparent to the ever-vigilant Sergeant that the man was a sexaholic, a sexual athlete even for his age, a man of Olympian proportions and a deviant. But then in the course of their conversation, it turned out that Sergeant Delaney had never ventured further than Brighton beach for a holiday and a dismal club in Soho for the odd bachelor night out or leaving party. So, anything verging on enjoyable propagation of the human race by casual sex might shock him into becoming a jealous zealot.

Delaney went on to relate how Tai Hock used the London house for his sexual frolicking and, to use all of his very considerable wealth and trappings to ensnare clients or people who were useful in influential positions. This in turn would be used to his-own advantage throughout the world.

'For instance,' the Sergeant continued 'did you know that last night the very evening we unceremoniously met at the end of a pick helve...' he smiled.

Kit did not return this expression of endearment.

'...That a high-ranking Minister was a guest at the house and it was not the first time he's been there either?'

Kit was suddenly interested.

'Not the first time you say?'

'No not the first time, I've seen him there once or twice recently, indeed one evening I thought I overheard a huge argument, certainly heated conversation.'

'About?'

'Well, I'm not too sure, it didn't make sense. It seemed to be all about his, er, usual subject; women. Then it moved on to photographs and in the next breath aircraft, fighter aircraft. During the shouting, it appeared that he, Tai Hock that is, apparently wanted to buy some aircraft and could not for the life of him understand the reticence of this Government. He said the French would sell him anything for the benefit of their industry, but the British as ever that was another matter.'

'So why did he not just go to the French, Sergeant?'

'Well I'm not sure. I'm no businessman, no intellectual, but I did gather that his clients already had British aircraft, er, the Hawk jet and I presume wanted more a continuation.'

Kit thought to himself, 'Hawk jets, basically a trainer and used by the RAF and the British display team the 'Red Devils' they were produced by British Aerospace, Hawker Siddley Division, hence the name 'Hawk'. Although just a trainer in Britain, it was so good some countries do use them for active service it's a handy little jet.

Indonesia instantly came to mind. It was rumoured the military had used them to snuff out an independence movement in West Papua, a former Dutch colony – and that was right in Tai Hock's patch!

'Thank you, Sergeant, most useful. Incidentally did you hear anything said last night?'

'Well no, not really. Apparently, the Minister was very demanding earlier hence Tai Hock sent Kotez to collect him, but neither would he see him straight away. He talked over the house phone for a while and although the Minister was trying to keep his voice down; it was a bit heated, to say the least. I mean he was accusing Tai Hock

of being a fucking murderer, excuse my language'
Kit nodded and looked up at the Sergeant.
'You sure?'
'Yes absolutely, he accused him of being a fucking murderer, I suppose because of wanting to buy more fighters to fuel a war, being an arms dealer and all that.'
'Possibly,' Kit said in his own monosyllabic style, now deep in thought.
'Did you see him in the leave?'
'Well possibly, but I'm really not sure, after the problem with yourself they seemed to keep me away from mainstream events, kept me busy in the house with trivia, but there was a lot of comings and goings.'
Another ten minutes and it was obvious the Sergeant did not have much more to add, but they would keep in touch. He glanced at Kit's bruising once again before the answer to Kit's unseen bell arrived and Sergeant Delaney was ushered away downstairs to the door.

Sue immediately put her head round the door,
'Sir Edward is busting a gut upstairs. He wants to know what the hell you are doing! Oh, and Sheeka is here waiting to see you.'
'Tell him I'll be there just as soon as I can. He

of all people will want a proper update and I am still not there,' Kit instructed.

He's not changed, thought Sue.

At that moment, Sheeka came striding into the room. Sue watched her figure thoughtfully from behind, glancing at Kit who caught her eye, just as Sheeka thrust a cassette at him, slapping it into his hand.

'I've just left Streak,' she exclaimed. 'We had coffee together, in Shepherd's Market again. She, er, likes the little Italian boy there, but that apart, today it was a somewhat bemused Streak. Just listen to it.' Sheeka nodded at the cassette. 'If that were me I would have been in shock, or care! Least of all having coffee. I was lucky but only thanks to you. We sat in a small alcove in that Italian coffee shop where no one could hear. Streak didn't know but I was able to record the conversation.

'Is it relevant?' asked Kit

'Please just you listen to this.'

Sheeka excitedly looked around for a cassette machine, Sue discreetly left the room. Kit placed the cassette in the double machine and added a new cassette. It would automatically make a copy. Pressing 'play' he walked over to the window, stared at the Thames and listened to the tape:

** 'You were lucky your stomach let you down again. Anyway, after you'd gone I was stuck with the three of them in this big super-luxury apartment, they gave me all the usual drinks although I wasn't sure which one of them I was supposed to be with, or maybe the bloody lot! But what the hell! Then the tall good-looking one, you know, he looked a bit Arabic, remember? Anyway, he suggested we have an 'E' or some-thing, you know, break the ice a bit. Well I can handle that, I've had em' all before so no problem. Mind, that's what everyone says, then it's too bloody late. So, we had a few drinks, quickly, you know, like we were in some bloody rush, which was unusual as they'd paid a fortune for the whole night for us both, remember?

It's usually us who are in a rush! Then there were these bloody pills. Very soon it all goes wrong and I started to feel weird really weird, but I have to say very happy sex.

It was certainly, on my mind, you know looking forward to it an' all that, which is unusual for us lot, isn't it? We haven't got the time to like it, feel it, no it's just a job, right?'

At this point, Streak, had started to sob so Sheeka had passed her a handkerchief from her handbag, at the same time making sure that all this was being taped.

'Sorry. Anyway, I was lying back on that big settee thing when the shorter of the two got hold of me and Christ, the tall one the bastard shot a needle into my arm. I tried to scream, but couldn't. I couldn't even move; they were so strong. Then within seconds, whatever it was they shot me with made me feel terrified, and I mean terrified. It was unbelievable. Then I was suddenly freezing cold, shuddering. I pissed myself with this feeling of terrible fear. I started to shake so much I couldn't control myself.

I knew I was going to die. Then suddenly, as if from nowhere, the tall guy hit me again with a tiny little syringe. I specifically remember the needle because it was so short and stubby. Within seconds I felt fantastic again, again unbelievable.

Then it happened – I felt my nipples getting hard, so hard the pain was excruciating – excruciatingly beautiful. They lifted my dress off and I slipped out of it like a slippery wet eel; my nipples were so hard they had bled, they stood out like bullets. I've never seen anything like it – on anyone. They lifted me up to stand and suddenly I realised that my genitalia felt swollen too. You know, I could actually feel the area had swollen, my – oh God! How can I tell you this?'

'Go on,' Sheeka had said, holding Streak's hand across the table.

'My clitoris stood out like a dart, it was hard and it hurt like hell. I was like a little boy.

I could look down and see it stuck out. I just

couldn't believe it. I stood there with my labia actually moving, trembling, I swear, and worse, they were salivating like a Boxer dog waiting for a bone. I could feel my vaginal fluid dripping, no gushing down my legs, and what's more I didn't care!'

Sheeka had to smile at Streak's descriptions. Some tape.

'I'll always remember it, Sheeka. I was quite naked and everything about me was swollen and different. I didn't even care when they all ogled at me, standing there in the middle of that room. I started to play with myself, couldn't stop. I was soaking, in torrents, and for some terrible reason I was enjoying it.'

Streak then started to cry again, this time quite badly, whereupon Sheeka had surreptitiously turned the tape off. She was having some form of withdrawal problem. After a while Streak had a long pull of her brandy and with a deep breath continued:

'They led me through into another room, tits wobbling all over the place, my nipples stuck way out, rock hard, and my clit protruding everything so swollen I could hardly walk.

The room was all sumptuous, you know, silk

drapes a huge bed and a bath you could near swim in; well you could it was set into the floor; there were steps down into it, and it was steaming. They closed the door behind me.

'For a moment, I stood there feeling light-headed and strange, floating even, hips gyrating wildly. Then another door opened and in walked a small man. He was bald or shaven and appeared to be quite old really, then again, I was in no condition to judge, but a picture of Yul Brynner in the musical the 'King and I' flashed through my mind! He was wearing a sort of ruby-red silk gown with yellow and blue Chinese dragons on it.'**

Streak was now becoming more under control and calmer as the brandy took effect.

** 'He moved slowly toward me and slid out of the robe. Curiously I watched it fall to the floor; it seemed to take a long time, as like a leaf in autumn it fell to the floor in a pile of colours like a flaming dragon, things were in slow motion I might have got it wrong but there was a strange smell, a smell of cats! Well actually, cat's piss, ugh!'

Amyl nitrate, Sheeka thought.

'When I looked up, Sheeka, I could not believe it, seriously! He had a penis like nothing I have ever seen. Well, once while on holiday in Rhodes, they have some mythical god or whatever. Priapus the Greek God of procreation, I think it was. You can buy these model artefacts in tourist shops to take home, half horse half man, or something where the dick passes their knees. Believe me it was huge.

No! That is not the correct word, it was abnormal, deformed even. It must have been made by plastic surgery, or have been operated on, or something. It was bigger than a donkey and appeared semi-erect. But being so long it could never be erect, or so I thought. The sheer weight, it was very swollen and deep red, with nodules under the skin of the shaft. The swollen end of it shone purple with a viscous droplet hanging from it.'

Hell, amyl nitrate, Sheeka thought again, that would be it for sure.

'He then gestured me to the bed and like a fool I moved over there willingly.

So willingly! I wanted everything! He moved slowly towards the bed, his penis dangling, lolling back and forward as if nudging his knees, willing him forward, goading, encouraging him into action. Then he stooped and from the ornately gilded bedside table he took the plastic tools of, er, I remember now what he said, he said, 'foreplay and pleasure, my dear.' Dildos, vibrators and the like.

The cheeky old bastard! He played with me for ages, things buzzing up me,

under me, round me. Front and rear! I remember that for sure, I'll remember it forever, I could never forget.

'After a while, and it was actually some considerable time, not to mention a

bit of a struggle, he held his solid penis upright, rock hard against my clit – as if to burst it. The pain – oh, the glorious pain! I just couldn't believe it. Then in an explosive crescendo of exotic agony he entered me, my head spinning as I

tried to scream; words would not come so in silence I passed out; missed all the fun.

'When I awoke sometime later the room was empty, there was not a sound. I

believe the others or friends of his may well have had their way with me too. That is, er, when The Man or boss, should I say, had gone, had finished with me I suppose. But I don't really know, haven't a clue'

There was a long pause, she continued:

'But the terrible thing, Sheeka, was that I, er, awoke masturbating, and defiling myself from the front and the rear, with his 'toys', just as he had done. I was lying there like in a vegetable patch, and should have been disgusted, but no! I was enjoying it. When I recovered from the shock of what I was doing to myself, the drugs were obviously wearing off. I felt ghastly, but pulling myself together, I used the bath, or should I say pool, and promptly left. There was not a soul in the place, no clothes either. Nothing to say anybody had ever been there, nothing but the five grand in notes, our agreed fee. I was totally nonplussed.'

As Streak finished speaking, she had dug into her handbag to give Sheeka her share of the £5,000 fee.

'No, no, keep it. Keep it all, hell Streak, you deserve it. I did nothing but be sick,'
Sheeka had said, in a horrified voice, aghast at Streak's story and amazed that she did not seem too much the worse for wear.

There was a click as Sheeka leant forward and switched off the instrument. She looked up at Kit with a sigh. He showed no reaction, still staring out of the window, looking out across the Thames and London.

'Well that's that,' Sheeka said, lifting her eyebrows, trying to goad him into some sort of response.

He did not speak for a while, but when he did his voice was sombre. He turned away from the window his thoughts returning to the room.

'Mm, that's an old Russian trick, mean too. We

reckoned they used something like that in interrogation in the late 1950 early 1960, during the Cold War. 'Friend and Fear' it was nicknamed. It's usually a 'happy', social drug that would give an immense feeling of 'well-being'. To start with some friendly type of person would administer it, someone trying to gain the recipient's confidence, if that were possible! Then when the poor bastard thinks life is all wonderful, he or she is given a shot of something to instil a terrible and all-consuming, nerve-shattering fear and the interrogator is changed, and so on. I've seen it work – the effect is just terrible.

Then after a further ten minutes or so – that is if they live and the heart has stood up to it. – It is then followed by a truth drug, something like sodium pentothal. In this particular case, some frightful cocktail for sure has been devised, for sex. Produced to achieve a massive sexual desire, followed by outstanding ecstasy and satisfaction. Rough on the girl, though, she could have died.

Yes,' he went on thoughtfully, 'penis adornment or extension is a traditional male speciality in Indonesia. The Dayaks of Borneo used palangs – I think that's what they called them. The penis is cut or drilled behind the glands; the wounds are then filled with **palang**, a hard wood, or even ivory pins. All for the man's prowess and supposedly, for the benefit of his partner. There is an interesting side issue though, if the woman is found to be unfaithful sharp flints or blades can be attached to the adornments and administered as a punishment and probable death.'

'Charming, you're a mine of information, but how horrible.' Sheeka said aghast

'Such is the price of male ego' Kit said

There was another silence. Neither of them spoke for a while, as both were now deep in thought. Kit spoke first,

'That is a hell of a tape and sadly there is many a man in high places who has experienced most worldly desires but is looking for more. Now that Hock has proved it works he can ensnare his target. To provide a woman like that could open some big doors in very influential circles'

'I see what you mean, if he has developed that drug technique it gives Tai Hock power over his quests'

'Exactly'

'Phew!'

'So where does this take us Sheeka? It would be difficult to prove that Tai Hock did anything illegal, as we don't have a witness who was compos mentis. In any event, it may be nothing to do with us; once again it could be a matter for the police, but as I have just found out, they don't want to make a move just yet and neither do we. Our net is cast much wider and we don't know yet what or who we are going to haul in!'

Kit thought for a moment of the events the comings and goings of the evening. A great deal had happened.

'Did Streak mention any other guests?'

'Well, as you heard, she thought there had been others, but to be fair she just didn't know.'

Kit had yet to mention that he had seen the Minister in the back of Tai Hock's chauffeur-driven limousine. Had he taken part? Or had that been some impromptu meeting on his demand, and then he'd left? Missed the party! But hardly a meeting, Kit thought, not the way Tai Hock was dressed.

So, had the Minister been a spectator to this spectacular performance? It often happens, but Kit felt not. Although he did not like the Minister he gave him better credit than that, he doubted that he was a voyeur and Hock himself an unlikely player as it would demean his authority.

So, had Tai Hock delayed his games till after the Minister had left? Probably so.

The direct-line phone once again shrilled, its green light flashing on top of the pale cream instrument, like an angry Dalek vibrating on the desk. Kit glared at it and looked back at Sheeka just as Sue put her head round the door enquiringly.

'Well Sheeka, sorry, but I'm going to have to

go and see Sir Edward, then I'm off to Hereford. So, spend the rest of the day getting together the skeleton of a report for me to give to Sir Edward; I'll read and add to it when I get back. Then Sue will type it up for us. Sir Edward is bound to ask for it. If we are forearmed it will then give you and I time to crack on, whilst he digests. It's getting interesting, isn't it?'

'You call that interesting? It would be if I knew as much as you; so how can I do a proper report?'

'Do as much as you know, then we will meet and I will add mine'

'Not the most efficient way; sir.' He glanced at her and nodded, knowing that she was curious to know what he had in mind.

'For the moment, it will have to do. I have a feeling that things are going to change rapidly anyway, just look industrious till I get back.'

With a click from the machine the tape jumped out; he handed back Sheeka her original, the copy went in the safe, the code number of which had surprisingly not been changed.

Eighteen

With no time to climb the stairs, the lift doors hissed open on the eighth floor. Kit hated lifts as they meant meeting people he did not want to see, this time he was lucky. He strode off down the corridor, enveloped in his own thoughts.

Even in the modern building, the smell of wax polish and Brasso cleaner hung in the air, a smell that seemed to haunt the floors of senior government. The light above Sir Edward's door was already flashing, indicating immediate entry. The cameras followed his progress from above. As he went in he looked across at Sir Edward's secretary who returned his inquiring look with one of anxiety.

'He's very up tight; why have you not made contact?' he was about to speak when she quickly went on, 'No, we haven't time, go straight in!' By now she was smiling, relieved that he was there. Kit went straight into the lion's den. Sir Edward was glowering from behind his leather-inlaid desk; not a pretty sight.

'Morning, sir,' Kit said pleasantly.

'It's damn near lunchtime, it's well after twelve!' He said, flexing his wrist and glancing at an old gold watch on a crocodile strap. 'Don't you know it's Thursday? I always have lunch with the PM and he wants to know if there was any truth in this damned rumour.'

'Rumour?' Kit lifted his eyebrows.

'Yes, for God's sake, man! The rumour of Stevens having an affair.'

'Oh, I see.'

'Well, is he?' Sir Edward snapped.

'Where are, you having lunch?'

'Number Ten.'

'Good fayre?'

'Lamb, it'll be lamb, it always is.'

'English I hope, not New Zealand.' Then realising he'd been sidestepped, Sir Edward fired back. 'Never mind my bloody lunch. Is he having an affair, or isn't he?' he snapped back again.

'I hardly think so at the moment,' Kit answered quietly. His mind went back to the remains of the disfigured body that had lain in the mews, and the charred corpse in the Cabriolet in Dorset – one and the same, now lying in some morgue like a burnt cold roast.

'No sir, I don't think so, not at the moment,' he repeated lugubriously.

'Yes, yes, I know that,' Sir Edward snapped,

realising the stupidity of his own question. 'But was he then, you know, before all this?'

'I think that he would like to have thought so,' Kit replied laconically.

There was long pause, an all-pervading silence, save for the ever-ticking grandfather clock in the shadows.

Kit had listened to it so many times before; a pendulum, segmenting time inexorably away, a dusty heartbeat in this hall of secrets, Sir Edward's office.

Kit spoke first, his voice clear and precise.

'Did you know, sir, that she was probably his son's girlfriend? The girl, sir, was Charles's girlfriend.' Pausing a moment for maximum effect, he then put in a broadside. 'Your godson, I believe?' The question hit Sir Edward as would a mallet; he reeled back in the leather Windsor, exhaling heavily.

'Charles's girlfriend? He was with Charles's girlfriend?' Sir Edward repeated with an incredulous look spreading over his face. 'I just don't believe it.'

'I believe it is correct, sir.'

'How do you know?' He was still disbelieving.

'Last night, Miranda, the, er, Minister's wife told me. They had all met several times at the Minister's behest, at the Penthouse. Once for dinner, with two of Charles's other pals from

Hereford and their respective girls. It appears that the Minister was very drawn to her, and she herself did not seem to resist or object to his attention. Indeed, after the first meeting she seemed to 'court' the relationship. Miranda was not oblivious to the fact, but hardened, one must presume, to her husband's philandering.'

'The bloody fool.'

'You can say that again,' Kit went on. 'Because the son, Charles, caught them soon after the last dinner party having an afternoon canoodle over 'afternoon tea' at Browns in Albemarle St.'

'Seems a tall story! What the hell was Charles doing in Browns? He was suspicious then? Had he been following them, and for how long?'

'Miranda says apparently not. He was on leave and it was just luck, bad luck. He'd just been to Asprey's in Bond Street, where they'd recently opened a sporting gun department. He was purely looking at what they had on offer. On his way, back to look again at Purdeys in Audley Street he walked through Browns as you can get from one street to another, and there quite by chance the reality of life was played out before him.'

'Did he approach them?'

'That, I will have to find out, er, later today, but I don't think so. No, he can't have done. According to Miranda she thinks he was too shocked to approach them, he was devastated by her duplicity, hated her for it and he does not get on with his father anyway; the scene was apparently quite embarrassing and he was livid. It's odd, I know, for a man of his calibre, but apparently, he's actually still quite afraid of his father, not physically, for sure, but mentally; it stems from his childhood.'

'So, armed with this knowledge, I am going out to his base at Hereford, where I hope at least to see him and discuss the matter.'

'Miranda knows of all this?'

'Yes, it all came from her. He confided in his mother about the assignation. They're still very close but as yet she thinks he's not approached his father. Actually, may not as it would cause a row at home, ultimately one from which his mother may come off worst. He will just brood and that for him is dangerous.

'His father, or as we now know it, his stepfather, would have denied it anyway, and would have said that there was nothing in it, so there would be little point. I repeat, they're not at all close and don't get on. He well knows his father would have found some glib 'ministerial' reply to deny it all.'

'I didn't know, and Miranda how did she take it?'

'She said it would just blow over, it always had, and her advice was for Charles to forget it and the girl. She had reservations about the girl anyway, and she told Charles this – he was taken aback at his mother's remarks. 'She's far too worldly wise for you, dear,' she'd said.

Typical mother's advice in these matters.

'She thought Charles didn't have great experience with women, mothers never do. Of course, she added that he'd mostly been concentrating on his career, which as we know, sir, takes men off round the world.'

'It never restricted you,' Sir Edward grumbled, but he still shook his head in disbelief.

Kit continued.

'Eventually Miranda and I touched on the subject of adoption. Or let me put it another way, sir, I managed to bring the subject up as you might say.'

Kit's mind wandered back to the bedroom. 'Had it caused pressures within the family I asked??? Did Charles know who his parents were etcetera? She smiled and told me a great deal, including that she was his real mother! And continued to say that his real father was an aristocrat living in a huge pile in the country. I even asked if Charles knew who his real parents were. There was a long, awkward silence then Miranda smiled back looked at me deeply. 'He does now,' she said.'

'But she never told me exactly who the father was, just that he was an aristocrat. She must have told Charles her son to get her own back on her husband David as she said he, David, had no knowledge of this whatsoever, just believing that Charles was an adopted child.'

'She was tired of his carry-ons, his fleeting affairs, and maybe now was time for a change. It was time now that Charles, her son, knew who his real father was anyway it was nearly too late sorry it had taken so long. She even thought he might inherit.' Kit looked up at Sir Edward.

'But then sir, you would know all about this wouldn't you.' Sir Edward moved uncomfortably in his seat. He cleared his throat a little.

'Yes, I'm Sorry, Kit, I do.'

'Are you going to tell me, sir?'

'I can't see that it will help, but I believe its Lord Strutt of Gouthwaite Hall in Yorkshire.'

Sir Edward waited to see if this information made any impact on Kit, but of course there was none, not visibly anyway there never would be.

In any case, through his own and Sheeka's investigations Kit already knew the answer – he was just playing the devil's advocate, knowing that it was a dangerous game with Sir Edward. But he needed confirmation, and to find out how much he already knew, for the moment he was satisfied.

What he did not know and was not prepared for was Sir Edward's next statement. One that was delivered with the utmost seriousness.

'I surmise that will mean little to you.' He looked up a little superciliously. Kit could take the attitude, but wondered whether it was a question or statement. He did not rise to the bait, but bided his time, as if he had not heard.

Sir Edward continued.

'Lord Strutt was one of the original members of the Special Air Service. Of course, not in the guise of Lord Strutt, no that title was inherited later from his father, another distinguished military man. He was then Lieutenant Colonel Carmarthen, a career soldier of great bravery and vision.

'After the war, when others wanted to disband the service, he was one of the few who banged the drum for its continuance, he was adamant of its need, a tireless promoter of its virtues, and he succeeded, don't you think?'

Kit nodded in agreement.

Sir Edward then wrong-footed him completely.

'I presume because of all this you're now pointing a finger at Charles,' he boomed, 'for the murder, and with just cause, you might say a jealous young man venting his fury on his harlot of a girlfriend who had succumbed to his hated father's desires.'

It was certainly in Kit's mind but he was surprised that he had come out with it so soon. Sir Edward could have had no idea of the weapon missing from the barracks at Hereford. Neither could he have known that Kit had the weapon.

Kit was just about to answer when Sir Edward burst forth again.

'Just think of the media, the headlines 'SAS man murders girlfriend, his adopted father's mistress. His father by adoption, David Stevens, a Minister. His real-life father found to be Lord Strutt, a founder member of the SAS. Then, to cap it all, his godfather is the head of SIS or MI6, British Intelligence, call it what you will. Gracious, the list is endless; the media would love it. More heads would roll than we can count'

Kit could have added the Minster's possible blackmail and, Tai Hock to the list, but he said nothing.

Sir Edward once more shook his head gravely with a sigh. He appeared to be ageing by the minute.

Kit thought for a moment; the media, Charles, Miranda, the Minister, his superior and friend Sir Edward, now looking crestfallen in front of him. Was he feigning? He was after all a man of many faces. He had to admit the situation did not look too good.

'Do you think the wrong person was shot sir?

I reckon I would have shot the father not the girl,' Kit said.

'I suppose you would, I expected that' Sir Edward grumbled, knowing Kit's taste for the ladies.

'We've come a long way from investigating a ministerial affair, haven't we, sir?' Sir Edward nodded in silence. 'Time for your rack of lamb, I believe, sir, and time for me to speak to young Charles.' Kit rose to leave.

Unusually Sir Edward let him take the lead, saying.

'Go carefully, don't scare the prey, as yet anyway. I don't see it as being so clear cut – there's got to be more to come.'

'If it's any consolation, sir, I entirely agree,' and with that he withdrew, closing the door behind him. He already knew more than Sir Edward, and it did not look good.

It was good to be out of the air-conditioned building and away from the electric light, but even for London the air by the Thames seemed fresher it energised him, maybe the move was not all bad after all.

The Jaguar down below in the garage had been cleaned as always, with all levels checked. The engine would already be warm and ready for immediate use. The car's interior smelt of walnut and leather all helping to lower the levels of stress that he felt as he wove his cosseted way northwest towards Hereford in the lunchtime traffic.

Late afternoon saw Kit approach the gate of the camp where he showed his identity at the guardroom and asked for Colonel Simon Stewart. To his surprise, he was asked to wait and the gates remained firmly shut. Within five minutes Colonel Stewart arrived, walking across the concrete to greet him. The double gates were opened and the poles lifted one by one. Although pleased to see Kit, Simon looked solemn.

'Come on, drive me up to my office,' he said as he climbed in. Once there, Kit removed a briefcase from the boot of the car and followed Simon into the dark brick building. The office was not typical of the military, being less formal in appearance.

Kit looked out of the window into the fading evening light. The view was of the camp proper. Most of the people he could see appeared to be in civvies, including Simon. It suited him. He had always dressed a little differently.

Kit remembered with a smile that he had a penchant for cowboy boots and today was no exception – as he swung round in his battered chair, one boot arrived with a bang on the desktop; he could not have cared less. Kit could see his suntanned calf and the top of the embossed boot; from the maroon leather seam a small, engraved, silver dirk protruded.

'You don't change,' Kit said with a grin, eyeing the silver encrusted top of the dirk.

'Neither do you and remember this, Kit. That's why 'we' are still here, still alive and on this bloody planet,' he retorted with a snort.

Kit did not pursue the subject but placed his briefcase on the desk, opened it and produced the Tokarev pistol, the one he'd acquired so unceremoniously in the mews. He ejected the magazine into his palm, pulled back the slide and passed the empty weapon across, handle first for examination. Then he rolled the silencer across the desktop towards Simon, who only looked briefly at the pistol. The serial number had been removed, leaving only file marks where it had once been.

Simon stood up, left the desk and asked casually.

'Are you still drinking whisky?' Kit nodded enthusiastically. Whereupon Simon produced a bottle and two glasses from a filing cabinet, poured two glasses of about three fingers each and slid a soda siphon across the desk, before finally saying, 'Well, it's a bad business, but it looks like the one we're after.' He sighed as he looked at the pistol again. 'Anyway, the armourer will confirm it first thing in the morning.' There was a pause to get Kit's attention as he looked at him before continuing, 'It appears I also now have another weapon missing. A model 89 Beretta 9mm.'

'Careless of you,' said Kit cynically. 'Is it related' Simon didn't answer.

Kit stood up quickly and said, 'If they were here, at the camp, who were they booked out to?'

'That's a little difficult to ascertain at the moment, but it seems there were four of them – Stevens, Riley, Duncome and Faisley. The last two, who are not on leave, say they've no knowledge of this and anyway they never used them on the range. But they believe Stevens and Riley might have done. Needless to say, I did not mention they'd gone missing.'

'Is Charles Stevens here?' Simon looked at a board with numbers, dates and varied coloured lines that was screwed on the white wall. No names were evident, just random numbers – numbers that would change frequently, with a code needed to link a name to a number.

'You know very well if he is here or not, Simon. You've no need to look at that,' he joked. Simon looked back embarrassed.

'You're right, of course I do. No, I can tell you that unfortunately he's on four day's leave starting today.'

'Convenient' Kit muttered.

'Well, a few of the lads are off and they deserve it.' He looked up at the board again, 'So's his pal, 'Wiley' Riley; they often go off together.' Then as an afterthought, 'Well, he's supposed to be out, but I saw Riley when I went down to the gate to pick you up. It's late but Mm, I'll just check.' With that he rang the guardroom.

Yes, Sergeant Riley had just left the camp, he did mention he was late checking out, but he'd had a bit of a lie-in this morning and had some paper work to do this afternoon came the gruff reply.

'Some bloody lie-in,' said Kit. 'Is that why you rang me today about the missing weapon? On the very day when Stevens wasn't here, come off it?'

'Just coincidental, really.'

But he didn't believe his friend. Simon, just like Sir Edward, would protect his own until he was absolutely sure of some misdemeanour. SIS and bloody mind games, but then they both knew that.

Simon continued, 'But I would obviously prefer to talk first, before you go blundering in. If that's your intention.'

'You forget, Simon, I'm not a policeman, I'm just trying to sort this bloody mess out before it goes public, for all our benefits. I'd like to look at his quarters, well, need to really.'

'Now Riley's gone, I suppose you can,' Simon

answered unhappily. 'But if anyone's around we must abort!'

'Obviously,' said Kit a little superciliously. Simon stared at him, shrugged and walked towards the grey-painted door, which by now Kit was holding open for him.

'Are you absolutely sure he's gone?'

'Well, the gate says so, but it is a bit odd him being still here when on so-called leave, I have to admit, most are usually off at the crack of dawn.'

As they strode leisurely across in the direction of the other buildings there were few people about and fortunately all was quiet when they approached Charles Stevens' quarters. Simon closed the door after them.

It was a small room and in need of a coat of paint through constant use. Charles Stevens could not have kept much here, as there was little cupboard space and the wardrobe was small. Classic car magazines were in an orderly pile on his bedside cabinet, as were the 'Shooting Times' and 'Autocar'.

Charles's immediate interests other than the Army were obvious, and just, as Miranda had described them. He also appeared to be a tidy individual.

There was sadly a lonely silver-framed picture of Verkuska displayed on the windowsill. She was laughing and looked beautiful, yet somehow the laughter seemed affected if not contrived, as if an act, as a model would for a photo call. Kit stared at it thoughtfully.

There was little in the bedside cabinet and nothing unusual; the wardrobe was the same. Kit sat on the end of the bed and looked round the room thumbing through a few of the magazines, a standard military shell; he'd seen enough of them and it depressed him.

'Happy now?' Simon said.

'I suppose so,' he said, rising from the bed, but as he did so, as he pushed himself up from it, his hand felt something hard on one side of the mattress, which was unusually unyielding. Carefully he rolled back the mattress and to his horror there before him was a grey plastic laptop computer, a 'Digital'

'Oh shit,' he said quietly as he covered one corner with his handkerchief and bent to lift it from the bed, between finger and thumb.

The Colonel looked on curiously.

'So, what it's just a laptop, many of the lads have them. I have one just the same, in fact exactly the same. The lads don't leave them lying around on view either, there is nothing unusual about hiding it under his mattress.'

'Maybe not,' Kit cautioned. 'But I know of one that's gone missing – his father's.'

'Oh God!' Simon uncharacteristically muttered. 'Do you think---?'

Making sure his fingers were protected, Kit opened it and pressed the 'On' button at the side. It flickered into life with the 'Password Protected' flag plainly visible. He sat looking at it for a moment.

'Simon, you've just told me that you have one exactly the same, correct?'

'That's right.'

He then suggested that they substitute one for the other, and if Simon's was not 'Password Protected' then to make it so. This would give him time to see if the one they'd just found was the Ministerial one or not. If Charles Stevens were to return there was every chance he wouldn't notice it had gone, therefore would not know it had been exchanged.

Kit carefully placed the laptop between the pages of a magazine, and looked up at the Colonel.'

'Well?'

'Er, yes, fine, a good idea,' the Colonel spluttered in uncharacteristic fashion. 'I have mine here and it's 'Password Protected' also. There's little in it anyway.' With that the Colonel went to get it.

Kit waited in the room, staring out of the dirty window at the drab buildings, tarmac and hard standings of concrete in the now fading light. The leaves were now falling and blew in gusts round the buildings, all-adding to the bleak scene. Autumn had well and truly arrived in Wales.

The Colonel soon returned with his laptop concealed in a battered black leather briefcase, string holding it together, the catch long gone. They did the switch and left as quickly and inconspicuously as they came. With a lot of the lads on leave.

They were lucky.

Nineteen

Charles Peregrine Stevens

Charles Peregrine Stevens had had a good life. Idolised by his mother and tolerated by his father, he had happily accepted his harsh public schooling. Although not particularly academically bright he enjoyed accumulating knowledge and had an enquiring and inventive mind. But without doubt he had excelled at sport, his favourites being rugby and distance or cross-country running. Little did he know that these would stand him in good stead in years to come?

He had an affinity with animals and loved to be on his own in woodland, come rain or shine; he was happy camping out overnight under the stars. He would not admit to being a loner, but he enjoyed his own company.

His adopted mother encouraged him all she could and he loved her dearly; they were very close. His adopted father, on the other hand, concentrated on his own career; becoming an elected Member of Parliament and he and Charles were not close. He worked late and they saw little of each other.

If Charles questioned his father's judgement, he was chastised without any real explanation. Like many people, his father would take the opposite view just for the sake of an argument and to dominate the boy. Charles took it in good heart and put up with it, but a wound was there and getting deeper. Curiously never felt as one with his father in the same way he did with his mother; there seemed to be no family bond between the two of them.

As far as he was concerned university was not a success, although most undergraduates lapped it up. He achieved a degree with good grades in his chosen subject, Psychology, but he disliked the 'professional student' element, which to his dismay surrounded him.

Charles Stevens was different. Somewhere deep in his soul was a restless gene, a spirit held back which wanted action. When considering his future, he thought of the RAF, which he would have loved, but it just wasn't physical enough for him. No, it had to be the Army. As ever, his father argued against his decision. He just couldn't understand it at all. The military indeed! Quite, quite, ridiculous.

Charles had matured into a big athletic man, with powerful hands and strong legs. He was tall and broad, square jawed with a slight bronze complexion from a life spent out of doors whenever possible. With his dark hair and dark eyes, it was difficult to read his thoughts, until his features burst into an ivory smile.

His dress was in the style of brown brogues, Clydella shirts, Irish tweed sports jackets and coloured flannels. He had a very county look and in that way, he was different from his immediate friends; he didn't know why but he felt comfortable in this attire, it was natural to him.

Apart from his more physical hobbies, he had always had a leaning toward guns and cars. Classic cars meant much more to him than modern, computer-generated cars, which all seemed the same to drive. To Charles, old classics often handmade, breathed life.

After three years in the Army his request to go for selection for the SAS was granted; he felt that an honour in itself. If only he had known the horrors of what lay in store! The sheer mental and physical effort, even for a man of his fitness, the hours and hours of training and preparation were unbelievable, mind-blowing. The sheer, total pain, the blisters, tattered feet with little useful skin remaining. The absolute agony of trying to harden the torn remains with vinegar and a hundred other potions – all recommended by the knowing and all to no avail.

He would never forget the webbing straps of his heavy Bergen cutting into his back, or being soaked through to the bone, never dry on the mountains; the endless physical pain, the discomfort, which never diminished.

In the end, it was his tenacity, his willpower won through and dominated the pain, allowing his mind and body to keep going; just.

To him jungle training in Brunei was seventh heaven; a relief in spite of being blistered and bitten, forever wet, with suppurating sores, ones, which he dare not report for fear of being sent home. He had never known he was such desirable food.

All that now behind him, a new future dawned.

And now love? His new-found girlfriend, a little older than he and amazingly sophisticated, she was right off the shelf and an absolute stunner to boot, but she had been a little over the top for his pals, just too much for them to believe. 'Wiley' Riley – all sinew and tendon, his friend who had got through selection at the same time as he – had been completely amazed. Charles had dominated the scene; Charles, who had never been out with someone like this before. In fact, there had been very few at all, but this one was not going to slip through his grasp.

His virginity had disappeared with little difficulty at university and he still kept returning to the same well-endowed girl to curb his carnal desires. The first time for him had been in the back of a car. He would never forget her enormous breasts, large protruding begging nipples searching upward for him. They were forever etched in his mind, always waiting, begging, looking up at him from the back seat.

But this time it was different; the past paled into insignificance and he looked forward eagerly to seeing Verkuska again. He knew his mother would be proud of his catch, and perhaps even his father too, though he had yet to congratulate him on getting through selection and that hurt. But this lady, this treat to the eye, he could not help but notice and would surely be pleased for him at last, proud.

Charles had been a little taken aback at Verkuska's forwardness. After his father appeared to get over the initial shock of meeting her they got on like a house on fire. In fact, she seemed to enjoy talking to his father more than to him, which annoyed him. She openly admitted she liked older men, 'they're more interesting'. In the weeks that followed it irritated him even more that he could not always see her when he had time off, it seemed she was not always available.

One day he decided to exercise his passion for fine guns. He had for some time been considering the purchase of a 'Best' English side lock shotgun, a twelve-bore. He was able to do this by his thrifty saving and a legacy that some years before had been mysteriously left to him 'for later need.'

Charles had no real inclination to stand in a field and turn pheasants into a ball of blood and feathers as they attempted to fly over him and a line of other guns. He would use it for the odd clay shoot and for him to admire its aesthetic beauty, to clean and enjoy. It would be a gun that was a tribute of the gun maker's art, an engraved investment, a marriage of walnut and steel, all cased by Brady's in leather and English oak.

With this in mind he paid yet another visit to James Purdey & Sons at South Audley Street, London. On entering the premises, he was immediately met by a polite gentleman dressed in a morning suit.

'Good day, sir, and how may I help you? Mr----?' the assistant said searching for a name and looking deeply at him.

'Charles Stevens. It's a big decision, if I may I'd like to look again at some of your shotguns,' Charles replied.

The assistant then looked at him more closely, studying his features, before saying, 'Indeed, sir, er, Mr Stevens, you said? Oh, I'm so sorry, I mistook you for someone else, but you do remind me of someone we know here at Purdeys. Your father shoots perhaps?'

'My father does not shoot,' Charles answered quizzically.

His second stop was to be Holland & Holland at Bruton St, then on to Asprey's in Bond Street, where they had just opened a new showroom.

Then it happened. His first gut-wrenching shock that day occurred whilst he was enjoying the walk from Purdeys, striding out in the autumn air. He was taking a short cut through Browns Hotel in Albemarle Street, which you can do if you wish to get from one street to another. He went in with the intention of perhaps getting a coffee, not knowing what fateful hand had led him there. But what he saw was to change his life forever.

It was about 3.30 in the afternoon and tea was just beginning to be served. English cream teas were being pushed around the ground floor, snug to snug, china cups and saucers rattling about on old polished wooden trolleys that were laden with buttered scones and pots of Devon clotted cream with strawberry preserve.

As he walked through the lobby he glanced casually around. What he saw stunned him. The scene that was unfolding and being played out before him sickened him, shocking him to the core. His training kept him moving robotically, moving slowly and sadly to the exit door and into the street. He felt hot, angry and sick.

His father, David Stevens, the Minister, had been enjoying afternoon tea in the company of none other than his girlfriend Verkuska. The scene was so intimate, almost vulgar, and it left nothing to the imagination. The amorous blatancy of the man, this, his adopted father, it appalled him – as it had before, many times.

The second bombshell of the day happened when either through bitterness or the fact that he was tired of his father's indiscretions, he knew not which, but after much deliberation, he told Miranda, his mother, of what he'd seen at Browns. Amazingly, she was not surprised and seemed to take it in her stride. That in itself shocked Charles; she was obviously upset but had learned to accept these indiscretions. Charles had not and would not. Verkuska after all had been his. He would avenge.

As for Miranda, she was secretly relieved that Charles would probably no longer see this lady. But Charles himself was miffed with his father to say the very least, and could not, would not forgive as easily as his mother. Somehow, soon, he knew he would get even and resolve the matter forever.

Then two weeks later, whilst on weekend leave, it happened, the biggest shock of all. His father was away at a meeting in his constituency. His mother seemed nervous, preoccupied with something and on tenterhooks. Then, as if she had finally plucked up courage, she asked him to sit down in the lounge. He poured himself a drink and chose the settee, crossed his legs and looked out over the harbour and Chelsea. He was in for an ear bending.

Miranda, his doting mother, sat opposite, her head bowed. After a long silence in which she was still visibly gathering sufficient of her inner strength, she told him. Miranda told him that she was his real mother! In tears, she leaned over and kissed him, held him close. After some time, had elapsed she continued saying that there had been some falsifying of the adoption papers, an intentional fiddle. She was ashamed that she had not told him before; would he ever forgive her? The real reason was that his father didn't know either and he was not party to these irregularities. David didn't even know that Miranda was his real mother.

She explained that as a baby the gamekeeper's wife at Gouthwaite Hall had looked after him, so that his adopted father never knew the true circumstances.

That was the biggest shock of the day, or was it really? Deep down in his subconscious he was not too sure that it was such a shock to him.

He was obviously confused but what really annoyed him was why it had taken his mother so long to admit. The next revelation really stunned him as his mother went on speaking quietly with her head bowed. His real-life father it seemed was no less than Lord Strutt of Gouthwaite Hall, a country gent of some considerable repute, who she had met at university. The name meant nothing to him, but after all this time what should he do? Was Lord Strutt still alive? Miranda answered proudly that indeed he was. He could see that she still had considerable feeling for the man.

With that look on his mother's face he knew exactly what he had to do. The next day was Sunday, the last day of his leave, he would set off immediately and drive to Gouthwaite in Yorkshire, 'for better or for worse'. For now, with that look in his mother's eyes and the softness of her voice etched in his mind, Charles knew that he needed to see his real father.

The Alfa Romeo not being available, he would hire a car for the trip.

It was a long pull up to Gouthwaite, about 240 miles straight up the A1 to Yorkshire. The Ford he had hired was quite quick, but not to his liking – a computer product. He found Gouthwaite easily and took a room at the village pub, the sign of which was a shield depicting the Strutt coat of arms, 'Virtuous in Adversity'. The pub was noisy and he slept little, dominoes clattered on the tables below till the early hours. His mind was in turmoil as to what awaited him the next day when he went to see his real father, would his father know him, would his father recognise him?

He found the gates and the two lodges at the entrance to Gouthwaite Hall without difficulty. They were imposing, he had to admit, although they looked to be in disrepair and the drive snaking away into the distance was full of potholes. It was typically English, a grey windswept day, with low clouds rushing across the horizon; he found it a bit depressing to visit this obvious relic of the past. There was no sign of anybody as he drove with some trepidation through the entrance.

As he rounded a corner the sight laid out before him was not what he had expected. It was the same one that had impressed Sheeka some days before; an unbelievable stately home in the Palladian style, its huge grey stone columns of the entrance hall reminding him of the classic grille of a Rolls Royce. He saw the overgrown lake, the balustrade bridge and the flaking stone of the temple on the hill close by, he drove slowly on.

Parking under the shadow of the entrance built so that years ago, a coach and four could be driven under it and out of the English weather, he went up the steps noting that one of the double doors was part open. He was going to knock but realised it would have been futile with such thick, heavy doors and the house so large so he walked through and into the enormous entrance hall. He stood there dwarfed by the sheer size. It was cold and smelt the spores of damp. To the left a door was open and he could see a figure with its back to him, so he called out loudly, 'Excuse me.' The figure straightened but did not turn, as if in disbelief that its privacy had been invaded. Charles called out again. 'Excuse me.'

This time the figure slowly turned; he could see that it was a tall if slightly stooped man wearing a tweed jacket with leather elbow and cuff patches, old, worn, baggy, cavalry twill trousers, brogues and odd socks. Charles walked a little nearer.

'Excuse me,' he said yet again, 'I'm sorry to---' but was cut short as the man bellowed, 'What!'

'Sir---'

'Speak up, man, I'm deaf – and who the hell are you anyway?'

'I'm trying to tell you. I'm Charles Stevens, Charles Peregrine Stevens, sir.'

Lord Strutt's face fell, his jaw dropped, he blinked and looked long and hard at Charles, scrutinising every feature.

'Oh dear, dear, dear,' he exclaimed, his voice losing its customary edge. Unsteadily he walked out of the library to greet Charles. They shook hands cordially. Then His Grace suddenly put his arms around Charles in a great bear hug, which he did not resist. Considering his age, he was still powerful. For a while there was total silence between them then His Grace spoke, his voice no longer gruff, wavering hoarsely.

'Charles, I am so, so sorry. I've waited for this day for so long and now I just don't know what to say.'

'Say sorry,' Charles answered glibly, but with a forgiving smile.

'Sorry? I am, more than you will ever know. So, after all these years Miranda has told you? I wish she'd warned me,' he said quietly his voice fading away.

'Mother told me, yes. It's taken a long time. How much longer might I have waited; how much longer might it have taken?'

His Grace, now clearly under great emotion and embarrassment, did not answer the question. 'It was all my fault, nothing to do with your mother, you must never blame her,' he said, clearly accepting all guilt.

'It takes two,' Charles pointed out, a little ruffled, but he was still smiling broadly. 'What the hell,' and he shook his father's arm again. They walked into the study where a 12-bore shotgun, a Purdey, was lying open across the old battered desk, its barrels straddling an open diary, deep red paper case cartridges scattered about among the papers.

'Pigeons,' His Grace said by way of explanation, glancing casually at the shotgun whilst continuing to gather his composure. 'Time of year; damn things come for the peas in the garden; I'll have no bloody peas left.'

Charles looked wide-eyed around the room, taking in the scene of centuries. It was a bit like a bric-a-brac shop, yet it had such character. He looked out through the sash windows, across the rolling parkland and the lonely statues that were once surrounded by gardens; some of the boundary walls were still there. Far to the left a huge mass of laurel hedge lay untended, no doubt once a maze.

'Welcome home,' Lord Strutt said quietly, nearly under his breath.

Charles just heard and perceptively nodded.

'Drink! I think this deserves a drink,' His Grace announced. 'Any objection?'

'None whatsoever,' Charles replied willingly.

'Then come with me, my boy,' His Grace said happily.

With that they walked out into the entrance hall and took a small corridor into the centre of the building, obviously designed more for staff rather than the owner or guests; there was little lighting. They came upon a heavy oak door with bolts driven in, which His Grace opened to reveal stone steps that led down to the cellars below;

cold moist air came up to greet them; a brace of partridge hung on a rusty nail.

Once at the next level, many steps down, Charles was amazed, impressed even; he had seen nothing like it. Beautiful stone arches and pillars supported the vaulted roof. Leading off in all directions were passages lined with iron racks containing bottles and wooden trestles for barrels from Oporto, Portugal. As they went, the lighting being poor, His Grace lit a taper from large tallow candles that rested in wrought-iron holders.

'The wine cellar,' he announced proudly as he wandered about looking at various labels and handwritten notes that hung from dusty bottles. After searching for a while His Grace stopped to point out a rack of dark bottles, the labels now nut brown. 'Your grandfather's favourite, Chateau Laffite. He put these down. It can be a little light for me thin even, but he would approve of your homecoming, so Laffite it shall be. OK with you?'

'Certainly' said Charles in total awe of the situation.

With that His Grace carefully selected a bottle of 1934 Chateau Laffite Rothschild, gently holding the taper behind it to examine the contents. 'Just perfect,' he uttered in quiet reverence. 'Just perfect.'

The wine was decanted and poured into to antique claret glasses, which they took with them as they went for a tour of the main Hall. Charles was shown dusty paintings of his ancestors staring back at him from drab oils, a frightening bunch he thought. Rooms that had not been opened in years were un-shuttered and exposed to the light. Rip van Winkle came to his mind as they peered under moth-eaten dustsheets; there was even a Steinway grand, long out of key, on which His Grace played a few notes.

The stable block was beautifully built with its arched entrance and clock tower in the centre, hands that had stopped long ago. Inside, surrounded by leather tack, a crested coaches, gig, and trap were sadly rotting.

Hours later, after his father had waved him off after making him promise to return, he was driving south to London, a happier and much wiser man.

Twenty

As Kit, had previously found out, Hereford did not boast a particularly good restaurant or for that matter a really good hotel – at least not to his taste – but he was far too tired to be concerned. With little sleep from the night before and after the long drive to Hereford, he was immune from thoughts of self-indulgence.

Carefully placing the computer on the rickety bedside table, he showered and slept fitfully, his mind repeatedly returning to the Charles Stevens problem. It didn't look good and he needed a meeting first thing the next day with the Old Man to discuss his recent findings.

With this in mind he'd rung the Old Man and requested an 'immediate' for the following morning. It was agreed they would meet at ten, about as immediate as it would get.

At 7 a.m. Kit drove east on the A 438, enjoying himself in the relatively light traffic of early morning in the country, all so different to London, his pulse quickening slightly as he settled into the drive. He drove in a relaxed manner, arms at three-quarter length and with his hands on the wheel in the classic 'ten to two' position. His eyes glanced in the mirror and across to the dials with metronomic consistency.

Then suddenly, whilst approaching a corner and applying the brakes, the bonnet diving down toward the tarmac, he checked the mirror once again. As if his dream had been broken, his eyes were transfixed by the car that was exiting the corner he had just left. Its central, inverted, triangular grill was unmistakable, an Alfa-Romeo, in yellow. Its tail hung out as it drifted easily away from the inside line it had taken, nearly moving into the other lane before the driver corrected it. He watched, curious, as its bonnet lifted and the power returned.

Charles Stevens? It must be. The chance of another Alfa and in yellow so close to the camp would have been unusual to say the least. Kit tried to assess the situation. The driver was obviously in a hell of a rush, although he could have been enjoying himself, just like he was himself.

If it was Charles Stevens, did he know then that Kit had been to the camp? Was he in fact trying to catch him up to offer some sort of explanation? Had his CO approached him? There had to be some sort of connection, so he slowed a little whilst still maintaining a reasonable pace.

The Alfa could easily have overhauled the big

Jaguar at its reduced speed, but instead its driver stayed a discreet distance behind as if waiting. Even at that Kit could not make out the identity of the driver through the tinted glass of the windscreen.

He glanced at his watch, deciding he could not hang about playing games; maybe he was mistaken. So, without further ado he put his foot down, relentlessly powering the Jaguar on towards London, now with one eye on the road, one eye on the mirror and with the little nimble Alfa playing in pursuit.

The status quo stayed like this for some time until suddenly, whilst going into a corner the little Alfa was upon him, so low on the road that it was barely visible in the mirror. Just the dark hood was visible, darting about behind him, the car virtually tucked under the Jaguar's long, majestic boot. It took him by surprise, at this stage of the corner it would have been fatal to brake; as it was he poured on more power and tried to drive out of the situation. The power steering went light as the Jaguar moved into under steer, so he backed off and collected the big car up again, its front end now diving back into the line of the corner its long tail stepping out; gravel rattled on the bodywork. As if glued the little Alfa never left him.

Driving harder still into a slight bend the rear of the big Jaguar once more stepped out of line.

Then to Kit's amazement and annoyance the two cars touched, the Alfa viciously nudging the rear of his car, pushing the Jaguar with a smart crack further off the driving line. The big car, already at its unwieldy limit, virtually lurched into a spin. But for steady nerves it would surely have done so.

Kit had expected the larger engine of the Jaguar to pull away from the little Alfa, but was disappointed. Its weight was a disadvantage so the little Alfa was able to hang in there, tenacious to the last. Even from within the cosseted interior, Kit could hear the scream of its little 1750 twin-cam engine; its four domed pistons sucking deeply through twin choke Weber carbs to retain power, fire and pressure. The race was now really on!

What he was not prepared for was to be out braked into the next left-hand corner; there was no bang, no jolt to the rear of the Jaguar, no anticipated foul play. Had the rules suddenly changed? The Alfa screamed past on a blind bend, power on, and tail well down, it's chrome Abarth exhaust trembling, as if shaking a fist. The front wheel looked light and was starting to patter. The droop nose now strained upwards in a tortured angle of defiance, as the driver kept the power on. He momentarily glimpsed the bare flesh of a broad, white-sleeved arm hard at work. They were so close he caught the flash of a stainless watch. He can drive, Kit thought, but he's either lucky or stupid. Blind corners are for dead men.

Kit followed hard on his tail, then as a hump-back bridge came into view, he had no alternative but to back off as he knew that the soft suspension would destroy the Jaguar on landing the other side. Then suddenly and disconcertingly he could also see the cab top of a large truck approaching the bridge. Prudence must prevail and he stabbed the softening brakes twice. As he went over the bridge the Jaguar felt so light he thought he had misjudged it, but grudgingly it weaved and snaked as the suspension took the strain.

To his horror, on the other side of the bridge, some way ahead, the Alfa had stopped dead, its red brake lights glaring back through its tyre smoke. The truck towered high amongst its own noxious fumes, a mass of aerials and coloured fairy lights, grinding its way inexorably towards them and the bridge. The road was now blocked by the Alfa and the truck, 86 mph. was registering and there was nowhere to go! A typical understatement flashed through his mind: Not good, he thought, not good at all. He grimaced with his jaw set and stamped hard on the brakes throwing the inertia of the car forward. After a split second, he let them off again and flicked the wheel over, then stamped hard on the tired brakes again; hot, distorted discs shuddered.

NO REPLACEMENT

The big Jaguar picked up her skirts from the rear and slowly moved into a spin, which quickened as the weight of the long saloon created a pendulum effect. Kit sunk lower in the seat, bracing himself for the heartrending crash as he and the Jaguar together would surely obliterate the little Alfa, simultaneously hoping desperately that he had timed everything right and that he would spin backwards into the other car thus giving his body more support.

He waited for the crash but amazingly it didn't come. The Jaguar spun on across the polished summer tar, as if in freefall. He saw the shadow of the diesel truck, smelt the fumes, heard the roar of the engine, the blast of the air horns and felt its vibrations as it hurtled by.

Just as suddenly as it had all started, the car landed with a jolt facing the wrong way on the grass, its engine stalled. Kit surveyed the scene. The truck had gone, there was no sign of the Alfa and all was quiet. Kit got out to relieve himself and looked back up the road. To his left was a small B road leading off into farming country; dust was being thrown up from a low and hardly discernible car that was being driven quickly away. He'd been pleased with his own skills and timing, but that guy was something special.

It was very close and had been deliberate. The driver of the Alfa had tried to kill him, Charles

Stevens, if that was who it was and, maybe not for the first time? He stood there thinking, listening to the sounds around him, the ticking of hot and tortured metal as it cooled, the smell of scorched asbestos and brakes. A little green antifreeze water ran away from under the front of a near-boiling Jaguar.

He would leave the driver of the Alfa, Charles if it was, for another day.

Meanwhile London called.

Twenty-One

Kit had not been in his office three minutes when Sue popped her head round the door without knocking.

'Someone to see you,' she said pleasantly. He glowered up from his desk, one that he had bought many years earlier in a London sale, though strangely he had left it behind when he had resigned.

He had no time for this; he was not in a good mood.

But the fact that he could see Sheeka hovering behind Sue cooled his temperament, a sight he could not resist. She just had this effect on him.

'Come in and a coffee for all, eh,' he called, looking down at his laptop computer with a bemused look.

'Too late, as usual just trust me,' Sue smiled, efficiently bringing in two large thin China cups and saucers, the dark coffee visibly showing through the bone China. I'll have mine with the staff,' she winked wickedly, closing the door.

A lucky man to have such an efficient secretary

and an understanding one at that, Kit thought as he clacked the computer keys to no avail. He looked infuriated as he pushed it to one side with a pencil and peeled off a pair of white cotton gloves whilst throwing a yellow duster over it; he looked up at Sheeka.

'Your report, sir,' Sheeka said with a smile. He took it and started to read. 'Anything new?' she asked impatiently, looking at the half-hidden laptop.

'Mm, quite a bit actually, but I have to go and see the Old Man at ten.' He uncovered the laptop and carefully opened it again.

'Trouble, sir?' she asked.

'This damned thing is 'password protected', and I can't get into it. I also need to send it to Forensic for prints. Sheeka, I'm in a dilemma as I need to find out whose exactly it is and I need to do so quickly, just in case I have to return it. How are you on computers?'

Sheeka shrugged. 'They're straightforward, no brain surgery needed. If what you are looking for has been put in and is still in there then technically speaking there is no problem getting it out. Other than time that is.'

'I haven't got much time,' Kit grumbled, stopping her in mid-flow – or nearly.

Sheeka continued,

'As I said, if the information has been put in

and is still there, then it can be retrieved – quite obviously. We will need to install a program of sorts, that is, a 'Digital' brand,' she nodded at the computer. 'This particular one, if I remember right, will need an external disc drive and I do have a program, well several actually.' She smiled and carried on with some more computer jargon. Kit was impressed but didn't show it.

Still pushing it by the same corner he slid it back into a transparent plastic cover and pushed it over the desk to her.

'Mm, it looks like a ten-inch colour, one of the first,' she said casually looking down at it. 'So, it'll be slow.' Kit nodded.

Sheeka picked it up and pushed the file across to Kit, saying, 'I'll have it checked for prints and then I'll work on it, OK? So, see you after your meeting, sir, if I may?' Self-assured she moved to go out through Sue's office; as she went she heard the electric bolts of the outer door slide as Kit left too.

'Communicative, isn't he?' Sheeka said out loud.

'Communicative? Hardly a word I would have used,' Sue said wryly as she sorted through files, files that bore the mark and stamp of the now disgraced and dead Liam. She was trying to bring the section up to date, to make up for her absence. Every single file would have to be analysed.

They both looked at their watches the greeting between Kit and the Old Man was quiet and short. Kit did not sit as bidden; rather he stood pacing a little as he brought his superior up to date. Half an hour or more of uninterrupted factual speech followed, which Kit was aware was unusual as the Old Man usually interrupted him in full flow, but now realising that he was in deep thought whilst considering all the ominous implications. Then after an unusually long silence when he had finally finished, Kit decided to take the plunge.

'Well sir, to sum up, I would recommend that Special Branch should be brought in to arrest and frighten Charles Peregrine Stevens, the arrest could be for the murder of----' He never managed to finish his sentence.

'Would you now,' was the loud and angry reply. Kit looked at the Old Man; in the background the clock ticked. He mellowed a little before continuing.

'You may of course be right but where would that put the Minister and our old friend Tai Hock? They may not be involved but we must not forget them. Do we know what the Minister was doing going to see Tai Hock that night? No! We don't and Kit, I bloody well want to know! I'm afraid I may well be guilty of forestalling the arrest of my godson, but neither do I wish to scare off what may be bigger fish involved in who knows what. That is if there are any. I just feel, always have done, that somehow there's a lot more to this than meets the eye.'

It was Kit's turn now to consider the facts.

'Someone is trying to prevent this enquiry proceeding sir. Someone's trying to hinder the investigation and even get rid of me, by killing me if necessary and uniquely I'm not sure they know who I am yet, or more to the point who I work for, but nevertheless it's someone who's trained to kill and won't mind doing so. It could well be Charles?'

'Kill you? Well my sincere condolences. I'm so sorry I do apologise, Kit,' he said cynically. 'But surely you should be quite used to that by now!' He added

'Thank you, sir, for your concern it makes me feel so much better. But it is something that you never do quite get used to!'

'I am delighted you're on your toes' Sir Edward laughed, 'but seriously why do you say kill; why should anyone at this moment wish to kill you?'

'I've been trying to work that out too, sir, so let's think about it. The murderer of the Minister's lady friend tried to shoot me on the night, that's a fact, right? If the gun had not misfired, he would have succeeded. At the time, I just thought it was natural reaction, for his own self-preservation covering his tracks. But now I think maybe not, there's more to it.

'Was he expecting me to burst in? Or did he even know that I was already there? Did he know the house was being watched? And if so, how? Had he had a tip-off, if so by whom?' Kit looked hard at the Old Man, but there was no reaction.

'How could he see you? How could he know you were there?' Sir Edward asked.

'With night glasses, he could and this man would have access to them, just the same as I. But once there he just sat it out, he had no need to move. Was he watching me before the girl arrived? Probably. He knew I was not after him or I would have moved sooner, so I must have been there to watch the Minister and his girl frolicking about, not knowing what part he was about to play.

'As yet he doesn't know who I am, or where I'm from. But what he does know is that I was the witness to a murder. If I'm right, I'm no longer the hunter, but the hunted!'

'It's possible, just possible but I doubt it,' the Old Man interrupted. 'Anyway, nobody at that time knew that you were back in London. Only you and I knew we were going to put some form of surveillance on the Minister.'

'Maybe so, but then there was the girl's apartment. There was little in there in terms of incriminating evidence, yet it was an absolute time bomb. Whoever set that up was not necessarily trying to destroy evidence, as well they were trying to eliminate whoever might come after them snooping about and, that someone was me. He'd missed me the first time, with the misfire, so he'd succeed the second time from a distance.'

Then Kit's mind flashed back to the night he'd taken Sheeka for dinner in Soho, the night he thought he was being followed. He clearly remembered that flat sound, a sound like a wet leather thong hitting a sofa, followed almost instantly by a soft thud. He'd thought little of it at the time, but…

'Then we have today's attempt, this morning's clever little driving trick with the Alfa,' he continued thoughtfully. 'An Alfa I believe I've seen before and maybe even the one I saw parked near to her apartment. We know who possibly owns it, especially as having seen it at Hereford too. In my book, it all points to one man, and that man, sir, is once again Charles Peregrine bloody Stevens. However, if you want me to look at Tai, so be it.' He shrugged. 'Mind you, I have to say I don't like Charles Stevens being at large and if I have to take him out to protect myself, I will!'

The Old Man winced and gave a big sigh.

'I've listened to what you say and I have to agree with you. If the man in the apartment opposite you that night was able to see you and just sat it out, to use your own phrase he's 'got some bottle'. He's a professional although it does point to the fact that as yet he doesn't know who you are, hence this little game of charades. You may well be right,' the Old Man said thoughtfully. Then he said 'Kit, I've known you since you were a young man and I knew your father before you. It is this, don't you understand, this sort of situation that you thrive on and brings the results.'

And if I take him out, how will you think then, my friend? Kit thought to himself before returning to reality.

'Thank you, sir,' he said. He was not enjoying the bullshit, or the stilted conversation. It was most out of character. The Old Man must be holding something back; he must know more. He just didn't want to admit the obvious that it was Charles, his own godson.

The Old Man continued, 'If Tai Hock is still in London, and I believe that he is...' to Kit this was the first sign there was more to come as he would know damned well if Tai Hock was around or not 'find out why the Minister is involved with him, that is if he is. We do know that an eastern country, Indonesia I believe, made representations to Hawker Siddley concerning the Hawk jet over which there have been many political difficulties. I'm sure that Tai Hock would be involved somewhere along the line.'

'The original request, though, would have

to be referred by British Aerospace or Hawker Siddley to the Government, would it not?'

'Yes, it would become a 'procurement request from the Indonesian Government', with I surmise, Tai Hock as an intermediary. An export licence would have to be granted; a lengthy document, which I'll bet initially, would be passed to who else but David Stevens, the Minister of Defence? So, Kit for now put Charles on a little ice, but watch him and meanwhile find out what you can about Tai Hock and the Minister.'

Kit nodded in agreement.

'You know he'll remember me, don't you? Tai Hock that is.' Kit said.

'That's why he may even see you; remember the rule that you once told me?' The Old Man looked deep into Kit's eyes. 'Mind games you said, mind games. Your favourite I believe was **'Hold on – by letting go'**. Did you not once say that to me, Kit? You did and that's why he will see you again; he won't be able to resist.'

Kit smiled, knowing the Old Man was right. He got up clasping the file and made for the door across the thick pile carpet.

'I'll see what I can do. Ironically now the same applies to Charles, doesn't it?'

"Hold on – by letting go'?' the Old Man said. 'Mm, I suppose it does.'

Just as Kit reached the door he was called back.

'Sorry, Kit, I nearly forgot,' and with that he slid a clear plastic jiffy bag across the desk. 'This was sent up for you from Forensic. I, er, didn't want it lying around downstairs. It's a pistol round, a 7.62, low velocity by the look of the rifling, probably out of a Russian Tokarev. Good job it was only low velocity otherwise it would still be going. Oh, it was dug out of the half-burnt corpse yesterday.'

'Lucky for who? Certainly, not her, low or high velocity, dead is dead,' Kit replied as he took the packet. 'Thank you.' He placed it in his inside pocket and left, knowing full well what the gun was.

A troubled and sombre mood, all pervading, enveloped him as he walked back to his office. At the same time, he could not help thinking about the evening he met Sheeka in Soho those few nights earlier, at Topo Giggio's, not for the enjoyment of it, but for that odd feeling of being followed; it stuck inexorably in his mind. For years, he had relied on his premonitions, his second sense.

His own description preyed on his mind; 'The sound of wet leather being thrashed', a sound so similar. That evening somewhat belatedly he would act on his second sense, he would go back to Soho and investigate. What irked him most was that he had not paid more attention to it at the time, but such is a woman's charm.

Looking out over the Thames, across and towards the West End, he dragged the phone to the window for a better view and dialled Simon's number in Hereford. The phone was answered and he was put through almost immediately.

'Simon, I need a sample of slugs from your firing range. I---' He was harshly interrupted.

'The Armourer says that almost for sure the Tokarev is one of ours and---' It was now Kit's turn to interrupt.

'Sorry, not good enough, Simon, it must be a hundred per cent and what's more I need a selection of spent 9mm rounds from the range.'

'You're crazy. Have you any idea just how many tons of lead and copper there is out there on the range? Many thousands for sure! And why now 9mm'

'Later – but there won't be that many rounds from a 7.62 pistol, relatively speaking that is, so that should be easier. But I take the point. However, those thousands of rounds you talk about have been fired by relatively few weapons. But Simon, I'm not going to argue with you, I just want it doing, understand.'

'Kit, as good a friend as you are, I don't believe your rank or position give you the authority to order me to do anything,' Simon replied huffily.

'Oh, quite right,' Kit snapped back, 'but I'll get authorisation, believe me. Then half the department and network will get to know, not to mention leaks from some clown, and then the media. The world would love to know that we may have an SAS guy gallivanting about; brandishing stolen weapons, not to mention the probable shooting of his girlfriend, his Father's lover. Oh, yes they'd love it.'

He listened to Simon's laboured breathing; the atmosphere could be cut with a knife. Then he spoke.

'Is that what happened?'

'Yeah, perhaps.'

'So why do you want 9mm slugs as well?'

'You have a pistol missing, a Beretta – yes?'

After a pause, Simon spoke,

'Yes, we do, you know damned well we do.'

'Then I have an idea who's got it and I'm about to prove to you and others that it's been recently fired in the city of London.'

'What the hell! Are you serious?'

'As serious as I can be, so Simon, you'd better get those cowboy boots on and get digging!' There was no reply. Kit quietly replaced the receiver; Simon did not ring back.

There was a knock on the dividing door from Sue's office, when Kit called out in walked Sheeka looking pleased.

'One open computer,' she announced placing the laptop on his desk.

'I'm impressed,' Kit smiled at her. 'Anything in it? I mean anything immediately interesting?'

'More to the point, there's nothing on it, I mean no prints, not a single fingerprint. Not even a sign of one. It just looks as if it's been wiped clean.'

'Are you absolutely sure?'

'Perfectly sure, the report is here.' She leant forward and passed over a report to him.

'So, don't keep me in suspense, what is in there?'

'Phew, that's going to take a lot longer to go through. I thought I would just tell you the news. Anyway, among many other things he has downloaded some information on to it regarding the so-called 'Spy Site' up at Menwith Hill in Yorkshire. I only know that because it was, by date, the most recent. But it all looks mostly routine; I doubt he could get into anything sensitive anyway. He's created a file which looks more like something he was preparing for answering technical questions in the House.'

'Anything else?'

'Sure, there's loads; it's going to take time as I said. But there is just one thing. He does his banking through his computer – on line. He's with the Royal Bank of Scotland using their 'Royline' system in Windows of course.'

'Of course,' Kit nodded knowledgeably. 'And?'

'Well, I shouldn't have really as that was password protected too. But it might have been a front, so I opened it – after a bit of hassle, I have to say. I've no doubt it's coincidental but what was the date of the shooting in the apartment?'

Kit thought for a moment. 'The twenty-seventh of September, a Thursday I think.'

'Right, well on the twenty-fourth of September he drew £100,000 from the bank – money that had only just been cleared into his account. It had only just arrived. So why did he need the money, I ask? Had he by then bought the apartment? Or was it a short lease, is that what the money was used for? It's a big amount, although in these circles that in itself may not have been too unusual.

'It would then appear to have been wired on to another account, as there is no cheque number against the withdrawal, but you can see that the money has gone. I'm not familiar with the Royline codes but it does look like it's been wired, or maybe turned into cash.' As she spoke, Sheeka clicked on the logo and the blue screen of 'Royline on-line banking' came on screen. The Minister's account flashed up, with it Kit felt a twinge. He steadily flicked through the private pages. The only thing abnormal was the transaction of £100,000. A large amount yes, but not abnormal for some.

'The bank would have confirmed all this in

writing to him, as he would have to sign a document for it to happen. Or he could have used their special code system to send it direct from the computer, but they still send a receipt after the transaction. We need his file,' Sheeka said.

Kit frowned. The Minister himself would have all the paperwork, which would not be easy to get at. Suddenly the phone burst into unwelcome life. Sue informed Kit that it was Colonel Stewart on the phone from Hereford.

'That was quick,' he said a little more cheerfully.

'Have you quite finished?' then after a pause 'I thought you might be interested to know I've just had a request put forward by Charles Stevens and his oppo Riley for two week's leave, to include the four days that they're now enjoying. Technically they're not owed that much, but I can bring forward some of their next year's entitlement. What do you think?'

'Where's Stevens, back at Hereford?'

'No, he rang in, he hasn't been back since you purloined his computer. Which could all fit in rather well – give you more time to check it out and return it, eh?'

'Are you absolutely sure he was not there this morning?' Kit asked, thinking again of his epic duel with the Alfa.

'Of course, I am. There's just Riley coming and going, sick of kicking his heels, wanting to go and meet up with Stevens, then they're off to Magaluf, or somewhere equally ghastly, I suppose. Anyway, it'll give me more time to deal with your bloody request!'

For sure he and Sheeka needed more time. 'Ok, I agree, let em go.' Then the words came flooding back to him: **'Hold on – by letting go.'** Only time would tell.

More games. He smiled to himself. So where was young Stevens now? A holiday coming up must mean a change of clothes, more civvies, and that must mean home and Miranda's. He had to be in London.

'Something wrong?' Sheeka asked as he put the phone down.

'Not in the slightest.' He looked at Sheeka in silence for a moment.

'Yes?' she said questioningly.

'Well, young lady, do you fancy some action?'

'I'm not going to be a whore again, am I?'

'Again?'

She glared at him, hands on hips, her long fingers beating her hipbones like a drum in unison.

'No, Sheeka, I hope not. Is your passport up to date?'

'It's a standard requirement – of course it is.'

'I want you to get all your travelling things together, pack a suitcase for a trip, er, the Med area I would think so not too heavy and for not much more than two weeks. I don't yet know where to, in fact I imagine that you will have to find all that out for yourself. When you get there, you'll need a car, so take your driving licence, credit cards, a couple of surveillance bugs, a radio transmitter, camera, mobile phone, and a self-protection kit of goodies. I'll go through it all with you and sign it all out to you.' Then he faltered. 'Mm, you're not cleared to carry arms, are you?'

'I have all the training – passed everything,' Sheeka said, breathlessly trying to follow what he was saying. 'I have just never signed myself off with an instructor, that's all.'

'Then do it, for Christ's sake!' he said sharply. She moved nervously back from him. 'No, sorry for that,' he apologised for his abruptness. 'OK, I'll attend to it for you, I'll get you a light weapon, check you out and get you signed off. It's for your security only, though you must understand that I want you armed.'

'I just would like to know where and what I am supposed to be doing.'

'Oh, that's the easy part, Sheeka! You're going to shadow our Mr Charles Peregrine bloody Stevens.'

'When?'

'Now, right this very day.'

'That's great, but hang on, I don't even know what he looks like!'

'That is also a teeny problem cos neither do I, well not really, not in the flesh that is, but I have a pretty good idea and I know exactly where there is a picture of him.'

Kit of course actually knew where there had been two, but the one at the Minister's apartment – Miranda's picture – seemed to be the only one to get hold of relatively easily now. He continued, 'If you follow me later to the Minister's Penthouse at Chelsea, I'm sure I can get a photo out to you,' he said with a wink and a laugh.

'Then may I ask you, what you are going to do?'

'You may, I'm going after the Minister himself, try and unravel some of his affairs, but first I am going to pay our friend Tai Hock a visit.'

'Pervert!'

'Hopefully not. But for the moment Sheeka you and I have a little job to do. I need you to get some badged council overalls for yourself and two typical hard site hats, one for me and one for you, a clipboard to take notes and look official. Speak to Harold in the garage; we will need to use the Ford Transit van, the one registered to the Council and with their logo displayed.'

Sheeka efficiently scribbled all this down.

'Just give me a call when you're ready,' he said by way of dismissal; Sheeka left. When she was gone, he looked into his briefcase and removed a Swiss Army knife, one that had been modified for him many years before by a gun maker in Yorkshire. The man had removed the red plastic side covers and replaced the backing plates to the blades and accessories with thinner, stronger titanium; this would increase the strength and reduce the size. In addition, certain parts had been changed; the corkscrew for one was finer, sharper and of exceptionally hard tensile, an instrument, not necessarily for removing corks. He had used it many times for the retrieval of bullets. If a bullet was roughly dug out it could damage the rifling marks imprinted on the sides of the copper jacket of the round as it passed through the gun barrel, thus destroying vital evidence to match the gun's fingerprint. Kit had had the instrument made so he could twist the strengthened corkscrew into the soft lead at the rear of the bullet and withdraw it away cleanly.

Within half an hour Sheeka rang; all was ready.

Twenty-Two

As they drove down Park Lane Kit could not help thinking this was quite like old times, using a disguised van in the name of a council department, one that would have its registration changed once or more a week. It had gone on all through the years of the Cold War when there was continuous surveillance of Eastern Bloc diplomats and their embassies. It was a game. They watched us, changed their cars and vans, we watched them, one big party.

Sheeka still did not know where she was going as they entered Soho; it was only then that Kit spoke.

'Remember when we had dinner here at Topo Giggio restaurant and I mentioned that I thought that I'd been followed?'

'Er, yes I do.'

'Well I never said anything to you at the time, in fact to be honest I only thought about it later, but as we were talking and greeting each other I heard a sound, a sound that should have put me on immediate alert then, but it didn't. After all, surveillance of the Minister should have been so simple, there was little reason for me to think otherwise, especially here in London.'

'So, what was the sound?'

'Rather like wet wash leather slapping something. It sounded dull and heavy.'

'A silenced bullet?'

'Exactly.'

He pulled over to the kerb of Brewer Street, pointing in the direction of Rupert Street, the way he had walked that evening, he set the hazard warning lights going on the van – to the casual onlooker it all looked official.

'OK, here is where we start looking,' he said, putting on the white plastic protection helmet. 'Today we're playing council inspectors. I'm looking for any indentation, any hole, ricochet mark or splintering of wood. Don't get bored, it's going to take time.'

'Kit, do you seriously think that you were shot at, here in the streets of London? It just sounds incredible to me.'

'You're right, it does, but remember at the beginning of all this a girl was shot and killed. So, whoever it is isn't playing games. What's one more to them? It may be nothing but I just have to eliminate this nagging doubt I have.'

After an hour or so of peering closely at cement

rendering, brick, stone walls and window casings, Kit was beginning to have doubts. Maybe he was overreacting and Sheeka was right. There was no sign of anything and more to the point he noticed that there was no obvious firing position. Try as he might, he could not see where a man could take a shot without being seen by anyone. So maybe Sheeka was right, why would anyone want to take a pot shot at him anyway? Was it just paranoia on his part? He didn't constitute a threat so why at this stage would anyone want to take him out?

He was just about to turn away and go when he looked along and across the road for the last time, just able to make out a multi-storey car park set back at an angle. The man would not have followed him in a car as Kit had been on foot, but it was a position a gunman could have used to take a quick shot, elevated and there was ample cover, especially from the second floor. He went to investigate, leaving Sheeka to tap wooden window frames and make notes.

Once on the second floor he could look out onto the streets below. On investigation, there was a possible firing position, just one, although not a particularly good one – the angle was difficult and the timing would have been critical, the operator would have had to overtake Kit on the other side of the road and get into position, Kit would possibly have had to wait at the junction thereby creating time for the hit, it was a possibility. From where he now stood the backdrop was of the famous Chocolatiers 'Floris' shop painted in light pastel blue and gold but with a great deal of plate glass; it was a non-starter as they had looked it over earlier.

So less than hopeful Kit returned to Sheeka and once again they went over the externals of the shop, so much so that this time the manager came out to ask them if there was a problem.

'Rot.' Kit declared then, taking a gamble, 'the Company, er, Floris, has applied for a grant; it's a listed building and there's some rot, well apparently, there is.'

'Seems bloody silly to me, we've just had it painted,' the manager shrugged and walked effeminately back in to the premises.

'First step in the right direction,' Kit nodded to Sheeka. 'It's just been painted, so look harder, look for any filling work, a sunken putty hole or the like in the window frames and shop front.'

Sheeka immediately called him over. She had found one indentation but Kit could see it was an impossible angle to have come from the multi-storey and on closer inspection he could see it was a shallow hole. Casting his eyes toward the car park he walked back and drew an imaginary line to the window frame. There was no indentation but after a few minutes he found a soft area in the wood, his fingernail sank into the putty. Without further ado, he scraped off the new paint and removed the putty to reveal a ragged hole in the hard wood, one that had been recently sanded and filled. One they had missed earlier. It could have been a rotten knot filled by the painter, but it was worth investigation.

'Sheeka,' he called quietly. 'Have a look at this.' He pointed and scrabbled about in the putty-filled hole. He took out his modified knife and selected the slim 'corkscrew' designed for this very purpose. After poking around further he felt the metallic object he was looking for, about two and a half inches into the frame, about right for a low-velocity bullet. It seemed to have entered and stayed the correct way up, without having turned. Pushing hard and turning he could feel his corkscrew grip and bite; within minutes he was holding a copper-coated 9mm bullet. He unscrewed it and passed it to Sheeka for examination. The hardwood frame and the extraction had done little damage to the barrel 'print' on the bullet.

'I'm impressed. Very! I would never have believed it,' she exclaimed. 'Quite unbelievable.'

'Never doubt me,' he smiled, taking the bullet back and looking at it, holding it between his fingers.

Game on! he thought, some low-key surveillance! A 9mm bullet being whacked at him round Soho? From now on he too would be armed and alert. The moment he was back at The Block he would draw out his old weapons again.

With that they returned to Vauxhall, Kit with his bullet, Sheeka with her thoughts of what lay ahead. What was Charles Peregrine really like?

By six o'clock that evening Sheeka had got her personal items together, having been issued with more equipment than she thought she would ever need. To be on the safe side she had requested and been granted a small Heckler & Koch pistol, the one she had done the majority of her training with; she was very familiar with it, and liked it. With Kit's help, it would be her standard issue from now on.

In the meantime, Kit, had made contact twice, checking on her progress. 'For a woman to pack anything takes time,' he had said as the hours of preparation dragged on. But now she was ready and she found him, he was pacing the office irritably when she arrived.

'Nothing to do with you,' Sheeka he had muttered, 'but finding that bullet has made me step up a gear. I don't like being shot at, no not at all.'

On his desk were two pistols and several magazines Kit was checking the spring tensions and re loading, there were a number of other gadgets, which he had obviously been getting ready. Sheeka had never seen anything like it. She was fascinated.

'A collection from way back,' he commented, noticing her curiosity, 'mostly made exactly to my specifications it was a hobby as well as a job, we're all different, after all, and I don't like imperfections in my equipment.'

'Really,' she laughed.

He raised his eyebrows and changed the subject. 'Have you got your car sorted out?'

'The Rover, same as before, but he's bound to be flying so I'll leave it at some airport,' she replied.

'Good, I want you to give me a lift out to Chelsea, to the Minister's, well Miranda's. I'm banking on him still being at Westminster as I want to go unannounced and don't want to use the Jaguar again. When we get there. I will try to get you a photograph of Charles while you wait outside in your car. I want no contact between the two of us; somehow, I'll get the photo to you. Take a print of it please and make sure Sue gets it, she'll meet you anywhere.'

He slapped a full magazine into the grip of the larger of the two pistols, the copper and brass of the rounds easy to see, slotted it with practised ease into his shoulder holster and buttoned his jacket with a happy smile.

'It's just like coming home. OK, let's go a 'hunting.'

It was the first time she had seen him really happy; he had got his toys back and was a different man.

On their way to Chelsea Kit briefed Sheeka on how he thought the 'trail' of Charles would go, where she should start, how she should keep in touch.

He was to be so wrong.

On Kit's advice Sheeka chose a position in the car park between the other cars, but one from where she could still see the doors leading to the Minister's penthouse. Kit was just about to leave the Rover when to his surprise a strong handsome figure dressed in some sports jacket and tan trousers walked out through the glass doors of the penthouse building.

He was much bigger than Kit had expected and certainly different to the Minister, but as he now knew, that was no surprise. He had not met his real father, but if he was anything like his son he must be some man.

'We're in luck,' he said quietly. 'I believe we have Charles Stevens, no less. His photo doesn't do him justice, but that's him all right.'

'Gosh, he's handsome hulk, I won't forget what he looks like in a hurry!' Sheeka exclaimed.

'Who needs a bloody photo? I expected someone looking like a crook, an army thug.'

'Thugs can be good looking as well,' Kit replied as he watched Charles walk unaware and unconcerned across the car park.

'He doesn't look evil, troubled yes, but not evil.'

'Perhaps not, but what I can tell you is that some of the worst people don't. Does he look the jealous type? I always think that a good-looking man does not like to be let down, it hurts his pride, dents his ego. Don't forget that it was his supposed father who was with his girlfriend, well, under her actually. That's some humiliation, you must admit. He would certainly not have been amused.'

'Pissed off big time, I'd say,' Sheeka smiled impishly. 'Yes, he would be dangerous, look at his set jaw'

Kit nodded.

'According to his mother, she was his first real love, er, Charles's that is,' Kit chuckled.

'So maybe you're right, maybe he really was that jealous, not the best of circumstances to find your father in,' Sheeka murmured as Charles strode purposely out of sight down the ramp, out and on to the street.

'OK, Sheeka, this is where we part,' he said quickly. 'Follow Charles, he's all yours I'll take a taxi back. Keep in touch, ring me any time tonight.'

He watched Sheeka drive off down the ramp, in pursuit and into the evening, wondering what it would have in store for her. He had been going to pay a call on Miranda but now with the turn of events he decided not to, that pleasure he would save for another day. He waited in the shadows for a short while, and then walked down the same ramp and over the bridge as Charles had done earlier. Kit then stopped a taxi for the West End and Tai Hock. There was no sign of Sheeka or Charles.

Fate plays many tricks, had Kit turned left instead of right and walked deeper into the maize of Chelsea; he would have come across an unexpected sight.

Charles had walked away at a brisk pace and after several streets he had slowed as he unconcernedly passed number 14 in Harbour Street. His long stride faltered and eyes flashed guiltily for a cursory glance at the property, his head barely moved as he strode past and on, but move it did.

At the bottom of the street he turned right and nearly fell over a girl at knee height who was struggling to fit a tyre jack under a small Rover car, its front tyre flat. She was a pale blond, and looked up at him with an infectious, mischievous smile. She was too well dressed to be changing a tyre and making a mess of it at that. He could see that the car was quite likely to fall on her and was momentarily nonplussed by the situation.

Sheeka had quickly realised that to follow Charles at his walking pace was impossible and risky. He was after all not an amateur, but a skilled operator and would be bound to notice. If she left the car he would still probably spot her, as the streets were just not busy enough and she was not so naive to realise that she would not go unnoticed clicking along in high heels. So, she would take the bull by the horns; she would blow her cover.

Decision made, she drove past Charles and at the next turning, just out of sight, she leapt out of the car. With a biro, she instantly deflated a tyre through the valve. Working quickly as he was only some two or three hundred yards from her, she threw the jack under the car, purposely fitting it in an obviously incorrect and precarious position.

She then sat on her haunches, all thighs and white knickers but immaculate and looking bemused with her hands on the dirty jack and flat tyre; hoping to hell that Charles would arrive. She had not taken into account that if he did not, she herself was now immobile.

She cursed.

Twenty-Three

It was near dark when Kit's taxi dropped him off close to Marble Arch. He paid and walked off down Bayswater Road, past the Lancaster Gate Hotel counting the streets as he went. From memory, the house that Tai Hock had presumably leased was in the fifth street on the left, Hyde Park being on the right.

Once there he recognised the street and the trees. The old ivy-clad house, not unlike a nunnery, was set back behind high walls and from memory would be a further two hundred or so yards further down. Right on cue, he saw Brushmore Place through the gloom. This time he would ring the bell, which was illuminated in a small stone alcove situated in the high wall.

To one side of it were the tall wooden gates set in a stone arch, a small tradesman's door either side. He looked up at the watching camera, smiled to anyone viewing and pressed the bell, knowing that somewhere, in some office in the rambling house, he would be on screen. At the second attempt the speaker above him crackled in answer, demanding his business.

'Kit Martin for Mr Tai Hock,' he announced.

'Have you an appointment?' Came the curt reply. He replied to the voice that he did not believe he needed one. It was then pointed out curtly that Tai Hock would not see anyone unless by prior arrangement. 'Good night, sir.'

He quickly asked if Tai Hock was in residence, only to be told that it was none of his damned business. 'Good night, sir,' came again.

There was a click and the speaker went dead with a crackle. Kit continued to press the bell, but in vain as moments later its location light was switched off and he was left standing in the all-enveloping darkness at the entrance.

As his eyes adjusted, he walked down the street to where only days before he had entered the property. It all looked much the same, so with a short run and a jump he landed halfway up the wall, found a footing and maintaining his impetus he rolled out flat on the top, lying there watching, listening. His Beretta and shoulder holster dug into his ribs.

They probably already had him on camera and therefore knew he was there, so he swung off the wall and, landing softly, sprang to his feet and walked straight to the main door at the top of the short drive.

Knowing Tai as he did there would certainly be some form of security scanner if he gained access to the house, perhaps an airport-style metal detector fitted within the door frame. Or even some form of X-ray within a seat in Tai's inner sanctum. Either would show up his holster and gun on a miniature screen somewhere on Tai's desk. With this in mind he moved forward away from the camera above the door, and slipped his Beretta into one of the two earth-filled Ming-style vases that contained flowers either side of the entrance. He must not take chances because after all, he came in peace. But with his undoubted awareness for potential enemies Tai would be as alert as ever and would not take any chances.

Kit again began to ring the bell. Without warning the door was opened noisily and flung open so that it banged on its stop. At the same time, papers blew off an inside table by the door. Delaney stood there blinking at him in surprise, his mouth moving, his tongue flicking, but no sounds came out. Quickly recovering from his surprise at seeing Kit standing there, he realised that he would have to say something appropriate as there would undoubtedly be someone listening to the ensuing conversation.

He continued angrily.

'I just said Mr Hock is out. But now you're here, you can come in and wait whilst I phone the Police. We don't take kindly to trespassers, or burglars for that matter.'

'I'm neither, I just need to speak to Mr Tai Hock,' snapped a recalcitrant Kit.

'Without an appointment – impossible' was the curt reply.

Kit looked into the entrance hall. If this is what Streak and Sheeka saw, he could now understand Streak thinking that it was virtually unoccupied. It was so bare, no carpets, just a marble floor. In the centre was what looked like a large round sundial, set into the floor in brass or gold even? He could imagine that a sunbeam would light it up from the domed glass skylight above, or more sinister perhaps, a moonbeam on a clear night for some devilish ritual.

In an alcove across the hall sat a large gold Buddha, its distended tight belly glistening, either side of it a double door with gold handles. His eyes moved past the Buddha taking it all in. He had seen what he was looking for; one eye of the Buddha was just discernibly different. It was flat, not convex, as was the other, a camera for sure.

Quietly to the right of it, a door opened slowly and a figure dressed in a pale blue silk suit, with white collarless shirt emerged. His baldhead glistened and he was broad for his age; Kit imagined he was still quite fit. He took an instant dislike to his snakeskin shoes – as said Kit liked snakes.

'You are remarkably persistent, Mr Martin, annoyingly so.'

'I am glad you approve, Mr Hock.'

'You have trespassed, you are unwanted and I have it all on video. I could prosecute you. You are clumsy, Mr Martin.'

'I'm here to see you by politely knocking on your door. I'm not hiding anything,' Kit explained, coming fully into the entrance hall. The metal detector, if there was one, did not go off; Delaney looked on, not knowing what to do.

'Mr Martin, you have aroused my curiosity. Why do you want to see me so much?'

'I think we should talk about David Stevens, your friend the Minister.'

'Is that all? You disappoint me he is no friend of mine. How uninteresting, I thought you would do better than that, Mr Martin,' he murmured, turning as if to leave.

'The other night he came to see you, Mr Hock.'

Tai Hock continued to close the door.

'He was in the back of your limousine,' Kit went on quickly.

The closing of the door faltered and Tai Hock turned to look him full in the face.

'You are a nosey boy, aren't you, Mr Martin. Or do you prefer Kit,' he snarled sarcastically.

'Do you prefer Tiger, or Tai?'

'I am both, of course.' A sickly smile trickled over his tight yellow face.

'Tigers are becoming extinct, people seem to shoot them.'

'Have you come just to annoy me?' he continued.

'You tell me the Minister is not a friend of yours, yet you let him ride in your car, you don't deny that?'

Tai Hock walked further into the room, leaving the door open behind him.

'Please come in, Kit, and close the door after you.'

Delaney stood there watching him go in, his face expressionless. Kit wondered if they had had the wit to bug the place – probably not, which in turn meant that any conversation that he had regarding the Minister would be reasonably confidential.

'So, what is your relationship?' Kit asked casually.

'You have no right to question me, I've done nothing wrong. I am not even a British citizen.'

Suddenly Kit thought of the tape that Sheeka had brought him; Streak's testimony to her sexual oblivion at the hands of Tai Hock and others.

'I would have thought the procurement of prostitutes and the administering of drugs against their will was indictable in most countries, wouldn't you?'

Tai Hock was visibly shocked; his face blanched. But he countered the accusation with an immediate denial and bodily expressions of horror. Once he had him on the run Kit continued. 'I could promise you fifteen years at least, for possession. Then of course there's administering drugs to another person without consent, probably more. You would spend the rest of your miserable life in prison. Especially if I did a deal with the Judge,' he continued, enjoying the effect it was having.

Tai exploded, 'Impossible, I---'

'Not impossible, only a few nights ago,' Kit quickly interrupted, 'you had two girls here; one left, sick. The other stayed, drugged by you, for your own seedy, carnal desires. He threw a cassette on the table. 'Would you like to listen to her experiences?'

Tai glowered back at him.

Kit continued.

'You're a frustrated old man suffering from rampant impotence and with an enlarged penis to fend off the feared day, hardly enough strength left to lift it. An operation, was it? That's sad and no doubt bought by blood money. I might also point out that it is attractive to no one but to you and your failing ego. No, Tai, it will provide interesting evidence. I think your manipulations and corruption; your arms dealing days are thankfully over. The boys will love you in prison'

Tai Hock did not speak which annoyed Kit. He knew that he must not give him time to consider his predicament.

'Of course, if you tell me about the Minister, you can keep the tape,' he said, pushing it a little nearer.

'You will have a copy,' Tai countered quickly.

'I do, but it could also be yours.'

'Why should I trust you? You have just invaded my life for no reason.'

'Every reason, but better to trust me than the alternative?'

There was a long pause in which Tai Hock looked decidedly uneasy; one of the few times in his life when he did not hold all the cards.

'I approached Hawker Siddley to buy their Hawk jet trainers for a customer in the East; sixteen of them actually. Hawkers in turn had to apply for an export licence. As usual your government prevaricated and I was getting no clear signal as to whether they would allow it or not. So, I approached your Minister, and I understand he has been lobbying on my behalf or so he says, I often wonder if the request ever left his desk.'

First standing then pacing back and forth behind the desk, a smile came across Hock's inscrutable oriental face, the skin like old parchment, tight and yellow, the type you would see on an old table lamp.

'But of course, we all have little tricks to play, Mr Martin, and you are not on your own. We are in a way in the same business.'

Kit did not comment.

With that Tai Hock bent and opened a small drawer in his desk. His hand flicked out, holding what looked like photographs, most of which he scattered across the desk in front of Kit.

'The last time I spoke to your friend the Minister,' growled Tai, 'I asked him how things were going, in the matter of my request for an export licence. He huffed and puffed, prevaricated as normal saying 'just at the moment it's impossible', and after all I have, er, given him. He complained that his 'hands are tied', or so he said and as you can see indeed they were!'

Kit looked down unhappily at the photos.

Several were obviously of the Minister, naked and tied by ankles and wrists to a bed, not dissimilar to the one in the mews. The Minister obviously had a certain proclivity for bondage.

Kit instantly recognised the girl, it was Verkuska, in all her naked glory. She straddled him, her head thrown back in ecstasy, mock or otherwise, whilst holding her extended nipples towards him.

He looked back at the photograph of the Minister tied under her, unfortunately God had not been generous with his manhood.

'I, er, introduced them so to speak, she needed a passport and I just knew he would want to help,' Tai gave a sickly grin. He had an even set of teeth but with pointed tips, and curiously yellow, like cut turnip set in an oriental dish.

'She was one of my girls if you know what I mean. So, Mr Martin, we both now have a little something to trade.'

'Does he know you took these?'

'I think he may now have a general idea,' Tai Hock chuckled. 'The man's a self-opinionated fool.'

'You are of the worst kind Hock, you are just a common blackmailing crook.

'Blackmail is common word Mr Martin it does not cover or match my intelligence – the wistful intrigue of which I can bring to bear.'

Kit, let it drop there was no point in the argument he was not yet one hundred percent sure.

'Did she get her passport?' Kit knew the answer.

'A passport? As she was his passport to happiness, I am sure she did or will. What a naughty boy.'

'Or will'. The word 'will' sent alarms flashing through Kit's mind. It was either a red herring thrown in to deceive, or Tai genuinely did not yet know of her demise. He studied him keenly. Tai Hock's inscrutable expression gave nothing away. 'When things were becoming difficult between us, he knew I might be a little indiscreet if he did not deliver and I needed to apply a little pressure.'

'Then why are you telling me all this?'

'The other evening the stupid man asked me to send a car for him, which I did, willingly. I was at last expecting some good news. As you now know he was interrupting my evening however, after sharing my hospitality yet again and with his enjoyment once more satiated, he had the temerity to tell me as pompously as ever, that after all this time the Government would not sanction my request for an aircraft sales agreement. He made some excuse that they had intelligence information that the country in question no longer used their Hawks for training as per the previous sales agreement, but instead had their existing aircraft converted to carry weapons for warlike purposes, keeping down the rebels I was told.

Mr Martin as far as I am concerned I have finished with the man, that is why I tell you. I say again'! His voice raised 'Yes, I have finished with him.'

'Even I can understand that you are annoyed, blunted in your evil world. But why did you tell me just now of the passport? You had no need.'

'Ah yes, your natural Caucasian curiosity of the Oriental mind does you some justice Mr Martin. Quite simple, just so that you know, so there is no mistake, I intend to inform your Prime Minister, anonymously of course, of the procurement of a British passport for an illegal immigrant and who was at the time used as a mistress by a minister.'

'You're an evil bastard.'

'You're quite right, on the second count anyway. I never met either of my parents, never will, never can. That, Mr Public School Martin, is what has given me the edge, the lead in life. That is why I am extremely wealthy and intend to become even more so.' His yellow teeth flashed again. 'I am, after all, a businessman. Our Mr David Stevens will be forced to resign and soon, as he is of no further use to me, a hindrance, in fact he now stands in the way of my progress.' After a pause for thought he continued. 'Our Minister Stevens will naturally be replaced and of course I know 'who' that man will be. I have already had a word. His financial and bodily needs are conveniently even greater than those of Stevens. It's all quite marvellous really – he's just waiting for the call and so the world turns. Mr Martin, I will get my aircraft'

'And the photos?'

'Oh, just an insurance in case he wriggled, on the first count, so to speak. I like them well hooked' he chuckled

'And the girl?'

'Oh no, Mr Martin, I was the provider so to

speak and that's his affair now, I never go back on my word. Do you?'

Kit rose and turned to the door, at the same time trying to contain his anger, both at Tai Hock's arrogant manipulation of people in high places and, of the Minister for his stupidity and greed.

He swung open the double doors and strode out into the entrance hall. Delaney was standing lamely by the main door.

'Good night, Mr Martin, I do hope that we meet again, when, er, your manners have improved.'

'I'm sure we'll meet again,' Kit mused.

Delaney held open the door with a quizzical expression on his face. Kit deftly retrieved the Beretta out of the Ming vase, checked it had not been tampered with and slotted it back inside his jacket, walked down the stone steps onto the gravel and out into the night.

As soon as Kit got back, he immediately tried to contact Sheeka, but to no avail. He had been asleep for over an hour when the phone rudely shook him out of his now much needed slumber. On the other end of the line was a very positive and excited Sheeka.

'You were asleep, how can you!' she exclaimed. 'Do you want to hear this?' she gasped with obvious elation.

'I was, and I do,' he mumbled, full consciousness returning.

'I've just had dinner with Charles Stevens.'

Kit shot up in bed and blinked at the wall; for a second he thought it was some sort of peculiar dream.

'You've what?' he roared, incredulous at her statement.

'I've just had dinner with Charles Stevens.' Sheeka then proceeded to tell him how she had feigned a flat tyre by jamming a biro into the valve and then looking a complete prat squatting on the pavement with the jack in her hand. Charles Stevens had virtually fallen over her as he rounded the corner in full stride, tweed jacket open and flapping. How she could see his eyes nearly popping out of his head as he saw her, dressed to kill, all thigh, knickers and silk, trying unsuccessfully it seemed to change a wheel.

His offer of help had been gratefully accepted and she had stood beside him engaging him in intelligent conversation whilst he changed the wheel.

She explained that she was very late seeing a friend at the Canteen Restaurant which she'd never been to before but 'It's somewhere around here.' She had said looking around vaguely.

Charles had replied that he knew exactly where it was; pointing out that it was also very good. Being close to his parents' home he'd often eaten there when he was 'at home'.

'At home?' she'd said questioningly.

He went on to explain that he was in the Army but his parents – here he had faltered, nearly saying something else, she thought, but he'd continued by just saying, 'Live here,' his voice she thought perhaps trailing away just a fraction, as if some distant thought had kicked in.

He had swiftly changed the wheel for her and as he finished he had asked if he could show her the way to the restaurant, adding that if she drove, he could direct her. She had readily accepted the offer.

As they had approached the restaurant which overlooked the harbour, he asked if he could escort her to the bar area to see if her friend had arrived. Once again, she had accepted. It was obvious he was a gentleman and it would have been a long wait for her fictitious friend. What was more she had found that she liked him, she really did. He was handsome, dressed from a different age and was a complete charmer, a gentleman, all very refreshing.

Embarrassingly they had waited at the bar for some twenty minutes before she had plucked up feigned courage and had said that it was now doubtful if her friend waited. She was after all now over an hour late. To compensate for this disappointment, he had offered her dinner; 'A shame to waste the experience,' he had said, very persuasively. She had accepted.

'So much for undercover surveillance,' Kit pointed out.

'Don't damn me yet,' Sheeka defended herself. 'Think about it, there was no way that I could follow him, either in a car or on foot without getting noticed.' She continued unabated, with little time to draw breath. 'Anyway, we had a fabulous meal and he really is very nice, believe me, you must.'

'I wonder if his other girlfriend thought that,' Kit said, with a twinge of jealousy running through him.

'I don't think he's that type, the type to kill someone.' Argued Sheeka

'Neither did she, I'll bet,' Kit commented wryly.

Sheeka warmed to her task, once more pointing out that 'Today is Wednesday and apparently, he has some leave. He's going away with his pal Riley over the weekend just for a few days. But more to the point, I'm seeing him tomorrow for lunch! Beat that.'

Kit felt like asking her to the hotel to discuss things then and there, but her comprehensive report over the phone made this unnecessary. Her sudden soft spot for Charles Stevens had also deflated him somewhat. She needed time to cool off.

'Don't get smitten by our quarry,' he warned. 'You must be careful, try to record or remember everything that's said or happens and we'll then see if he's spinning you a yarn.'

'He's not spinning anything; he's just a very straight, county guy. Even though he is in the Army.'

Kit suddenly felt more tired than ever and decided to end the conversation. They would meet in the morning by which time he would be able to think more clearly.

So, with these thoughts he cut her off in full flow, apologising for doing so and asking to see her at ten in the morning.

'Get some sleep,' he ordered wearily, 'you're going to need it. And more to the point, I need to think.' He had a feeling that things were now going to happen and, rather fast.

His instincts were rarely wrong.

The following morning Kit's arrival at the office was greeted by the delivery of a large and somewhat grubby box full of spent bullets, all in varying degrees of damage. At a glance, they all appeared to be 9mm. He took the bullet from his top pocket, wrapped in a white handkerchief where it had been since its discovery in Soho.

Placing it in an envelope he passed the whole lot through to Sue who would send everything immediately to Forensic. He then opened the letter, which had been Selotaped to the soiled box and read its contents, smiling.

Before the meeting with Sheeka he urgently needed to see Sir Edward. His sleepless night had born fruit. The next step forward would be painful for one or two people and he needed the go-ahead from on high.

Luckily Sir Edward was available and would see him straight away. Kit knew that he was going under false pretences, as Sir Edward would be expecting news, which he was not going to divulge. Sue would have to delay Sheeka, but not for long as he knew the meeting would be short.

'What would you say, sir, if I asked permission to view the Minister's bank account?' The look on Sir Edward's face was one of disbelief.

'I would be most unhappy! But why, for God's sake?'

'What would you say if I said I was suspicious of Tai Hock's relationship with our Minister. How would you feel if I told you he may well have been bribed? I also believe he may have been indulging in certain sexual activities all part of the bribe and that a considerable amount of money may have been involved.'

'What an earth have we got ourselves into Kit,

we only started looking at him to see if he was having an affair.'

'Some days ago, sir, you said, 'Find one and you may find them all.' I now believe you could be right. I don't want an official enquiry yet, just the bank statements, and correspondence with his bank for the last, say, six weeks?'

'I ask you, how can I do that? Anyway, he is a friend of mine, well was.'

'So? This is an enquiry. You can, sir, you've done it before, on the QT.'

'I have?'

'You have.' Sir Edward looked decidedly uncomfortable. 'Just a statement or two and any relevant correspondence, that's all I need.' Sir Edward's expression changed and Kit immediately sensed that he was going to be refused. 'Sir,' he said quickly, 'would you as a compromise, ask your contact if there has been any large, or unusual amounts of money deposited by Stevens recently, where and why.'

'Hardly likely to have it sat in a UK bank, is he?'

Kit thought of the £100,000 that had appeared on the Minister's laptop when they opened his account with the Royal Bank of Scotland's on-line banking service. It was evidence, but not enough.

'Well, any movements of money then?'

The silences in that room were always daunting, and today was no exception. Then it came.

'It is illegal and immoral,' Sir Edward complained, getting on his high horse.

'I could only do it by going through the proper channels and I'm hardly likely to compromise my friendship with the Governor of the Bank of England or any other banking colleague for that matter. Clubs are clubs, Kit, and there are certain standards one must stick to. I don't like it.'

'I think, sir, you may like it even less if we don't catch this falling star, so to speak.'

'The Minister is a falling star?' Sir Edward looked at him quizzically, annoyed at his analogy. 'Is that all?'

'No, as a last resort I would like permission to search his home.'

'For?'

'One of the same.'

'It's most unlike you to ask.'

'But as you keep telling me, he's a friend of yours, sir.' Kit saw that it hurt.

'I will pretend that I did not hear that.' Then after a pause, 'let me know what you find straight away, no games please, Kit.'

The meeting had been tense, but he'd expected it to be. On returning to his office he immediately rang Miranda, the Minister's wife. She was delighted to hear from him and even more delighted for his repeat offer of lunch at Harrods. She would be there a 1 p.m. on the dot.

Sheeka meanwhile was waiting to see Kit and was quite miffed when he just said.

'See you later in the day and don't let him take you to Harrods for lunch.' He was sorry to cut Sheeka short, but the truth was he just did not have the time.

'Why not?' Came the stubborn reply.

'Because I'm taking his mother there!'

Her eyes opened wide as Kit smiled from ear to ear. Sheeka shook her head, incredulous, as Sue smiled too, but unlike Sheeka knowing that there would be a very good reason.

Twenty-Four

Kit had to pull out all the stops to arrive at Chelsea Harbour before the time he estimated that Miranda would leave the penthouse. He parked the Jaguar in a side street and then approached on foot. At about 12.15 he watched Miranda leave the building and climb into a waiting taxi.

He walked quickly from his cover and approached the high-rise apartments, hoping by now that Charles her son would also have left for his lunch date with Sheeka. A clear playing field that's what he liked.

Before entering the foyer, he checked through the glass that the lifts were vacant, nothing moving, no numbers flickering. The last thing he wanted to do was arrive inside the foyer just as a lift opened and Charles Stevens or Miranda came out.

Everything seemed quiet. Normally he would go to the floor above and walk down to the apartment in question, making certain that the floor was empty, but the penthouse being the top one made this impossible. The lift whisked him skyward, the doors opened with a hiss and the corridor was clear, he breathed easy. By the door, he slipped on a pair of ultra-thin chamois leather gloves and listened intently; there was not a sound from within. The lock wasn't easy, but moments later he was standing in the hallway breathing slowly. There was no sign or sound of life, just a reminder, the tantalising scent of her perfume.

The last time he'd been there he'd noticed that on entering the premises Miranda had not turned an alarm system off, nor had he been able to detect any signs of one. However, just in case there was an alarm system using the phone line as a relay, he immediately took the receiver off the hook.

The rooms were just as he remembered them, modern and immaculate with lots of light streaming in. He made swiftly for where the Minister's study was; a small room next to the lounge, which also looked out across the Harbour. Quite stunning views, if he'd had time to enjoy them, with the backdrop of London. High above aircraft criss-crossed in the traffic-laden sky.

The Minister's inlaid rosewood desk stood proudly taking up the major part of the room. The walls were lined with impressive leather-bound volumes indicating an educated man.

He quickly sifted through the drawers and

trays but could not find what he was looking for. Exasperated, he went into the lounge and checked a writing bureau that was in an alcove bedecked with flowers, but still to no avail.

Time was short, the clock was ticking and there was always the chance he could set off an alarm he had not yet noticed. At that very moment some helmeted security organisation might be beating their way to the door.

Desperate for a result, he set off towards the bedroom to look for a safe. 'They always seem to be in bedrooms,' he muttered to himself. As he crossed the room, he glanced at the open door and noticed a briefcase in the hallway which he had not noticed before, as it was half hidden by a table. Instinctively he knew.

It was quite heavy so he placed it on the polished table that had so nearly hidden it. Predictably it was locked, which to him caused a delay of about three seconds. It was full of papers, fit to burst, but more to the point, he soon found some letters from Barclays, which he read as quickly as possible. One of them was particularly interesting, although not what he had expected. There were no statements, just the bank's letters of acknowledgement.

A few weeks earlier it appeared the bank had sold some £100,000 worth of shares for him, the letter now in Kit's hand confirmed that the money had been credited to the Minister's account, at the same time offering financial advice regarding reinvestment if he needed it. But a later letter confirmed the sending of the money by them to another bank account, which was only referred to as an account number and bank sort code – 'As per your instructions of your letter dated ----'. Kit photographed both letters twice with a Minox 3c and replaced them, locked the case and placed it back on the floor just as it had been.

There had been no evidence of documentation regarding Tai Hock. But where had he sent the £100,000? It was a large sum of money.

He glanced at his watch, nearly 1.0 pm, time to ring the Oyster Bar at Harrods and to apologise to Miranda for the unavoidable delay! 'Oh, how embarrassing, the traffic---'

Just as he was about to leave he looked across into the kitchen, to the other side of the breakfast bar, where there was a stylish tapestry stretched across a board on the wall. Upon it and held by coloured pins were the many social invitations and events befitting a minister and his wife of their standing. Along the bottom, in brass was a row of hooks on which to hang keys, one of which had an Alfa Romeo key fob dangling from it, the red cross on white background with serpent insignia plain to see; the Alfa badge designed in 1910 by Signor Merosi, 'The cross of Milan and a four-fold snake of the Visconti family.' On closer inspection, there were two keys, both identical, one of which Kit removed and placed in his pocket.

So, is Charles not using the car today? He asked himself. Being a classic, it was perhaps not ideal for everyday use and he remembered that Miranda had told him that he didn't always use it.

Before he opened the door into the corridor he placed his ear against it and listened, but there was no sound, no lift wending its way up to meet him.

Quickly across the corridor and once in the lift, he hesitated as he read the list of floors, then Basement, Garage, etc. He pressed Garage.

Like all basement parking areas. It was poorly lit but within a minute he had located what he was looking for: 'Penthouse Parking'. In the four white-lined spaces were two cars, a new Toyota Celica, Miranda's, and a yellow Alfa Romeo Spider. He approached the Alfa, somehow in awe of the little car, which sat there like a shrine to some previous involvement, identical it seemed to the one that had chased and very much like the one he had seen a few days before here in the street close to Verkuska's. If only it could speak.

Once again, his mind was thinking of alarms. But these keys along with the other one left in the Penthouse were the only two keys; there was no separate alarm key. The lock clicked and the button popped up, no alarms sounded.

To his surprise the car felt warm and indeed when he turned the ignition on to check, the temperature registered halfway along the gauge. The interior was clean and tidy, just as he had anticipated. If Charles had done all the reconditioning, he had done a very good job.

He sat there for a moment contemplating, then feverishly started to search the car, but the glove compartment, ashtray and door pockets revealed nothing of interest. Before getting out to check the boot he put his hand under the seat. There was very little space as the seat was virtually on the floor pan, but his hand froze and his heart missed a beat.

He knew exactly what the familiar object was, instantly recognising the sinister shape of metal as he pulled out a black Beretta 9mm pistol from underneath the seat. It was loaded and had been modified to take a silencer, as had the Tokarev. Unloading it, he carefully wrapped it in a yellow duster, which he took from the glove compartment. Feeling again under the seat he resignedly removed an open box of latex surgical gloves. Only a few individually packaged pairs remained.

Sheeka meanwhile was once again enjoying the company of Charles Stevens. He had chosen for lunch a restaurant very much to her liking, San Lorenzo in Beauchamp Place. It wasn't easy for her, but she was aware of her responsibility and was committed to probe for snippets of information. Yet, try as she did, she soon realised he was no fool as he gave nothing away.

Charles was obviously a 'very aware' man, saying nothing without giving it thought. His speech was not deliberate but he obviously preferred fact to tittle-tattle, which Sheeka rather admired. In some ways, he reminded her of Kit himself, preferring a corner table, liking good wine, game and seafood and even reading the same daily paper. He told her he thought he was too young for the gentlemen's clubs in London, but maybe some time in the future. Her assessment of him was that he was a proud man, a true Englishman in the full sense of the word, enjoying the old Establishment and remnants of colonialism. He had thought of the Foreign Office for the future, or after his time in the Army some form of intelligence involvement, perhaps MI5 or MI6, he'd said.

Sheeka had been surprised at this revelation, as he appeared so honest, so open and uncomplicated with her. Yet here she was in the Service and undercover, searching for any clue to his possible involvement.

She felt a real heal for what she was doing,

but remembered Kit's words: 'Don't get smitten by your quarry.'

He could be right, maybe all this from Charles Peregrine Stevens was a carefully thought-out smoke screen. He was very deliberate and more than capable of it.

Charles for his part could not believe his luck – virtually stumbling over this gorgeous girl in a street and what's more being able to take her out for dinner and then again for lunch. She was amazingly attractive, yet she seemed to know little of her ancestry; she was an only daughter, brought up in a small country village, by strict parents, in Cornwall.

Interestingly for Charles, her father had been at the Foreign Office and had wanted a son. She described her mother to him as a village socialite, from bridge to bring & buy. And she too would have preferred a son. So, was Sheeka a tomboy? She'd seemed interested enough when he talked of guns, calling them 'a necessary evil'. In fact, her knowledge had surprised him.

When the conversation had drifted into country life, she hadn't complained about game shooting 'Providing one doesn't abuse it' she had said and her knowledge was intelligent in her country observations.

Yet for all that, he felt she was much too

inquisitive for his liking, her questions being too probing – as if she had some inner knowledge of him, even for an intuitive woman. So, although he appreciated her interest in his present employment, he was on his guard. But his new commanding officer had always said, 'Say as little as possible, people and the media will always be curious as to your position and what you have achieved in life.'

He found that he was in an awkward position, for he was rapidly becoming infatuated with her. Yet for him it was all coming at the wrong time; he was not prepared. His life was the military. So, who is prepared when it happens? He wondered, and on top of all this he was supposed to be going away for a few days with 'Wiley' Riley which he'd been looking forward to for some time. He needed the break.

There had been considerable problems with his adopted father and, now to crown everything his real father had come to light. Would she wait for him? Hell, why should he even think like this, he had only just met her? But as far as he knew she was unattached, and had only just come up to London, she had said. However, in this city she would soon be snapped up if he let her out of his sight.

A plan now started to form in his mind. He already had leave granted, so would cancel going away with 'Wiley' Riley and take Sheeka instead

– a far better idea – that is if she would go. He'd take her out into the country, go North for the weekend, separate rooms of course, separate hotels if necessary – but in the same village, his father's village? Why not? The countryside there was spectacular. Better still if he dared to take her to see his real father she would be impressed. But what if his father didn't like the idea so soon? Well so be it; next stop would be Paris. He must make sure that she had her passport. He would suggest it all when the moment was right.

But the sooner the better.

Twenty-Five

To protect against possible prints Kit carefully placed the gun in the outer packet, the one that had previously contained the latex gloves he then put the unused packets back under the seat. He locked the Alfa Romeo but kept the key; it was too risky now to go back to the penthouse. He was also very short of time. Miranda would be waiting, hungry, but for what? He smiled to himself.

As fast as he could, he now made straight for Harrods and his lunch date. He was very late, but was hopeful that he'd be able to talk her round.

Once at Harrods he parked the Jaguar at the rear on the yellows and scribbled a note that said 'Garage Aware' which he put under the wipers. He would only be gone for a few minutes anyway, as now he owed Miranda a far better lunch. It would be at his old favourite 'Kaspia's' at Bruton Place came to mind.

Once at the Oyster Bar on the ground floor of Harrods he looked around, but there was no Miranda. He cursed silently, he was not all that late. The manager suddenly noticed him and took out a lilac-coloured envelope from under the bar, which he handed to Kit; it was sealed and smelt of perfume. He opened it and read:

12.55
Sorry, have to cancel our date. David rang me on the way here; he needs to speak to me urgently, damn! So, can't stop. Call me.

Love Miranda
XXX

As much as he would have liked to see her again, nothing was lost, he decided. He had achieved everything he needed to, but what did David want!

Back at The Block, Vauxhall he immediately sent the Beretta to Forensic, for a fingerprint check, and also to have it fired into a snail drum receiver so that the bullet could be retrieved and the marks could then be checked against the one he'd found in Soho, plus the ones which he had sent from Hereford, some of them might match. He gave instructions that he wanted to know immediately they had any news, and that meant 'in the next hour'.

His next call was to the estate agent who had sold the mews apartment to the Minister. Predictably he was out showing property, but the secretary would make sure he called immediately on his return.

He called Sue, asked her politely for a coffee and threw her the tiny Minox film he had used at the penthouse, adding, 'I need these developing as soon as possible – like now!'

Four coffees later and almost exactly one hour later the phone rang. After being put through a slow and toneless voice from Forensic informed him that there were no prints on the gun, nothing. As for the bullet, they would need a little longer, that was if it were to be challenged in court by an independent expert. But as far as he was concerned, at the moment it was certainly a match. At a glance, several of the others in the cardboard box also were too, but he would need much more time.

Just as Kit was about to put the phone down, the voice droned on, 'One other thing, the gun and the lap top computer you sent down, are they both related in this case?'

Kit said that they probably were and there had then been a moment's pause. He could hear the man breathing at the other end. The 'voice' started again, 'It's just that if you asked me, in my opinion that is, I would say that they have both been cleaned in the same way and with the same cleaner, something like Johnson's 'Mr Sheen' spray polish, oh and with a yellow duster, in fact I am sure that was what was used.'

Kit scribbled down what he had said and thanked him for being so prompt. When he put the phone down he called through to Sue to send the man a bottle of whisky. 'I think that's his tipple.'

Sue called back that there was a call holding on line two; a firm of estate agents from Knightsbridge.

He took the call, only to find out that the Minister had not actually bought the mews property, but had agreed only to rent it for a year, with an option to buy at a later date. Dead end!

So, what had he spent £100,000 on? Maybe it was just a normal transaction, just moving his investments round?

He cursed at not having written down the account and sort code numbers from the Minister's bank letters rather than have to wait for the film. He was just about to call through to Sue again when she walked in and gave him the photographs of the bank letters, a relief which solved that particular problem, but would the bank now give him the name of the account to where the money went? If not, it was a job for Sir Edward. Probably a reluctant Sir Edward.

One thing that niggled him was why the gun and computer had been so meticulously cleaned and yet left where they were, it did not make sense.

Twenty-Six

The evidence stacking up against Charles Stevens was now considerable and Kit started dictating a report for Sue to type out later. After he had recorded all the facts on tape he replayed it; it did not look good for Charles, not good at all. He made an appointment to see Sir Edward the following morning at 11.30 a.m., Friday.

There was a knock on the door, which he did not answer but instead picked up the phone to ask Sue who the hell it was and why she had not fore warned him?

'Er, it's Sheeka,' was the reply, as if that explained everything, which it did. In she walked, perhaps a little nervous, but smiling and as happy as ever, or so it seemed.

'So, the wanderer returns,' Kit gave her a big smile to reassure her.

'Yes, a lovely lunch at San Lorenzo and about fifty yards from the bloody agency in Beauchamp Place! I nearly died. Anyway, guess where I'm going next, that is, if you agree,' she said swinging her hips. He looked quizzically at her in silence, waiting for her to continue.

'OK then, I'm off to see his bloody father!' she exclaimed. 'Well he wants me to go off into the country for a short break and possibly see flipping Lord Strutt, no less. That's going to be just great, isn't it?'

'A quick worker and no you can't go, I forbid it Sheeka. He'll recognise you straight away; your cover will be blown so far away you won't have any.'

'I could dye my hair black and wear---' She said jokingly but never allowed to finish.

'Don't be so bloody stupid.' He cut her short.

Her eyes flashed back at him. She could see he was a little annoyed, as indeed he was – miffed by her obvious liking for Charles, and for the unusual manner of her surveillance of him. The way that she had achieved it was all very irregular and of her own volition. But it was working and maybe it was that that irked him most. She thought like he.

'But seriously, there is a way,' she went on. 'When I visited Gouthwaite, Lord Strutt told me that he and Sir Edward,' she cast her eyes to the ceiling and to the offices above as if heavenwards, which in a way it was. 'He said they were good friends, indeed 'Sir Edward has shot here,' he told me. So, if Sir Edward could speak to him and warn His Grace that I was accompanying his son, perhaps we could get away with it.'

'I'm not too sure their new-found father and son relationship could cope with this sort of thing. If and when it all comes to light Charles would never trust his father again – he's probably barely forgiven him for the last twenty-odd years of silence. We'll think about it, I don't want to be too hasty; there are too many people involved. What else happened?'

She was disappointed that her idea was pushed to one side however she could bide her time, she continued.

'Well, for the record, I still don't think he's our man, but that said I'm certainly not as sure as I was! He's very possessive, bordering on being jealous. We've only just met and you get this strong feeling of dominance and possessiveness from him. I think if it became a relationship like the one he had with Verkuska, there could be real problems.'

'Could he kill someone?'

'Of course, he could, he's trained to. I also think that deep down he could be highly volatile a time bomb, yet he does not appear irresponsible. A very difficult mix to describe'

Kit said nothing but just looked at her thoughtfully.

'More interestingly,' she continued, 'I met his

pal 'Wiley' Riley with him here in London – he joined us for a coffee after the meal. Now there's a character, just as complex but noticeably jealous of Charles's upbringing, for sure has a chip on his shoulder about Charles's money, his obvious class, his accent and what have you. I just can't imagine what Riley will feel when he finds out that his best mate's proper father is a real live Lord, complete with a stately home in Yorkshire. He'll explode. It's a shame as he's a great guy, typical Army though and a bit rough round the edges. He comes from Liverpool so he's had a pretty tough upbringing. Full of blarney, he should have been called O'Reilly; well, he probably was years ago, He's annoyed with Charles too, for cancelling their trip abroad. So, he's sworn to go off on his own, there was actually quite an undercurrent'

Kit let out a big sigh as he looked at Sheeka.

'You know, Sheeka, it would have been far better if you had not got involved. If you hadn't, you could now have gone after them both to see what they get up to on their trip, which was my original intention,' he muttered unhappily.

Sheeka said nothing, as she couldn't disagree with him.

There was no point in belabouring the point, what was done was done. Kit became serious and broke the news to her of how he had found the gun and latex gloves in Charles's Alfa Romeo. She was quite shocked and her face visibly dropped. She pursed her lips as if to whistle and exhaled.

'I just can't believe it,' she exclaimed. 'He seems so straight and correct.'

'Those are the worst kind. You said earlier that he was possessive and could be a jealous type, even volatile you said and we both agreed that he could kill.'

'Without a doubt, I can't argue with that. He's certainly a strong character and I've not yet decided how I'll handle him.'

'There is one odd thing, well two really,' Kit pronounced, 'and that is that both the gun and the computer have been wiped absolutely clean, there are no prints; any thoughts?'

It was now Sheeka's turn to be quiet and to think. When she answered, she spoke slowly, 'Only if someone was trying to set Charles up would they have wiped everything clean so that when Charles touched these items, his would be the only prints on them.'

'But if this someone put the gun under his seat, Charles would hardly go looking for it, would he?' pointed out Kit

'Good point, but it depends on what game the other person is playing – one phone call and –'

Kit had to agree, but it worried him that Sheeka continually tried to justify or support Charles. She seemed to be taking his side in the whole business, when as far as he was concerned there was already enough evidence to arrest Charles, which in his opinion is exactly what they should be doing. Put him under pressure and see what might transpire; get some answers come what may, before something else went wrong and another body appeared.

Mind made up that was precisely what he would suggest to Sir Edward in the morning. It had been some time since the murder and the longer it was left; the more it would look like a cover-up. If the culprit was not where the arrows pointed, then the real murderer was getting away and the scene growing colder by the hour. They had to act now.

Sheeka went on to say that she was not seeing Charles until the following day, sometime in the afternoon, when they would drive north in a hire car.

Kit thought of the warm engine in the Alfa when he had visited the penthouse earlier in the day, and of the attempt to create a fatal crash as he left Hereford. They mulled the situation over together for a while before Sheeka made a move to leave, she had her own file to bring up to date.

For a moment, Kit wondered if she would like to join him that evening, purely to discuss the situation of course, but not wanting to be disappointed and knowing it would be inappropriate, he sadly decided against it.

Next morning Kit got up later than usual, having finally convinced himself that he needed the sleep; in any case his appointment with Sir Edward was not until 11.30. His phone had kept ringing earlier but he flicked it to silent, ignored it and turned over.

It was not until halfway through a hearty English breakfast that he realised something was wrong when the bellboy arrived at his table carrying a polished brass plate, especially when the young man leant forward to speak to him quietly.

'The lines have been red hot for you, sir,' he said as he proffered the brass plate, on which were several pieces of folded, handwritten messages. Kit took them with thanks. It appeared that Sir Edward had rang several times, Sue also; apparently, she'd been told to find him urgently.

Within minutes he was speaking to Sue, who did not know what the problem was, only that Sir Edward was leaping about trying to find him. Should she put him through?

He agreed and waited whereupon it transpired that Sir Edward had been summoned to an urgent meeting with the Prime Minister, having left instructions for Kit to come to the office immediately.

He signed for breakfast and left the hotel by the back entrance. He would get a paper and hail a taxi for Vauxhall Bridge and The Block.

It was not until he was walking out through Shepherd's Market, down past the antique shop, the silversmith and left at the Grapes that he came upon the news-stand; there staring him in the face, written in broad marker pen, was the headline for the first editions. The morning papers were piled up in the newsagents, with headlines in bold ink: **'Top Minister due to resign.'**

Kit stood there momentarily stunned. He bought a copy of 'The Times' and continued on his way, his pace quickening.

When he arrived at his fourth-floor office, Sue was waiting by the door for him looking uncharacteristically flustered.

'Sir Edward is back, you can go straight up. I, er, told him you were on the phone.'

'Thanks,' Kit nodded, turning on his heel exiting briskly.

Even though he was in a hurry he ignored the lift and raced up the stairs two at a time to the silently waiting corridor with the forbidding door at the far end.

'Go straight in,' Sir Edward's secretary ordered, holding the door open as he swept past without a pause.

Sir Edward was at his desk surrounded by the morning papers; two phones were flashing, but he ignored them and looked up at Kit.

The figure of a man sat cross-legged in the

chair to one side of the large desk; he turned to face Kit, who stopped in his tracks. Without a jacket and tie, and perhaps unshaven the man looked totally different. His hair appeared greyer than normal, his whole appearance somewhat dishevelled; an open briefcase was at his feet. It was the Minister. They exchanged glances, both expressionless, neither saying anything.

'So, it's all been in vain,' Sir Edward grumbled. 'Where in the devil's name have you been?'

'At the Park Lane having breakfast and living out of a suitcase, all for you, sir.' He spoke coolly, looking from one to the other.

The steam also went out of Sir Edward's voice as he started.

'You've read the papers, I trust? They say that David Stevens here, the Minister, is tipped to resign today and it's in the damned press, before the PM even had an inkling.'

'I just don't believe he did not have an inkling,' the Minister's comment fell on stony ground.

Sir Edward spoke slowly.

'Apparently, the press was told late last night that it was going to happen, by a series of anonymous phone calls and faxed statements. After some inquiries, including to David himself, it seemed there was a real possibility that he might, so they decided to run it. David rang me late last night having had a phone call from someone he didn't recognise about half an hour before the papers started to ring him at about one a.m. in the morning. It seems they'd been given his private number; probably by the same person. Anyway, the man said that he was in a position to tell the PM and the Press about an arranged passport for a certain lady, and if that didn't lead to his resignation, the caller promised that he had further information that certainly would.'

'Tai Hock? The bastard,' Kit muttered quietly.

The Minister heard him and looked up, his eyes flashing wildly. Had he heard Kit correctly, Tai Hock?

But Sir Edward continued speaking, as if he hadn't.

'David here was beleaguered in his home this morning, surrounded by the vultures. As a favour, I sent a helicopter in to lift him out, got him off the top and brought him here. Now I want to move him out into the country, to a place where he's not so easily recognised, if that's possible.' Sir Edward looked at Kit expectantly.

'Anywhere in mind sir?' said Kit

'I may have,' he said with a most uncustomary wink. 'David likes walking in the country, particularly the Yorkshire Dales, and needs time to consider his position.'

'Whether he should resign or not?'

'Yes, something like that, just to give me a

little time to sort it all out correctly and not in some mistake giving rush.'

Then out of the blue Sir Edward changed the conversation.

'Kit why do you mention Tai Hock?'

The Minister began to fidget in his chair, now dreading any further enquires. Were his lies, his stories to his good friend Sir Edward all about to be exposed? He began to sweat; the puffy gin bags under his red eyes began to glisten and perspire.

'I don't think that time is on our side. I wonder how much the Minister has told you so far, sir?' Said Kit preparing the metaphorical gauntlet

Sir Edward now looked across at the Minister questioningly.

'Have you told me everything, David? I do hope so, as I'm right out on a limb for you. Do you appreciate that?'

David Stevens visibly squirmed in his seat, unsure of himself and of just how much Kit knew. He ignored Sir Edward's last comment.

A hollow perfidious man, Kit decided, looking across at the Minister. Kit now proceeded to bring Sir Edward up to date, mostly with the last forty-eight hours. There were one or two points though that he did not mention, preferring not to show his full hand, well not just yet.

Sir Edward listened intently, absorbing the amazing facts. Every now and again the Minister tried to interrupt, but to no avail as Kit held up his hand to silence him, adding.

'One moment, please Mr Stevens, you will have your say.' Sir Edward made the occasional note as Kit continued with his report. Then, as he was drawing to a close and about to sum up, he rose from his chair.

'Could you please excuse me for a moment, sir?' And even as he spoke he surreptitiously placed a minute transmitter between the leather of the arm and the squab of his chair. Sir Edward spotted what he had done as a warning pinhead of red light began flashing in the concealed console of his desk, this to indicate that a transmitter had been activated in his room. He glanced at Kit with an imperceptible frown.

As Kit left the room he nodded his apology to the Minister. Sir Edward could now gently quiz his friend on what they'd both heard and in a more relaxed atmosphere, man to man. As far as David was concerned, the person who was threatening his very existence was gone for the moment. Now he could talk more freely.

What he did not know was that Kit would be sat in the office next door, with Sir Edward's secretary, monitoring the conversation and she would be taping all that was said.

When Kit knew that a definite lie was given in answer to any questions, he would press a tiny button on his receiver and a further hidden pinhead of light would glow red on Sir Edward's desk. If a question was answered truthfully, then a green light would glow.

After ten minutes or so, Kit would phone Sir Edward and bring him up to date with events, before returning to the office a few minutes later as if nothing had happened. The system had worked well in the past. Between them they had used it in-house many times and had caught out more people than they would care to mention.

The Minister was desperately sorry for his small lapse, his shameful affair. But things had not been good at home and for the sake of the party he had not wanted a divorce. Kit was not too sure but for good measure he gave him the red light. 'Good Lord no,' the Minister continued, he had no idea that this lady was his son's girlfriend. What a shock (red light on).

The passport? Oh, absolute rubbish came the answer (red light). Tai Hock, any involvement there? Any other girls? No never came the reply (red light) Was money or any other favours ever given? Even a day at the races? 'No certainly not,' came the outraged reply.

Kit was not impressed by this dishonesty, but so it continued for a good half hour or more. When Sir Edward asked the first question again it was a sign that he was running out of steam, so

Kit excused himself from Sir Edward's secretary, returned to his own office to collect some items and then went back to the meeting.

He knocked and went in carrying the Minister's digital laptop.

'Your laptop I believe,' he said handing it over to the Minister, who for a moment looked aghast, and then very relieved. Life was not quite so bad for him after all, he thought. This man had told them what he knew, and now the laptop had been safely returned. So, was it not a good day? He was on the home run at last. Things looked brighter, a lot brighter.

Kit calmly started on the Minister again.

'Having found it for you, I have to say that I had a look at it.'

Sir Edward looked across at Kit, he was somewhat bemused, wondering just where all this would lead and he settled back in his chair as Kit continued.

'Otherwise of course I would not have known it was yours.'

'But it's 'password protected'.' Said the Minister

'Unfortunately, technology works both ways. I apologise, but I did look into your files, particularly your Royline banking account, purely routine of course.' The Minister was about to say something, but Kit quickly went on, 'I noticed that some days ago, you moved £100,000 around – could you tell me what that was for?'

The Minister exploded in a tirade of abuse. This was totally out of order. He had no right. These were his private affairs. He had no warrant. He would now leave immediately to see his solicitor.

As mediator Sir Edward held his hand up with a genial smile.

'Come, come now, gentlemen. I am sure there is a logical explanation.'

'I am sure there is,' was Kit's retort. 'What was the money for, Minister?'

Quick as a flash the Minister replied.

'You will remember I foolishly bought a mews apartment.' Once again, he had gained his composure and confidence.

'Of course, of course,' Kit answered. 'Forgive me.' The Minister seemed to relax slightly as he too settled back with a trace of a smile; he thought he had won that round. The smile, it did not stay for long. 'You couldn't buy much for £100,000 in Knightsbridge,' he continued. 'It must have been a very good deal.'

'It was, it was,' the Minister exclaimed eagerly, once again seizing on the opportunity presented to him. 'That's the only reason I bought it, of course,' he simpered.

'So, good was it, Minister, that you only signed

a contract to rent and an option to buy at a later date! What was the money really for Minister?'

The Minister rose, looking furiously at Sir Edward.

'This is outrageous, Edward I thought you were in control here! This man is out of order,' he said shaking a finger at Kit. 'What's more I'm leaving, I'm not staying here to be insulted, to hell with Yorkshire'

Sir Edward was a little taken aback by this outburst and looked questioningly at his subordinate for guidance.

'It wasn't intended as an insult, more of a question, Minister.'

The Minister started to gather his things together and place them in his already full briefcase. Creased papers fell to the floor.

'I don't think you should walk for a cab, David,' said Sir Edward. 'Not while this resignation thing hangs over you, the press will be everywhere.'

'I've nothing to be ashamed of,' he snapped. 'I'm not going to resign, never!'

Both Kit and Sir Edward looked at each other, incredulous at such a statement considering his position.

'Seriously, will you not resign, sir?' Kit asked.

'That is nothing to do with you!'

'I think you should,' Kit said directly to him.

Sir Edward now looked on in horror as Kit tightened the screw.

'What!'

'I think you should resign. Because, Minister,' he said as he took an envelope from his inside pocket and opened it. 'Here's the passport in question, the one the press seem to know about, the one Tai Hock presumably informed them about, the one your expression acknowledged to me several nights ago, in the mews. You seem to have forgotten that I had it. This is Verkuska's passport, the girl who died in your arms, the girl introduced to you by Tai Hock. Amongst other things Minister, it has your prints on it. It's a sham, Minister, a disgrace and a fix.'

As Sir Edward had no prior knowledge of all this, he looked on in amazement at the passport which Kit now held aloft; he was shocked at what he had learnt, but at the same time impressed.

'What are you hiding, Minister?' Kit glared at him. He then continued. 'You have already tried to lie on the purchase of the mews apartment your love nest, so what else is there in your cupboard of deceit?' But Kit did not let him answer that one. 'And there's another thing that troubles me. This young girl was blown away off the top of you and yet to date I've not seen you show any remorse whatsoever. I saw a major part of her on the wall, not a pretty sight.' The Minister winced, while Sir Edward frowned, but he continued, 'I then saw her once beautiful body cooked to a crisp in her car, a car that I believe you bought her Minister.' He looked across at the Minister for some reaction. 'At this very moment, she lies in a mortuary in Dorset, and the local police are getting very twitchy.' He waited a moment for it all to sink in, before going on, 'We for our part,' he looked across at Sir Edward, 'We, for our part have done our best to suppress the inquiries made by the police. Sir Edward even asked for this to be a private investigation, but now it's obviously gone too far. We can't keep this bottled up forever. Meanwhile, you Minister seem unconcerned. As if she was some sort of disposable item. So, what else is there, Minister, what else are you hiding?'

The Minister rose from his chair with indecent haste, so that it rocked badly, nearly falling over. Like a spoilt child, he made no effort to stop it. He stood there shaking, clutching his briefcase from which papers protruded untidily. Then he spoke, trembling as the words came out in a torrent, his lips wet with saliva, dancing spittle hung in the air.

'I don't need to sit here and listen to all these accusations, to be insulted and degraded by you. I am after all a minister of this Government, and a friend of the PM----'

'We know all this, so let's try and be reasonable,' said Sir Edward in a conciliatory and friendly manner, at the same time still digesting what Kit had said.

Kit took the view that it was long past the time to show friendship, after all he now knew far more than it appeared that Sir Edward did. So, he applied more pressure – gently as he did not want to offend.

'The word, sir, is 'was' a Minister,' he added, 'I'd say your time is over, finished.'

'Steady on, Kit,' growled Sir Edward, startled. 'We don't really know that yet, we don't know if all this is true,' he added, a bit lamely.

The Minister who was now visibly distressed didn't want to hear any more and was already halfway to the door. Contemptuously and in a black mood he strode out, not bothering to turn as he wrenched open the door. Sir Edward fumbled for the buzzer that would alert and send his secretary rushing to his aid and an escort to take the visitor out of the building.

'Well, Kit, what now?' Sir Edward said, folding his arms with a scowl. 'What the hell do we do now?'

Kit looked up with a smile.

'We wait sir we wait.'

Back at his desk Kit immediately rang Sheeka.

'Can you speak?' he asked quietly.

It appeared that she was just packing,

preparing to leave for Yorkshire. Charles was picking her up at about one o'clock and had booked two single rooms for them at the village pub in Gouthwaite. They were going to meet his real father on Saturday afternoon, when he would show her the Hall. She was dreading it. But more to the point, she wanted to know about the Minister? She'd read the morning papers and had tried to get hold of Kit, only to be told he was with Sir Edward. She was shocked at the speed of change.

She had then rung Charles to say how sorry she was about the news that was just breaking about his father, but he was surprisingly non-committal, almost as if he was expecting it, as if he already knew.

Kit questioned her again on his reaction and without hesitation she confirmed he had been quite indifferent. He was just not bothered, far more concerned for his mother and the possible embarrassment and repercussions it might cause her.

'He was in a foul mood too, a different man completely,' she said, as apparently, he'd had a big argument with this mate Riley about not going off with the lads for a few days.

'You're a wimp,' Riley had told him as he slammed the phone down. Some wimp Sheeka thought.

The phone conversation with Sheeka prompted Kit to call Sir Edward. He'd had a brainwave.

'Sir, I believe the problem of Sheeka going up to Gouthwaite has been solved for us.'

'Continue,' he grumbled into the phone.

'Simple, Stevens has done it for us. His Lordship will have seen the news about his son's stepfather and his possible resignation. You could now quite reasonably ring His Lordship and say quite legitimately that we've had the Minister under surveillance. To this end, we put Sheeka in. Who he already knows is investigating something. You could say that she came into his son's life, so to speak, by mistake, whilst inquiring into his stepfather's situation, no need to expand. But ask him not to upset things, at least not until we get to the bottom of it all. Their relationship is quite genuine. If you are your normal diplomatic self, he should go along with it and that way Sheeka's cover for the moment will be secure.' Kit waited for some reaction.

'It's a bit weak and I won't be dishonest. It's his son, after all,' Sir Edward pondered.

'You won't have to be. It is weak, I know. Wishy-washy, yes, but the better for it, we're not giving anything away, leaving it all to be surmised and anyway their relationship is genuine,' Kit argued.

Then at last Sir Edward agreed.

'I'll make the call.'

Kit relaxed; it was like a weight being lifted; he could move on. With that he started to read the memos that had arrived during the meeting. The second one down was from Sir Edward's secretary, what few bank details she'd been given were making it difficult to trace the name of the bank, although that in itself was not a problem as the sort code indicated an offshore bank in Guernsey, possibly Fleming's. But it was going to be difficult if not impossible to trace the account holder by the number held by them, as the bank's business in Guernsey was based on confidentiality.

He promptly spoke to her.

'Don't mess with them tell them exactly who we are,' he said, 'and say that we believe it to be laundered money from a drug ring. Tell them the drugs are going to children on the streets. Frighten them to death. But say we will keep it confidential if they go along with it, if not it's in tonight's press and that'll do Fleming's a lot of good I'm sure.

'Can you do that?' she said, knowing the answer as the words left her lips.

'Just watch me,' he replied. 'I'll have the 'Evening Standard' ring Fleming's in Guernsey in a minute just for good measure, that will give them the 'wakeup call.'

'Who do you know at the 'Evening Standard?' she asked out of interest, to which he replied with a laugh.

'Trust me.'

She did.

Soon he would know precisely to whom, why and where the Minister had sent the money. It might just be his offshore account, of course. Yet another Ministerial blunder one, which the press would undoubtedly, love.

Sometime later and with the news now common knowledge, Kit rang Miranda to convey his sympathies for her husband's problems, the pressures of public life, and the probable resignation from the Government of her husband David. As he dialled the number, he cursed for not doing it sooner.

Surprisingly the phone was not engaged and was quickly answered by her. She sounded as effervescent and cheerful as ever.

'Now you can come and see me all you want,' she bubbled.

The alarm bells rang immediately in Kit's head, he was not sure why but instinctively he knew it was for more than one reason.

'Why is that?' he queried nonchalantly.

'Because the bugger's gone! And not before time,' she laughed. She had obviously been drinking, either through relief or remorse it was hard to tell which. 'When I got back he'd packed his bags and gone. He must be serious too, as his best set of golf clubs has gone with him; thank God. He was so bloody interesting that even the press has left the car park and have gone too. The who-ha, it didn't last long did it?' she joked. There was an ominous silence, but he knew what was coming. 'I feel so lonely now, don't you?'

This was a serious development. Not so much that she felt lonely, that was plain dangerous. But more to the point the bird had flown, the Minister had fled the nest, disappeared.

'Any idea where to?'

'Oh Mallorca, I should think. Well, actually I'm sure it's his favourite bolthole; he always runs there when in disgrace! The house keys there have gone so it must be Mallorca. He just left me a note saying he'd ring tonight.'

Kit immediately rang Sir Edward who was astonished at the Minister's sudden departure. They both took stock of the situation, agreeing that their kindly approach had not paid off, and might even have instigated a very serious situation.

But to the Minister himself, Kit's revelations had been the final straw; they had turned his mind.

Kit's own mind however was now in overdrive, he was looking for maximum damage limitation. They would have to find the Minister and take control of the situation before it got any more out of hand, he was now 'a very loose cannon'. But Kit was torn in which direction to move. Decision made! First, he decided to follow Charles and Sheeka to Yorkshire and Gouthwaite Hall. The minister may now be temporally out of the way sat in the sun, but Charles was on home territory. Gouthwaite it was, where he would confront Charles Stevens in front of Lord Strutt who would act as a witness. He would then bring him back to London for further questioning at least that would be one problem out of the way.

He told Sir Edward what he intended doing and as ever there was a long pause, but then with a sigh and obvious heavy of heart, his mind made up, Sir Edward said slowly.

'Do as you think fit. I will warn Lord Strutt of your impending arrival, all in complete confidence, of course. His son and his honour are at stake, so I'm sure he'll help. I won't tell him much, Kit, so it's up to you, just be tactful and careful.'

'We have been far too over-cautious, sir. But hopefully I'll bring him back to London or Hereford for questioning, after which I fear it may well have to be the police.'

'I understand.' The phone was put down quietly and without its customary clatter. Sir Edward clearly felt sick at heart.

Twenty-Seven

By the time that Kit had made his call late in the day to Miranda, the Minister was relaxing high up in the sky, at 37,000 feet to be exact.

He had carefully left the apartment block by the service entrance at the rear in a pre-ordered taxi, hounded by only a few of the media, not as many though as were waiting at the front. His instructions to the driver were to 'drive like hell'. Moments later as the reporters drifted away, a commercial-looking TV repair van arrived. Two men from the hire company started moving his personal items out of the service lift in the basement and into the van. These in turn were to be shipped out to an address he had given them, 'somewhere in Spain,' he'd said vaguely. 'They're all labelled.'

He had seen people escaping tight situations in films and with these in mind he changed into a set different clothes from an old duffel bag and donned a small grey party wig that smelt of perfume.

After fifteen minutes of hell driving and without warning, he paid the cabby at some traffic lights and, leaping from the taxi with his bags clutched under his arms, he sprinted across the central reservation and caught a taxi going in the opposite direction. He changed his clothes yet again and watching out of the rear window all the while, ordered the cabby to take a circuitous route to Heathrow.

He was amused at his own dexterity in changing his identity and by the fact that there were no signs now of being followed. A good friend in the VIP staff at Heathrow, one that he had paid many times, saw to it that he went unimpeded through the VIP channels with the minimum delay.

He naturally travelled first class to Mallorca, content in the knowledge that for the moment his problems were behind him. A holiday, a rest, would do him good and who could deny him that? When things had settled down and this silly woman thing had all been 'put to bed' – he could not resist a smile at his own little pun, – he could surely return to public life.

He ordered a glass of champagne and as the stewardess bent to serve him, he looked lecherously at the airhostess's legs and figure. She noticed but was not impressed. Her forced smile was one hewn from chalk.

He dismissed her and snuggled back into the luxury of the leather seat, swirling the sparkling liquid in its frosted glass.

There would be another day.

Twenty-Eight

Sergeant William Riley had been somewhat dismayed, even shocked to learn of the problems with the Minister. He'd seen the resignation suggested in the morning press just as he was having a big greasy fry up at the Watford Gap service station on the M1 motorway. He was truly shocked. He had thought such a man totally invincible, with his education, position, life style and more than anything else his money. The Minister had everything that he had ever craved for.

That very morning, he had rang several times to speak to David, Charles or even Miranda if he could. Just to ask if it was true. After all, they were such good friends, but the line was always engaged.

Charles, his supposed best friend had not returned his calls, probably because he was suddenly head over heels with this bloody girl and the last conversation he had had was that Charles would not be coming for a lads' weekend at Magaluf in Mallorca; a true bloody bore.

Anyway, who cares, he had thought. He didn't need him, what with his fancy airs and graces, not now anyway. He would stay in a B & B, or a motel near Luton airport and get the flight out in the morning. He was not looking forward to being crushed like a sardine in a sweating tin. But what could you expect on a cheap charter flight? He had always been used to them, always had to be careful with his money, always jealous of those who did not; they were so wasteful, when he had to be so careful. Yet they were so lucky. One day soon he would fly first class.

But he was unhappy for another reason as this particular holiday was in a small way a celebration for him. His new bank manager had approved one of his life's desires: a gold credit card. To him it was like a gold medal. He had craved one for years; been jealous of those including his friend Charles who could flaunt them in restaurants, impress the girls. So, eaten with envy was he that he had hardly deigned to look. He so dearly wanted to use it in front of Charles so that he would be the first person to witness his triumph. After all, they were equals.

When he had eventually got through to Miranda, he had been surprised that David had actually left the penthouse and with such speed. He was disturbed by the resignation now confirmed in the press. What was it all about? He was even more shaken to learn that the Minister had apparently gone to Mallorca, his own destination the very next day.

He had memorised the address of the villa or finca in the hills, resolving that he would pay a visit to it; just to see that all was well.

It worried him.

Twenty-Nine

In spite of all the problems Kit had had a good night's rest at the George Hotel, Stamford Bridge, an old and historic coaching inn half way to Yorkshire on the A1. He rose late on the Saturday morning and had breakfasted well on traditional fayre, not intending to be at Gouthwaite Hall much before 2 p.m., which he estimated would be an ideal time for an impromptu meeting with Charles Stevens.

As he drove north he admired the scenery, his mind wandering. It was now October, a Saturday, and there were plenty of horseboxes and trailers on the A1. This was middle England, the shires, famous old hunting country. They would doubtless be returning from early morning cub hunting. He was in no rush but as he returned to reality he wondered how best to tackle Charles, what his reaction would be, not to mention Lord Strutt, who knew nothing of what his son had been up to in recent weeks.

Three hours later, after a steady, uneventful drive,

Kit spotted the forbidding gates of Gouthwaite Hall, flanked by the weathered stone lodges. Stone eagles glowered down from the pillars either side at anyone daring to enter. It was a daunting scene but one, which impressed him, just as it had Sheeka and more recently Charles. They had after all been doing so for centuries.

He avoided the potholes up the long winding drive, but noticed that the water had splashed out of some of them, which he hoped indicated the earlier arrival of Charles and Sheeka.

He had been prepared for the first sight of the hall, but it did not diminish the spectacle of the huge neo-classical style house, set back in grounds laid out centuries before; it was truly awesome. The whole scene was surrounded, just as Sheeka had said, by high hills, wooded slopes and moors of faded heather.

In front of the house were a battered Range Rover and a smart sporty Ford, a Cosworth. It seemed Charles was in the habit of using hire cars, reserving his Alfa being for more interesting days! The Ford had to be his. It looked totally incongruous in front of the house on this aged decaying estate, as if it had landed from another planet.

Kit was not put off by what he saw, having graced the steps of many a stately home at one time or another, so he climbed the worn but clean stone steps two at a time, walked through the pillars and knocked briskly on the high half-open door which creaked open further. The sun had suddenly come out and was casting shadows through the columns into the entrance hall.

Eventually a dusty old retainer arrived, older it seemed than time itself. His morning suit may have fitted him once, but not anymore.

'May I help you, sir?' Came the wavering enquiry, as he clutched onto the doorknob, quite obviously more to steady himself than to open it fully for Kit.

'Indeed, you can, Kit Martin for Lord Strutt. I believe he's expecting me.'

'He is expecting someone, sir, I do recall,' and with that he started to wrestle with the door, Kit came to his aid.

'I'm old you see, sir. I was here with his father and for that matter his grandfather,' he explained. Together they walked into the great domed entrance hall.

Suddenly, with a long creak another high door to their left opened, letting more sunlight briefly stream into the hall. But it was soon dimmed as a big man dressed in scruffy tan cords and a collarless shirt filled the doorway. The collar looked as though it had been ripped off. He was wearing odd slippers, one with a hole in the toe. A dog forced its head between his legs and the door, a grey muzzle twitching, its eyes dull. Collecting all its energy it gave a muffled 'woof', whereupon it subsided into a heap at its master's feet; it too was very old.

'Ah, Martin I presume,' boomed His Grace, his commanding voice echoing as if on stage around the entrance hall; a pigeon's wings clattered as it left the roof above. His Grace climbed over the now recumbent animal and came towards Kit to greet him, shaking his hand firmly. Lord Strutt ushered Kit into the room ahead of him.

It was the library and obviously, Lord Strutt's den or office. There were wall-to-wall books mixed with the odd trophy; an ill-fated lion, a stuffed pike in a glass case and others. An old Purdey shotgun lay open across the huge worn and untidy desk, while a fishing rod and landing net were propped up in the corner. Kit caught the classic scents of age, cigars and the port wine of generations, leather-covered books bound with old brown fish glue, horses and dogs; all contributing to this cornucopia of history.

A large silver tea service had been placed precariously on a small table with a selection of teas and sugars; cane, demerara, and molasses. China cups were at the ready; a very slight aroma of bergamot oil from a pot of Earl Grey tea drifted in the air. The scene was set of the gentry of long ago.

A couple stood by a tall sash window looking

out across the park, towards the overgrown lake with its brown bull rushes now bending in the breeze all overlooked by the round pillared temple on the hill.

Turning slowly in unison they looked at Kit, the unexpected visitor. It was Charles and Sheeka. They made a remarkably handsome couple. Lord Strutt cordially introduced them but he did not shake their hands and Sheeka showed no sign of acknowledgement.

It was the first time he had seen Charles close to and noticed that like his father he was a big man, rugged and fit. He watched for any recognition by Charles but there was none, not a flicker of an eye, no expression of surprise, no resentment showed. His jaw was set and his eyes ice cold. He smiled but only at Sheeka.

Kit tried to recall the body form in the shadows that dark night in the mews. He was bigger than he thought, but it was quite possible that it had been him, yet neither seemed to recognise the other.

'Martin here,' Lord Strutt announced with a nod at Kit, 'has, I have been told, come to ask a few questions.' His Grace moved away, seating himself behind the huge battered desk, as if to preside over the local court.

There was suddenly a look of genuine surprise on both Sheeka and Charles's faces.

'You didn't say anything earlier, sir,' said Charles questioningly to his father.

'No, I did not, as I have only just found out although I know not what it's about,' he explained in a cautious and lugubrious tone. 'I am in the dark just as much as you.'

Kit was not known for his subtlety and during the drive up he had changed his mind, deciding not to waste any further time, enough had been lost already. He intended to take the bull by the horns, but he still addressed Charles Stevens in a relaxed manner and with a smile.

'I'm Kit Martin, late of MI5 & MI6,' he said easily. 'Technically I'm retired, but recently I was dug up by Sir Edward Ferrensby and asked to look into a rumour, a rumour that your father, David Stevens minister of this government, was having an affair.' He waited a moment for maximum effect; there was little apparent reaction. He looked at Charles before continuing. 'If there was any truth in the rumour and he was, then as he was a minister a damage limitation exercise was to be put into effect immediately. He was to be warned off seeing her and perhaps it would all go away. The Prime Minister was not amused when he first heard of this lowering of standards by a senior minister. He wants as he puts it 'squeaky clean' government with no more scandals!

But as you know, events have moved on. Your

father has now resigned and we have the very scandal breaking that we had hoped to avoid. Sir Edward is most unhappy and we have a certain amount of egg on our faces.' Kit paused for effect.

'Indeed Charles,' he went on, now turning and looking fully at him, 'I believe after talking to your mother that your father flew yesterday to Mallorca, which is not very helpful to the situation.'

'Typical, but at least it was a woman he went after,' said Charles glibly. 'A change for a minister it would seem,' and he gave a nervous laugh, which was totally out of character.

'I didn't say that it was a woman,' Kit observed.

'Oh no, don't give me that,' Charles said, regaining his composure. 'He's no puffter, he's girl mad.'

Kit let the statement ride for a moment before continuing.

'Girl mad? Your girl, Charles, is that what you mean?'

Charles visibly shook for just a moment, his Adam's apple moved as he swallowed and then became stiff. Suddenly he looked dangerous, his eyes blackened with internal rage, his body like a taught spring. Sheeka sensed this and edged away, just a little. The change and reaction within him had been amazing.

'Yes, your girl, Charles!' Kit continued, now

going for the jugular. 'The one that you saw him with in the hotel, Browns in Albemarle Street, wasn't it? Wasn't she your beautiful girl, Charles?'

'It wasn't my girl,' he said more to Sheeka than anyone else, whilst moving closer to her again.

'It! Charles that's not very polite. But let's continue see if I can jog your memory. Oh, and relax, I'm not a policeman and I have little authority in this sort of situation, that will come later. But Charles can you recall using a Beretta 9mm and a Tokarev 7.62 recently, both fitted with sound moderators? You drew them out of the armoury at Hereford, along with some other weapons? You can't deny it as I've spoken to Colonel Stewart. If you don't believe me, you can ring him if you wish.'

'I don't need to. I used them, yes, but so did three others and we have done several times recently. Why?'

'Because, Charles, on this particular day the pistols were not returned. Indeed, it would appear none of the other weapons were until a day later and minus these two.'

Charles's face was expressionless, inscrutable, giving nothing away.

'Then give me the date and who signed them out,' he snapped.

'You did, Charles.'

'No, I did not; the date please?'

'But it's your signature, your name.'

'That may well be, but it proves absolutely nothing. I say again, I did not sign them out.'

This was something Kit had not bargained for.

'So, what are you saying then? That you used them on the day with the others, but did not sign for them?'

'I am and that would make me not responsible for them.'

'Then who did, Charles?'

'You're the one playing detective, Mr Martin, so what was the bloody date?'

Lord Strutt shuffled restlessly behind his desk, disapproving of his son's discourteous manner. Kit didn't much like it either. Charles was getting hot under the collar, cross, his neck red and he was sweating he seemed irrational and to Kit that spelt danger.

'Do you really not know why I am here, Charles?'

'Actually, I have no idea at all,' he answered, his manner changing yet again and becoming superciliously unconcerned, just as if he was losing interest. 'But what I do know is that you're ruining my afternoon.'

'I haven't yet but I am certainly going to!' Kit articulated, his voice becoming more forceful and filling the library. He glared at Charles who glowered back angrily.

Lord Strutt stood up from his desk and walked

uneasily to the other side of the library to get some fresh air from the window; he looked out at the estate. His son had returned and now this; he felt careworn.

'Your girlfriend Verkuska.' Kit said, it got his immediate attention. Charles winced again. 'Your girlfriend was murdered, shot of top the of your father whilst in a mews bedroom, a love nest rented by him. Unfortunately, I saw it all happen from the house opposite and trust me, it was not pleasant, Charles, I smelt her death. The gun used was a silenced Tokarev, the one you, Charles, had signed for at Hereford.'

'But I didn't!'

'I believe you knew of the mews, of the meeting, this assignation, this---'

The sentence was never finished.

'How could I?' Charles exclaimed, flamboyantly opening his arms like a Jewish trader, feigning to talk to his father, wrong-footing those watching his clever display. He moved sadly as if to go to the window to explain, as if to find some form of condolence from Lord Strutt.

But he never got there. As swift as a cat, he spun on his heel, was round the desk in one movement, and snatched up a handful of cartridges and the open Purdey from on top of the desk. There was the dull ring from the Whitworth steel barrels as the varnished paper and brass cartridges were rammed into the chambers, there was a sharp metallic snap as the Purdey 12 bore was shut tight.

Three shocked people the other side of the desk were now looking down the threatening 30-inch barrels of the menacing twelve bore. He held a spare cartridge between the third and fourth finger of his right hand, the brass and deep red cases glistening evilly, effectively turning the weapon into a four-shot weapon.

'Don't be such a bloody fool,' urged Lord Strutt, now making for his son. With an ear-splitting explosion of smoke and flame, the corner of a bookcase Lord Strutt was about to pass suddenly erupted in a shower of antique polished splinters; fragments of paper, book bindings and dust swirled in the pungent sulphur-laden air.

The Purdey sprung open and the red cartridge was ejected; even as it rolled somehow aggressively across the floor, quick as a flash the gun was reloaded and snapped shut. Another cartridge from the desktop replaced the one momentarily missing from between the fingers. Two in two out, a four-shot again. Lord Strutt tentatively sucked out a splinter from the back of his hand; blood dripped. The gun slowly traversed the room again.

Kit looked on; taking risks at the wrong end

of a twelve bore at this range did not make sound sense! It could easily cut a man in half and this guy he was good after hours of training somewhere; he would not miss.

'I'm sorry, desperately sorry, especially for the library, Father,' Charles said calmly and apologetically. Oddly, at that moment, he did seem genuinely upset at the wanton destruction in the library. But his mood quickly changed.

'Nobody move! now, Mr Martin, listen hard. I've no doubt you're carrying a gun. As a gesture of goodwill, I will not humiliate you by taking it from you, and I will not even search you for whatever else you might be carrying. Father, I don't doubt for a moment you also have some World War II memento lying around in this museum of yours, all loaded and tacky with Young's .303 oil, kept for just such an eventuality. So please, don't even think about it! If you do, Martin, I will kill you, as it will be self-defence. I trust you won't be so stupid.'

He did not mention what action he would take with his father.

Sheeka had turned a little pale for she too was armed. She looked hesitantly across at Kit for direction but his eyes indicated a firm 'no', for which she was very grateful.

The atmosphere and mood in the library now started to calm down a little; nobody moved.

'Right, now if that's quite clear,' Charles continued, 'I am going to leave by car and I shall be taking Sheeka with me.'

'Leave the girl out of this,' Kit snapped. Lord Strutt nodded his agreement.

'Unfortunately, gentlemen, for the moment I give the orders. She will be perfectly safe as long as one of you does not start shooting or trying to follow us; after all that's why she's coming with me. She guarantees my safety. Oh, and by the way, contrary to what you might be thinking I'm not running away but as was once said, by Captain Oates, I believe, 'I may be some time'. I intend to return and when I do I shall be looking for you, Martin, believe me, I shall be looking for you.'

'Where are, you going?' Kit asked, stalling for time.

'That, Martin, I'm sure you know or can guess,' answered Charles, aware that any more time wasted could cause complications. So, saying he grabbed Sheeka firmly by the arm and led her towards the door, pushed her through it and closed it after them. Holding her tight, he grasped the large key to lock the library door. As he glanced down he noticed the old chipped ceramic doorknob. It was white within the glazing, were small blue flowers, forget-me-knots.

Charles smiled; surely, they would not.

Kit heard the key grate and turn in the lock before being thrown noisily onto the stone flags of the entrance floor. He also heard Charles bolt and lock the huge outer doors with a dull thud.

Rushing to a side window, he looked out; it was some fifteen feet or more above ground level and there was a six-foot gap and a further drop to allow light into the cellars and kitchens underneath. It would be an impossible leap, even if the window opened fully, which he doubted, not to mention being fired at with a shotgun.

He watched helplessly as Charles and Sheeka ran down the steps, noting that Sheeka's movements were reasonably free; she was not being dragged nor did she appear to be resisting – in fact she seemed almost eager. He hoped she knew what she was doing.

Then to his horror he saw Charles swing the Purdey and drop to one knee to take a shot. He ducked, but he was not the subject of his attention, from a crouch position, Charles fired one shot into the rear of the Jaguar. Kit now knew why he had adopted the crouch, from that angle he could take out the rear tyre, but more to the point also the fuel tank. From inside the library the shot was not so loud. He watched the Jaguar drop to its wheel rim as fuel flooded out onto the gravel.

Charles did the same to the Range Rover.

Neither car caught fire; they rarely do, that is reserved for films. Then he opened the Purdey, ejecting the spent cartridges to the gravel, and placed the shotgun carefully and correctly open on the Range Rover bonnet, along with the remaining cartridges as if on a grouse butt. He had immense cheek or nerve.

Lord Strutt cursed loudly in Kit's ear as he urgently pulled at the cord behind the curtain for the old butler. Oblivious to all that had happened, a bell would be ringing in the butler's pantry somewhere deep in the great house.

'I'm afraid the old bastard's stone deaf,' Lord Strutt said by way of apology as they watched the Ford Cosworth blast its way down the long drive in a cloud of mud and dust. 'Main gates don't close either, haven't done for years,' he went on distantly. 'Did you get the registration number?'

Neither of them had.

Thirty

Charles apologised profusely to Sheeka; this was all most unfortunate, a total misunderstanding, he tried to explain. But she said little, preferring to watch and await developments, as somehow, in spite of what had just happened, Charles seemed straight and maybe her best course of action was to let him lead.

Charles, for his part, didn't have a problem with the car. They would try to trace it, he was sure, but he hadn't used a credit card so there could be no immediate trace there. He always preferred cash for that very reason. Neither was it from a major rental firm and there were plenty of Ford Cosworth's about, so they were not conspicuous.

He had hired it from a friend with a backstreet car lot outside Hereford. They would get to it in time, he knew, but the garage was shut on Sundays and there were only a few hours of trading left today. Monday they'd work at it, but with luck it might be even Tuesday before they made contact. The gamble, of course, was whether Martin had taken the registration number when he arrived? It was unlikely as there was no need to do so at that time.

He had made up his mind in the library, he desperately needed to get to his stepfather and he had to get there first. He was the danger. Wherever he was, that would be where he, Charles, needed to go. He could not ring his mother to verify where his stepfather was, but Martin had given the clue; he had said Mallorca and that fitted. 'Old habits die hard'.

His stepfather would surely not wait, or hang around to be hounded by the press. So, Mallorca was the most likely bet and it was after all their holiday home, a secluded retreat in the hills, little known and difficult to get to and an ideal hideaway to use while the dust settled.

He knew Sheeka had her passport and he had his. But would she go quietly through an airport and customs control? He doubted it; she'd squawk, could they get a flight instantly? That was also doubtful. He had enough cash and an account that he could draw on abroad, his stepfather after all had kindly seen to that.

His mind focused as he began to formulate his plan. He was sure they would expect him to go south; they would also expect him to go to see his stepfather. He must therefore, at all costs, get there before Martin. That was imperative. He was positive Martin would go south in search of him, probably London, then Heathrow. That was once he had transport. But Martin could no doubt summon up a chopper although Charles doubted that he would, sensing that their investigation for some reason was not yet at that level. His stepfather had messed things up for them too. He must out think them and with that he drove to Hull and the ferries. Charles told Sheeka of his plan and that he intended to drive down through Europe, to Barcelona and then take the overnight ferry to Mallorca. He had to get to his father at all costs, he told her.

Charles reckoned he would be well out of the country whilst they were still looking for the car and checking airports. They could be in Hull within the hour and aboard within two. Martin would hopefully still be at the Hall, it was a risk but one worth taking.

He suddenly and unexpectedly grabbed Sheeka's inner thigh hurting her and she gave a slight yelp, but he did not let go as tears welled up in her eyes.

'Stop it damn you you're hurting!'

He ignored her cry.

'Now listen to me,' he growled, his mood changed again 'I'm sorry but like it or not you're here. I'm sorry I got you into this, but in it you are and we can make this easy or hard, it's up to you, the choice is yours. You can go through customs as you are, a beautiful girl, or you can go to sleep. If you go to sleep, you won't wake up till Paris, that I can assure you,' he smiled callously.

As he let go of her thigh, she could feel the pain but he did not apologise again. Sheeka shuddered as she wondered if her judgement had been right, but it was a bit late now and her curiosity still had the better of her. She knew as far as Kit was concerned that she was in the front line and this was just a job, she had to be strong as this was her first real test. She hoped to God that she was not searched at customs; some of her belongings would take some explaining to Charles, let alone the customs, not to mention her cover being blown. So, with little practical alternative she agreed to go along with him.

Thirty-One

Meanwhile Kit had not been quite as inactive as Charles had estimated. Within moments he had rung the RAF base at Leconfield close by, the other side of the A1, and had spoken to the Duty Officer. Twenty minutes later, after several more calls to the base and up and down the country, a fast Aerospatiale Gazelle, a military helicopter of French manufacture, was fuelled and inbound to Gouthwaite Hall.

The unique, high-pitched, cutting whine of the jet turbine was plain for all to hear as it screamed round in a tight curve to one side of the lake and descended nose up in front of the stone pillars of the portico. Kit watched enviously as the sleek machine settled on the grass, before turning back to speak to Lord Strutt. After a moment, the rotors wound down and the pilot and his navigation officer climbed the stone steps to meet them.

'Thought I was in Athens, the bloody Parthenon,' the pilot said as he climbed the steps looking up at the Palladian structure of the building. 'I also thought you were in a rush, sir, but you didn't run out so we've shut down, OK?'

'No problem. I've just been having a word with Lord Strutt here, as I needed to finalise a few details. He wants to come along for the ride, any objections?'

The officer looked quizzically across at His Grace's clothing and down at his odd slippers.

'I intend to change, damn you!' he barked back, visibly rocking the officer on his feet. He then stormed off up the huge stairs, which encircled the entrance hall, knocking an old gilt picture frame with his shoulder as he went. It shimmered in a cloud of dust and plaster. The butler, who was fluttering and hovering nearby like a dusty bat, adjusted the painting of a man on horseback.

Moments later His Grace returned. He hadn't had time to change his clothing much but he carried an old olive-green army satchel, the webbing frayed.

The flight south to the centre of London was thankfully quick, the military helicopter being very noisy even when they were wearing headgear. From a thousand feet, the two men flew with their own misgivings, watching the land and spires of old England flash by below.

A helicopter which develops a mechanical problem is basically irretrievable when flying at less than 600 feet; Kit noted that the pilot therefore had a 400-foot margin of error, mere seconds. Not being at the controls, he hoped the reactions of the pilot at this height were spot on.

Lord Strutt was subdued, not because of the flight but because of the disgrace his new-found son and heir had seemingly brought on him.

Sir Edward himself met them at the heliport, along with his driver. He and Lord Strutt greeted each other like the old friends they were, being immediately engaged in deep conversation. Kit promptly seized the opportunity to use the car and its communications to speak to Colonel Simon Stewart at Hereford on one of the two contact numbers he'd been given. Stewart answered the second one, the clipped military voice easily recognisable.

'Simon, it's Kit, remember the booking out of the weapons, those involving Charles Stevens and Co?'

'How can I forget? I'm trying to keep the peace at this end, but I don't like cover-ups!'

'Don't worry I have a feeling that we're nearly there, but could you check the signatures to see if the weapons really were all signed out by Charles, you see he denies it!'

'Then get him back here!' Stewart protested. 'I'll soon fucking well find out.'

'I'm sure you would, but how come it wasn't noticed that they had not been handed back that night?'

'Could have been night training,' was the guarded reply, as if deep down he was remembering something and something very important.

Suddenly Kit's voice quickened, his mind also racing.

'Simon, check where Charles was on the twenty-seventh of September.'

He could visualise Stewart sat there, dragging his cowboy boots off the desk top as he swivelled to read a wall chart or fumble through some coded diary. The answer came surprisingly quickly.

'I have no need to, the twenty-seventh, Kit, sorry, no luck there he was with me.'

'With you!' Kit said incredulous.

'Absolutely yes, he was with me, we had a practice operation in the City that night, five of us, well four actually as I was just the observer.'

'Who the hell were they? Why didn't you tell me before?'

'You didn't ask me directly. These things are classified, you know.'

'Bloody hell, now you tell me!' Kit almost shouted down the phone. For a moment, Stewart, did not answer.

'It was Charles Stevens, William Riley, Kit Duncome and Adam Faisley. They nearly always work together as a team, part of the 'Squadron' formula. Normally, I suppose Charles would lead but that night Riley did. The weapons would not be handed back to the armoury straight away, as when we returned the armourer would not have been on duty.'

'What was the training? And if you say classified, I'll get in this car and knock you all round your bloody training ground.'

'You think you still can?'

'Why not I may not be able to run like you lads but I can fight; remember?' Kit muttered. There was another silence as Stewart digested his comment.

'They were to break into and remove certain selected cars, 'ours' of course, ones that we had placed on public streets; they were to take them without being noticed, without causing alarm. They were to use the weapons on a special night range, shooting moving targets from the moving cars, they were -----'

'Great. Thank you very much, all because of a lousy date. The twenty-seventh.'

'Stevens and Riley are very good operators, they're good at it.'

'I am sure they are. Would Charles have access to night goggles?'

'They all would, standard kit.'

Kit slammed the phone down.

As he climbed out of the car he noticed that both Sir Edward and Lord Strutt were standing there looking at him, waiting for him to finish. His mood and the noise of the phone going down had startled them.

'Problems?' Sir Edward asked curiously. Kit shrugged, still thinking.

Sir Edward then slowly removed a piece of folded notepaper from his inside pocket and handed it to Kit. He nodded at it and watched intently as Kit unfolded it and began to read:

The Bank of England
London

Governor's Office
14–10–00

Sir Edward

As requested: The name of the bank account you were querying,

i.e. Code No. 12–34–33 Act No. 45545 343434
Relates to:

Fleming's Investment Bank, St Helier, Jersey.
The account holder: Mr William Riley,
14 Thames View,
Battersea, LONDON.
Regards
Brian

Sir Edward waited for some reaction, but did not get one for several moments.

Thirty-Two

For Charles and Sheeka the customs either side of the channel were non-events, Charles had made good time and by mid-evening he was driving hard, south towards France and the Riviera. He would then route right and across to Spain, then relentlessly on to Barcelona using the coast road where he would board the overnight ferry for Mallorca.

He knew now that the chances of being apprehended en route were slim. But Barcelona itself could pose a problem, for if Martin and his team accepted they were heading for a confrontation with his stepfather and when they realised that they had not boarded an aircraft, the alternative had to be by road, the route unfortunately being obvious. His gut feeling was that Martin would also head for Mallorca and a showdown, rather than Barcelona, where he might miss them.

Sheeka had been cooperative at the customs and had given him no problems, which was a relief, as he did not relish the idea of forcing her to keep quiet. A girl who had been knocked out was not a pretty site.

For her part, she had said little, her mood of mild resistance being tempered to match his aggression and to make sure she was there at the finish, wherever it might be. In no way, did she want to be dumped at some service station along the way, especially as she had engineered herself into this position. But what she did have to do was alert Kit as to her and Charles's whereabouts, as they were quite obviously way out of range of her communicator.

As the trip dragged on kilometre after kilometre she slept, only to be awoken from time to time by the sound of fuel being pumped into the car. Each time she thought of an excuse to leave the car and use the phone, but she realised she had no Euros to make the call, and layback defeated. Then just as night turned into day somewhere below Montelimar, she looked across at Charles who was equally tired and now showing the signs of stubble. He stared ahead with bloodshot eyes, in his relentless pursuit.

'Are we ever going to stop?'

'Only for fuel,' he said curtly.

'Food?'

'Sheeka, we have no time,' he snapped back at her.

'Well, you may not, but nature calls. I need the loo; and desperately.'

'Tough.'

'Don't be a prat,' she laughed out at him trying to inject some friendship into the conversation, trying to win him round. 'Think about it; you're going to need fuel again soon,' she said leaning over to look at the gauges. 'When you stop, let me have a pee and I'll get some food so we can at least eat on the hoof. You'll need food to keep you going at this rate. We need energy, remember that!'

It struck a chord as Charles saw the logic of her argument and within fifteen minutes they were flying up an exit road and into a service station, arriving with a screech at the pumps. He quickly threw her a handful of Euros that he had changed on the ferry.

'Don't forget the oil,' she hollered as she ran across the forecourt towards the café. She saw him take the bait and move back to the interior to pull the bonnet catch. It would give her the time she needed. Unnoticed and as a precaution she had also palmed the car keys.

She did not spot the telephone booths straight away but luckily, they were in a corridor and on the way to the toilets, out of immediate sight. Moments later she was leaving a message on the number in London that was constantly monitored and recorded; there was no time for conversation. But Kit would be alerted almost immediately.

Just as she put the phone down, Charles suddenly came into view marching toward her down the corridor.

'Where're the fucking keys, and where's the food? What have you been up to, you bitch?' he snarled, losing all of his public-school charm.

She turned, ran into the toilets and locked the cubicle; a woman screamed as Charles undaunted pushed past her, entered and battered at the door. Had he seen her on the phone? She couldn't be sure either way.

'I didn't know what you ate,' she screamed back, 'I was coming to ask.'

'Give me the fucking keys,' he yelled as his shoulder started to crash into the door; wood splintered as the lock creaked. 'Give me the fucking keys.' He roared

She was suddenly aware he hadn't mentioned the phone!

'Let me finish, for Christ's sake. You go and get the food. A tuna sandwich or something like that's fine for me,' Sheeka called back calmly, and started rustling some paper. 'Go on, Charles, we're supposed to be in a bloody rush!' The banging stopped, as once again he saw her logic.

'You've got just two minutes,' he shouted, giving the door a final kick in disgust. With a snort, he promptly left. Sheeka gave a sigh of relief.

When she entered the café, she saw him

standing by the doors waiting for her, clutching a bag of food. He turned on his heal and headed purposefully back in the direction of the car.

As she passed the startled cashier, Sheeka put a handful of Euro notes on the counter and took two bottles of red wine and a pack of glasses from the display.

When she was back in the car she handed him the keys, glaring at him. Charles glared back, but handed her the bag of sandwiches and some French cheese.

'I thought you'd taken them, the keys that is and were trying to get away,' he muttered, by way of apology.

'I thought you might leave me here in the middle of bloody nowhere, you hardly need a hostage any more. I was only looking after myself.'

There was no reply as Charles gunned the car back onto the autoroute. He looked in mild amusement at the two bottles. She sensed he was not really annoyed.

Looking at the wedge of Brie and French rolls, Sheeka pointed out that she had not got a knife, whereupon Charles leant forward and from his shin brought out a knife; he flicked the blade open.

'A present from my Commanding Officer,' he said passing her the knife. She looked at him oddly. 'Don't worry, I doubt you will try to kill me at this speed,' he smiled, his eyes going back to the road.

'Do you have a corkscrew in the same place?'

'No corkscrew' he answered distantly, as driving took his concentration.

So, with that she forced the cork into the bottle, spilling wine onto the floor as she did so. She poured a glass and passed it to him.

'Drink and drive? This is bloody ridiculous.' But he drank deeply, and laughed for the first time in twelve hours. Sheeka took a sip of wine and passed him his food as the car hurtled on. The tension seemed to be broken, maybe now she would learn more.

Thirty-Three

Sergeant William Riley, gold card or not, had a torrid flight. Saturday morning, Luton airport and of course the flight was delayed! To his annoyance, it was typically crowded, bustling with fraught, overweight and late holidaymakers. He wondered if next time he should travel first class; he'd always wanted to, but not from Luton! The Minister had often mentioned Heathrow and that made him envious.

With a flying time of only a couple of hours, it seemed effortless in the big silver Boeing 757. As he glanced casually out of the window, lying serene ahead of them amidst the deep blue of the Mediterranean Sea was the humid misty mountains of Mallorca.

The approach and final descent was from the northeast, out over Pollensa Bay and Alcudia then down the south side. He looked down with interest at the Palma plain, windmills slowly turning, pumping the water that would be taken greedily by the parched earth of summer.

The Boeing kissed the tarmac and after a short

taxi came to a standstill. Once stationary, everyone as usual stood up, at once creating chaos. He scowled at the melee, preferring to wait for the aircraft to empty before collecting his things.

His polished shoes clicked on the aluminium gantry in the sudden warmth as he descended from the aircraft and walked across the tarmac towards one of the largest air terminals in Europe.

Mallorca was still hot and humid, even now in mid-October and the sun beamed down out of a clear blue sky, the mountains of Puig Gros de Bendinat a patchwork of colours in the background. To the right Bellver Castle stood guarding the bay, with Mount Galatzo behind, and the Tramontana range pointing gracefully skyward all completing the picturesque scene; it indeed was a tonic to the system. He would find a good hotel, relax, soak up some sun by the pool and prepare for the notorious nightlife.

Yet for all this, to his annoyance, deep down, try as he would he just could not relax. On the aircraft, his mind had been in turmoil, something had gone wrong and he was mystified over his friend David's resignation, which he could not understand. Until now he had thought the man invincible.

His first task, after acquiring a rent-a-car and booking in to a hotel, must therefore be to locate David. So, taking his travel tickets out of his jacket, he reread the scribbled address that Miranda had given him. 'Finca sa Murterra between Andratx and Estellencs, about four miles out of Andratx he would find a little track on the right, difficult to see,' she had said and it's about half a mile along. 'But of course, you must call in, cheer him up, he'd love to see you.' He wondered just how welcome he would be. But he would call there anyway; he of all people now had to.

He quickly hired a car, not the one he had wanted which also annoyed him, however he could change the little Fiat later for a car of his choice; he was told a Suzuki Vitara perhaps, take the hood off and get a tan. Like the one he'd acquired in Brunei, now faded.

His luck changed when the first hotel that had been recommended to him had vacancies. The Villa Mil at Paguera was quality, had a magnificent balcony overlooking the bay and served a superb champagne cocktail, so he had been told and he could not wait.

Thirty-Four

Kit meanwhile had received Sheeka's message almost immediately. He was not surprised by Charles's action. The long drive down through Belgium, France and Spain, and on to Mallorca it was a natural, it made sense. But what worried him was that this was the route a person carrying a weapon would choose in order to miss the stringent security checks at airports. So just how dangerous was this man? Why the sudden urge to see his stepfather? He had no need to leave the Hall the way he had. Something could have been arranged but now he, Charles, had put his head on the block; technically he was a wanted man, a fugitive.

He held the piece of headed paper that the Old Man had given him. It was on expensive paper with the address in embossed black letters. It read 'Confidential the Bank of England' and typed below was the information: Sergeant William Riley indeed! It was not the estate agent who had been the recipient of the £100,000 from David Stevens, but Sergeant William Riley, no less. So, had the Minister tried to set up the mews apartment in Riley's name as a cover? Possibly, but then the estate agent would surely have said so. The Minister's solicitor could probably answer that one, as the details would be in the lease.

Sue, Kit's secretary, was now on full alert, set to monitor any calls from Sheeka and to pass on any instructions to her. For the moment, Kit had no direct contact with Sheeka whilst he was away from the office in London, or indeed abroad and this was the only place she would call.

He had to get to Mallorca urgently, preferably before Charles and his stepfather met. Should he warn the Minister of his unstable stepson's imminent arrival? Somehow, he felt not, as a chance meeting would probably produce the best results, as long as he was there, and time was short.

Sue booked him on the first available flight out of Heathrow on the Sunday morning, a direct first-class flight on Iberia, the Spanish national airline. A hotel booking in Andratx was also made for him at the famous, luxury Villa Italia; the only suitable hotel close enough to the target.

He calculated that Charles would catch the midnight ferry the same day, from Barcelona to Palma, arriving at 7.30 the following morning, Monday, giving him twenty-four hours to find David Stevens at his villa, or finca.

That evening he selected what extra items

he felt he might need and packed them away in a screen-proof travelling case designed for this very purpose. Most items never left the case; they were always ready at a moment's notice, as were his toiletries and clothes which were identical to those in his wardrobe. On his return his clothes would be washed and ironed by his 'lady' and the toiletries checked and re-packed in the case just the same, ready for the next time. He hated packing and liked to leave instantly.

To anyone else, the case just looked like a piece of up-market leather luggage, yet it boasted intricate workmanship, was double sided and with a false base and top, a gift from a grateful friend.

Once more the mountains of Mallorca could be seen out of the port window as the aircraft approached its destination. It was a beautiful sight, the same rugged mountains that, unbeknown to Kit, Sergeant 'Wiley' Riley had seen only some twenty-four hours earlier.

He finished his coffee and removed a small flask with a flourish, watching the ground get closer; he sank back into the seat and relaxed, thinking of the potential problems which lay ahead. There were many, it was certainly going to be interesting. A wistful smile flickered on his face.

The baggage claim was quick and efficient and the customs seemed not to exist at the huge modern airport.

A hire car was booked, and yes, they had 'tried harder' the requested Cabriolet had been urgently found, a Ford XR3, which would be quick and nimble on the Mallorcan roads.

As he filled out the forms the irony was not lost on him, this was the same model of car even to the colour that he had seen burnt out, a jacket of death, just a few weeks earlier on a lonely Dorset road.

Some sixth sense alerted him and for no particular reason he idly watched the large expanse of glass, the travellers moving to and fro, the gentle hiss as the automatic doors opened and closed. He was about to look away and complete the booking forms, when he was surprised to see a figure he knew as 'Wiley' Riley. He carefully watched him saunter to the green 'Europcar' kiosk further down the airport.

Casually lowering his head, Kit signed the hire form and the Visa payment chit that was clipped to it. He thanked the smartly uniformed girl as she passed him the keys and saw from the addendum that the car was parked on the fourth floor of the nearby parking lot.

'No,' he said, when asked to wait whilst they brought the car. 'There's no need, after the flight from London the walk will do me good.' Surprised she passed him the keys and showed him the direction of their park area.

As he moved off, with his head eyes and body locked together as one, his eyes casually swept across Riley, who was patiently waiting two kiosks down. It was important not to show any sign of recognition, not to observe for a moment longer than was necessary. There was no falter he moved as a radar would sweep eyes focusing and absorbing without locking on; it takes a lot of practice.

But as he turned Riley saw him and although he couldn't be sure, he had seemed to recognise him. He found that interesting for as far as he knew they had never met; yet Kit instinctively knew that he'd been spotted. Without hesitating Kit continued to turn away making for the escalators and the crowded shops on the first floor of the airport, desperately looking as he walked for some sort of mirror so that he could watch his back, but there were none.

He knew that Riley had originally wanted to have a break on the island with Charles, a lads' weekend in Magaluf. He therefore presumed that Riley, already having a ticket, must have come to the island anyway, determined to have a break and why not, but he was surprised? Alarm bells rang in his mind with this new twist. It seemed to him to be a 'gathering of the clans', so to speak. What then was his involvement with Charles? Now that Riley was on the island, there was no way Kit wanted to lose him, he was confident that Riley did not realise that Kit had 'clocked' him.

Thirty-Five

Sergeant 'Wiley' Riley, on the other hand, unknown to Kit 'had' indeed seen 'that man Martin' almost as soon as he entered the building. He had after all been walking in the same direction and to the same batch of car hire kiosks.

Martin, Kit Martin. He had known who this man was for some time. One day whilst he had been preparing to go on leave from Hereford he had seen him arrive. Curiosity getting the better of him, he had watched the man in his flashy Jaguar drive up from the gate with the CO, Colonel Simon Stewart, by his side. His interest was aroused and he had delayed his departure, watching them go to the admin block and later enter Charles's room. They were in there some time, which he found very strange and, it was then as they came out, that he took a somewhat poor photograph of him.

To take a photograph through a closed window, quickly and without adjustment means that sometimes the auto lens will focus on the glass, not the subject, this leaving the image the other side of the glass sadly out of focus. To get the shot Riley had to stand back in the shadows of the room that he was in, with predictable results.

He was not without friends and the photograph had been quickly developed, scanned and faxed to a friend of his via his desktop computer; the friend had touched up and improved the quality of the picture and later had it checked out. Within an hour or two, the call came.

'The photo is almost certainly of one Kit Martin, ex-SIS, probably of MI5, but later he moved on in a reshuffle, possibly to MI6, where I believe he was friendly with its head, Sir Edward Ferrensby, in many ways his private spook. He's a gentleman, a classic dresser and gourmet and a 'bon viveur,' but don't be fooled. He is also dangerous and known for his preference to operate on his own hence Sir Edward's indulgence; he doesn't like having people round him, doesn't tolerate fools, his few friends being carefully chosen. Information now says that he's apparently retired after losing his best friend, a chap called Stuart Kilburn, killed in Oxford during an operation that ended up somewhat explosively in the Mediterranean. I am told it was coded Carlos II,' said his informer.

With this information to hand, Riley had become suspicious. What the hell was this man doing at Hereford, and now, more to the point what was he doing here in Mallorca?

Riley's car hire forms had already been completed and it was only a matter of a signature and a changeover of cars. The girl recognised him as she handed him a set of Suzuki keys saying that the vehicle was on the fourth floor, lot 210, where most of the hire cars were kept. He tossed her the keys to the Fiat, which rattled noisily on the desk.

'Should I go and get the Suzuki?' she asked as he impatiently signed his name.

'No, I'll walk,' he replied gruffly. 'The Fiat is up there too, just where I found it, fourth floor lot 206,' he called over his shoulder as he moved off, but changing direction, he went over to the Avis kiosk and spoke pleasantly to the girl. 'Excuse me,' he said, feigning breathlessness, 'a friend asked me to meet him here, a Mr Martin, but I'm late.'

'Oh yes,' she replied, 'he's just left, but if you hurry he'll be coming out of the car park in a moment in a Ford Cabriolet.' Although she knew what car he was in, out of habit she held out the form out that Kit had only moments earlier signed. To her surprise, Riley grabbed it and read the information on it. Ford Escort Cabriolet, blue, registration PM 1486 CD. He memorised the vital details noting that the address given was the Hotel Villa Italia, Port Andratx.

He needed to follow Martin in order to check and recognise the car and to ascertain where exactly Villa Italia and Andratx were.

There was actually a lot more he needed to know and soon he would find out. Martin needed sorting, once and for all.

Kit walked into the mirrored 'Cigar House,' a large cool humidor that was virtually opposite the escalator he had just ridden. The gamble was whether Riley would follow. He could not afford to lose him, but why this apparent interest in him? Kit wondered. How did he recognise him when they'd never met?

Surveying the rows of Cuban cigar boxes and their accoutrements from Havana was a mouth-watering experience; he gazed at Montecristo, Punch, Partagas, Bolívar and many more. He could see his favourite in the top corner, the best of the best in the world of cigars; Cohiba.

It is rumoured that in more peaceful times Fidel Castro asked his friend and fellow revolutionary Che Guevara, to find and produce the 'Best of the Best' of Cuba. It had to be a Havana cigar of course and it had to be created using only the very best choice of wrappers and fillers. The reason he wanted them was for personal consumption, but also to offer them as very special gifts to high-ranking diplomats from countries that were friendly towards Cuba.

As Kit handled a box of 25 Cohiba Robustos with a certain fond reverence, he saw Riley's head come slowly into view as he too rode the escalator. Kit had cleverly laid off the reflection of this from the mirrored shop wall to a small convex mirror held tightly to the box of cigars, which he was studying. To look at the mirrored wall would have been far too obvious.

In any event, he always carried the tiny mirror, convex one way, concave the other; it could be clipped to his pen as a tiny extension or direct to his glasses, allowing him to examine his fellow travelling passengers.

Riley was obviously watching him as he left the escalator and oblivious to Kit monitoring his progress. He walked over to the paper stand and busied himself looking at the foreign press while Kit paid for his box of Cohiba's and set off for the fourth floor of the car park that was accessible from the same floor. Riley followed.

The two bags of luggage that Kit was carrying seemed to be heavy and twice he put them down to read his car hire details, not so much for a rest but to monitor the progress of his mirrored follower. Once inside the multi-storey car park Riley vanished, but he knew it would not be for long.

As he left Palma airport in the Ford Cabriolet, so did the Suzuki, following him five cars back.

Hood down, enjoying the sun and with one eye on the mirror Kit drove quickly through Palma and along the sea front, the Paseo Maritimo.

On the right, towering over the bay, stood the

magnificent cathedral created by King James the first of Aragon, in memory of his deliverance in 1260 from a tempest at sea, it is said, whilst he was on his way to invade this very island.

On the left a huge harbour and marina complex disgorged masts, fly-bridges and aerials skyward, the whole place housing the toys of the rich and famous, legends in their own imaginations.

He passed the Victoria Hotel where only a year earlier he had looked out over the docks, anxiously waiting for the arrival of the merchant vessel 'Carlos II'. He accelerated up the hill away from Palma docks, heading for Andratx. In the mirror, some cars back he could still see the little Suzuki panting after him, its white plastic hood billowing outward with its speed.

Suddenly his mind flashed back to Hereford and the little Alfa Romeo hurtling after him. He instantly looked back to the mirror half expecting to see the Alfa there, but of course it was still the Suzuki. Could it be that the driving style was the same? It was impossible to tell, but there was something that tugged deep down in his subconscious.

To the left, behind old fortifications, the Spanish flag was flying high from a pole above the Marivent Palace, a former residence of the President of Chile, now a holiday home of the royal family of Spain, some of who must have been in residence. The motor yacht, 'Fortuna', captained by an Englishman, would no doubt be below in the Naval Yard at Porto Pi.

Within twenty minutes of leaving Palma, he was driving past the colourful fishing boats and the lines of restaurants that adorn the harbour front in the picturesque Port of Andratx. Further on towards La Mola he could see the 'Villa Italia', so named after its original owner and builder who was an Italian. With its unmistakable Italian design, it looks as if it has been transplanted from the mountains around Lake Garda in Italy.

Many years ago, now, Mussolini, a friend of the original owner was supposed to have stayed there with his mistress, Clara Petacci which all adds to the hotel's mystique, beautifully situated as it is looking out onto the bay of Andratx.

He slowed quickly, purposely giving the persistent Suzuki little time to realise that he was stopping, a pale face glared out behind the windscreen as he swerved to avoid the braking Ford. It shot past him like an annoyed gnat, away and up the hill, engine screaming.

Kit had caught a glimpse of a sinewy man hunched over the wheel, so that was Riley close to? Not a very subtle character. Kit could not help wondering why he had hired such a small vehicle, although he knew that some people found these little 4x4 jeep-type vehicles trendy, with their gaudy customised colour schemes. He, for one, did not.

The entrance gates to the hotel were tall and narrow in a typically northern Italian style, with steps leading off to the right and left joining together a multitude of terraces and fountains. He was impressed as he climbed out of the car and looked across the bay.

The manager spoke impeccable English, and he was shown to his room; it was classically decorated with a view out across the small bay to the expensive villas opposite. Many yachts were at anchor, some it appeared on permanent moorings, as large buoys bobbed up and down in front of them. To his right, he could see the white structure of Club de Vela, the yacht club, its flags flying and its tables laid, covers blowing in the breeze.

When his luggage was delivered to his room Kit was already on the telephone to the Europcar rental office at the airport in Palma. As he waited for the phone to be answered he idly opened the complementary half bottle of champagne.

When he got through, he explained that he had been supposed to meet a friend there at the kiosk that morning, believing his friend had also arranged to change his car for a Suzuki Vitara. However, his plane had been delayed and they had missed each other. He apologised and asked if it would be possible for the girl to tell him where

Mr Riley was staying as he had lost the note and hence the address given to him in England. Within moments she gave him the information.

'Your friend the client in question is staying at the Villa Mil Hotel in Paguera, that is according to the booking form. Do you also want a car?' she enquired. Kit politely declined, but smiled at how easy it had been to get the information he wanted, although he hadn't yet decided how he would use it. He should really concentrate on Charles; Riley was nothing more than a red herring.

He locked the door; old habits making him place a chair against the handle, closed his eyes and lay on the bed to think.

Later that afternoon the phone rang, it was Sue from London with confirmation that Mr Charles Peregrine Stevens and Miss Sheeka Thomas had booked onto the Transmediteranea Ferry at Barcelona, bound for Mallorca tonight, their car a Ford Cosworth. The ferry was due to leave close to midnight and they would be expected to arrive at Palma at about seven in the morning.

The timing was perfect.

Thirty-Six

Charles and Sheeka arrived in Barcelona at about four o'clock in the afternoon; two very tired, hot and grubby people. Charles's mood had calmed during the long drive and he was now more of the gentleman that Sheeka had first met. After making a reservation on the car ferry to Palma, they booked into an adequate hotel close by.

Charles then insisted that he buy Sheeka a new set of clothes and any toiletries that she may require. He insisted she must also buy her favourite perfume. Impressed by his thoughtfulness, together they shopped also to buy some clothes for himself more suitable for the Mediterranean climate.

So, with carrier bags emblazoned with store logos, and full of practical clothing, they returned to the hotel. Charles ran the large bath and added some of the hotel's foaming bath oil, the scent of which was both pleasant and relaxing as it wafted through the rooms.

'Ladies first,' he said with a wave toward the bath. 'Oh, and sorry, but leave the door open please.'

'That's not very nice,' complained Sheeka.

'No, maybe not, but it's necessary; having got you this far I don't want you disappearing into thin air.'

'Where the hell do you think, I am going to go?' she shouted slamming the door.

The pleasantness she thought she had experienced whilst shopping had vanished; his mood was just the same, aggressive

'Don't lock it,' he ordered, his temper rising once more as he quickly moved towards the door, 'or it will be off the hinges faster than you can blink.'

'As a compromise, then,' she offered, opening the door and glaring at him, 'here are my clothes and I will leave it ajar.'

'Fine,' muttered Charles his expression like granite. 'I'm sorry but it's necessary. I don't want any mistakes and it may yet be for your own good.' With that he walked across the room to the balcony, opened the doors and looked out onto the busy street below. The Spanish siesta was now over and people were returning to work.

Charles stared out past the huge column of Columbus by the harbour, out over the sea and Mallorca, thinking of what lay ahead, the delay with the ferry was infuriating but there was nothing he could do, it was a race against time and he knew why.

He could hear Sheeka humming in the bath. She was a cool customer and beautiful too, outstandingly so. He was quite sad that he had to act toward her in this way, but needs must. She was a hostage and he must not lose sight of that. Yet sometimes he wondered why she did not really try to get away she seemed to want to be with him and that unnerved him, who was she really?

Digesting these thoughts, he eventually turned, pensively, to walk back into the room. It was then he noticed that the bathroom door had opened with the faint draught from the balcony doors. Sheeka lay there staring at him, her bare breasts protruding tantalisingly out of the bath foam. He glanced at her tousled near-white blond hair and cheeky wide smile as the vision hit him like an axe.

'Pass the towel,' she said. He did and to his amazement she stepped out of the bath.

Round one she thought.

Thirty-Seven

The moment the call from London ended Kit swung off the bed and looked again at David's address which Miranda had given him, 'Finca Sa Murterra'. He would not make contact yet, preferring to watch and wait, let events take their course. There were too many players coming onto the stage for him to intervene – they must be left to play their parts and he must be in position when the curtain was ready to come down. But what he did need to know was precisely where the finca or villa was, as he had to have a prime seat for the first performance.

Twenty minutes later he was on a good road out of Andratx town, one that is sometimes used for a hill climb, a form of motor racing against the clock, which led into the mountains heading in the direction of Estellencs. As he drove he kept an eye out for a rough track on the right, there were many but eventually he spotted a small wooden sign, barely visible and built into an old stone olive terrace, proclaiming 'Privado – Casa Sa Murterra'. That was it. At the entrance to the track ancient olive trees stood guard with twisted branches, they reminded him of gnarled old men and it seemed with sticks raised as a warning to him.

The track was virtually impossible for the low Ford Cabriolet to negotiate and after many scrapes and bumps from underneath the car he found a small clearing that would allow him to turn around, or if necessary for another car to pass. He could drive no further without damage to the car, so the rest of the way would have to be on foot.

He walked on for perhaps another 300 metres or so, keeping to the tree line, until he came upon visible signs of cleared and rotated ground, cultivated with olive and almond trees that stretched away on terraces into the lee of a hillside opposite.

A positively idyllic finca lay before him, looking for all the world like an English country cottage covered in honeysuckle and ivy, but in this case terracotta tiles with bougainvillea and flowering cacti growing in abundance, and what appeared to be grapes hanging from the vines that entwined the traditional pergola over the terrace. A dusty Land Rover was parked under a lean-to of coloured creeper. In a rocking chair, slowly rocking, sat David Stevens quietly reading a paper. This was an Englishman's retreat.

Kit was fascinated by what he could see and

watched from the shadows of the pines for quite sometime before eventually backing away silently into the woods and so back to the car.

On the way, back, he has second sense. Kit, felt he had been watched too, was the watcher now the watched? As he approached his parked car he could smell rather than see dust from the arid earth hanging in the air. The earth around his car looked scuffed, torn by all-terrain tyres. He now stood stock still listening, was he mistaken? Or could he just make out in the distance, above the constant racket of the crickets, the whine of a tortured engine, a vehicle being driven hard away like a mad gnat? He believed he could.

That evening with excitement brewing for the morrow Kit went for a walk round the port of Andratx to stretch his legs, get a meal and try to relax. The port was busy, noticeably full of overweight German tourists searching for oblivion from alcohol. He was hungry and after some deliberation he chose the Miramar, a restaurant on the front in Andratx, overlooking the harbour, choosing it not so much for the menu, but more for its interesting wine list, to ponder whilst enjoying the restaurant's prominent position.

He ordered a local dish of green beans, with mint and ham, 'Habas con menta a jamon,' followed by a spiny lobster stew, 'Caldereta de

Langosta,' all gently washed down with a pleasant local red wine, a chilled Mont Feruch by Miguel Oliver of Petra, Mallorca.

Some people find eating in a restaurant on their own purgatory, but Kit never felt that way, indeed he enjoyed it to read a newspaper in peace and watch the world go by. The evening passed pleasantly enough. But it was 7.0 a.m. the next day and the arrival of Charles and Sheeka, which really concerned him.

He paid the bill and strolled along the front, back towards the hotel, resolving to have an early night, but he would call London again to check for any news. Little did he know that when he called London it would not be quite so routine.

It was as he walked in the shadows of the final hundred metres to the hotel that he began to feel uneasy, his senses rarely let him down. A slight sound from behind warned him, but not soon enough, as he turned he saw a figure springing at him from behind a parked car. With reflex action, he moved to ride the force of the attack so that the man only hit him a glancing blow to the side of the neck, a failed rabbit punch. Turning, he drove his fist deep into the stomach of the attacker who seemed to ride the punch well, countering swiftly with a blow to the side of Kit's head, it glanced off as he sidestepped but he slipped momentarily floundered on the rough ground.

The attacker saw his chance and closed before hitting him again hard, this time managing to get a head lock on Kit as he was dragged dizzily towards a car so that his head could be rammed painfully into the metal body. He realised what was coming and kicked the man's legs from under him sending them both crashing in a cloud of dust to the ground.

The moment they hit the ground Kit let go, pressed his palms on the crumbling tarmac, did a handstand and popped out of the headlock like a cork from a bottle. Free now he instantly spun round and drove the side of his foot hard into the face of the other man; the sound of splintering bone was not pleasant as something gave way. He followed this kick with another, the force of which jarred him so hard that he felt it through his tibia, femur and right into his hip. The attacker rolled over with a groan and now laid still, his breathing no more than a gurgle.

He moved forward to examine his attacker when suddenly he was forced to the ground by the sheer weight of what appeared to be two heavy, sweating men, both surrounded by a halo of garlic. Before he could react, he felt the harsh pain of cold steel being forced hard, into the back of his ear, the soft tissue and the bone nearly giving way. He heard the well-known sound, indeed he felt the clawing vibration of the hammer on the pistol being drawn back all the way; two clicks no room for error. The foresight of the pistol dug further in, as he lay motionless. The three men breathed heavily as the fourth one on the ground groaned more as he returned to consciousness and his bloodied snuffles became more controlled.

Kit felt handcuffs being clicked firmly on as he was pushed against the side of a car. From behind they unceremoniously delved through his pockets, throwing everything that they found onto the bonnet of the car, a room key fell to the ground.

When at last he managed to stand up and turn to face them, he found he was looking at the green uniforms and faces of the Guardia Civil; neither of whom had been to keep fit classes in recent years. But a man in handcuffs is easy meat for anyone, then for no reason and without warning he was hit fully in the stomach; winded he bowed, but he did not give them the pleasure of dropping to his knees. Straightening to his full height, he smiled. Surprise registered on their faces.

Trying to analyse the situation was not easy, although it was plain they thought that he was the attacker. All his identification was in his wallet, which they could not or would not read properly, and it was all taking up considerable time.

During the ensuing argument, they heard a car start, causing all three of them to turn and watch a Suzuki Vitara driving erratically away. The 'victim' had gone leaving a pool of blood on the road as a reminder. Kit knew exactly whose it was.

Three hours later and after several phone calls to the British Embassy in Palma, Kit was released from the Guardia Civil headquarters in Andratx town and driven back very apologetically to the Villa Italia.

Thirty-Eight

By six o'clock the following morning he was sitting in a small, bustling marinero's café, the Jamon, opposite the ferry terminal in Palma and enjoying a strong coffee watching and waiting. Even after the scuffle of the previous evening, he felt good. For Kit action was his drug.

At seven o'clock with a flurry of dock activity the huge white and green Transmediteranea ferry came into view, she slowly came alongside and by 7.30 the first trucks were rolling off, down the ramp and onto the crowded quay. As the cars slowly began to nudge their way forward, Kit moved to his car, this time with the hood up, allowing the tinted glass to blend him into the gloom of the interior. He knew Sheeka would be looking out for him, and wondered if she would notice, as somehow, they had to make contact.

When eventually the low-slung Ford Cosworth finally appeared, he was surprised as to just how travel stained the car was, very different from when he last saw it. But he could clearly see the two occupants as the car slowed to climb tentatively over the hinge at the end of the ramp.

The car was called forward and guided carefully over the metal hinge by a member of the blue-clad crew, sounding noisy as the engine revved; Charles Stevens slipped the clutch as he moved across down and away. Once on the dockside the car's indicators flashed, and he drove confidently with the obvious knowledge of direction.

Kit pulled out into the early morning traffic and took up position about five cars behind the Cosworth, whilst simultaneously keeping a sharp lookout for a Suzuki, of which there was no sign. What he did not expect was for Charles and Sheeka to pull in at the French Coffee Shop at Puerto Portals. But it gave him the chance to try and make some form of contact with Sheeka.

As they selected a table under the faded canvas shade he had time to park almost opposite amongst the many cars in the area reserved for Marineland. Taking a newspaper that he had bought earlier he punched a small hole through it with a ballpoint pen, knowing that Charles or Sheeka could not possibly observe the peephole. But the paper he now held close gave him adequate cover for a short while, whilst providing a means of unobtrusively observing them. Slowly he lowered the window down. His fingers momentarily drummed on the fabric of the roof, then relaxed as he held on to what would be the rain channel. He was not far away which made it quite unnerving as he watched and waited as they gave their order.

It was not long before what must have been a much-needed breakfast arrived, making him somewhat envious of their order as the smell of bacon drifted on the morning air. But he also knew that he would not be able to stay in the same position for too long as this sort of cover would always arouse someone's curiosity after a while, especially when dealing with a man of Charles's calibre.

Then, just as he was about to move to another position, Sheeka looked up and faltered momentarily. Charles followed her gaze, but she covered well by standing up to pour him a coffee; as he thanked her, his concentration went back to his plate.

After taking a sip of coffee Sheeka started to wind her watch idly, looking across at the Ford Cabriolet, a look of increasing relief on her face. Kit smiled, knowing she had recognised his watch, one that she had commented on whilst having dinner at Scallini's in London. It stood out unmistakeably, an unusual large but tasteful gold Audemar Piquet.

When a tourist coach came in to the parking

area, belching diesel fumes and with its air conditioning roaring away, Kit started the car and drove off, when Sheeka next looked up he was gone.

Kit did not have to be an Einstein to know that Charles's next port of call would undoubtedly be his stepfather's finca. There was an outside chance that it might be a hotel, but either way it would be in the direction of Andratx. With that in mind he waited up a small slip road leading to Calvia, and it was not long before the dust-streaked Cosworth shot past. He started up and pulled in leisurely pursuit, following at a safe distance, knowing exactly where it was going.

They were soon out of Andratx town and on the winding road up into the Tramuntana Mountains, once again out toward Estellencs. Kit held himself well back so that Charles would not see him in his rear-view mirror. The small track eventually came into view on the right, the wooden sign 'Privado – Casa Sa Murterra', nearly hidden in the centuries-old stone terracing, confirming the position.

The gnarled and twisted olive trees either side of the entrance, 600 or more years old, seemed to be even more sinister than the day before. A fine dust cloud hung in the air along the track, far above a bird of prey circled, watching the scene below.

After taking all this in Kit drove carefully along the track, half expecting at any moment to round a corner and come across the abandoned Cosworth straddled on the rocks of the track, with Charles and Sheeka walking on in the distance. However, when he came upon the same clearing he had used the day before, he stopped. Further on down the track dust still swirled in the still air, thicker now, scuffed earth and upturned stones lay strewn about. Without total disregard to the Cosworth. Charles was certainly in a hurry, he thought?

Kit drove the car as best he could into a small gap in the pines and walked carefully through the trees, the pine needles soft and spongy underfoot. When he got to the more open cultivated ground by the Finca he could see the Cosworth parked at an angle, virtually on the veranda, its driver's door open. On the veranda two men were having a loud animated argument, the rocking chair was swinging violently at their side. As Sheeka stood there watching stepfather and stepson she glanced over her shoulder to the trees but saw nothing.

David Stevens gestured angrily for them to move inside which they did, Sheeka going in first. When the door closed, Kit waited a moment then came out of the trees; still using whatever cover he could to cross the 200 metres or so to the side of the house. As he got nearer he could plainly hear the raised voices of a violent row developing, with Charles seemingly getting louder and more out of control all the time.

Straightening the rocking chair, Kit sat down under the hanging grapes and rocked himself as he listened to the heated exchanges.

'You bastard,' exploded Charles again to his stepfather, 'How could you date Verkuska, she was bloody my girlfriend, how could you?'

'Verkuska, bloody Verkuska! You stupid fool, she was no girlfriend, not to you, or to anyone else. She was just a prostitute as you well know, a lackey of that bloody man Hock'

'You're a liar, you're sad twisted she was no such thing,' Charles shouted.

'Wise up boy, the first time you met her, in er, where was it? Yes, that restaurant of Marco Pierre White, she was with an old man then, entertaining him! You told me so yourself, so did your friend 'Wiley'.'

'So? That doesn't mean she was a prostitute!'

'No? Hell, you're a naïve, boy,' his stepfather bellowed back. Then with an unfeeling shrug, 'Anyway it's over, as you've just pointed out, she's dead,' he said haughtily.

'She is, and what's more she died with you, you bastard. Who the hell shot her?' he yelled. 'Did you arrange her murder?'

Kit now listened with acute interest.

'Don't be ridiculous,' David laughed again. The laugh though sounded a little nervous, 'how can you say that?'

'Because I believe the man who told me, the man who came to see me at my father's house in Yorkshire just two days ago, I believe him. What's more I believe that you've tried to implicate me in this whole thing. I believe that you tried to set me up, me your stepson, or son as I was then, you bastard.'

'You're the bastard,' his stepfather laughed at him cruelly.

'I'll kill you for that, just for that alone'

With that Charles turned and grabbed a long and deadly Spanish kitchen knife from the table, he moved swiftly towards his stepfather. Sheeka screamed at him and he faltered. There was utter silence; he stood there, chest heaving, the knife glinting in his hand. Then as if reasoning, Charles seemed to collect himself together gather his thoughts and the tension eased a little. He lowered the knife and continued to speak, but much quieter now.

'Your computer was found in my quarters at Hereford, and a gun was found in my car. Now that's really sad, my own stepfather trying to implicate me, his stepson. That is why I had to leave Yorkshire in the manner I did; I've had to help myself in this world. It's difficult to disprove guilt from inside a prison, especially when you of all people would have been on the outside, helping to keep me in. How many more malicious tricks have you got up your sleeve?'

'Don't be so ridiculous, you're crazy Charles, how do 'I' know that it's not you who is trying to set me up, trying to make me out to be the murderer, how do I know it's not you trying to switch the blame on to me?'

'I'm not being crazy. It's you, it's you who's tried to set me up as a murderer.'

'Not at all, it was----'

At that moment, Charles's patience, finally broke. He let go of the knife, which fell to the floor with a clatter; he suddenly slapped his stepfather with the back of his hand. David's head snapped backwards and he went down on his knees before struggling to his feet, a drop of blood trickling from the corner of his mouth. Sheeka discreetly kicked the knife well away from them both.

'You're insane Charles, you're just like your bloody father, if only I'd known, all these years I wasted with you, harbouring you like some bloody cuckoo in my nest,' his voice trailed away as Charles moved nearer, a murderous look now on his face, his eyes searching the room for the knife.

'I'll ask you one more time.' Charles said, 'Who shot her?' he said coldly, lips curled back in a snarl.

'You're a schizophrenic; you did, my boy and you can't even remember, you took my computer and it was your gun in your Alfa, was it not,' he spoke with a confident, all-knowing smirk.

Charles forcefully grabbed his stepfather, only to look up in total amazement as the door to the finca burst open and Kit walked in. Charles let go and stood to his full height. His stepfather fell back and all three-stood staring at each other, blinking in the bright sun that outlined Kit in the doorway, its rays lighting up the room like shafts of quartz. It was like something from a spaghetti western as a dusty stranger enters the saloon, there was silence save for the lone call of the buzzard circling high above.

David spoke first.

'How the hell did you get here?' Stammered David, he was genuinely taken aback. 'But anyway, thank God you did, this boy has finally gone mad. He's schizophrenic and in my view, he always has been,' he proclaimed, jabbing a finger at Charles. Then gathering up his pompous ministerial pose he said, 'I'm sorry sir but I've forgotten your name. You must be following Charles to be here. Phew! my guardian angel, for God's sake arrest him and take him away before he does any more harm,' David our minister begged, now puffing out his chest with obvious relief at his saviour.

Kit spoke carefully and deliberately.

'As I said before, sir, I'm not the police, far from it.'

'Then we'll ring the Spanish Guardia, they'll arrest him' David suggested as a compromise whilst moving for the phone.

'Maybe you shouldn't,' Kit interrupted. 'I'm very tired of all the deceit, Minister.'

David faltered.

'Deceit? There is no deceit here, just a very dangerous man, a jealous murderer I shouldn't wonder, one who needs to be locked up forthwith, for our safety and his, or maybe put in a home even, that would be less embarrassing to all and a better solution all round. I can arrange it.' He made a stride to the phone again. There was a sudden silence as his words sank in.

It was Kit who spoke next.

'I'm sure you can, Minister, I'm sure you can arrange anything that you wish to.'

'I can, I can,' he said excitedly suddenly seeing light at the end of the tunnel, and a solution to this predicament, which Kit did not.

'Minister, why would you want to give a Sergeant William Riley, Charles's friend and fellow soldier, £100,000? I'm interested, very, so please do tell me.'

'What?' exclaimed Charles incredulously, moving forward again. Sheeka looked up at him as Kit held up his hand to continue. Charles stepped back, his eyes flashing round the floor, searching.

Then suddenly there came the sound of uneven footsteps from outside, the possible dragging of a limb. The wooden door creaked open and once again a man stood there.

'You're extremely irritating, Mr Martin,' came the distorted, nasal voice from the now open doorway through which Kit had entered moments earlier.

They all turned to see a horrifying sight, although it was somewhat amusing to Kit who could not help but raise a little smile. The apparition standing there in the door way was more akin to a giant Panda, a black and white face. The problem was it was a dangerous giant Panda that stood there with a revolver firmly in its hand. The weapon Kit mused looked like a snub-nosed Smith & Wesson style .38 Special.

'Wiley' Riley he could only presume, stood there, a white plaster cast was covering most of his face and head, black hair spiked from the top; two bloodshot eyes peered wildly out from within. He walked in slowly with a shuffle and closed the door behind him. He was breathing hard from under his mask.

'Well, at last we have everyone here, all the players; all the cast and all in one room,' came the strange muffled voice from within the plaster cast. 'Everyone that matters anyway,' he waved his arm in the general direction of the group, then after a pause 'are you three annoying my friend here?' he slurred painfully whilst looking across at David his friend.

'Riley what the hell are you doing here?' Charles asked, bewildered.

'Originally Charles you may remember, that is before you fell in love again we were coming on holiday,' he said cynically whilst looking disdainfully at Sheeka. 'So, quite obviously, I had a ticket, remember? But now there has been a change and more importantly I've come to see your father, David,' he said waving the little .38 in his direction.

'Keep quiet, Riley,' David ordered nervously.

'Oh, don't worry, David, we can say what we like, indeed anything we like, you see information is quite useless to dead people.'

Kit moved slightly, but Riley turned on him in a flash, the .38 pointing at his belly.

'Ah yes, Mr Martin, I have no doubt that you're armed. Take it out, please, using the thumb and third finger only; if another finger touches it, even by mistake Mr Martin I shall shoot you in the shoulder, er' and don't think I'm being soft Mr Martin, it's just that I need you to walk away from here alive, so that your death, or should I say your tragic disappearance will be a mystery. Do you like boats Mr Martin? I do hope so.'

'What the hell are you getting at, 'Wiley'?' shouted Charles. But he never got chance to answer as Kit butted in.

'So, Sergeant Riley, you're the real perpetrator of these crimes. I've been thinking for some time that you might be.'

'Cut the crap; the gun, Martin.' Riley jabbed the muzzle of the .38 in Kit's direction. 'The gun.' Riley pulled the hammer back on the .38 and Kit saw the fluted chamber rotate, all six rounds patiently waiting. Carefully, between finger and thumb, Kit as instructed, lifted out the Beretta 9mm.

'Place it on the floor and kick it over to me,' croaked Riley from behind his plaster mask. Kit did as he was told. The other three stood motionless, watching. The gun rattled across the uneven stone-flagged floor. Riley bent painfully to pick it up but watching all the while. Deftly he flicked the button on the left side of the weapon and the magazine fell to the floor with a clatter, a single round sprung from the magazine glinting momentarily as it rolled noisily away across the stone flags. Kit watched it roll to a stop. Riley cast the weapon aside which slithered to a standstill under the wood-burning stove, it was still just visible.

Kit was unflappable at best but now his heartbeat quickened a fraction, now he knew that somehow this battle could be won as Riley was not thinking straight. Only a fool would cast aside a fully loaded 9mm Beretta and leave himself hanging onto a snub-nosed .38 and a poor quality one at that. It looked like a 'Star', a cheap Brazilian copy of a Smith & Wesson. A slug from a .38 did not worry him too much as there was a good chance of survival. It should have been a backup in Riley's belt and the Beretta in his hands!

Riley saw the bemused expression on Kit's face but still did not grasp the full implication of what he had just done.

'Ah yes, of course, the gun,' he smiled contentedly 'You're impressed? Me, a supposed holiday-maker with a gun? But there are always guns for sale in a seaport such as Palma, it was easy,' he said smugly. Kit nodded in agreement as if to congratulate him on his skill and, for the first time looked across at Sheeka whose face was expressionless; she bowed her head slightly to look at her lower leg. Kit knew what would be strapped to her leg under the flairs of her tight-fitting designer jeans, but getting to it unnoticed would be another thing.

'So, you've sunk to a new low of being a paid hit man have you, Riley? Your lust for money and status has finally got the better of you.'

'Not intentional but I was er' persuaded you might say, anyway it will seem that Charles here was the murderer, not me,' he answered.

'So, it was you, you bastard,' exclaimed Charles. 'Now I understand that feigned cock-up of stealing the wrong car, the BMW, then swapping it for the Ford. Where did you go that night on training? You were away for an hour or so and I had to cover for you; and where did the Ford go?'

Riley ignored the questions and continued somewhat patronisingly.

'Dear Charles after all the furore it will be presumed that you caught your father with your girlfriend and did you not?' He laughed 'Then shot her in a fit of pique, rage I'd say, eh? It all figures. His stepfather's computer was stolen at the scene, government secrets maybe? Perhaps to be used to trade for your freedom. After all, it was found, was it not, in your room at Hereford?' Riley chuckled at his summing up of his thoughts. 'I shall also say that you left the exercise in London on the night of the twenty-seventh for a few hours, er, for reasons best known to yourself.'

'You bastard,' Charles muttered again.

'I presume then it was you – Riley in the Alfa,' Kit observed.

'You presume right. Dear Charles every now and again allowed me to borrow his pride and joy.'

'You repay the generosity of your friends well Riley' Kit said cynically 'but I will say this of you, you're not a bad driver,' knowing now that Riley liked a bit of flattery.

'Thank you, that from you is a compliment.'

'Of course,' Kit nodded equally conceitedly in agreement.

'Charles, my dear friend here,' Riley waved condescendingly at him, at the same time looking at Kit, 'He was kind enough to lend me his Alfa several times; I didn't have such a luxury item. You first saw it near the girl's apartment in Chelsea. The day you should have blown yourself sky high, which would have made it easier for us all. You would not have interfered.' He laughed. 'I didn't know who you were then, but no matter, we're all here now, nice and cosy, a final chat'

Kit cast his mind back to the gas-filled apartment, a time bomb waiting to explode. But what he did not know was why David Stevens should have gone to such elaborate trouble. He needed to keep Riley talking until he made a mistake and gave him a chance.

'So why, Minister, did you have to kill the girl?' Kit asked.

'I don't know what you're talking about,' Stevens said, maintaining his pompous air of denial, at the same time sitting down on a nearby settee, crossing his legs and folding his arms. As

Riley, did not object to this, it was quite obvious to Kit that they were in collusion.

It was the man's sudden mannerism, the way he held his head that gave him away. Kit's mind went back to the time he had seen him in the back of Tai Hock's limousine, that arrogant posture, head held high reading the 'Times'. Then it all started to fall into place as he remembered Tai Hock's words.

'Tai Hock,' Kit muttered.

'Of course,' Stevens uttered, visibly flinching.

'But you got it wrong, didn't you Minister? You thought it was Verkuska who was blackmailing you. Get rid of her and avert a scandal, you thought. Remember the photos, Minister? I've seen them too.'

'There's no such thing,' he snorted, 'quite ridiculous.'

'In return for favours, his applications for export licence were to get your stamp of approval, Tai Hock provided you with girls and the nights, didn't he? Verkuska was one of those wasn't she and as Hock pointed out to me, you said, and I quote, 'My hands are tied Mr Hock.' And if my memory is correct, indeed they were, weren't they minister?' Kit said sarcastically

'Rubbish, I ----'

'And so, you paid an astronomical sum of £100,000 to Riley here to rid yourself of what you thought was the blackmailer, Verkuska. But big mistake she was not the real one.'

'Not an astronomical sum but a neat deduction,' complimented Riley.

'Quiet! For God's sake,' Stevens whined.

It was at this point that Charles decided to make his move. He could just see the Beretta sticking out from under the wood-burner; it was like a sweet to a child, it beckoned him. Charles knew that although the magazine was out of the weapon, kicked across the room, there would still be one round left in the chamber. At that range and with his training he would only need the one.

He waited until Riley looked across at Kit, weighing up what to say next. It was then he made a dive for the weapon, arm outstretched he dived, fingers reaching out for the weapon. It was a fatal move. He never made it; his fingers never touched cold steel. Before he could get there, an equally well-trained man – Riley – spun round and fired.

With a blinding flash and deafening explosion, a .38 slug hit Charles full in the chest. Horror registered on his face as he fell with a gasp, air from a punctured chest cavity began to leave him, his lungs were collapsing, his eyes rolled white in disbelief as nausea raked him, he knew that he had been unlucky, his brave gamble had not paid off this was a lethal shot and that he was dying. Blood welled up from his lungs quickly filling his mouth, making him re-ingest. His body went into shock, colours of yellow and blue filled his brain, large at first like the flaming sun, then the coloured orb in his tortured mind shrunk away from him, leaving him. It was becoming dark. The hole in his chest burbled as did his lips, Charles lay in the dust of a foreign country, on the floor dying.

Sheeka screamed and as she bent to help Charles, simultaneously she reached for her ankle and produced a small polished stainless pistol from under her trouser leg. She swept the weapon up into a rough aim and got off two shots in the same well-trained movement, a double tap. Riley exhaled in amazement, grasped his stomach and fired back, but he was unbalanced, staggering and the round went wide of its mark. Sheeka fired again wildly, this time hitting him in the wrist, which caused Riley to drop the .38 to the floor. Sheeka tried again but the little automatic jammed.

Kit remained controlled, he could see the gun was jammed an empty brass case stuck upright proud of the chamber and slide. Gasping from shock and increasing pain Riley stooped to pick up the .38, and in a flash Sheeka kicked it a few feet away from him.

Bowed and holding his stomach he hobbled after it, then as he straightened up painfully from the crouch, the .38 in his hand he groaned aloud. Sheeka's first two shots had hit him twice at an angle in the abdomen, cutting across his stomach Riley's sudden exertions had done the rest, a long red tear appeared across his shirt front. Even as the others watched horrified, his abdomen wall tore, his intestines began to spill out slowly at first, a little grey bulge at the start, but growing all the while like a bag of silver grey light bulbs, glistening and bulbous. With one hand, he tried desperately to hold in his innards as best he could, dark blood spurted freely from his injured wrist, dripping down the .38, which he was now starting to raise. His mind was in shock as the horrifying truth of his predicament began to dawn on him.

Kit seized his opportunity and dived for the stove and the Beretta, rolling rapidly on and across the floor to where it lay by the wood-burner, only to see Riley amazingly come awake and spin back with the .38 in his good hand confused but about to shoot at Sheeka. Late he'd seen Kit's rolling dive to make a grab for the Beretta and Riley changed his aim. The .38 swung round at Kit and bucked violently, but Riley was badly hurt and the round missed its mark. He struggled to re-cock it with his injured hand. Even as he did so Kit had the Beretta to hand and as lightening the hammer came back with practised ease, the explosion from the 9mm ear shattering in the small room. A neat hole with a puff of chalk appeared instantly in the centre of Riley's cast – his forehead, a pink exit mist exploded out behind, as the copper-jacketed slug continued on its destructive way, driving into the wall and plaster. The Beretta, its single shot fired, was now empty, the wall behind a mural of red wash.

Grotesquely, Riley smiled, his teeth bared and like small blunt turnip chips, Halloween yellow stumps still unclean from the blood of the night before. He was dead on his feet, the remnants of his brain searching in bewilderment for contact with life but fading into oblivion. The failing body, now out of control, took a step forward staggered momentarily still smiling in muscular confusion his body twisted and hit the floor.

Sheeka crouched, watching in shocked silence, the Minister now shook uncontrollably.

For a second nobody moved, Sheeka then sprang to Charles's side and took his hand. There was no movement, no pulse, no life; she began to cry, quietly at first then in great sobs. Kit surprised at her reaction took her other hand as if to draw her away, but she would not move, sadly he let it fall.

He looked down at Charles's broken body, twisted shrunken where it lay. Then suddenly he knelt down, although the blood had dried around Charles's mouth, the blood round the chest wound still seemed to be just flowing. He felt the artery in the neck and wrist, but there was no pulse, surely there had been a faint movement in the chest cavity.

Moments later he was talking urgently to the Embassy in Palma requesting a medevac helicopter to be dispatched from 'Medico Balear.' The helicopter was rotating before the call finished. The short time it took to arrive seemed interminable. Half an hour is no time at all but it seems forever when you are doing your best to resuscitate what appears to be a corpse. During the wait, Kit tried everything he knew to induce life, but still there seemed to be no movement. It seemed hopeless and was more for Sheeka's benefit. When he opened the lids, the eyes lay back in hollows, dim and vacant.

The paramedic team of Medico Balear tried hard, but to no avail. They did not want to take the corpse in the helicopter, as by tradition it would be bad luck. But because of the heat Kit argued strongly that Charles's body should be taken to the hospital in Palma; after all, if there was any life whatsoever when they arrived at the intensive care unit then they would not have been carrying a corpse. They said there was no life, so Kit asked the simple question:

'Is there anyone here who can sign a death certificate?' There was not, so he went on, 'In that case if there is life and we don't save it, who do I sue?'

Somehow it worked. During the short flight, they would continue to carry out all the normal resuscitation procedures, and the body would not be declared dead until examined by a qualified doctor.

The helicopter lifted off in a swirl of dust, carob pods battering the Perspex screen. Sheeka stared out into the blue beyond as she held a cold, unresponsive hand. Kit watched the instruments of the craft and the pilot at work, he then looked across at Charles's body, Sheeka and the medics, sadly he thought as he had many times before.

> 'Death follows me, palm open like a persistent beggar.'

Thirty-Nine

Four hours later and against all practical odds Charles Stevens was technically still alive – just. The medical team had seemingly performed a miracle, slight blood pressure having been achieved, complimented by a weak, inconsistent heartbeat, which barely kept pace with the machine; but it was beginning to settle.

The .38 bullet, after colliding with the sternum and scything down the right side of a lung, opening it like a red silk purse, it had then travelled on its evil twisting way to be finally lodged in the heart wall against the left ventricle causing tissue and muscle damage. The heart until removal of the bullet could not function properly and after removal was marginal in function at best, but it would heal. Because of oxygen starvation they were told the likelihood of a normal recovery was remote, if not impossible. Brain damage was unfortunately inevitable.

Sir Edward and Lord Strutt back in England were immediately informed of events and that Charles's faint hope of survival hung in the balance. Within the hour, they were aboard a private HS125 jet en route for Palma, Mallorca.

David Stevens, having been left in the finca with the body of Sergeant Riley, was paid an immediate visit by the Guardia and also removed to Palma for questioning.

For five days, they maintained a helpless vigil beside Charles's bed. Sheeka never left his side; food came and went but she ate little, so much so that she herself was becoming a figure of considerable concern.

Kit paid frequent visits whilst trying to sort out the problem over the Minister, who on Sir Edward's arrival was released from the Guardia, after it had been agreed that he did not kill Sergeant Riley, therefore there was no charge against him under Spanish law.

As for the others, it had been self-defence. Although the British Embassy received a curt letter saying it would be appreciated if permission could be sought in future when any British Intelligence personnel were required to work and carry arms in Mallorca. The reply was apologetic but pointed out that whenever an investigation was started, things could move quickly and no one knew where it might end. If the Spanish Government had a similar problem, it would be the same in reverse. Subject closed.

After his arrival, Sir Edward spent four days

and many hours in deliberation with David Stevens and hours with Kit, which had led to queries as to his use of Sheeka, she had after all not been authorised by him, should she now not have returned to England? Having eventually come to an agreement with all, David Stevens flew back by a scheduled airline back to England, where an enquiry would take place.

Lord Strutt had arrived in a typically gruff mood, dressed as if he was returning to India or some other British colonial outpost now long gone. He had even shaved – in places, but his brogues had odd-coloured laces and of different lengths.

After an hour's conversation with Kit, a debriefing he called it. His Grace then took on a totally different attitude, becoming almost human and showing considerable concern for his only son and heir. He was also more than curious as to why the attractive undercover girl 'Sheeka' was still here and why she was so obviously concerned with what had originally been her 'target'.

Charles meanwhile had not moved or shown any encouraging signs of returning to normal life; the doctors were showing increasing concern over brain damage or permanent coma. The life support machine ticked away by his bedside and a decision was necessary from Lord Strutt as to whether to turn it off or not. Sheeka had pleaded 'no' but on the evidence, they had, there was little point as no activity could be detected, except a weak heartbeat prompted by the machine.

On the ninth day as a nurse changed his dressings she thought there had been a flicker of an eyelid. A doctor had been called but no further movement was detected and he poured scorn on the happening.

The following day Sheeka swore that there was an improvement in Charles's colour and she gauged there was some reaction however slight to her touch. Others disagreed. There was no hope.

On the eleventh day, London called to request Sir Edward's return. Then quite by chance as he came to the hospital to say farewell, Lord Strutt, Kit and the ever-vigilant Sheeka were gathered sadly round the bed of Charles to consider if there was to be a final decision, how long would they wait. On quietly entering the room Sir Edward had held back a little to survey the sad scene. One by one Charles's visitors sensed his presence and turned to greet Sir Edward in a sombre fashion.

Then suddenly on possibly hearing their voices an eyelid of Charles flickered, the movement was barely discernible but Sheeka was holding his hand and felt it grip hers feebly.

The group moved back as the medical staff summoned now busied themselves around him.

Some fifteen interminable minutes later Charles's head moved a fraction his eyes half opened to look up through dim, clouded eyes at Sheeka, weakly his hand started to grip hers. When mind and eye recognised her, in a hoarse whisper, his mouth dry, they were just able to make out his words:

'W-w-will you marry me?' She could not answer as the tears flowed.

'Brain damage, definitely brain damage,' Kit grunted with a wry smile.

Sir Edward's gimlet eyes shot him a killer look, although a suggestion of a smile played also on his tight British lips, as had happened once before, Lord Strutt turned to the window, his handkerchief in hand.

'Are you going to answer?' Kit asked quietly

They all turned to look again at Charles, who had now slipped back into a relaxed sleep. Eyes rose as they looked expectantly at Sheeka.

'It depends' Sheeka said slowly rising and walking with moist relief out into the corridor.

Fourty

When Kit arrived back in London the office in the 'block' seemed tame by comparison to recent weeks. Although the last few weeks had not been in his normal and preferred line of work it had been interesting to say the least, and for him it was not over.

Sheeka for her part had not seen too much of Kit since their return they had both been busy in their various ways, they had had dinner once and it had been intimate yet somehow cordial, it was difficult to explain she had wanted to see more of Kit but the following day he had been called away. Then almost simultaneously as Kit had returned she learned that Charles had been flown home privately and much earlier than expected.

A few days later Kit's phone rang; it was Sheeka, 'may she pop up to his office for a coffee?' He was more than delighted to accommodate.

As she was shown into his office Kit was standing by the panoramic window thoughtfully looking out across the Thames. When she entered, he did not turn immediately and as she approached him she could not help but notice that on his desk lay a pile of papers one of which was a recent copy of the Mallorcan Daily Bulletin. When she looked up she took a breath, he was watching her. His face expressionless now burst into a smile but there was some silence before Sheeka spoke.

'A good trip?'

'Fair' he answered non-committedly

They both now looked out at London and beyond. Sheeka spoke first, she told Kit that it appeared that Charles had been flown back to London and that he was now in Hospital here, indeed he had been so for four days, during which time it appeared that he had been trying to locate Sheeka. He had left messages for her but as yet she had not yet been to see him or spoken to him. She waited for a reaction but there was none, yet she noticed that somehow Kit did not seem surprised of Charles's quick return. 'A strong man' he said.

'Yes, but he will never be fit enough to join his regiment, again will he?' Sheeka said

'He will be fit again and will find something, something that I may be able to help him with.'

Then suddenly Sheeka had turned to face him.

'Sir, no damn er' Kit, do you think anything about me, even in your dreams?'

For Kit such a sudden verbal blast was a bolt from the blue.

Then after a pause he answered slowly.

'More than you will ever know, but that is all it can be Sheeka, for me just a dream.'

She visibly saddened, she did not know what to say, she would never plead and there was a long silence before she spoke again.

'Kit, will you let me go?'

'Of course, you must go see Charles immediately and ----' He never finished.

'That is not what I mean. I mean Kit will you let me go?'

'I have no hold over you.' He said quietly

'You have and you know it.'

As a gentleman, he apologised.

'I'm sorry,' said Kit quietly.

As he looked down into her sapphire eyes he inwardly knew what she was telling him. But he would not allow himself to admit; he had for her sake to change the subject.

'We were a good team,' he said.

The change of the unsaid subject didn't wash, she was shaking her head, her eyes were welling.

'You just can't admit it can you!' her voice was raised a little now.

He kissed her fully on the mouth and for the

first time in years he felt his resistance to a relationship lower.

Sheeka did not push away but she slid away gently quietly. Kit turned away, once more to look distantly mistily out over the Thames.

'You are alone in your world Kit' She held his hand, then let it slip away to his side, 'but I thank you.'

Behind him Kit heard the door click. He knew he had kissed her for the last time.

The Minister was now under investigation by MI5 for the payment of funds to a Sergeant Riley and, also for the procurement of a British passport for Verkuska Tronovich, a Russian citizen from St Petersburg. He was naturally, denying both charges.

Sergeant Riley was of course no longer available as a witness. In turn, posthumously Riley was being investigated for the murder of Verkuska Tronovitch.

As the weeks became months, Charles made a full and quite remarkable recovery, a tribute to his fitness, courage and determination.

One day a gold embossed wedding invitation, included on which was a prominent coat of arms, appeared on the Adam mantelpiece in Kit's new home in Knightsbridge. It was headed:

Lord Strutt requests the pleasure of the company of Lieutenant Colonel Kit Martin

The happy event it announced, was to be held at the private chapel in the grounds of Gouthwaite Hall, just as many others had been over the centuries, followed by a ball and a residential reception; guests to stay at the hall.

Kit was quite surprised when he read the covering letter from Charles & Sheeka requesting him to be best man; an unexpected honour. He placed the invitation in a prominent position, with all other invites and notices moved to one side.

His secretary Sue now also looked after the affairs of his house and made sure that the invitation retained pride of place.

Even more interesting was the announcement in the 'Times' of the forthcoming marriage of Lord Strutt to Miranda Gibbons, formerly Miranda Stevens of The Penthouse, Chelsea Harbour. Kit idly wondered if she was yet divorced, there being no mention of Mr Stevens, although he knew that it would not stop Lord Strutt doing what he wanted to do, or for that matter, Miranda.

The wedding of Charles to Sheeka was a beautiful and touching affair. The private chapel was in the grounds and within walking distance of the Hall, the path was lined with flowers, Sheeka was in white and Charles in full military attire, making a striking couple.

As Kit mingled with the other guests, Sir Edward joined him and after a few moments said,

'A happy ending, Kit?'

'Indeed, sir but we should not lose track of him; he is a useful and resourceful young man.' Kit continued walking, adjusting his stride to Sir Edward's.

'What are you going to do now, now that the dust is beginning to settle?' Sir Edward asked.

'I have one or two things on my desk, unfinished business sir if you see what I mean, but why do you ask?' he said, turning to look curiously at Sir Edward.

'Well, it may be nothing of course, in fact I'm sure it's nothing,' then after an uncomfortable pause ------

'But, something has just cropped up and I was wondering if ----'

And so, to return.

Also by James Hayward-Searle

Featuring Kit Martin MI6

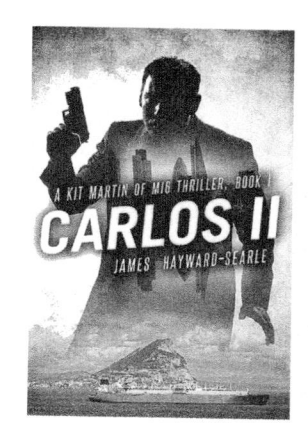

Coming summer 2019

'The Meeting'

www.spythriller.com

Printed in Great Britain
by Amazon